TAKEN BY

The elevator slowed, eased to a st.., ... quietly opened. Stepping into the private entrance of their suite, she swiped her keycard again and entered the silent condo. The lights were off and the sun was fading, painting the gray shadows in a muted golden tone. By the door her shoes dropped with a muffled clunk to the plush carpet, and she removed her scarf.

Dropping her clutch to the table in the hall, she began unbuttoning her coat and heading toward their bedroom. As she focused on the buttons, a shadow passed by the blurred edge of her peripheral vision. Turning quickly, she screamed as hands suddenly grabbed her shoulders, forced her pivoting feet to reverse, and pressed her front firmly into the cool papered wall.

"Not a word," a deep masculine voice whispered, soft lips pressing over her hair and into the shell of her ear. Panic gave way to relief as her ears recognized his voice at the same moment her nose registered his familiar scent.

Lucian.

"Your lover won't be home for hours and I plan on having you several times by then."

Also by Lydia Michaels

The Surrender Trilogy

FALLING IN
BREAKING OUT
COMING HOME

BREAKING OUT

lydia michaels

BERKLEY BOOKS, NEW YORK

THE BERKLEY PUBLISHING GROUP
Published by the Penguin Group
Penguin Group (USA) LLC
375 Hudson Street, New York, New York 10014

USA • Canada • UK • Ireland • Australia • New Zealand • India • South Africa • China

penguin.com

A Penguin Random House Company

This book is an original publication of The Berkley Publishing Group.

Copyright © 2013 by Lydia Michaels.

Library of Congress Cataloging-in-Publication Data

Michaels, Lydia.
Breaking out / Lydia Michaels.
pages cm—(The surrender trilogy ; book 2)
ISBN 978-0-425-27506-1 (paperback)
1. Triangles (Interpersonal relations)—Fiction. I. Title.
PS3613.I34439B74 2014
813'.6 —dc23
2014017705

PUBLISHING HISTORY
InterMix eBook edition / October 2013
Berkley trade paperback edition / November 2014

PRINTED IN THE UNITED STATES OF AMERICA

10 9 8 7 6 5 4 3 2 1

Cover design by Rita Frangie.
Interior text design by Kristin del Rosario.

For Duffy.

You told me to get on an elevator and I took my first real step to the top.

Thank you.

And to Leis for opening a door.
A million thank-yous are not enough.

evelyn

one
·····

THE JOB

EVELYN smoothed her clammy palms down the front of her pencil skirt. The narrow belt at her waist winked under the artificial, amber lighting of Patras's lobby. Reflections danced across the toes of her patent leather Mary Janes as her feet clicked over the polished marble floor, suddenly muffled when she crossed the threshold and the four-inch heels landed silently on the red runner. Dugan waited just past the gold tassels.

Her hands tightened the lapels of the nipped jacket she wore over her pearl-buttoned blouse as the brisk March air cut through her clothing. Dugan nodded at her and opened the door to the limo.

Silk slid over leather as she slipped inside the warmth of the car. The door shut with a gentle snick and she adjusted the nude lace at the top of her stockings. Nerves twisted her stomach into a spring that coiled and released adrenaline, heating her blood.

Dugan glided into the driver's seat. "Where to, Ms. Keats?"

Pulling in a slow breath, she carefully exhaled, forcing away any trepidation. Her lips were done in a deep crimson shade one of the girls at the salon had suggested after she had them style her hair in a sophisticated French twist that morning. She was very aware that she looked nothing like her normal self.

"Patras Industries," she said with as much confidence as she could muster.

Dugan's untamed brows lifted to the brim of his hat. She had never been inside Lucian's office. It was a part of his world she didn't like to trespass on, but after their conversation this week, she knew it was time to cross into that part of his domain. After all, he had brought so many of her fantasies to life that it was time she returned the favor.

Dugan maneuvered the limo carefully away from the curb and eased into traffic with practiced skill. The pearls at her neck hung low in her cleavage. Her fingers twirled over the opalescent, heavy beads. Her mind toyed with images, predictions of Lucian's expression as she unveiled her surprise.

Her legs crossed and uncrossed as the limo navigated through the busy streets of Folsom. A jolt of nerves had her questioning her motives. What if Lucian was busy and became upset when she interrupted his day?

She pushed the thought away. This was one of *his* fantasies. He'd taught her to be adventurous. As much as she worried he would be upset with her brazenness, she couldn't truly imagine her handsome exhibitionist being too put out.

The corner of her mouth pulled into a secret smile. Breath filled her lungs as excitement spun wildly in her belly.

The limo pulled up in front of Patras Industries. The glass façade reflected a distorted version of the car back at her. "Would you like me to phone Mr. Patras and inform him you're here?"

She tensed. "No. No, thank you, Dugan. I'd like to surprise him."

"Would you like me to wait?"

Her palms again smoothed her skirt. "That won't be necessary. Lucian will see that I get home safely."

"Very good, Ms. Keats."

Dugan exited the car and came to her door. Sweet anticipation
had her knees softening. Sliding out of the car, she stood and
found her footing in her high heels. She was doing better with the
walking in heels thing. Her clothing adjusted with gravity and her
eyes momentarily widened as she became suddenly aware of a
minor wardrobe shift down below. Heat rushed to her cheeks as
the gusset of her panties sagged under the damp weight of her
arousal. She was already starving for him. Luckily, no one could
see her panties. Yet. Lucian would know soon enough how excited she was.

She cleared her throat. "Thank you, Dugan."

He nodded. "Do you know where you're heading?"

"Fifteenth floor, right?"

"Yes."

Taking a deep breath, she pivoted, and stepped through the
revolving door. The lobby was quiet. A man sat on a chair beside
the elevator, typing something into a Blackberry. Evelyn's manicured finger pressed the elevator button, and it instantly took on a
golden glow.

The man looked up from his phone, his gaze traveling from
her heels, up her stocking-clad legs, around her curves barely con-
cealed by the tight skirt, and settled at her breasts. Her lips tightened as she watched the antique metal arrow clock the floors.
When the car arrived, she breathed a sigh of relief and stepped
inside the elevator, away from Sir Staresalot.

Knuckling the button for the fifteenth floor, she stepped back
and ran a quick hand over her clothing and hair, making sure
everything was in place. The car alighted with a luxurious purr

and slowed just as the arrow reached fifteen. Shutting her eyes, she took a calming breath.

Showtime.

The metal doors parted and Evelyn carefully stepped out onto burgundy carpet. Phones rang and quiet voices carried. A woman in a brown skirt and ivory blouse leaned flirtatiously over the reception desk, a ballpoint pen twirling in her dainty fingers as she whispered to the young man who manned the area.

He cleared his throat and his visitor straightened. She stood up, stepping aside so that Evelyn could be seen. "May I help you?"

Evelyn smiled. "Yes, I'm here to see Mr. Patras."

The man stilled, glanced at his computer, and frowned. "Did you have an appointment?"

"No."

His mouth opened and snapped shut. "Mr. Patras only sees people with appointments. If you'd like to leave a name—"

"Could you please just let him know Ms. Evelyn Keats is here?"

The man's eyes bulged. "Ms. Keats?"

She smiled, seeing recognition in his eyes. "You must be Seth. It's a pleasure to put a face to the name."

He seemed suddenly self-conscious. "The pleasure's mine. Let me inform Mr. Patras you're here." He pressed a button on the receiver at his desk. "Mr. Patras?"

"Yes, Seth?" Lucian sounded harried.

No backing out now.

"There is a lovely Ms. Evelyn Keats here to see you."

There was a momentary pause, and then his voice sounded, tinged with curiosity. "Is there? Please, send her in."

Seth smiled and pressed a button. "You may go in."

"Thank you."

She carefully stepped to the door labeled President and turned the brushed nickel knob. Lucian was coming around his desk to greet her. "Evelyn, is everything all right?"

She smiled and quietly shut the door. "Everything's fine, Mr. Patras." He raised a brow at the use of his formal title. "I came for my interview."

Pausing, then extending his arm, he gracefully invited her into the lion's den. His face split with a slow grin and he nodded. "Ah, the interview. I'd forgotten. Please, have a seat."

He returned to the executive chair behind his desk, this one just as messy as his desk at the condo. The lavishness of the office compensated for its sloppy surface. She slid into the butter-soft leather chair facing him and crossed her legs. His gaze followed the action and she hid a smirk.

Folding her hands over her lap, she waited for direction. He waited as well, the pregnant silence tightening her muscles as each second ticked by.

He cleared his throat. "Why don't you tell me a bit about yourself," he suggested. Easing back into his chair, his steepled fingers hid his mouth. Her own lips twitched with a sense of playfulness, but she shut her eyes and drew in a slow breath. Fantasy was about fulfilling a psychological need with physical illusions. In other words, she needed to be convincing in order to do this right.

She licked her lips, again drawing his attention to the subtle movement. "Well, I'm told that I have an aptitude for taking direction. I'm a fast learner, I like to please, and I do well with praise."

"And if there is need for correction?"

His eyes darkened and she drew in a slow, heated breath. "I do well with that too."

It was nearing four o'clock, and his throat showed shadows of a day's growth as his Adam's apple bobbed slowly. "I'm quite particular with my expectations, Ms. Keats. I do not tolerate anything less than perfect."

Her mouth went dry. "I understand."

He leaned forward and gathered some papers on his desk, stacking them haphazardly and tossing them into a tray to the right. "Let's take a look at your briefs."

"Pardon?"

"Come here, please."

Her lips parted as she rose to her feet. Slowly, she stepped around the edge of his desk. Heavy brass wheels rolled slowly as his gaze traveled over her outfit. "You are looking quite professional today, Ms. Keats. I like it."

"Thank you, sir."

"Show me your briefs."

Her fingers glided to the hem of her skirt. She slowly lifted the fabric, exposing the lace of her stockings, the snaps of her garters, and the pale pink lace triangle of her panties. Lucian's eyes darkened and his nostrils flared. Her gaze slipped to the bulge beneath his Armani belt buckle.

"Very nice." He made no move to touch her. "Remove the garters."

Carefully, she bent and undid the beribboned snaps holding her stockings in place. They hung like the seductive branches of a weeping willow. Once the last was undone, she stood.

"Did you bring duplicates?"

Her brow pinched and he nodded toward the apex of her thighs. He was referring to her panties. "No, sir."

He tsked. "I'm afraid you will have to leave the originals then, Ms. Keats."

Her chest rose and fell with shallow breaths. "Yes, sir. I apologize for being unprepared."

"I believe in correcting employees immediately after an infraction. Please hand me your briefs."

Her fingers fit under the string of her damp panties and slowly lowered them. Rising once again, she held the garment from her pinky and offered them to him. He caught the shred of silk and brought it to his nose, inhaling deeply.

"These are wet." He crumpled the fabric and slowly stuffed it in his pocket.

"I'm sorry, sir. I was excited for the interview."

"Come here, please."

There wasn't much room between him and his desk. She took a small step forward. The weight of his palms circling her hips caused her to sigh with pent-up relief. Since morning, she'd been starved for his touch. He turned her. "Palms on the edge of the desk, Ms. Keats. I'm going to look over your proposal."

Her hands pressed into the fine wood of his desk as his palm caressed the rounded cheek of her ass. Chills raced up her spine, curling her toes in her Mary Janes and causing her heart to gallop in her chest. She arched and his palm lifted, coming down quick and sharp on her rear. A delicious heat bloomed at the surface and seeped deep beneath her skin.

A sharp gasp of excitement slipped past her lips as she jumped and his fingers gently scraped over the sensitized skin. "This is an office, Ms. Keats. Discretion is important. I'm going to have to ask that you keep your voice down."

Sucking her lips between her teeth, she bit down. His palm slapped upon her flesh again. She hummed quietly, drawing her shoulders back. Her neck rolled, her head tipping back.

"You take direction very well, Ms. Keats."

"I aim to please, sir."

His palm came down a third time. Her flesh was alive and needy. The blunt tip of his finger followed the line of lace around her thigh and traced the seam down the back of her leg to the heel of her shoe. He wrapped his fingers around the heel and lifted her foot off the ground.

Her weight shifted as he bent her leg back. "These are new. I like them."

"Thank you, sir."

"Spread your legs." He released her and she widened her stance. His palm pressed like a brand into her lower back, easing her slightly forward. Her spine stiffened as his fingers bit into the rosy cheeks of her ass, spreading her wide. His tongue licked up her crease, over her waxed folds. "Fuck, you're sexy."

She moaned. He released his hold on her ass and bit her sensitized flesh. Her heart raced and arousal flooded her sex. Her lungs sucked in a breath as his finger breached her folds and entered her. He quickly withdrew the digit and replaced it with two.

She was embarrassingly wet. The sound of his fingers fucking her could be heard all around the room. His other hand reached around her hip, bunching up the front of her skirt gathered there. The first touch of his fingers to her clit had her jerking her body forward.

He was suddenly on his feet, his mouth biting through her blouse, into her shoulder. "Don't move, Ms. Keats."

She loved the way his body managed to hold her in place as he tortured her so sweetly. The press of his arousal through his suit pants, and the sensation of heat added to the thrill of his thrusting fingers.

"You see," he said in a gravelly voice as he blanketed her from behind, "I seem to have made a mistake with my schedule. I have a meeting in about two minutes with a man from accounting. I'd hate to cut your interview short. I've yet to test your oral skills."

She was breathless as he plucked at her clit. Her knees trembled. "I'm told my oral skills are quite notable, sir."

"I'll be the judge of that." His hands suddenly disappeared. The echo of his zipper was followed by the clank of his silver belt buckle coming undone. She was pressed forward until her breasts grazed the surface of his desk through her silk top. "But first I'm going to fuck you. Don't make a sound."

His cock nudged her opening, and then he filled her in one swift movement. She bit down on her lip, stifling a moan as she went up on her toes. Spine arching, her upper body lifted from the desk.

He grunted and grabbed her breast roughly over the silk of her shirt. His mouth sucked at the tender flesh of her neck. His tongue slid over the pearls as he pulled them between his teeth.

He thrust hard and she couldn't help the moan that escaped. The weight of his palm settled over her lips, fingers curling gently into her cheek. His breath beat at her ear. "Shhh, Seth will hear you."

His other hand slid down her front and found her clit. He pinched the sensitized bud, and she squeaked, eyes going wide. He thrust faster and tightened his hand over her mouth.

His warm breath tickled the shell of her ear. "Is it good, Evelyn? You want to scream, don't you? But you can't. If you make a noise I'll spank you again, this time until you come."

Her body tightened. Breath rushed out of her nose, over his fingers.

"You want to come, don't you, baby?"

She quietly moaned her agreement. "All right. Because you performed so beautifully during the first part of your interview, I'll let you come. I need to come too. Then you're going to suck me hard again while I meet with my accounting rep. When I come the second time you're going to swallow every drop, never letting anyone know you're here."

Her body gushed around him, pulsing and tightening. He

rubbed her clit rapidly and her muscles locked. As she came in a rush, he moved his grip to her hips and fucked her relentlessly, groaning softly as he filled her with his release.

When he withdrew from her sex, she was trembling. He cradled her on his lap and kissed her temple. The intercom buzzed.

"Mr. Patras?"

"Yes, Seth."

"Mr. McElroy is here from accounting."

He glanced at her, tipping her chin back so he could see her face. "How are you, love?"

She smiled dazedly. She was wonderful. "Mm, I'm good, Mr. Patras."

"Would you like to proceed with your interview?"

"Oh, I don't plan on leaving until the job is done."

He grinned. "You know what I expect."

She gently kissed his lips, then slithered off his lap, lowering her body to the floor. He stood and zipped his pants and fastened his belt as she fit herself beneath his desk.

Lucian leaned forward and pressed a button on the phone. "Send him in, Seth."

The door clicked open and Lucian greeted the man from accounting. Evelyn quietly backed farther into the niche beneath Lucian's desk. The other man said a quick hello and settled into the seat she had originally occupied at the start of her "interview." The fine leather on the chair squeaked beneath his weight. She wanted to peek under the small space to see the other man's shoes, but was too afraid of inadvertently bumping her elbow or accidentally making a noise that would give her away.

"Let's see what you have," Lucian said, his tapered legs coming back into view as he lowered himself into his chair. His shiny shoes eased forward, his chair gliding him closer.

Evelyn fit herself between his knees and was comforted when

his hand lovingly petted over her hair and down her cheek. Like a cat, she pressed into the caress affectionately.

His hand disappeared as the sound of papers shuffled above her. Their voices were muffled. Her cheek grazed the tailored thigh of his pants. She'd never done anything like this before. Swirls of delicious, erotic tension knotted in her belly. Perhaps she was turning into an exhibitionist too.

Lucian had taught her early on just how much he enjoyed an audience. When he'd explained his fantasy of having her in his office for the day, servicing him like this, she knew it was the idea of being watched that made the fantasy so erotic for him. It didn't matter that the other person had no idea what they were witnessing—at least she hoped they didn't.

Shaky fingers steadied as they coasted up the inside of his thighs. Her body still bore the results of their last coupling, making her thighs sticky. She rubbed them together with pleasure, reveling in the sensation, Lucian's mark of possession. She found his belt and bit down on her lip as she quietly fed the leather through the small metal buckle. His torso elongated purposefully, giving her easier access.

The space under the desk grew warm, and her range of movement became limited as he hardened. Once the buckle was undone, she pushed it to the side, wincing as the clip accidentally clanked against the metal catch on the other end. Lucian cleared his throat and continued talking. She had no idea what he was saying.

Her fingers found the tab of his zipper and slowly lowered it. The sophisticated snap of his pants was inside his waistband. She frowned as she worked to unlatch it. Once she had his pants undone, she spread the material into a wide V.

With nimble fingers, she unbuttoned the lowest three buttons of his shirt and spread the material wide. Lucian's muscled

abdomen twitched beneath her gentle touch. Her lips pursed playfully as she teased him by blowing softly over his tight stomach.

Knowing she wouldn't be able to get him out of his briefs, she
smothered a laugh. He had *her* briefs—she ran her fingertip along
the front seam of his underwear until she found the opening.

His knee jerked as she fed her fingers inside and withdrew
him. It was no easy task. He was already fully aroused. Once she
had his length in her hand, she gripped him, marveling at the
softness of his skin over steel, the firm weight filling her palm.

Easing up on her knees, she took him in her mouth and had
the satisfaction of hearing his voice shift in timbre. Her lips
stretched over him as she pressed forward, taking him to the back
of her throat. His knees clamped into the sides of her body,
squeezing her tight, restricting her breathing.

The other man's muffled voice filled the office as she wrapped
her fingers at the base of Lucian's cock and quietly pumped him in
and out of her mouth. He eased back in his chair and there was
suddenly a tapping sound rattling over her.

Her brow knit with confusion. Releasing him, she turned her
face and looked up. He was rapidly twiddling a pen between his
fingers, tapping the edge of his desk. She smirked. It must be killing him, having to keep his hands to himself. Lucian was very
hands-on when it came to oral sex, or any sex for that matter.

Knowing she was making him insane only made her go at her
task with more zest.

*Ms. Keats shows great enthusiasm for tackling objectives on
the job.* She giggled.

"Did you hear something?" the muffled accountant's voice
asked.

There was a sudden pinch at her scalp as Lucian's hand tightened over her snugly wrapped hair. "My apologies, McElroy. I
skipped lunch," Lucian quickly explained. His warning touch

was gone before the other man could notice Lucian's hand disappearing beneath the desk.

She returned to her task a bit chastised, but also a bit cocky. The meeting continued, and she wondered if Lucian would really allow her to finish him in front of the accountant. She had no idea how he would manage to keep a straight face.

She sensed him getting close when his thighs lifted. Voices continued to travel overhead as he toed off one shoe. She frowned and released him as he shifted his legs. She eased back, unsure of what he was doing.

His right leg adjusted in the cramped space, the tip of his socked toe fitting between her knees and extending until he found her core. She jumped at the contact. Breath stuttered out of her as his socked foot grazed her clit and her labia. She bit her lip to keep quiet.

There was a sudden clatter. "Pardon, I dropped my pen," Lucian apologized. Her eyes dropped to the carpet and spotted the pen. Dark eyes suddenly had her pinned. They creased with mirth. He smiled and reached for her.

She was huddled against the back of his desk. Her eyes widened, unsure what he was doing. Since his foot had joined the play she'd grown incredibly distracted.

His fingers wrapped around the back of her neck and drew her back to his lap. *Oh, okay, keep going then . . .*

He rose just as his fingers swept up the pen. "My apologies. Got it."

The other man continued talking. Her lips slid to the base of his cock as his palm pressed her head low. He held her there a few seconds. When his grip on her disappeared, she bobbed up and down quickly. He was being a bit brazen. She could be brazen too.

She relentlessly went at him. His foot continued to tease her. "Well, this all looks great. I'm going to call over to Shamus now and fill him in." Lucian's voice was strained, but barely. He had remarkable self-control.

The other man made a muffled good-bye. The sound of footsteps faded and there was a click as the door closed. His cock popped from her lips and his chair propelled back. She was suddenly dragged out from under the desk, and he was on her.

The rough carpet burned her sensitive rear as his lips crashed over hers, his body pinning her to the floor. "So fucking hot, Evelyn," he growled as his tongue knifed into her mouth. His fingers hooked beneath her knees and wrenched them up. He filled her almost violently.

The moan was unavoidable. He pounded into her, chafing her backside as he fucked her, propelling her from behind his desk. There was a sudden knock on the door.

Evelyn's eyes bulged, her head jerking toward the door and, as if in slow motion, the knob on the door turned. She smacked at Lucian's shoulders, but he was like a man possessed.

"Mr. Patras, is everything okay? I thought I heard . . ."

Evelyn screwed her eyes shut and turned her face away from the door and into his shoulder. Lucian suddenly stilled. "Not now, Seth," he growled.

"My apologies!" Seth made a fast exit. The door practically slammed shut.

Neither of them moved for several heartbeats. Lucian's shoulders shook. He was laughing. She was mortified and he was fucking *laughing*!

She shoved at him. "It's not funny."

His shoulders trembled as he sucked in a deep, audible breath, and loud laughter spilled from his lips. She rolled her eyes. Her face was likely the color of the burgundy carpet. When she attempted to squirm out from under him, he stilled and frowned at her, his body locking down on hers.

"Where do you think you're going?" he asked, all humor gone.

"I'm embarrassed and you're laughing. We were just caught."

His mouth spread into a tight, satisfied smile. He was too beautiful. At the moment, his attractiveness irritated her.

With complete seriousness, he said, "Ms. Keats, the interview is far from over."

She narrowed her eyes and his crinkled with humor. He rotated his hips and she groaned. No matter how mortified her brain was, her libido was still raring to go.

Her head dropped to the carpet. "You damn exhibitionist pervert," she grumbled.

He chuckled. "You know you love it."

She did, but she'd never freely admit it. Her chin pressed into her chest as he awaited her reply. "I'll never be able to come here again."

"Nonsense," he teased. "I plan on making you come here at least twice before I take you home."

She mashed her hand into his face and shoved him. He laughed and kissed her. It wasn't long before she gave in and they were at it again; this time, however, there was no rushing. He made love to her, slowly and thoroughly.

The arrogant bastard was right as usual. She came twice more before he took her home.

two
.....

HOME SWEET HOME

"WHAT are they?" Lucian's sister, Toni Patras, asked as she grudgingly edged closer to the vendor's table dressed in a dated blue cloth.

The vendor stood back, his tattered duds flapping worn hemlines like frayed flags with each teasing wind. His stained fingers remained hidden, tucked deep within his crossed arms. Apparently, he was aware that some of the company found his presence wanting. Evelyn's gaze met his, an empathetic curve to her mouth. She hoped his ego wasn't too wounded by Toni's hypercritical appraisal. Of all the Patras siblings, Toni's silver spoon was the largest, and in moments like this, Evelyn wanted to rip it out of her mouth.

The sidewalk sale was part of the Irish festivities that marked every March in Folsom. Participating in the revelry from this end was such an extremely different experience than what Evelyn was used to. All her life, she awaited the lull of the Annual Folsom Celtic Festival, because it gave way to a smorgasbord for the homeless. Half-eaten foods and bins of discarded toddies sometimes spiked with something to ease a bit of the nip in the air awaited the empty bellies of the less fortunate. Forgotten jackets and hats littered the sidewalks alongside the trivial bullshit that rich folk wasted money on, like necklaces and bobbles that glowed for a day. Even now, Evelyn couldn't help but spot some of those forgotten pieces of trash that would soon become another's treasure.

This had always been her favorite time of year. After the parade came through the beribboned streets of Folsom, thorough-fares were littered with suckers and taffy and plastic jewels, all sorts of treasures a kid on the street never was handed in life.

Evelyn's memory of her small, dirty hand gripping the waxy wrapper of a long-ago found chocolate taffy transcended to her now manicured hand holding a collection of blue gems. *My, how times have changed*. Well, not times, but situations. Hers certainly had.

Unable to tear her gaze from the bobble she now held, she tried to answer Toni without losing patience. "I don't know."

The sunlight caught on the various swirls of green and blue buried in the smooth stones, waves trapped in time.

"That's sea glass," the vendor chimed in. Toni eased back as the vendor smiled toothlessly at them, his unclean odor wafting in their direction over the cool breeze. Evelyn smiled, finding great amusement in Toni's discomfort. This man was really no different than Evelyn, but Toni wouldn't know that. While the Patras family was not overtly snobby, they would never become used to those who lived a much rougher life. Toni was the most sheltered of them all.

"It's beautiful," Evelyn complimented. Her gaze was trans-fixed on the various hues. She'd never seen the ocean, but she'd seen pictures. It was as if the stones had trapped those wild, ra-diant mercurial blues, entombed them together in a piece of glass.

She found each little stone to be its own breathtaking work of art. More impressive that it was made by nature. Man could only attempt to imitate such beauty, but this was authentic, something that had been touched by the ocean.

"That there is real silver," the vendor said informatively, drawing Evelyn's gaze from the enchanting stones to the other merchandise on display.

Toni gave the dealer an insincere but polite smile and returned the spoon she was holding to the cloth-covered table. She shifted her bag and sighed. "Come on, Evelyn. There's a sale at the Coach boutique I want to hit."

Evelyn looked back to the stones filling her hand, now warm from her own body heat. "Um, okay. Just let me get Dugan." She pivoted and found their driver already approaching at the mention of his name. "Dugan, I'd like to buy these stones."

Toni frowned at her, her face scrunching like that of a sharpei. "What are you doing, Ev? All this stuff's junk."

Irrationally, a twinge of offense on the stones' behalf filled Evelyn. Her embarrassment about Lucian's sister on the *vendor's* behalf was completely rational. Her fingers closed over the stones protectively as if to save their inanimate feelings.

"They're pretty," she said, slightly self-conscious of how uncultured she could be. There was so much about her she feared Lucian and his family would one day see as too weird to bother with.

Evelyn never had pretty things before Lucian. Clothes cost a fortune where he shopped, and she simply couldn't fathom the difference between a two-thousand-dollar pair of shoes and a ten-dollar pair. She humored him when it came to her wardrobe, knowing it pleased him to provide for her and see her dressed in fancy things, but this was different. A stone didn't have to be a diamond or a ruby to be pretty.

It was indulgent and silly, but Evelyn wanted it. "How much for these five?"

The vendor extended his neck and examined her finds. Motioning with a dirty hand to the grouping of other blue glass along the table, he said, "I'll give you all ten for five dollars."

Evelyn smiled as Dugan withdrew his wallet. "And what about these?" she asked, gesturing toward the eclectic grouping of silverware spread out along the edge of the table. There were other items too, jars of old buttons, broken earrings that looked dated, tattered old black-and-white photos, and some vintage typewriter keys.

Before the vendor could answer, Toni stepped in. "What are you going to do with a bunch of mismatched forks and spoons, Evelyn?"

She shrugged. "I don't know. They're neat."

"They're tarnished," Toni mumbled, her mouth drawn to the side in disapproval, dimple forming an unhappy divot in her cheek.

"They'll clean right up with the right type of cleaner, ma'am," the vendor offered pleasantly enough. She liked that he didn't back down under Toni's disapproval.

Dugan handed her a hundred-dollar bill, and Lucian's sister scoffed. "This stuff is all crap."

Evelyn frowned at her. The vendor obviously heard her. Now Toni was just being rude. She took the bill from Dugan and lifted her chin. "How much for all of it?"

With bulging eyes, the dealer said, "Uh . . ." He did a quick inventory of his goods. "Forty?"

"I'll take it all," Evelyn announced proudly, and Toni threw up her hands in exasperation, turning away from the table. The vendor grinned, wide and toothless, an expression of sheer joy on his haggard face.

"Do you have a bag?"

"I sure do, ma'am." He quickly reached under the cloth of the table and pulled out a stack of newspaper and a crinkled, plastic grocery bag. Evelyn smiled and made small talk with the man as he carefully wrapped her treasures. Toni stood a few feet away tapping the toe of her expensive boot.

When he handed Evelyn the bag, it was heavier than she expected. Dugan relieved her of it and silently stepped back from the table. She held out the hundred-dollar bill for the merchant.

His expression fell. "Uh, I'm 'fraid I can't break that, ma'am."

"That's okay," Evelyn said in good spirits. "You keep it. Go get yourself some lunch and maybe buy something nice for yourself now that your afternoon's free. I saw another vendor down that way selling gloves for a dollar, the nice warm kind."

He looked at her hesitantly, his eyes weighing her sincerity. His gaze returned to the crisp bill being offered to him. She extended her arm a little more. When he still didn't take it, she reached for his gnarled hand, opened his fingers, and closed them over the money.

"Thank you for all the beautiful treasures," she said, and turned to find Toni.

Lucian's sister awaited her with comic disapproval accentuating her posture. Evelyn had no regrets about her purchase. The change from the hundred dollars was worth the joy she put on that man's face. The bag of treasures was just a bonus.

Her gaze caught on a small yellow taffy at the edge of the curb. Evelyn grinned and bent to pick up the overlooked treat left in the wake of the parade that morning, its waxy wrapper spreading a warm, nostalgic heat through her chest. When she stood and faced Toni, it was clear the other woman thought she was nuts. Evelyn didn't care. The yellow ones were the best.

They walked from one end of Folsom's classier district to the other. Evelyn's toes were screaming to get out of her narrow-toed kitten heels by four o'clock. Thank God she had the good sense not to wear her dagger heels out today. If she had, she'd probably be leaving a trail of blood in her wake, which was still a possibility, even in kitten heels. Unless shoes had rubber soles she pretty much hated them.

By the time they neared the limo, Dugan was completely weighed down with boutique bags and designer boxes. Luckily, even the lacy wrappings of such a girlie outing couldn't detract from his manliness. Dugan was a tree of a man and loyal to the bone to Lucian.

At six foot five, roughly three hundred pounds and not an ounce of fat, Dugan was all man. His gruff, thin lips tucked within the handlebars of his mustache gave him an unapproachable presence that allowed him the solitude he seemed to favor. His eyes, however, sometimes hinted at a much softer man beneath. She'd been working on getting his freak flag up for a while, but so far no such luck.

"Scout?"

Evelyn stilled and turned at the sound of her name. Scanning the pedestrians surrounding them, her eyes landed on the familiar, bouncing curls of Lucian's friend Jamie. "Jamie, hi! What are you doing here?"

"I had a business lunch that was canceled, so I figured I'd walk around." He leaned in and kissed her cheek, his Irish eyes smiling. "No Lucian today?"

She sighed. "No, he had some things he needed to take care of. Luckily I was able to find a stand-in."

Jamie's gaze lifted and traveled past her shoulder. The moment he spotted Lucian's younger sister, a blank mask forcibly settled into place. Evelyn always got a kick out of observing the two of them dance around the sexual tension they shared. According to

Lucian's older sister, Isadora, Toni and Jamie had been playing this game of cat and mouse for years. However, poor Jamie was the mouse.

Do it already!

"Antoinette," he greeted coolly.

"Well, well, well, if it isn't Shamus the anus."

He pressed his lips together. "Mature, Toni. I can see you've grown up quite a bit."

Toni shrugged indifferently, but the proof of her embarrassment following her juvenile outburst was clear as her color rose and her lip quivered slightly. So much of that toughness was an act to hide her insecurities.

Looking back at Evelyn, Jamie asked, "Did you find some good sales today?"

Toni rolled her eyes and blew out a puff of air, clearly over her own issues. "I did, but Evelyn got ripped off. She bought some dirty man's trash."

It was Evelyn's turn to blush. Toni was twenty-three, just like Evelyn, but they had led two very different lives until recently. There was an immature quickness to Lucian's little sister that Evelyn wasn't sure how to take sometimes. She laughed nervously. "It wasn't trash. It was a collection of stones and eclectic silver spoons."

Jamie's jaw ticked. He was one of the few people who knew she had grown up on the streets. She never had the guts to ask him not to share that information. Evelyn looked at him pleadingly, hoping she wouldn't regret never having that conversation with him.

"Well, for those not born with a collection of silver spoons in their mouths, they have to buy them somewhere," he said succinctly, hitting Toni with a pointed look.

Toni let out a very unladylike sound. "You're an asshole, Jamie." She turned and marched away. "I'll be at the car."

Jamie rolled his eyes. "Don't mind her. She's too young to realize not everyone grows up with every request met at the drop of a hat."

Evelyn didn't see the point in mentioning she and Toni were the same age. She smiled tightly, acknowledging without words that he tried to casually come to her defense without giving too much away.

His eyes softened. "What did you get?"

Feeling silly now, she blew off his question as she swatted at a strand of dark hair blowing across her face and irritably tucked it behind her ear. "Nothing. Maybe it *is* junk."

Jamie's smile eased with understanding that felt a little too much like sympathy. Shame on her for letting all of Toni's comments get to her.

"If you liked it I'm sure it isn't junk." His long fingers lifted and tucked the unruly strand of dark hair tightly behind her ear. His fingers pinched the edge of her chin affectionately. "Send Lucian my best. Dugan." He tipped his chin at their driver before turning away, his blond corkscrew curls slowly fading into the melee of pedestrians shuffling over the pavement.

When she reached the limo, Dugan had already loaded their purchases into the trunk. Reluctantly, Evelyn climbed into the cab of the limo. Toni sat, arms akimbo, sulking on the far seat. Evelyn was tired. She missed Lucian and didn't have the energy for his sister anymore today.

Without wasting time, Toni snapped, "He's such a dickwad!"

Evelyn sighed.

"You know, I *am not* spoiled! I can't help it if I have better taste than most people. I mean people appreciate my taste. I bet you didn't know I was offered a job as a style consultant."

Evelyn did know, because it was something Toni brought up often. Before she could comment, the girl continued. "You know, Shamus used to be fun, but now he's just a miserable old fart."

Shamus, or Jamie as he usually went by, was not old. But there was no stopping Toni once she started.

"He needs to get laid. That's the problem. He dates all those plastic bimbettes and doesn't have a clue about what good sex is."

Evelyn thought about Toni's string bean boyfriend, Peter. No matter how she tried, she couldn't imagine him being able to masturbate satisfactorily let alone fuck above par. Toni continued to grumble and rant until they reached her apartment. The doorman stacked her purchases on a brass pull cart, and Toni kissed Evelyn's cheek affectionately.

"Let's do this again sometime, okay, Ev?"

Evelyn forced a tight smile. "Sure."

Although so much of her current situation was new to her, Evelyn was coming to learn she could do without all the indulgent excursions wealthy people filled their time with. She was grateful for everything she had. According to her track record, she was very lucky at the moment.

She was secretly in love with the most incredible man she had ever met in her life. Her mother was finally getting the help she needed thanks to said amazing man. Evelyn was growing more literate with each passing day. And for the first time ever, she had a roof over her head she could depend on. It was wrong to complain.

Still, sometimes Evelyn wished she could hide away in Lucian's condo forever, safely sheltered from the rest of the world. She'd spent her entire life outside of walls. Now she wanted to be within them and stay there. But she knew that wasn't healthy.

Being born on the streets, literally, addicted to the heroin that ran through her mother's veins like water, she'd slept on benches, under bridges, in barrels, on playgrounds, and many more unsavory places that would scare the shit out of a normal girl. It was enough to last a lifetime. She'd be happy with never going out again now that she knew what inside felt like. She was a homebody to the extreme. Maybe she should talk to someone about that, her obsession with home sweet home.

Her concern that she might be developing some sort of unhealthy dependence on her home was distracted the moment the limo pulled up to Patras. *Ah . . . home.*

She reached for the latch on the door just as Dugan pulled it open. He held out a hand and helped her to the sidewalk.

As always, the Patras Hotel was bustling with life. The place had a pulse of its own. There truly was no need to ever leave.

The hotel was its own little metropolis, complete with clothing stores, restaurants, bars, salons, art galleries, and over one thousand guest rooms.

She stepped onto the gold-tasseled red runner that no longer intimidated her, and Dugan followed her to the glass doors held open by Philippe, who was dressed in Patras livery.

"Good evening, Mademoiselle Keats. Monsieur Patras left instructions for your packages to be left at the front desk and delivered to your suite later this evening. He also asked that you meet him at Vogue for supper at eight." Vogue was the hotel's main restaurant.

"Thank you, Philippe," she said as she passed. Once they were a distance from the doorman, she turned to Dugan. "I only have the one bag. I can carry it. No need to bother the front desk."

Dugan, who looked tired after an afternoon of following Toni Patras from store to store, cleared his throat. "Better do as Mr. Patras directed, Ms. Keats."

She rolled her eyes. "No wonder you're his favorite."

The tiniest grunt of what could possibly be laughter sounded in his throat. "I believe the title of favorite has been given to someone else."

She playfully batted his shoulder and sighed. "Oh, Dugan, you sweet talker, you. Fine. I'll wait for it to be delivered."

"Very good, Ms. Keats."

She tipped her head at his unshakable formality. "One of these days I'm going to get you to laugh, like, really laugh. Pee-your-pants laugh."

"I doubt that, Ms. Keats."

She dug in her little clutch for her room key. "We'll see. Take it easy, Big D." Waving at him with her keycard, she turned toward the bank of elevators.

The sophisticated whispers of the lobby silenced as the elevator doors closed. She sighed and leaned against the bronze mirrored wall of the car as it rushed up thirty floors with a hushed hum. She loved the clean sent of the elevators, the way guests' perfume sometimes lingered in the air over the scent of the smartly polished tiled floor.

At the quiet ping announcing her arrival, the doors parted. She exited the elevator and took the hall to the private bank of elevators that led to the master suites. Sliding her room key through the slot, she entered the antiquated car that was more like a gilded cage than a means of transportation. Once she was on her way, she slipped off her kitten heels and moaned as the blood flowed back into her tired toes.

As she scooped up her shoes, fantasies of sliding out of her jeans and into her robe filled her mind. How long until Lucian would be home? If dinner was at eight she still had a few hours. Maybe she would nap. She hated when he wasn't around. He made everything more fun.

The elevator slowed, eased to a stop, and quietly opened. Stepping into the private entrance of their suite, she swiped her keycard again and entered the silent condo. The lights were off and the sun was fading, painting the gray shadows in a muted golden tone. By the door her shoes dropped with a muffled clunk to the plush carpet, and she removed her scarf.

Dropping her clutch to the table in the hall, she began unbuttoning her coat and heading toward their bedroom. As she focused on the buttons, a shadow passed by the blurred edge of her peripheral vision. Turning quickly, she screamed as hands suddenly grabbed her shoulders, forced her pivoting feet to reverse, and pressed her front firmly into the cool papered wall.

"Not a word," a deep masculine voice whispered, soft lips pressing over her hair and into the shell of her ear. Panic gave way to relief as her ears recognized his voice at the same moment her nose registered his familiar scent.

Lucian.

"Your lover won't be home for hours and I plan on having you several times by then."

Her breath hitched as a strong hand snaked under the material of her coat and gripped the apex of her thighs. Her body caught fire. Firm hips pressed into her backside, grinding and forcing her flat against the wall as his palm fit into the crease of her jeans. The heat of his palm bled through the denim of her pants. She regretted that he hadn't given her a chance to remove more of her clothing.

His grip on her thigh tightened, thumb pressing hard into a sensitive crease, massaging as she moaned, already growing aroused and needy.

"Shh . . . Lucian's not here."

Pressing up on the balls of her feet, she rocked into his grip and he chuckled. "Is that how it is? So ready to give yourself over to an intruder? Perhaps your lover hasn't been keeping you satisfied."

Her scarf was yanked out of her hands, the velvet a slippery tease between her fingers. Every bit of her flesh was suddenly hypersensitive and on alert. She gasped as her coat was jerked off of her shoulders, drawn back at the curve of her elbows, forcing her spine to arch, thrusting her breasts high. And that quickly he had her restrained.

The dim room suddenly went black as velvet covered her eyes, soft and cool over the arch of her cheeks. Her hair tugged as he knotted the scarf at the back of her head. Her heart ratcheted up as she could only anticipate what would come next. Would he be relentless, push her to the brink and tease her there until she begged him to finish her? Or would he be cruel and selfish, making the fantasy all the more real?

"Let's see how many times I can make you come before your lover returns," he growled, turning her quickly. The fast turn disoriented her. The wall pressed into her back and his warm lips crashed down over hers. Taking advantage of her startled gasp, his tongue breached her lips forcefully, taking from her greedily. Evelyn moaned and reached for his broad shoulders, but her coat was still in the way.

His lips tore from hers as a chill caressed her front, his touch suddenly absent. "Don't move." His deep voice was gravelly in a way he sounded only when highly aroused. It crawled over her senses like a physical touch and she shivered.

Breathing deeply, she pressed her back into the wall, fingers nervously opening and closing into fists. Wherever he was going she hoped he would be quick. Her eyes were adjusting to the darkness as her other senses sharpened. She could keenly hear his muffled footsteps over the carpet. They silenced as he paused and then slapped along the dark marble floor of their bedroom. He was barefoot.

She had barely seen him before he blindfolded her, catching only a flash before he was on her, depriving her of sight. She imagined him in the dark dress slacks he'd chosen that morning, shirt now wrinkled and rolled at the cuffs, collar undone and without a tie. Dressed down, buttoned up, naked, or bundled, Lucian always looked amazing.

The rich scent of coffee lingered from breakfast. The condo was cooler than usual. Did he lower the thermostat to heighten her anxiety, make the fantasy more genuine as though she were really walking into an abandoned suite with a stranger crouching in wait in the shadows? Once she considered the cold a chill took hold of her. Her shoulders trembled as her nipples tightened beneath her clothing.

The muffled sound of his footsteps drew nearer and she licked her lips, tasting his unique flavor lingering there. Anticipation shivered up her spine as her heart beat wildly in her chest. She wanted to be ravished. How would he take her? There was no doubt he would have her trussed up and at his mercy within minutes. This was Lucian Patras. When he saw something he wanted, he took it. Asking was child's play to him, something that took some getting used to for her, but over time she had learned to simply surrender where intimacy was concerned and she had never been disappointed. Even when Lucian took, he gave.

Would he be kind or relentless? Generous or demanding? He was a trespasser. Excitement allowed her to easily fall into the fantasy play. She focused on the sound of his breathing, the anticipation of him approaching. Her breath quickened as the heat of his body mingled with hers.

"What are you going to do?" she whimpered. It wasn't an act. He had her so excited that her voice quivered on its own.

A large hand gripped her jaw, pressing firmly into the soft flesh of her cheek, and tilting her head back to an incredibly vulnerable angle. "I said no talking. I have ways to silence you if you can't follow directions. Do I need to find something to occupy that sweet mouth of yours?"

Before she could answer, his tongue licked over the plump curve of her lips. She couldn't stifle the moan that followed. She was incredibly aroused.

There was an unspoken security in playing with Lucian that gave her the courage to surrender, allowing her to let go, give over to him as if he were truly taking from her with no concern for her comforts or needs.

It was fun to pretend with him, because she trusted him to stay in control, therefore giving her the gift of losing herself in the game. During her childhood she rarely played, so playing now, with him, was an endorphin rush she'd never known before. She loved it.

She wanted him to take. She wanted him aggressive. Her thighs pressed together tightly and she trembled with the sudden desire for him to rip her clothing away. She felt no shame. If things got out of hand, well, that's why she had a safe word. All she had to do was call *checkmate* and Lucian would stop everything.

Like a child with a stick, she poked the impressive beast, anxious to see what he would do. "My lover will be here soon, any minute! And you won't touch me. He's very protective of me and when he sees what you planned to do, he'll make you regret ever contemplating putting your hands on me."

Harsh laughter filled the quiet space between them. The puff of his warm breath against her cheek told her how close he was, yet he was no longer touching her. She wanted to lean forward and press into him, but held herself still, rigid and proud.

His laugh abruptly stopped and the sudden silence had her catching her breath. All calm slowly tingled away, replaced with the slight tickling of unease at the nape of her neck. Perhaps it was her blindness, but more than likely it was the absence of his touch.

Something shifted and reality wavered. How did he do that, shift the energy of an entire room? Her breath quickened as anxiety pressed into her thoughts. Rationalization of her situation became a blurry mirage in her mind, slipping through her grip.

"Lucian?"

"He's not here. Just me. Me and you."

She stiffened as his cool finger trailed over the crest of her cheek, past her ear, and down her neck. He had somehow transformed his touch, disguised it. Adrenaline coursed through her veins. It was him, yet it wasn't. How had he suddenly made her apprehension so real? She knew if she wanted to stop they would. All she had to do was say her safe word, but she didn't even want to think it in that electrified moment where she stood poised on the cusp of dark need.

Like the slight static of a balloon lifting the soft hairs on an arm, she felt him ease closer. Her lungs held as his breath echoed in the shell of her ear. In. Out. In. Out. She was glad one of them was breathing.

Like a top tightened on a string, he suddenly said the one word that threw everything into motion. His lips pressed over the soft curve of her ear and he whispered, "*Run!*"

Evelyn didn't think. She only reacted, knowing she might seriously hurt herself being unable to see, she shrugged her coat back over her shoulders, held her hands out in front of her, and bolted. It didn't matter anyway. He caught her before she barely had a chance to move.

She struggled against him and he subdued her every attempt to break free of his hold. The great thing about Lucian being so unbreakable was he never had a problem with playing rough. She made the trek to the bedroom as difficult as possible for him, catching her flailing feet on furniture and biting him through his dress shirt. She'd earned a few swats on her ass along the way, but it was worth it. She loved the adrenaline rush of roughhousing with her lover.

Her body landed on the cool, plush bedding and bounced with the impact. Hurried fingers attacked the snap of her jeans, and as they were yanked below her knees she twisted to her stomach and hastily crawled away. Like a manacle, fingers wrapped around her ankle and yanked her back to him.

Her heart raced as he laughed at her pathetic attempt. "That's it. Fight me. There's no escaping what I plan to do to you."

They tussled, but he kept a constant hold on her limbs. She loved that she could play rough with him. Adrenaline pounded through her veins as she wriggled under the strong body pinning her. She panted and pushed against him. Every time he reinforced his hold on her, her arousal doubled.

Once her legs were bare, her coat was roughly stripped away. Her hair had come undone from its clip and strands clung to her lips as she panted. His weight settled over her hips as he pressed her wrists into the pillows above her head. Warm breath coasted against the skewed collar of her blouse. The warmth of his tongue suddenly scorched the tender flesh of her throat as he licked a hot trail to her rapidly throbbing pulse.

"Are you planning on fighting me the entire way?" he whispered, pressing his lips to the corner of her mouth. She loved when he spoke to her like that, dragging his mouth over her flesh, as though drawing away for a few words was simply too much to bear.

Heat pulled low in her belly, tightening her loins as a wave of euphoric need settled over her, clouding her judgment, banishing all common sense. She pressed into his hold, trying to break free and growing intensely aroused at the fact that, no matter how she tried, he had her outmaneuvered.

"I won't let you have me," she hissed, pursing her lips to disguise her smile.

His weight lifted off her abdomen for a split second as he

transferred her wrists into one hand. As he settled back over her, cool satin banded her hands, leaving her palms kissing and her fingers with their long, manicured nails useless. The air of the bedroom cut away, replaced with the heady sent of him leaning over her. The soft, sensual fabric became a new experience in her darkened state.

The awkward bondage left her to discover how sweaty her palms had grown. Once she was sufficiently restrained she felt him ease back. She imagined his arrogant expression as he evaluated his work. She tugged, but the satin was clearly tied to something else, leaving her stretched helplessly beneath him.

The sudden shredding sound of fabric rent the air. Buttons popped and pinged around the room. Her nipples tightened beneath the lace cups of her bra. Her blouse, now a useless rag, was yanked open. Exposed and vulnerable, she squirmed. He had her pinned, plucked, and poised for his pleasure.

His touch, when it came, was reserved. Although he was taking what he wanted, he was caressing her like a stranger who had never seen her exposed before. It seemed almost reverent. The raw lust that traveled from his fingertip to her chilled flesh as it slid over the slight swell of her heaving breasts was foreign.

She knew he was doing this to mess with her head. He wanted her to fully experience the fantasy, view him as a stranger and feel the rush of fear colliding with the unknown. What a mind fuck, to take pleasure from someone she should be fighting off. It was a wicked game, this fantasy.

He explored her exposed flesh like a trespasser. Perhaps she should feel a pang of disgrace for finding it so titillating. Maybe another person would be ashamed, but this man above her had tutored her in all things sexual and as far as softer couplings went, she preferred him always taking her to that darker edge. Maybe she was a deviant too.

"Your lover is very lucky." His voice was hoarse, quiet. His touch grew bolder.

Her breasts plumped as he used both hands to create slack in the lace connecting the cups of her bra. A quick snap and tear and the support was pushed aside, leaving her breasts naked. The heat of his palms engulfed her flesh, squeezing, drawing a moan from deep within her.

He stilled. "Surely you are not aroused by a stranger touching you?" He played the game so well, always drawing a touch of psychology into sex, never allowing it to simply be a physical act. Her emotions only ran high where this man was concerned. In a way, he had programmed her to react so, conditioned her.

Regardless of her grasp on reality, his words made her cheeks burn. He was no stranger, but he also wasn't her Lucian in that moment. Fear that he might confuse the fantasy with reality skated through her mind. Was he fishing for reassurance?

"Only you . . ." she whispered.

He didn't comment, but the press of his forehead to her abdomen, the soft tickle of his dark hair on the underside of her breasts, proved he took stock in her words. He would never openly admit to having insecurities. No, they were for mere mortals and Lucian likened himself to the gods. She hid her smirk, loving that he only showed his more human side to her.

He scooted back and as his weight lifted off her hips her panties were peeled away. Her thighs were wrenched wide. She gasped and he tsked. An impersonal finger swept down her slit. "You're soaking wet," he remarked in a chastising tone. More heat rushed to her face.

The bed dipped and she heard him moving around, unsure what he was planning. She startled as his finger smeared over her lips. "Lick my fingers clean."

Lips parted, she swept her tongue over his two digits, then

closed and sucked them into her mouth, recognizing her own flavor. He grunted and withdrew his fingers with a pop.

She waited, wondering what he would do next. The scent of his rich cologne intensified as he ran a finger over the skin beneath her nose. She knew it was his finger, but his fragrance was suddenly so strong it reminded her of kissing his throat. Her brow knit beneath the blindfold. When he pulled away all she could smell was his cologne. He had put it there, why?

"I've invited some friends."

Evelyn tensed, all other thoughts floating away like dust. She and Lucian had discussed a myriad of fantasies. She had a safe word in case she ever felt unsure and he reminded her often that she could use it. Sharing was something she was not okay with and he knew it. He too admitted not being able to tolerate another man touching her.

Her heart pounded like a wild bird caged in her chest. Her tongue slicked suddenly dry lips. Was this part of the game or had he had a change of heart?

"Undress, boys. I believe we can each have a shot at making her come before her lover returns."

She sucked in a sharp breath. In the span of a second her confidence in his commitment to be the *only person* entitled to her body wavered, shoved back by her absolute certainty he would not push her too far. Still, she sought reassurance.

"Luc—"

His hand pressed over her mouth. "Quiet."

Then his touch was gone. She grew intensely self-conscious of her naked, exposed state. *He wouldn't. He would never share her. Not now, after they'd come so far.*

The sound of fabric shifting grated over her nerves like tiny blades. True anxiety announced itself and her breathing grew loud enough to overshadow the sound of the bodies moving. It was a game. He was toying with her and her rational self knew that, trusted him, but her imagination, that twisted part of the mind that fabricated nightmares, was really fucking with her certainty.

She fought for control, ordering herself to calm down. Sharp awareness of how much control she'd surrendered dominated her panic. She was helpless.

There was a shuffling of movement. The jangle of coins deep within silk-lined pockets, the clank of a metal belt buckle hitting the marble floor. She couldn't help but flinch when someone's hand wrapped around the arch of her foot and pulled it toward the edge of the bed. *Lucian. Lucian. Lucian. It's only Lucian.*

"Isn't she beautiful, boys? Look at that pretty pink pussy. It's just begging to be filled by a big, hard cock."

Evelyn trembled as her ankle was restrained with silk. Again, a hand wrapped around her other foot. The process was repeated and all physical contact ceased. She shivered, as she lay exposed, restrained, and completely vulnerable. Minutes ticked by like hours. The silence was deafening. She wanted to scream, but also refused to give over, thinking she could somehow outwit the hysteria that beckoned. He was testing her trust, she realized.

She did trust Lucian. He was purposely shaking her faith, that was all—fishing for more reassurance. Actions spoke louder than words. Knowing that he would watch her reactions, weigh her surrender, only calmed her more. He wouldn't let anyone else touch her. This was a test, to see if she trusted him to toe the line without crossing it.

As she lay there on the plush, cool covers she lost track of time. The weight of being watched pressed into her, tightening her skin, making her hyperaware she was not alone, yet at the same time she had never felt so unaccompanied. What was he waiting for? Trepidation choked her. No one else was there; she knew it because she knew him, sometimes better than she knew herself, but still, the anticipation of proof was torture. She didn't want to move past the game, but she *needed* to confirm she was right and it was only the two of them in the penthouse.

Blindly, she clung to the familiar scent of Lucian just under her nose. She became aware of only that one anchor. So engrossed was she in breathing in that recognizable scent that she missed the moment he climbed onto the bed. The tickle of mysterious soft hair along her spread thighs made her jump. Silk cut into her ankles and wrists as she tugged at her bindings, and then his mouth was on her.

She didn't have time to adjust to the onslaught of sensations attacking her. This was it. This was the mind fuck of having an unsolicited touch force pleasure on her. The game suddenly became a reality.

Fingers plunged into her wet core as lips tightened over the bud of her sex. Pleasure, no matter how much she protested it, built and washed over her with the sudden downpour of sweet release. Evelyn cried out, and before the fluttering waves subsided, the mouth was gone.

Insecurity and confusion warred with her lust-addled brain. Doubt and certainty reflected each other like a funhouse mirror. Where was Lucian? She was so disoriented, she couldn't place him in the room.

Her questions ceased as the mattress dipped again and a strong body climbed on top of her. Her chest constricted at the unknown. This was still Lucian's fantasy. He would not let someone else touch her, but the illusion he'd created was intensely real.

Trust him, Evelyn! Trust him.

Forcing a steady breath, she swallowed and waited. He had control. He had the power to call halt. He loved her. He would never push her too far.

It amazed her how much her trust for this man could calm her.

She never had such unwavering faith in someone else, never allowed herself to be so vulnerable. Trusting another to take care of her and know exactly what she could and could not handle was a new and frightening experience for her.

Heavy weight settled high on her torso, knees bracketing her rib cage. Evelyn waited. Hands encased her breasts, and thumbs flicked over her nipples. Her thighs fought to draw together, but the silk holding her ankles was without give.

Heat seared to the tips of her breasts as fingers clamped down on her nipples. Her lips pressed tightly, and her breath was audible in the silent room as it rushed in and out of her nose. Why was it so quiet?

His weight eased and a finger ran along her jaw. Every touch raced over her senses, prickling every nerve receptor she had. Fingers curled over her chin as a thumb gently traced her mouth, pressing down on her lower lip. Her mouth opened and the hand was gone as he leaned forward and pressed his cock between her lips.

Her tongue compressed under the hot weight, and she fought the urge to pull away. She had only ever done this with Lucian, and her mind eased as she recognized the feel of him.

Her lips stretched as the cock pressed deep. She was completely pinned and afraid of choking, but he quickly withdrew. The mattress dipped beside her head where he caught his weight. As he pressed forward again, she heard the sound of heavy breathing. He was not unaffected.

Her tongue curved around the cock foisting into her mouth, and she sucked. A sharp grunt sounded above her.

The cock withdrew with a pop, and his weight was suddenly gone. Her lips moved as she silently repeated his name like a prayer. *Lucian, Lucian, Lucian, Lucian . . .*

The slight flow of blood tingled to her toes, as her feet were untied. Her legs were drawn together and her body was pivoted and dragged over the bedding until a good portion of her limbs hung off the edge of the mattress. As her hips were hoisted and turned, forcing her to switch her weight from her back to her belly, she gasped. Barely given a chance to adjust, she was yanked lower on the bed until her toes grazed the cold marble floor.

She lunged forward as two hands spread her cheeks. If there was ever a place a woman could be violated—a tongue licked over her back entrance. Unexpected pleasure knifed up her spine. A moan laced with the sound of confusion escaped her. The stubble of a male jaw scraped over her flesh followed by the quick nip of teeth. Then the assault began.

"Lucian!"

Faster and faster, his tongue slid over her flesh. Her cries called into the mattress until she was practically begging for him to finish her. His hand gripped her cheek while his other hand teased at her back entrance. When a wide finger speared the tight pucker there, she shouted with acute pleasure.

Her body jerked as the digit fucked her. Her ankles were kicked out by bare feet, and hot thighs pressed against the backs of hers. The broad head of a cock slipped through the arousal covering her folds, and she experienced the unmistakable sensation of flesh on flesh. That's when her certainty was validated.

Lucian. It's Lucian.

She was, without a doubt, one hundred percent certain. Relief and pride washed over her that in those sparse moments of doubt she held strong to her conviction that it was him. Lucian could barely tolerate another man looking at her, let alone touching her. The lack of protection separating their bodies was all the proof she needed to ease her fickle mind. Her body stretched at the familiar sensation of Lucian's cock pressing into her.

He thrust into her, burying himself to the hilt and lifting her feet clear off the floor. Evelyn sobbed with renewed desire. His thumb pressed deep into her back passage as his cock withdrew and thrust again.

"Lucian . . ." She repeated his name like a mantra, again and again, but out loud. With each vocalization of his name, he fucked her harder. His movements echoed his own manly cries. Grunts and moans filled the air over the slapping sound of sex. Her skin heated and her blood slowly boiled under the surface.

"Say it . . ." he demanded. "Say my name . . ."

"*Lucian*," she shouted, her voice now hoarse as well.

"That's it. Say it. Know that I'm the only one who will ever touch you like this. Me, Evelyn." He forced his cock deep, withdrew his thumb and blanketed her body with his weight. "Me."

It was raw and it was coarse, but it was completely honest. His need for her flowed from his body to hers as his heart beat into her back. However she had imagined love, it was not this. This was not something soft and delicate, tied up in flowers and bows. This was wild and honest, durable and true. He loved her, and when his feelings poured out of him like this, it was so potent there was no denying they were real.

His breath beat at her shoulder. Her heart pounded into the bedding. He could be rough with her. She wouldn't break, and over time he had learned that. She smiled into the rumpled bedding as her body found contentment in this beautiful moment.

"You, Lucian. Only you."

She gasped as he suddenly withdrew completely. Her body was lifted and flipped. Again, she was lying on her back. His hips pressed between hers and his cock slid home. Belly to belly, they each sobbed at the unbelievable pleasure of being connected in such an elemental manner. Anyone could fuck, but she found it hard to believe many people knew what this felt like.

The blindfold was stripped from her eyes and she blinked into the shadowy darkness of the room.

"Look at me."

Lashes fluttering, she focused on the dark silhouette above her. As Lucian's messy black hair came into focus and his dark eyes bored into her, she had the wonderful sense of coming home. There was no need to search for others. They were alone. "I knew it was you," she whispered with a smile.

"Always me, Evelyn. No one else." His lips crashed down over hers and he delivered the most passionate kiss of her life. "I missed you today."

"I missed you too." Her knees drew up and cradled his hips. Fingers tugged at the silk tied to her wrists, and the fabric gave way. She fisted her fingers in the air, forcing the blood back into them, then reached for him.

Warm, damp muscle filled her grip as she dragged her nails over his broad shoulders. Grasping his arms, she stared at him. The words were there, but she couldn't say them. Fear that they might slip out had her leaning up to kiss him.

The urgency eased, but their need only grew. Slow intensity guided them. Her hands explored his body, gripped his neck, tugged at his hair. She latched her leg over his hip, ground her heel into his thigh, and they melded together as if they could somehow pass through each other.

Broad hands spanned her back, lifted her closer as he thrust deep. His strokes, now measured, were delivered in a way that said *never forget me*.

She never would.

"I love you, Evelyn."

Still unable to say the words, she pressed her face into his strong chest, gripped him with all the need and affection she had for him, the ever-present, all-consuming drive to be by him, with him, and showed her love the best she knew how.

three
.....

BREAKFAST OF CHAMPIONS

EVELYN'S drowsy mind told her it wasn't quite morning before she opened her eyes. Something had awoken her. Soft sheets twisted over her body cushioned her with pockets of heat. She stretched and instinctively reached for Lucian. When her hand came into contact with cooling emptiness, her eyes opened.

Frowning into the dark, she listened. In her mind, she saw him sitting in his chair, watching the early morning stillness just before daybreak crept in.

There is a quiet to night that only comes during the brief moment when the world is mostly asleep. Taxis are hidden away and even the nightingales have flown home. In a city like Folsom, these moments are fleeting and rare, yet Lucian seemed gifted in capturing them. As weightless as wishes drawn into a net, he somehow always knew exactly when these moments drifted by. They were as delicate as an untouched bed of new-fallen snow, and Lucian seemed to catch every single one before the world shattered that glimpse of quiet peace.

The condo was silent. She slid from their bed, cool marble

pressing into her feet. Her arms slipped into her robe. Padding softly into the common area of the suite, she stilled at the edge of the hall. Lucian sat in his desk chair just as she expected him to be, posture at ease, ankles crossed, fingers steepled beneath his chin, facing the window.

The blackness of early morning showed his reflection in the glass. With the ease of sand falling through an hourglass, black faded into deep purple hues. He appeared deep in thought. She smiled, enjoying the sight of her intense, beautiful man.

Even beneath the frown rippling his brow, he was incredibly handsome. His bare chest was naturally muscled. His legs, clad in only black silk lounge pants, were strong and long.

Lucian often awoke at odd hours of the night. It wasn't uncommon to find him there, contemplating one business deal or another. Evelyn wasn't much help in that department. Maybe someday she could be. Right now she was working on learning to read, so that day was far off.

This was his time. She'd come to think that he awoke at such an early hour because it was the one time of day he would not be disturbed. Lucian's life was unendingly busy, yet at the same time, startlingly lonely. She didn't like to think about him sitting up in the middle of the night before she came to live with him. There was a sadness to Lucian she was still figuring out. She liked to think she was easing it, filling that hole camouflaged beneath the image of perfection, but she was never really sure.

She quietly padded over to him, smiling softly the moment he noticed her. The tension tightening his expression eased, and he seemed to breathe a sigh of relief as if she were a welcome distraction.

His hand reached for her. "Hey, beautiful."

"Hey."

Evelyn lowered herself to the carpeted floor and rested her

head on his thigh. His palm immediately ran over the length of her hair.

"Did I wake you?"

She shook her head, the silk of his pants a whisper beneath her cheek. "I couldn't find you."

His sigh told her he had a lot on his mind. She wished she could ease his burdens, but most of Lucian's stress was far above her head.

"Did you have fun with Antoinette yesterday?" he asked, his fingers sifting softly through her hair.

She shut her eyes. "Mm-hm. Your sister sure likes to shop."

He laughed quietly as he twirled a chestnut strand. "Your shopping bag was delivered. What did you get?"

Evelyn remembered the way Toni made fun of her purchases. "Nothing."

"You got something. The bag felt heavy."

She shrugged. "A vendor was selling some odds and ends I thought were neat. He looked a little down on his luck and I thought some of his merchandise was interesting so I paid him a hundred dollars for all of it. I think the most valuable thing I got was his gratitude. The rest is probably worthless, but it felt really good giving him that money."

"Then mission accomplished. I give you spending money to enjoy; if giving it to that vendor brought you pleasure, I'm glad you did it."

Her heart fluttered at his justification. He was always so accepting of her, even when she did weird stuff like pay a hundred dollars for a bag of rocks.

"Your sister thinks I'm nuts."

"Toni's young."

"She's my age, Lucian."

"You've had more life experiences than most will ever see in their lifetime. Toni only knows what it is to live in the lap of luxury. She doesn't understand what it is to truly be hungry for more."

She drew in a deep breath, pulling his comforting scent deep into her lungs. The sky on the other side of the glass had faded to a deep amethyst. They skipped dinner last night, spending the evening in bed making love and munching on muffins and breads Lucian always kept on hand. She was hungry.

As if reading her mind, he said, "How about I order some breakfast for us and you show me your purchases?"

"Okay."

She stood and Lucian grabbed her hand. His dark gaze told her he wanted to tell her something. He looked at her for a long moment, but said nothing. Noticing the set of his eyes, she recognized a bit of the well-concealed sadness showing through.

"What is it?" she asked.

He shook his head. "Nothing. I just . . . I'm glad you're here . . . with me."

Warmth spread through her chest. Her lips curved. He had no idea how much he meant to her. Never before in her entire life had she put so much trust in another human being. Although she was terrified of admitting she loved him, afraid saying it would make it real and somehow more fragile, she knew he felt her love.

He had brought her here, clothed her, sheltered her, taught her, and loved her. Lucian *was* home, her home.

Leaning close, she pressed her lips to his and whispered. "Me too. Besides, where else would I be?" As she pulled away, worry still weighed on his face. Something was really bothering him. "Lucian, is something wrong?"

Immediately, his expression cleared. "No. I'm just being sentimental. Go get your things. I'll call down for breakfast."

She knew when he was being sincere and when he was being Lucian Patras, master of strategy, connoisseur of façades. She didn't enjoy feeling maneuvered like one of his business associates, but whatever was bothering him seemed to run deep. She'd give it a few days to surface before she asked again.

While they waited for breakfast, Evelyn had a quick shower. As she returned from the bedroom, hair wet and in her robe once more, she found Lucian sitting at the sofa, examining a blue stone. She hesitated, hoping he wouldn't tell her she wasted her money. Their covered breakfast awaited them at a small bistro table in the corner. She could smell the sweet scent of the maple syrup and knew he had ordered her favorite, French toast.

Slowly, she walked to the couch. Lucian turned the stone this way and that. "This is sea glass."

"I know. I probably wasted the money—"

"I think it's interesting. You can't get stuff like this so far in from the coast. They're pretty."

Such satisfaction filled her when he didn't judge her for buying rocks and glass. "I thought they were interesting too. Look at this one, with the green and purple swirls. That one's my favorite."

He smiled at her excitement as she scooted close to him on the sofa. They searched through the stones, pointing out various unique qualities of each one. "What are you going to do with them?"

She shrugged. "I don't know, but they seemed too pretty to let go. Is that weird?"

He grinned and pulled her close, his fingers pushing her damp hair away from her face. "As a collector and curator of beautiful things, I'd have to say no." He kissed her, his passion starting a slow burn, then quickly heating. "I'm hungry," he whispered against her lips.

Her mind went to the fluffy French toast waiting for them as Lucian's hand tugged at the belt of her robe. He eased her down on the couch. "Lucian . . ." She giggled.

"Hush."

The plush lapels of her terrycloth robe were drawn away from her bare breasts as he positioned her the way he wanted, hands resting above her head on the arm of the sofa. She tipped her chin to watch him.

Warm lips pressed into the tender flesh of her belly as he took his time working his way to her sex. Strong hands gripped her narrow hips, practically spanning her midsection, thumbs pulling at the flesh above her sex. By the time he placed a kiss on the bare delta of her pussy, she was a puddle of desire.

Soft hair tickled her belly, and her body coiled, seeking his contact. Slowly, his tongue licked over her clit and she arched. Everything was soft, sleepy; nothing felt rushed as he explored her.

He groaned in approval of the needy way she moaned and pressed into his touch. Sometimes Lucian desired her in a manner that was so intense she lost touch with reality and existed only for him. Other times he drove her to a point of need so slowly and acutely it was almost painful. Either way she loved it when he touched her. She had never had another lover, but was certain there was no one in this world who could pleasure her the way Lucian Patras could.

His tongue slid through her dewy folds, gently fucking her, sipping from her, nibbling her lips. Taking his time, for several long minutes, he simply made love to her with his mouth, drinking from her as if she were a sacrament.

Warmth bathed her sex as his tongue flicked over her clit. She moaned and begged him never to stop. He drew out her torture until she was sure even the slightest touch of his breath would make her come. It was amazing that such slow seduction could bring her to this point.

"Come for me, Evelyn," he whispered over her clit before kissing her there, pulling her gently into his mouth.

She arched as shivers racked her body. Limbs locking, toes

pointing, her legs slowly curled over his strong arms as her heart beat right down to the point below his lips. Warm waves of pleasure blanketed her, carrying her on an easy current to a time-less place of beauty and escape.

She sagged in his grip as he lifted her on top of him. Quickly he lowered his silk pants to his hips and seated her with a knee on each side of his thighs. Her sex rippled at the press of his hard cock. The wide head breached her folds and filled her, prolonging her orgasm before it could fade.

Lucian's hands brushed her tangled hair away from her face, and when his lips found hers she tasted herself. Her weight lifted as she slowly rode him, luxuriating in the fullness he made her feel. They kissed and fucked with an unhurried passion and she savored it.

His hands gripped her softer parts tightly, as though he needed to feel her everywhere. Fingers coasted down her spine, twisting and tickling up to her scalp where they locked in her hair, angling her head back.

His mouth sucked at the long column of her exposed throat. He kept her in the vulnerable position, hair fisted in his hand, other hand anchoring down her hip as he lifted his body into hers. Deep, needy pleas of lust whispered over her flesh as he filled her.

Her body peaked again and her hair suddenly released as his palms gripped her hips hard and dragged her down on his cock, impaling her, dragging her clit over the hard bone of his pelvis. She treasured making love like this, savoring every tender touch and intense whisper.

He filled her with his hot release. Her body fluttered and he began to rapidly pump his hips off the couch, thrusting into her deep. "I want one more orgasm from you, Evelyn."

Lifting from her wilted pose, she covered him, crying out as he drove her to the pinnacle quickly and she easily climaxed.

When she came, it was hard and forceful. She cried out and collapsed onto his shoulder, replete, tiny shockwaves of the aftermath jerking her body in tiny spasms every few seconds as she came back down.

The thump of his heart thudded against her ear. She smiled into his chest and giggled. "I'm gonna need another shower."

His chuckle was a slow rumble that expanded the smirk on her face.

She loved him.

four
.....

SNEAKING AROUND THE KNIGHT

"OKAY, read me the next one," Lucian said as he sat behind his messy desk, reading glasses perched low on his nose, and made notes in his ledger.

Evelyn took a deep breath. "*Cllll . . . Clep . . . Cleptone . . .*"

"Clapton."

"*Clapton In . . . Indeew . . .*" She blew out a frustrated breath.

"Take your time."

"*Clapton Indeew . . .*"

"It's a soft U, like in *under* or *umbrella*."

"*Clapton Induss . . .* I don't know it."

"That's because you haven't sounded it out yet. Don't get frustrated. Take your time. Remember how *ies* sounds at the end of a word."

He was so patient with her. She looked at the statement again. "*Clapton Indust . . . ar . . . ies.*"

"Now put it together."

"*Clapton Indust-ar-ies* . . . Clapton Industries!"

"Very good!" His eyes creased softly at the sides as he gave her a praising smile.

She grinned proudly from the club chair pulled close to his disordered desk. Lucian was a perfectionist and neat in everything except the way he kept his workstation.

This had become part of their Sunday morning routine. Lucian would order breakfast, they'd eat, she'd change into one of his shirts from the week that still carried his scent before the cleaners could wash it away, and she'd read through a stack of invoices as he recorded the names in his ledger. It was a task that would probably take less than ten minutes for him to do on his own, but it was good practice for her. She had come a long way from the illiterate girl she was when they met last fall.

He added the name into the ledger and placed his pen in the crease of the binding. It took Evelyn a while to realize most people did their bookkeeping on computers. Lucian told her he preferred the feel of the pen between his fingers and the appeal of the leather-bound ledger. She liked seeing him like this.

Stretching, Lucian let out a wide yawn that ended with a manly, animalistic-growl-type howl. "Let's do the rest later. Why don't you take a break? I have to make a few phone calls."

Evelyn left the invoices on the chair and stretched as well. There was no use putting the organized stack of paper on his desk. That thing was like a black hole.

As she snuggled onto the sofa and mindlessly hit buttons on the remote, she considered how much her life had changed from the endless struggle to survive it once was. Here she sat, toes warm in a thick pair of wool socks, fire burning in a glass insert ten feet away, television at her disposal, and a bracelet worth God only knew how much weighing down her wrist. It was bizarre.

She came across some Sunday morning cartoons and put the

remote aside. Adult programs bored her, although she did enjoy the *Gilligan's Island* reruns. Having never gone to school or lived in a real house, she simply couldn't relate to the shows women her age usually liked. Once she watched a court show where two friends fought over a pedigreed dog, and she wanted to reach through the screen and strangle them both. Some people just didn't know what real problems were.

Lucian spoke softly in the background, his velvety voice mingling with the pings and whizzes coming from the television, accompanied by her occasional giggle. A scraggly character showed up and her mind wandered to faces from her past, one in particular.

No matter how she tried to forget about Parker, she couldn't let him go. He'd hurt her the last time they spoke. His disapproval held more weight in her conscience than she was comfortable admitting. He basically accused her of being someone seduced by money. Of course he didn't know how deeply she had grown to care for Lucian at the time he made his accusation, but there was no excuse. His words hurt. They weren't true, but it took her a long time to convince her bruised pride of that.

Lucian tried convincing her that Parker only said those hurtful things because he was in love with her and jealous, but that wasn't true either. She and Parker had known each other for almost ten years. He'd come to the tracks when she was just a girl, probably around ten or twelve. Evelyn never knew when her real birthday was, so keeping track of her age was always a challenge. She assumed her age to be closer to twelve because she recalled that was the year she had just started to develop and get hair where she had none before.

He was fourteen, a couple of years older than her. He didn't look like he belonged on the streets. Parker had papers that certified his age and other important information, which he carried with him at all times. She had nothing like that. According to the government, she didn't really exist. Lucian was working on obtaining legal documents for her, but it was difficult when there was no record of her existence.

There had always been something about Parker that said he'd been on the other side, known what it was like. He'd somehow known money well enough to hold disdain for wealth. He could read heavy hardcover books and loved to. He was cultured in a way only educated people were. There was a lot to envy about him.

Evelyn decided at an early age she would not become like the rest of the John and Jane Does out there. It had been her life's objective to get a job and get off the streets. That was how she met Lucian. To those that knew her plight, it was easy to see how some might mistake her as a gold digger. But she and Lucian and those they trusted most knew the truth of it. Evelyn felt entitled to nothing of his wealth and had no interest in it. She only had a desire for earning her *own* money, not taking someone else's.

Although she gave up her job as a maid at Patras, that didn't mean she was turning into a kept woman. She had worked into the New Year, but her appearance in a service uniform began raising eyebrows when people recognized her as the woman on Lucian's arm who'd been wearing an evening gown the night before. It was sort of weird working for, and sleeping with, the owner of the hotel. And there was no way she was giving up Lucian. So she gave up her job. Lucian was ecstatic, but she needed to start looking for a new one.

Lucian preferred her not to work, and while there was no immediate need for money, she'd been without her own income for almost a month, and that was enough. Income meant personal security. It was time for her to find new employment. She dreaded that discussion.

Her gaze drifted to Lucian. He was sitting at his desk, speaking softly into the phone. His reading glasses hung low on his nose, and he needed a shave. No one else saw him this way, vulnerable, relaxed. Heat spread in her chest. He was hers.

As she turned back to the television, her mind returned to Parker. Unlike Lucian's strong presence Parker was . . . less intimidating. He was thinner, due to the difference in their lifestyles. Sometimes Parker had facial hair, usually in the colder months, but when he shaved, his skin still had a youthful glow Lucian's lacked. Lucian was a man. Evelyn still saw Parker as a boy only slightly older than herself.

Shortly after she and Parker met, he had come to her rescue. She could still recall the shock of seeing him attack Slim, a disgusting pervert who lived at the tracks. Slim had come into the abandoned mill she and her mother occupied. Pearl had gotten in the habit of trading herself for drugs, mostly heroin. One day Slim came by and Pearl wasn't there.

He entered what Scout considered their private space and seemed reluctant to leave. Scout wasn't ignorant about certain things, even at her young age, but she was taken off guard when Slim touched her. No one touched her in those places. She'd pushed his grubby hand away, repulsed by how filthy his fingers were, but he only pushed back. Instinctively, when his grip on her thigh tightened, she screamed and Parker came running.

She'd been so confused and upset she began to cry, something she never allowed herself to do in front of others at the tracks. After dealing with Slim, Parker held her and promised her she would be all right. He had become a force of his own to reckon with, shocking her with how lethal he could become when pushed. Nothing made sense that day. Parker somehow crossed into her personal space the way no one else on the streets ever could.

It wasn't until after the fact that she realized they were *friends*. On the streets she was known as Scout because she was excellent at scouting out good finds. She knew the underbelly of Folsom like the back of her hand. She was a survivor, determined to get out and make a real life for her and Pearl. Scout didn't have friends. Caring for those on the streets would only hold her to that unfavorable part of her existence. But Parker had become one.

A cold chill ran through her as she wondered where he was now. He was smart, smarter than the rest of them. It was Parker who taught her the basics of reading, giving her enough knowledge to land a halfway decent job. Television was unavailable where they were from, but the Folsom library was a public place. Parker spent most of his days entertaining himself with books. He sometimes took her with him. Those days were her favorites.

They'd curl up on the braided rug in the children's section and he'd guide her through children's classics. The first book she ever read a page from was *Green Eggs and Ham*. She was around eighteen, and it was probably one of the proudest moments of her life. She could only read very small words. Having Parker read to her was much more enjoyable than struggling to hear herself clumsily piece together letters.

Growing up within and never leaving a ten-mile radius, books opened a world of imagination for her. She saw things in her mind she could only dream of ever seeing in real life, the ocean, Egypt, the Big Top, all described in such thought-out detail she could taste the cotton candy and breathe the salt air without ever leaving that magical braided carpet.

He made it a goal to read her as many classics as possible, *The Catcher in the Rye*, *The Color Purple*, *Of Mice and Men*. She couldn't get enough. Scout became obsessed with words. Even if she couldn't read big words, there was no stopping her from saying them. She clung to every syllable he spoke, like a thief.

Then there were the more mysterious sides of Parker. When a person is homeless, there is little entertainment, so in the fall they enjoyed watching the little league practice and play games. The

T-Ball players were the cutest. She and Parker made a habit out of finding entertainment that was free.

One day she'd gone looking for Parker so they could find something to do together. He had a few places he hid out when he wasn't at the library. She ended up finding him in an alley, where she heard noises. When she peeked into the shadows, she wasn't prepared for what she saw. Parker was doing to another woman what Slim had wanted to do to Scout. However, this woman seemed on board with his plans.

Scout gasped, and Parker immediately turned and cursed. The woman gave Scout a nasty look that haunted her for days. She now was old enough to know that Parker was having sex. That afternoon, a world of mixed emotions opened up inside of her over the span of a minute. She supposed she'd always looked up to Parker in a way, found him admirable. She wasn't jealous of the woman. Sex scared Scout and she wanted nothing to do with it. Yet, there came a twinge of something she couldn't name when she realized Parker was doing it with that woman.

He chased after her, completely discarding the other woman. When he caught up to her, he grabbed her arm.

"Scout, what are you doing here?"

"I . . . I was looking for you."

His face was creased with frustration, and his cheeks were flushed. "You shouldn't have come here."

His words irritated her. She jerked her arm away. "I'm not a child, Parker. I know what you were doing."

"I know you're not a child. I just . . . I didn't want you to see that."

"Why?" She was truly curious about his reasons.

He frowned and wedged his hands in his pocket. Looking away, he mumbled, "It's dirty."

She frowned as well. "You aren't the only person who does that, Parker."

"I know. But I don't like it."

"Then why do you do it?"

He shrugged. "Guys are different. We need . . ."

She waited quietly for him to continue. His cheeks grew redder and he said nothing. She touched his arm. "It's okay, Park. I get it."

He shook his head and curved his lips into a barely there smile. "No, you don't, but thanks for trying."

Her hand dropped from his arm. "Thanks." She was insulted. "You know, you aren't much older than me—"

"I know that! God, Scout, I know that."

"Then why do you say things like that, like I'm some dumb kid?"

"Because you're a good girl and a good girl shouldn't see two people going at it like animals!" he hissed.

She drew back. Her understanding of sex was twisted. She'd seen her mother and other men. There was no modesty. She saw things no child should probably witness. She only needed to see it once to determine she never needed to see it again. But to her knowledge, there was no way to have sex that wasn't animalistic.

After they stood awkwardly silent for a while and the woman he had been with slunk away, he said, "Come on. I'll walk you back."

They walked in silence, she playing back what she'd seen, and Parker scowling about what he had inadvertently showed her. One thing she was sure of, he did not see her as a sexual being, but as more of a little sister. This pleased and irritated her for reasons she didn't understand.

Evelyn smiled, remembering how, after that, he made a point to read adult stories to her. They were never graphic, but sometimes they mentioned some of those less animalistic couplings he must have been referring to. He would sometimes blush when he read her the more adult parts of those classics.

That day at the alley was never mentioned again, but from then on, on those days he would sometimes disappear, she'd smirk and avoid his eyes upon his return, knowing exactly where he'd been and what he'd been doing.

Parker had definitely been her friend, the only one she ever had before Lucian.

Her present-day mind jumped to visions of her and Lucian. They could be quite animalistic, yet she loved being with him in that way. She preferred him intense and raw and holding nothing back. When he acted as such, she seemed to break out of her rigid skin and surrender, allowing him to guide her somewhere dark and freeing where only the two of them existed.

"What are you grinning about?"

At Lucian's question, Evelyn's mind snapped back to the present. Her lips trembled and fell into a more natural smile.

"I was just thinking about how much my life has changed." There was no point in mentioning Parker. Lucian didn't care for him and never seemed to regret the day Parker insulted her, as it conveniently removed him from her life.

She hoped he was someplace warm. Maybe he was curled up by the library radiators at that very moment, reading some spectacular tale. She told herself that was likely where he was, needing the comfort of believing him safe.

"Jamie called. You didn't tell me you saw him yesterday. He wants us to join him downtown for dinner."

Evelyn never minded spending time with Jamie. It was Slade, Lucian's other colleague, she hated. The feeling was mutual. Luckily, since she and Lucian settled into a more serious arrangement, Slade rarely came around. As a matter of fact, she couldn't recall the last time she'd seen him.

"Dinner with Jamie sounds great."

BY Thursday, Evelyn still couldn't shake her thoughts of Parker. The more she thought about him the more she worried something was wrong, as though an unknown force was putting him into her mind on purpose. Lucian had long ago forbidden her to visit the part of the city where the shelter was, because he considered it too dangerous. She'd tried to sneak back a few times, only to be followed. Each attempt ended in a fight she had no interest in repeating.

Lucian had a lot on his mind lately, probably some big business deal. She didn't want to cause a rift or bring him more stress by mentioning Parker or asking to visit St. Christopher's.

She knew the only way she could get to that part of Folsom was through sheer creativity and pretended innocence. The problem was, Lucian loathed any hint of dishonesty between them. She'd have to figure out a way to check on Parker while being honest and casually forgetting to divulge her true intentions. There was a run-down strip mall between St. Christopher's and the Folsom Library, and that was how her plan took shape.

"Do you think Dugan can take me to a craft store tomorrow?"

Lucian looked up from the checkered onyx, considering his next move. Chess was a way they often ended their evenings. She'd become quite good at the game. He lifted his knight and captured her bishop.

Bastard.

She scowled at the board. She didn't want to sacrifice her queen.

"What do you need there?" Lucian asked as she contemplated a very stupid move she would likely make in order to save the old girl.

"I was thinking about getting some wire and stuff. Maybe I can make something out of the sea glass I bought."

"Like a sculpture."

She smiled, knowing it took everything he had not to tease her. "No, not like a sculpture. Maybe a necklace or something."

"I'm not sure if I know where a store with that sort of stuff is in the city."

"There's one by the library."

He eyed her curiously for a long moment, and she hoped he didn't see through her request. She took great interest in moving her rook to a square that made no sense.

He pursed his lips, eyeing her, as he captured the rook with a pawn. "Are you sure wire is all that you're looking for?"

She swallowed and forced herself not to give anything away. Looking down at the board, she picked up a pawn without thinking and slid it forward. "Maybe some tools to work with too."

When she returned her gaze to his face he was still watching her. Without breaking eye contact, he captured the pawn she just moved. "Think about your actions, Evelyn. Hasty moves will get you into trouble."

He was referring to the game, but the knot in her stomach told her he might be commenting on more than that. He could read her like one of those books she longed to devour from start to finish. She looked down and frowned over her new predicament. "You've won." She moved her bishop anyway, knowing it was only a matter of two or three moves before he had her in check without an escape.

He slid his bishop forward, knocking out her most powerful piece and doing exactly that. "I always get my queen. Check."

• • •

EVELYN shifted nervously as they headed into the more unsavory parts of Folsom. Not being honest with Lucian didn't sit right with her, but she had become wholly convinced that something was wrong. She just needed to find Parker and see that he was okay, and then everything could go back to normal.

They were heading to the craft store by the library, so she hadn't lied, per se. Still, guilt chafed her insides. Lucian was a stickler about honesty, stating it was a fundamental ingredient to trust. She agreed with him, which made her feel like complete crap. But in this situation, her confirmation that Parker was fine would ease her mind. She didn't see the need for drama and justifying her actions when all she was searching for was a little peace of mind, especially when Lucian was already stressing over issues outside of their relationship.

Lucian always sent Dugan with more than enough money for anything she needed, but he also left an obscene amount of cash in her top drawer for things around the hotel. She rarely touched that money. It wasn't hers and she didn't think she would ever see it any other way. However, today she secretly skimmed two hundred dollars off the top in case she did find Parker and he needed it. As soon as she found a new job she would replace the money she took if that were the case.

Her stomach twisted as old familiar places came into view. It was a distasteful form of nostalgia. This part of Folsom lacked the hustle and bustle flowing around Patras. No one walked around these parts unless it was all they ever knew or if they were hoping to score a hit. She glanced into the rearview mirror and saw Dugan scowling over the wheel.

"Thanks for driving me, Big D."

He grunted. "Perhaps next time you need art supplies you

could shop online or at the craft outlet by Mr. Patras's permanent residence."

Yeah, that would probably make more sense. "This one has the things I'm looking for. I should only be a few minutes."

She was swallowing more than usual, and a touch of carsickness had her shutting her eyes. Being deceptive sucked.

As they neared the library, Evelyn perked up. Dugan was watching her and she grew paranoid that he suspected her motive for coming to that section of the city, but she came all this way to find Parker, and even Dugan's surly glances wouldn't stop her from trying. It would be stupid to come here and be too chicken to actually look. Besides, she could be looking for anything.

Her eyes scoured the alleyways and sidewalks, greedily searching for any flash of life. March was cold and wet, so there wasn't much more than litter traveling by. A sense of regret filled her as the limo passed the library with no sign of Parker.

They pulled into the strip mall and Dugan parked. There weren't a lot of shoppers. He came to her door and escorted her to the craft shop. The chirp of the limo's alarm engaging echoed like a lost crow in a desolate field.

Dugan was like a shadow, bigger than her, always there, always silent. She distractedly filled her basket with materials she hadn't the slightest idea how to use. She'd made the trip. She might as well get what she told Lucian she needed. Dugan eyed the merchandise quietly.

She turned when he cleared his throat. He held a packaged tool in his hand that looked like a drill.

"It's a solder gun," he explained. "If you're going to be making something with wire you probably want one to secure the ends."

She smiled at him. Dugan didn't say much, but he also didn't miss much. It was lonely sometimes, what with how often Lucian was pulled away on business. She liked to think that Dugan liked her. Moments like this made her believe he did.

She held out her basket. "Thanks, Big D. Put her here."

He dropped the gun in her basket. "You'll probably want gloves too. Wires have a way of beating up your fingers. Little girlie hands like yours . . ." His words faded off as his gaze darted back to the shelf. He cleared his throat.

Big softy.

They loaded her basket with so many things, Dugan eventually offered to carry it. She was distracted when they passed the poster section and she spotted black-and-white prints of the city. She flipped through the matted prints. It didn't take long to find what she was looking for. *Patras.* The hotel stood like a god among kings.

"Does Lucian have this photograph?" she asked Dugan.

"I don't usually take notice of what's on Mr. Patras's walls."

"Well, I think he'd like it, don't you?"

"I think he would enjoy anything you chose for him, Ms. Keats."

"Seriously, Dugan, call me Evelyn or Scout. No one even calls my mom Ms. Keats. It's weird, especially considering how much time we spend together."

"Very well, Ms. Evelyn."

Her lips pursed. Narrowing her eyes, she tried to express what she thought about his compromise, but she let it go. "I'm gonna get it for him."

They visited the framing department, and Evelyn selected a cherry frame that reminded her of the wood of Lucian's desk in the condo. An employee placed the photograph within a sheet of dark red matting.

"Would you like to inscribe anything on the placard?" the

clerk asked. "We have a machine that does it, so it only takes a few minutes."

"Okay." She hadn't thought about actually having the little bronze label engraved, but she liked the idea.

The clerk slid a scrap of paper over the counter. "Here, write what you want it to say there. Make sure you write it exactly as you want it to appear as far as capital letters and all." He turned to ready the machine.

Evelyn swallowed and stared down at the blank scrap of paper. It was incredibly intimidating. Her hand slowly reached for the pencil, her fingers tightly wrapping around the six-sided piece of wood.

Fuck.

Breathing in, she pulled the paper close and poised the pencil at the edge. The tip snapped and she realized she was pressing too hard. "Um, can I have another pencil?"

"Sure." The clerk slid another across the counter.

She knew she could ask Dugan to write something down for her, but she wanted it to be from her. She wanted to say something poetic and special, but she only knew how to spell small words.

Her fingers slid over the smooth wood of the pencil as her palms began to sweat. She wiped them on her jeans, cleared her throat, and leaned closer. Her mind played over the words she knew how to spell until she finally thought of the perfect word.

Carefully her fingers pressed down as the soft lead glided over the paper, one straight line, then another. She connected them. *H.* Next she formed a circle. *O.* Licking her lips, she turned the paper and began making the next set of strokes. *M.* Finally, she turned the paper again and made four neat lines. *E. HOME.*

She placed the pencil down with a shaking hand, and Dugan leaned over her shoulder, observing the word she chose. "What do you think?"

He smiled at her, a rare expression on his serious face. "I think it's perfect, Ms. Evelyn."

She slid it to the clerk.

As they returned to the limo, that same sense of hopelessness filled her. As Dugan pulled away from the dilapidated strip mall, it transcended into a physical ache. She'd come all this way and discovered nothing. The discouraging ache bloomed into panic as they eased out of that part of the city.

"Dugan!"

The limo slowed immediately. She hadn't meant to shout. "Ms. Keats?"

"Can we stop at the library? I think I want to get some art books."

His eyes narrowed, but the car turned, heading back in that direction. As he parked he didn't immediately get out like he usually did. "We will have to be heading back soon. Mr. Patras made reservations for the two of you."

"I'll be quick."

The moment they made it into the old library, her eyes combed the aisles. She deliberately headed toward the literature department, where Parker found most of the classics he enjoyed. Passing the children's section, she paused, letting her memories comfort her. Only then did she realize how much she truly missed her friend. She didn't expect the familiar smell of paper and books to hit her as hard as it did, bringing with it a sentimental twinge.

"I believe the art section is this way, Ms. Keats."

Already he was back to the formal title. Reluctantly, looking one last time for her friend, she followed Dugan. She selected four books, one on jewelry making, one on wire sculpture, one on metal work, and one on architecture she thought Lucian would enjoy. She made sure to get books with lots of pictures.

She had never actually taken a book out of the library so she needed to give the woman at the counter her information in order to get a card. It was the first time she ever told someone her address and hadn't needed to lie.

Before they left she looked back at the quiet library one last time. Parker was nowhere to be found and this was likely the one place he would be. The shelter wasn't open until nightfall.

Sighing, she returned to the limo. The ride home was made in deep thought, one resounding hope playing through her head. *Please be okay.*

five

THE DANGER OF DECEPTION

"EVELYN? Are you listening to me?"

She looked up from her plate. "What?"

Lucian tilted his head and frowned. "What were you thinking about?"

"I . . . I don't know."

"How did your trip go today? Did you get what you needed?"

She nodded tightly. "Yes. I even picked up something for you. When we get back you can open it."

"A present?"

"Yes. I hope you like it."

He placed his hand over hers and squeezed affectionately. "I'm sure I will. What else did you do today?"

"I went to the salon and met Patrice for lunch."

"And I assume you two behaved yourselves. Or should I expect another four-hundred-dollar bar bill?"

She rolled her eyes. Get drunk and buy a few rounds *one time* and she'd never hear the end of it. "Don't be silly. It was lunchtime, not happy hour. I only spent two hundred on drinks for my admirers today."

All signs of amusement disappeared. *Shit.* She was only joking, but clearly her barb fell flat.

"Did anyone else join you for lunch?" His whisper was dangerous, the kind that told her there was no room for sarcasm.

"I was joking, Lucian."

"Jokes are meant to be funny, Evelyn."

She stilled and frowned at his snide tone. "No," she said succinctly. "There was barely anyone else in the restaurant. Unless you want to nitpick over the waiter being male, I think I'm in the clear."

"Watch it, Evelyn. You're mine. I have a right to be territorial when your last excursion with Patrice ended with men drooling all over your shoes."

She rolled her eyes. He was being ridiculous. "Those men don't matter, Lucian, and you know it."

"Are you sure about that? I think you underestimate your appeal."

She met his gaze and instinctively pulled back in her chair. "Yes, and the same could be said for you."

He was in a mood. Lucian was an extremely possessive man, but she'd given him no reason to doubt her. It was a stupid joke. How could he have possibly taken it as anything more? Why was he looking at her like that? The fact that she'd been deceptive that morning was perhaps intensifying her guilt and making her a bit too prickly.

No. He was being the prick. Picking up her fork, she defensively whispered, "God, forget I said anything."

The waiter came and refilled their glasses. The rest of the meal was eaten in silence. Maybe it was time to ask him about whatever was bothering him. He'd been extremely temperamental lately.

"Lucian, is everything okay? You've been acting strange lately, like something's been weighing on your mind."

His eyes softened. "I'm sorry. I've been . . ." She could tell he was choosing his words carefully. "I've been distracted over this deal I made a while back. It's silly to worry. I'll stop."

"But if you've already made the deal there's nothing to worry about, right?"

He placed his fork on the gold filigree rim of his plate and folded his hands at the edge of the table. "It all depends how things work out. Believe it or not, Evelyn, sometimes I make very stupid choices."

"Well, what's the deal about?"

"Finish your dinner. Let's not waste the evening talking about things I can't change at the moment. Everything will work out in time."

He was being cryptic and she didn't like it. Her appetite had dwindled. Taking a few more bites of her vegetables, she pushed her plate away and leaned back as the waiter cleared the table.

"Would you care for dessert?" Lucian asked.

"No, thank you."

The waiter returned and Lucian said, "She will have a hot fudge sundae."

As the waiter turned, she scoffed and whispered, "I said, no thank you."

"You're being stubborn."

The accusation was uncalled for and she didn't appreciate it. His crappy mood had nothing to do with her. "You're being thick-headed."

His eyes narrowed on her. Her mouth twitched. She couldn't believe she'd just said that. With Lucian, she had wisely learned to choose flight over fight. She stood. "I . . . I need to use the ladies' room. Excuse me."

Quickly, she turned to find the restrooms. What was wrong with them? It seemed like every word out of their mouths was a lie, her with her quest to locate Parker and him with his stupid deal—his words, not hers.

The guilt she had over worrying about Parker was eating at her, and that was simply ridiculous. He was her friend. She was allowed to have friends, damn it.

As she washed her hands she scrutinized her reflection. Her auburn hair was down, its dark hues giving her skin an opalescent appearance. Her blue, nearly silver irises were darker than usual. She had too much eye makeup on.

Evelyn suddenly wanted to scrub her face clean. Her dress was bloodred and fit her curves like a second skin. For some inexplicable reason she resented everything she saw in her reflection. She looked so different from the girl she was only months ago, but she didn't really like her either.

Irritably grabbing her clutch, she turned with a huff to leave the fancy restroom. She gasped and stumbled slightly on her death heels when she saw Lucian watching her. He stood, posture lazy, leaning against the door, studying her. How long had he been there?

"Everything okay?" he asked in a monotone voice, face unreadable. He was being weird.

"This is the ladies' room," she hissed, stating the obvious.

"You seem upset. Something you want to talk about?"

He was acting cold and distant. "You can't be in here, Lucian."

"Who's going to stop me, Evelyn? I practically paid for this bathroom in tips alone. No one has the balls to ask me to leave."

A humorless puff of laughter slipped past her lips. *Arrogant much?* "Well, whether they have the balls or not, it isn't right. Come on. Let's go back to the table."

Her heart beat too fast as she walked past him. He was making her nervous. As she brushed past him, he grabbed her wrist, pulling her in the opposite direction. Her body spun and the cool wood of the door pressed into her back. His arms fit on either side of her face, boxing her in, and the lock to the door clicked into place. She stared at him, waiting for an explanation.

"I'm not ready to return to the table."

She couldn't wrap her brain around his polar temperament. "Lucian—"

"Take off your dress."

She gaped. "We're in a public restroom."

"Are you telling me no? There's a word for that."

Checkmate.

She knew the word. They had an agreement that with all things sexual she would trust him not to harm her, to know what was okay and what wasn't, but under no circumstances was she to tell him *no*. All she had to do was breathe her safe word and he would back off. That was acceptable, but the word *no* was not.

"Lucian, why are you acting like this?" Her voice wavered and she hated showing that he was upsetting her, but why shouldn't he know? He was being a jerk.

"Are you mine?" he snapped and she flinched. "Are you?"

Why was he behaving like this? "Yes! I don't understand—"

"Take off your dress."

Pressing her lips together, she drew in a deep breath. His scent was all around her. She knew he wouldn't hurt her. He loved her. But for some reason he was not being himself, and that made her worry something bigger, something she was missing, was wrong. There was something he wasn't telling her.

Lowering her gaze, her fingers reached to the back of her dress and closed over the tiny zipper. The slow glide of metal teeth filled the quiet room as she pulled. She swallowed and slid the straps off her shoulders, exposing her breasts, her stomach, and then her hips. She wasn't wearing panties. The dress was too tight. As the fabric passed her hips, she let go.

Lucian bent to pick up the dress just as she stepped out of the red puddle. He tossed it to the seat by the door. "Go over to the vanity."

She blinked then did as he said. The vanity was built into the wall. A flat porcelain countertop with a gilded mirror bracketed to the wall. He used his foot to move the cushioned seat directly in front of her. Evelyn didn't want to see her reflection in that moment. She was afraid if she saw the confusion in her eyes, paired with the antipathy in Lucian's, something inside of her would crack.

His hands pressed down on her shoulders. "Kneel."

She lowered herself to the cushioned stool, her palms automatically reaching for the vanity for support. The metal clank of Lucian's belt coming undone made her shiver. Her body had a Pavlovian response to such things and, to her chagrin, her sex contracted.

His palm pressed into the back of her shoulder, slowly easing her forward. She finally lifted her gaze to her reflection, needing to see his as well, and searched his expression.

His gaze was directed at her backside. His expression made no sense. He appeared almost . . . rueful. Evelyn studied her reflection, trying to see what he saw. Her breasts hung like twin pieces of supple fruit fresh for the picking, and her dark, wavy hair draped over her lily-white shoulders. In that moment she had a flash of Eve driving Adam to madness.

The queen has more power than any other piece. She can manipulate even the king to move from a distance.

Lucian was completely dressed, still wearing his suit jacket, his hard cock protruding from the opening in his pants. He stepped close and without a word, lined his cock up with her sex.

As much as she wished she could claim she was unaffected, she couldn't. Her body was ready for him, as always.

Without preamble, he thrust into her and she reflexively grunted at the force with which he entered her. Looking up, she found his eyes boring into her. After pulling slowly out, he thrust again, hard, as if to convey a message to her.

Her breasts swayed. His hands gripped her hips tight enough to leave bruises. He controlled her movements, sliding her body forward, coating his cock with her arousal as he withdrew, then slamming back into her deeply. It was as if he was once again showing her that she belonged to him. With each deep and purposeful thrust, he never took his gaze from her.

Her brow pinched in confusion, but she never looked at her reflection. She kept her stare solely on Lucian. She didn't come. Her body neared a point of pleasure that naturally came no matter how he touched her. Becoming more malleable, she went with his thrusts, but he never eased his grip on her.

He made not a sound. Even the slap of flesh was absent, the material of his pants muffling each hard contact with her ass. His thrusts grew closer together, faster, and with one final, hard slam of his cock he was filling her. His rigid length pulsed within her channel as warmth coated her folds.

She sucked in a breath as he suddenly grabbed her shoulders, pulling her back to his front. He gripped her jaw and turned her face to his shoulder, his mouth connecting with the curve of her throat. It wasn't a kiss. He sucked her flesh between his lips and teeth so hard she felt the blood vessels rising. He was marking her.

What did I do?

He sucked on her neck longer than necessary. When he pulled away, there was a purple mark about the size of a small plum. Her hand covered the bruise and she looked at him in confusion.

He swallowed. Uncertainty flashed in his eyes for the briefest second, and then his staunch confidence was back in place. He thrust one last time. "Mine."

Evelyn's heart raced. She was glad he said it, because in the last ten minutes her confidence had been shaken. No matter what he was going through, she didn't want to lose him.

He withdrew and her sex wept with the proof of their intercourse. Rather than clean her up the way he usually did, he reached between her legs, gathering the remnants of their coupling, and smeared it over the delta of her sex and onto her lower belly.

"I want you to leave that there until I wash it off you."

She nodded, not trusting her voice in that moment. Lucian left her there, kneeling on the stool as he went to clean his hands. As soon as the water shut off he was there with her dress. She stood docilely, allowing him to dress her. Bending at the knee, he lifted her foot, brushing his palm over the forced arch formed by her spiked heel. His actions were tender, loving, a complete contradiction to his behavior minutes ago, yet familiar to Evelyn all the same. Lucian loved her.

He stood, gliding the fitted red dress over her curves and feeding her weakened arms through the straps. His palms brushed over the flare of her hips.

"Turn."

She pivoted slowly, in a daze. The face she saw in her reflection was washed clean of all innocence. It was the face of a child presented with something they'd never understand, needing to be taken care of. She shivered as his fingers sifted under her hair and draped it over her shoulder. He slid the zipper slowly up her spine and placed a kiss at the nape of her neck before fanning her hair back in place.

The bill was apparently taken care of, because as they emerged from the ladies' room they went right to the coat check and out to the limo.

THEY entered the condo in silence, tension thick from their unusual evening. As Lucian flipped on the lights, he stilled. "What's that?"

Evelyn removed her coat and turned. It was the picture she'd bought for him, wrapped in brown butcher paper. Dugan must have had it delivered while they were out. "It's a gift."

He stepped closer to the thin package where it stood tilted against his desk.

Lucian was always peculiar when she gave him presents. For a man who had everything, he seemed to cherish the little things. "It's for you. I told you I bought it today while we were out."

His fingers gently traced the edge of the package. "What is it?"

She shrugged. "Go ahead and open it."

He smiled shyly and lifted the package, giving it a little shake. It was wide and cumbersome. He carried it to the sofa and sat, staring at the paper.

She slid into the seat across from him. "Well, are you going to open it?"

His grin was precious. One would think he was never given a thing in his life. The tear of the paper made a slow ripping sound as he peeled it back. The glass shone. When he noticed Patras Hotel in the frame, his smile doubled. "Hey, I know that place," he said teasingly.

The paper tore away in heavy scraps and he tipped the frame, balancing it on his knees. Evelyn stood and moved to stand next to him. His thumb traced the small brass plate at the bottom. HOME.

He glanced up at her. "Home," he whispered.

She nodded and the tense mood turned to something weighted and tender. He reached for her hand, gliding his thumb over the backs of her fingers much like he'd glided it over the plaque.

"Thank you for this."

Her throat was tight. "Thank you for giving me a home," she whispered in return.

He nodded and glanced back at the picture. "This *is* your home, Evelyn. You've made it a home for me, a sanctuary. This is a beautiful gift."

She lowered into the seat beside him. "We're okay, right, Lucian?"

His throat worked as he swallowed. "Yes, I believe we are." It was as though her gift had offered some much-needed reassurance to him, but she didn't understand where his need for such a thing stemmed from.

Leaning up, she softly pressed a kiss into his cheek. He turned and kissed her fully. After a while, he placed the picture against the wall and led her to bed. They made love languidly, each caress a slow unraveling treasure, and fell asleep in each other's arms.

Evelyn's last thought was that it was nice to have shelter, but it was Lucian who truly was her home.

six

EQUAL OPPORTUNITY

E VELYN made a conscious effort to not think about the Parker situation anymore. Whatever had been bothering Lucian on Friday seemed to have passed by Sunday. They did their usual routine of breakfast followed by ledger entries. As she read him the last entry, she lowered the pages in her lap and watched him make his notations. It always intrigued her that Lucian kept his own books.

"Is that the last one?"

"Yup."

He leaned back and stretched, swiping his glasses from his nose in the process. "What do you say we get out of here for a while? How would you like to take a ride to visit Pearl?"

Evelyn never turned down the chance to visit her mother, especially now that she'd somewhat forgiven Scout for checking her into the rehab facility Lucian found. "Okay."

"I need to read over this contract. Why don't you get a shower and we can go in a little bit."

Rather than stand, she watched him. As he realized something was keeping her there, he turned back to her. "Say it, Evelyn." He always knew when something was on her mind.

"I need to start looking for another job, Lucian." She had been dreading this conversation.

His expression tightened. "I'll talk to the concierge and see what openings he has."

"I don't want to work at the front desk. You know that. It's too much reading for me."

"I wasn't talking about the front desk. There are other, less high-profile positions."

"Less high-profile as in you invent a position, put a fancy title on it, and feel justified in giving me a paycheck every week? I don't think so. I want to find a real job."

"It *will* be a real job."

She deliberately gave him a knowing look, shoving her tongue in her cheek and rolling her eyes. "Come on, Lucian. I need to work. We've been through this."

"Why do you need to work? I provide everything you need. You have a heap of money in your top drawer and if you want something I'll buy it for you."

"There's a name for women who let lovers leave money on the nightstand." He gave her a warning glance and she amended, "I don't like feeling indebted."

"You aren't." His tone took on an offended ring. "I give you those things because I want to."

"Lucian, a man can buy a woman gifts, but only a whore gets money on the nightstand."

He glared at her. "Evelyn, don't. We aren't going there again. I have money. I spend it on those I love. End of story. Compare yourself to a whore again and you'll regret it."

"Well, I want money too. Money I earned, so that I can spend it on the people I . . ."

He looked at her, waiting for her to finish the statement. She couldn't. She never spoke words of love. Her experiences with love only taught her that it was the strongest weapon a person could wield. She'd loved her mother, and for twenty years Pearl did nothing but take advantage of her affection, use it to manipulate her. Every time her mother stood a breath away from death's door, Evelyn's heart was flayed deeply. She cared about Lucian in ways she never cared for anyone else, including her mother. She couldn't give him that kind of power over her. She would give him anything else, but not that.

She cleared her throat and looked away. "Please don't fight me about this. If you help me find a job I could probably land a better one. You know I have a hard time with the help wanted ads."

"Fine. But you wait a few weeks."

"Lucian!"

"Just a couple weeks, and then I'll help you. I'll ask around and see who's hiring. I don't want you working somewhere shady. Let me find you a job in a respectable part of the city with a boss you can trust."

She laughed. "Yeah, because my last boss didn't understand the definition of inappropriate behavior at the workplace."

He smiled evilly. "Very true and precisely why I want to know exactly who you're working for. Now come here and let's examine your skills."

Evelyn understood the playful look in his eyes and went to him willingly. She giggled and yelped as he pulled her into his lap and kissed her soundly.

VISITING Pearl was always like visiting a place remembered fondly. It never quite lived up to one's expectations and afterward it left one feeling incomplete and slightly off.

Pearl was quiet and subdued. When Lucian gave them some privacy she brightened a little. She looked weathered, but clean. Her hair was no longer matted and her usual sallow coloring had eased. She didn't have a healthy glow, but she looked better than she had in years.

There were those moments as a child when Evelyn could remember idolizing her mother, before she realized she was a vagrant and an addict and someone who sold her body to get high.

She assumed every child had those moments, when a mother, no matter who she was, was the most beautiful human being in the world. She also assumed every child was disappointed when they realized mothers were just as human and flawed as everybody else. Evelyn had once idolized Pearl as beautiful and flawless, but now she only saw the shell of a human being, too far gone to ever fit back in place.

Her jaundiced eyes focused on Evelyn as her mouth worked like a goat chewing over some straw. Pearl had barely any good teeth left. If she asked, she knew Lucian would pay for an oral surgeon, but Pearl didn't have much interest in such things.

"Where's your friend, Scout?"

"Lucian went to the lobby to wait."

"Nah him. Your other friend. The nice one," her mother said as she rocked too quickly to appear relaxed.

"Lucian's a nice man, Momma."

"No, he ain't. He got me locked up here."

They'd agreed it was in Pearl's best interest that she not know she had every right to walk out the front door. Luckily, she was nasty to most of the rehab staff so none of them ever talked to her much or educated her otherwise.

"Are you talking about Parker?"

"That nice gentleman of yours. Use to come to the tracks now and again. Brought me gloves once. He was a nice boy."

"I haven't seen Parker in a few months."

"Why?"

She shrugged. "I don't live at the shelter anymore."

"Oh, right. You a big fancy rich woman now. I barely recognize you in your fancy clothes."

Evelyn looked down at her lap. It was absurd to feel embarrassed for her nice clothing when all of her life she'd worn rags. "Your clothes are nicer now too, Momma. I know you like those sneakers I brought you."

"Yeah, they all right. But I ain't ever have no visitors no more so what do I care?"

"I visit."

She snorted. "You my keeper." She looked back at the door and stopped rocking. Leaning forward, she whispered, "Come on, Scout, let's get out a here. We can go back to the way things were."

Her mother's recollection of their previous life was skewed and nothing remotely close to reality. "It's cold out there, Momma. Look, you have a bed and blankets, and a big window to see the people going by—"

"I don't want any of that shit," she snapped, slicing her hand through the air. "They've probably taken all my stuff by now, ransacked everything. I'm gonna have to start new now."

Pearl didn't have stuff. She had a pallet of cardboard boxes, some dry, rotted rags that were once clothes, and a cart with a broken wheel. She also had a stash of heroin, but even Evelyn knew that was long gone.

"Do you want me to bring you anything, Momma?"

"Why, you talk to someone? You get me a hit?"

Hope crumbled in her chest. Of course her mother's mind would go right to that. Four months sobriety hadn't made a bit of difference. "No. I meant clothes or games or shampoo. Anything like that."

Pearl made a fed-up sound, turned away, and leaned back in her rocker. Evelyn knew it was time for her to go.

"You ain't worth shit," her mother mumbled as she rocked, facing the wall.

Evelyn stood and kissed her mother's cheek. "I'll be back to visit again soon." She left without being acknowledged.

seven
·····

UNWELCOME

EVELYN'S conscience fluttered awake at the press of Lucian's lips to her temple. "Have a good day, beautiful. Love you."

She rolled to her back, trapped in that dreamy place between being asleep and awake. "Mmm, don't go."

"Have to. I have meetings all day." His fingers coasted down the soft side of her breast as she stretched languidly. "But you have no idea how tempting you are."

She peeked at him from under her lashes. He wore a pressed white dress shirt under a pinstriped black vest and tailored slacks. The warm scent of fresh coffee steamed from the mug in his other hand, and his jacket was draped over his arm.

"I left you a little present in the hall. I have to get going. I have an appointment in twenty minutes." He kissed her again and as he walked out the door, longing pinched her heart. The sound of the front door closing behind him created an actual twinge of pain in her veins.

Sighing, she rolled out of bed and slipped into her robe. After using the bathroom she wandered into the hall to see what he'd left her. Her steps faltered as she spotted the enormous box wrapped in red glossy paper, and several other smaller, but still large, boxes wrapped and scattered around it. There was a black bow—so very Lucian—tacked to the top of the biggest box, with a tag.

She shouldn't be surprised this was what he considered a "little present," but she was. Shaking her head, still half asleep, she shuffled over to the boxes and looked at the tag. He had written in legible, boxy print using only small words.

CALL FRONT DESK. WILL BUILD. HAVE FUN.

~L.

She plucked the corner of the paper on the largest box carefully. She liked to save a scrap of the paper from every gift Lucian gave her. Her collection was becoming a bit of a hoarder's fantasy, but she couldn't help it. He always had things wrapped in such pretty paper.

Finding the folded seam, she pulled the paper back and frowned. The picture on the front showed a woman drawing at a big, square slab. There was a word she sounded out. *"Cruh . . . cruff . . . cruft."* She shook her head and tried again. *A says ah.* *"Crahfft. Craft."*

Looking at the picture again, she noticed the shelves of the counter were filled with baskets of paintbrushes, scissors, and markers. He got her a craft table? The phone rang and she moved to his desk to answer it.

"Hello?"

"Do you like it?"

She smiled. "It's a craft table."

"I know. Do you like it?"

"Yes. Thank you."

"I figured you could use it to do whatever you plan on doing with your collections. The front desk is awaiting your call. Get dressed and give them a buzz. Someone from maintenance is scheduled to come up and put it together."

"Where should they put it?" It was a large, square table, judging by the picture.

"You can put it in the guest room or put it next to my desk if you want. That way while I'm working you can work beside me."

Her face stretched to accommodate her smile. He was amazing. "Thank you, Lucian. I love it."

"I love *you*."

He'd been saying that more and more. Maybe she should just say it back. But she had this sickening fear the moment she said those words everything would turn delicate and shatter. "Thank you." She could only confide her love once she was certain she wouldn't regret it, but she knew there were no guarantees in matters of the heart.

He sighed and she hated, after everything he had given her, that she still couldn't give him that. "Have a good day, Evelyn. I won't be home until after seven. Go ahead and eat without me." The line went dead.

She quickly dressed in a pair of jeans and a soft periwinkle sweater, fixed her hair and washed up for the day, then called down to the front desk. A man by the name of José came right up bearing a toolbox and wearing a more serviceable Patras uniform.

Evelyn opened all the boxes. They were filled with beautiful baskets and jars to organize her stuff. José went right to work. The table was enormous, twice the size of Lucian's antique desk. It looked juvenile next to his fancy setup. She went to her room and pulled a tip out of the top drawer for José. He was done within an hour.

When he left, she stood staring at her new table. José had put some of her items from the craft store in various compartments.

Her stones and trinkets from the sidewalk sale filled pretty apothecary jars, catching the sun coming through the large window. She sat at the stool Lucian had bought to go with the table and stared at all her stuff, a bit afraid to touch it and mess it up.

Her fingers brushed the jar holding her sea glass. She turned it until her favorite piece showed and caught the sunlight. Drawing in a deep breath and releasing it slowly, her shoulders slumped. *Now what?*

She hadn't really thought through her whole craft project yet. The legs of the table were bulky shelves. José placed her library books there. Evelyn pulled them out and flipped through the one about jewelry making. Her fingers tapped the surface of the table as she spaced out, thinking random, weightless thoughts and passing a good part of the hour.

Finally, without giving it much thought, she went to find her shoes. Slipping into her leather boots, she wrapped a navy blue scarf around her neck. Opening the top drawer of her dresser, she pulled out two hundred dollars and stuffed it into the inside pocket of her Dolce & Gabbana purse. Zipping it tight, she found her coat and key, and left.

Evelyn took the gilded elevator to the thirtieth floor, then walked past the elevators that dropped guests into the lobby. She took the one delivering guests to the fitness center. Moving quickly, with her head lowered, she hurried down the hall, past the gym, past the indoor pool, and out the side entrance.

The cold March morning air cut down the collar of her coat and she tightened her scarf. She should have grabbed a real scarf. This one was nothing more than an accessory. Looking left, then right, she saw no one she recognized and quickly headed east, away from the front of the hotel.

It was still fairly early, and the morning rush of pedestrian traffic mostly moved into the commercial district to settle in with their first cups of coffee for the day. The sidewalks were mostly vacant, lacking the blending roar of the footed rush hour of Folsom. Cabs busily chauffeured people where they needed to go, and as the cold, blustery morning again cut through her clothes, Evelyn considered hailing a taxi for herself.

She didn't really have a plan. She only knew she had several hours until Lucian returned and this would likely be her only chance.

"Ms. Keats!"

Spine stiffening, Evelyn turned and saw a man in the unmistakable Patras uniform chasing after her. He held a phone to his ear and ran awkwardly through a cluster of pedestrians.

Are you kidding me?

Decision made, she threw up her hand and a yellow cab pulled quickly to the curb.

"Ms. Keats!" the man called again as she slammed the door.

"The old St. Christopher's church," she said as her heart raced. "Go!"

The Patras employee neared just as the cab pulled away. She felt bad for whoever the man was. Twisting in her seat, she stared out the rear window of the cab as his shoulders drooped and he spoke into a phone, despair clear on his face.

"You know that church ain't open no more," the cabby said. His voice spoke of too many cigarettes, and the scent of the cab's interior confirmed he was a smoker.

"I know."

"Girl like you shouldn't be in that section of town alone. You picking someone up?"

"I don't know." It honestly all depended on if she found Parker and how he was doing.

The driver was quiet the rest of the way as he navigated down the busy streets. She tapped her foot anxiously and fiddled with the zipper of her purse. If Lucian was in a meeting he wouldn't be disturbed. Seth, his assistant, knew better than to interrupt Lucian when he had important clients in town. She hoped whenever Seth got the call informing she'd left without Dugan that such would be the case. If Lucian was occupied she would at least have somewhat of a chance to find Parker and get back to Patras safe and sound so she could prove he had nothing to worry about.

Her cell phone buzzed. Unzipping her bag, she pulled it out and looked at the screen. It was a missed call from Dugan.

"Shit," she mumbled under her breath. People probably escaped the Nazis easier than one could escape Lucian's paid staff.

Not wanting the bother or the heartburn, she shut off her phone and stuffed it back in her bag. Twenty minutes later the cab pulled up in front of St. Christopher's. It was so familiar and at the same time different.

Lucian had funded a great deal of the renovations. The church and old school had new roofs, and the stone facing had all been repointed. The concrete steps were redone, and the dilapidated railing going up the center was now gone, replaced by a brandnew sturdy one. There were no cars in the lot, but she expected that. Residents had to be out of the shelter by eight and couldn't return until curfew.

"I told you. Nobody's here."

She reached into her pocket and pulled out a twenty. "Thank you." Handing the money over the front seat, she reached for the door.

"You want me to wait?" the driver asked.

There was no point in him sticking around. She knew Parker could be hiding in a ton of places by this time of day. She was going to have to walk back, but she'd made that walk a hundred times before.

"It's okay. Thanks though."

"Okay," the driver said reluctantly. "You be careful. A girl like you shouldn't be walkin' these parts alone."

"I'll be fine." She climbed out of the cab and watched as it slowly pulled away. Trepidation, having everything to do with Lucian and nothing to do with her surroundings, tickled her spine. She should have been uncomfortable in this part of the city, but she wasn't. It was home, her home before Lucian, even if he was her home now. Besides, she'd grown up at the tracks. St. Christopher's district was like a country club compared to the tracks.

She knew no one was there, but she tried the heavy doors anyway. Locked. Walking around the perimeter of the building, she searched for signs of the living. Sometimes people would find a place to rest in the empty flowerbeds, being that the brick embankments were slightly raised and could block a good bit of wind.

She'd forgotten how quiet this section of the city was. No cars rushed by. No pedestrians walked on the broken pavement the city council tried to pass off as sidewalks. Even the basketball nets were without the jangle of their netted chains. Once Parker read her a book called *How the Grinch Stole Christmas!* This section of Folsom looked like the Grinch had been by. Even the mice running over the storm drains looked emaciated and cold, without even a crumb to nibble on.

The sound of gravel crunching directly behind her had her pivoting quickly. She hadn't realized anyone was around. She squinted at the mangy face staring back at her and recognized the eyes belonging to a man who sometimes stayed with the rest of them at St. Christopher's. Paul or Marty was his name. She couldn't remember.

"I'll take that bag of yours there, missy," he said and Evelyn noticed, gripped within his dirty fingers peeking from the frayed tips of his gloves, was a small, but very sharp, knife.

She frowned at him, in no mood for nonsense. "Do you know where Parker is?"

"How you know Parker?" He didn't lower the weapon.

"I'm Scout. You remember me, right?"

He looked her over, his gaze snagging on the bracelet Lucian had given her. When his eyes met hers again he said, "You don't look like Scout by the way you dressed, but you got her eyes. I ain't seen Parker in months."

Months? Evelyn's stomach dropped. Oh, God. Was he dead? Her voice shook. "Do you know where he went?"

The man shrugged. "Maybe I'll be able to remember more if you give me that bracelet."

Anger had her clamping her jaw tight. "Look, I'm trying to find my friend. You can either help me or not, but you aren't getting a damn thing from me. If you tell me where Parker might be I can give you enough money for something decent to eat—"

"I think you confused, *Scout*. You see, I gots me a knife and all you gots is some fancy clothes, new jewelry, and that big expensive pocketbook where this money you talkin' of is probably hidin'. I'm thinking with all that I can get more than a decent meal. Now hand it over."

"Or what? You'll cut me? I don't think so."

His dirty face darkened and he took a step forward. Evelyn immediately stepped back, her hands balling into fists. She didn't spend twenty years on the street not knowing how to take care of herself. This motherfucker was going to lose a hand if he came any closer with that dingy knife.

"Last chance, Scout. Give me—"

There was a strange click. "Step *the fuck* away from her."

Evelyn spun on her heel and came face to barrel with a handgun. "Jesus!" She jumped out of the line of fire and saw Dugan looking fiercer than he ever had.

"Go get in the limo, Ms. Keats."

"Dugan, I—"

"Now."

She looked back at Paul or Marty or whoever, who looked about ready to piss himself, and decided it was time for her to leave. She quickly walked back to the limo and found it unlocked. She clambered inside, suddenly sick to her stomach. This was not good.

The front door of the limo opened only a minute later and Dugan climbed behind the wheel. He stuck his gun in the glove compartment and lifted his phone to his ear.

"Dugan—"

"Not. A. Word."

"Dugan, please . . ." The privacy glass went up. The doors clicked, all locking on command, and the limo pulled away. *Well shit.*

eight
.....
CHASTISED AND THEN SOME . . .

UNLIKE normal kids, Evelyn never had a room to be sent to. There was never a specific age at which point she could cross the street, because that would be like marking a time for a toddler to cross the kitchen in a typical home. She never went to school, so she never really could get into trouble there either. Her life followed the simplistic cause-and-effect patterns of nomads, and every consequence she ever faced had been a natural one.

Her knee bounced anxiously. Dugan stood across the common area of the condo, arms braced over his broad chest, scowling at her. She'd given up trying to reason with him. The uncomfortable nausea that swirled in her belly, a mix of panic and uncertainty, battled with the indignity of being treated like a child.

"I wouldn't have let him rob me," she snidely said to her chaperone. His eyes narrowed, but he said nothing.

Unable to match his stare, she lowered her gaze to her lap and waited. They had been sitting there for over thirty minutes. She knew they were waiting for Lucian, but she didn't know for how long. He had meetings all day and didn't plan to be back until seven. It wasn't even lunchtime yet.

Long ago she'd given him her word that she wouldn't venture into that section of the city alone. Today she broke her word. That bordered on lying, something Lucian had zero tolerance for.

The private elevator to the master suite pinged softly in the hall. The mechanical buzz following the swipe of a keycard sounded. Evelyn's breathing accelerated. Maybe it was just house-keeping. The sound of Lucian's briefcase hitting the hall table told her it wasn't. She sat up straight and waited.

Lucian walked around the corner, jaw set as though it were made of granite, eyes a stormy shade of the darkest onyx, and his movements stiff as stone. He didn't look at her.

Dugan moved from his post at the wall and nodded to Lucian. Lucian walked right past her, somehow avoiding making any eye contact, and moved to stand in front of the glass window. She didn't turn or say a word. The air seemed to be escaping the condo by the second, making it harder and harder to breathe.

Facing forward, she could only make out his shadow in her left peripheral from where she sat on the sofa. The door to the condo clicked shut. The elevator gave a muffled ping, and then took Dugan off to wherever he was going. Evelyn had no idea what having a father felt like, but seeing Dugan go sort of felt like her last hope of any champion was abandoning her.

Silence.

As the quiet consumed her and everything else around her, she began to notice sounds she usually overlooked. Traffic, thirty-two stories below, whisked by in a shushed hum. The clock on the accent table actually clicked with each second. Lucian's breathing was measured and heavy, but slow as well.

"Do you mind telling me what *the fuck* you were doing there?"

She jerked in her seat as his initially quiet question ended in a shout. He turned and faced her from behind his desk.

"I—"

"You could have been killed!" he bellowed, his hand sweeping across the messy surface, taking everything, including the antique lamp perched at the corner, with it.

She instinctively flinched, her back pressing farther into the cushions of the couch.

"I share everything with you! My homes, my possessions, my staff, my money, I even give you my goddamn heart, but you can't even offer me the truth!"

He was shouting in a way she had never heard him speak before. Lucian didn't raise his voice. When he spoke softly he was menacing enough to demand the attention of an entire auditorium. Her throat constricted and even if she had something to say she wouldn't have been able to get words past the lump choking her.

The hot burn of an unexpected tear flipped over the edge of her lashes and skittered down her cheek.

"Say something!"

"I don't know what to say . . ." she whispered in a voice so constricted she could barely hear it herself.

"How about telling me *what* you were looking for?" Then his face contorted and he sneered, "Or should I say *whom*?"

Be honest. "I wanted to find Parker, to see if he was okay."

"And you felt the need for secrecy *why*?"

She shrugged stupidly. "I knew it would make you angry. I didn't want you to worry about anything."

"If there was nothing to worry about, then why not tell me what you were really doing? Why be deceptive?"

"I wasn't trying to be—"

"Bullshit." He was suddenly in front of her, leaning over her, boxing her in. "You purposely tried to keep this from me. Why, Evelyn?"

"I don't know!" she sobbed.

"You know."

"I don't. I didn't want you to be angry—"

"Tell me the truth!" he snapped. "Say it."

"I don't know what you want me to say!" She pleadingly reached for his face, but he ripped his body away before she could touch him. "Lucian, please—"

"Just admit it."

She didn't understand what he was trying to get her to admit. "Admit what?"

"You fucking love him!"

Her breathing stilled and her mouth opened. She stared unblinking at Lucian's back as her mind tried to wrap around his words. Finally, she croaked, "What?"

In a voice sounding defeated and all too quiet, he whispered, "You love him."

"Lucian . . . *no*." How could he think such a thing?

"Then why?"

"I don't know why. I was worried about him. That's all. I swear it. I don't see him that way. *Please*, believe me. I haven't seen or talked to him since we had that fight last fall. It's been months. The man at the shelter said he's been gone for a while." Her voice broke as she cried. "I'm worried he's . . . what if something bad happened?"

Lucian turned on her, his face haggard, but his eyes again narrowed on her. "And what if something did happen? What if you found him and he said he needed you? What would you do then, Evelyn? Would you go to him?"

"That's not a fair question."

"*Would you?*"

"I'd want to help him if I could, but only because he's my friend."

"And what if he was just fine? What if he somehow made it off the street just like you did? Would that change your feelings?"

She shook her head. "Parker has no one. I don't think that's what happened. Lucian, I swear, I only went because I can't shake this feeling that he's in trouble, like something bad happened to him."

"Do you intend to continue to look for him?"

He seemed to hold his breath, as did she. There was no right answer to that question. She couldn't look at him. Lowering her gaze to her hands fisted in her lap, she whispered, "I need to know he's okay."

There was no sound. No reaction to her words. Minutes passed. They seemed to reach a stalemate. Finally, Lucian sunk into the chair across from her.

She peeked at him from under her lashes. She was completely unprepared for the desolate look in his eyes. Instinctively, she went to him, but as she reached for his hands, he flinched away from her touch. "I need you to not touch me right now, Evelyn. Please go away."

Pain crushed down on her chest. Air choked off as an agonized whimper left her throat. Her hands began to shake so violently even her shoulders trembled. Tears fell unchecked from her eyes, skittering down her cheeks and dropping onto her knee to mark and soak the fabric there. She wiped at her suddenly runny nose with her cold fingers and sat back, nodding.

When she found the strength, she stood and awkwardly walked to their bedroom and sat on the edge of the bed, unsure of what to do.

Should she pack her things? Move her belongings to the guest room? She'd never known such an ugly, unwanted worthlessness.

Her voice spilled past her lips in a sharp, gasping sob. She didn't know what to do.

Thinking things couldn't get any worse, she realized just how stupid she was. The sound of the front door opening and slamming closed echoed through the empty condo. She had finally pushed too hard. He hated her. And he'd left.

nine
· · · · ·

UNCERTAINTY

IT was after two in the morning when Lucian finally came home. Evelyn's eyes opened, the only light a green glow coming from the digital clock on the nightstand. Her lashes felt glued together with dried tears, and her nose had run so much she could barely breathe through it. As she heard him moving around in the common area, there was a thud and he cursed.

She peeled her tear-dampened cheek off the pillow, forced herself out of bed, and quietly walked to the hall. Standing at the edge of the hall in the dark, she saw Lucian examining his sock-covered foot. She squinted into the shadows and saw that the antique lamp he had knocked off the desk lay shattered. He must have stepped on it. Wanting to help, she stepped forward.

"Go back to bed, Evelyn."

Her steps faltered and her jaw trembled. "Are you hurt?"

He placed his foot on the ground and grimaced. "I'm fine. Go back to sleep."

"I was awake."

He sighed and pinched the bridge of his nose. She waited for him to look at her. When he said nothing she asked, "Do you want me to leave?"

In an exasperated tone, he said, "The last thing I want you to do is leave. Now, please, go back to bed. I'm tired and I can't do this right now."

This? As in her? "I'm sorry," she whispered.

He started cleaning up the papers around his desk and tossing the shattered pieces of the lamp into the canister on the floor. She was clearly dismissed.

Evelyn returned to bed and waited. Her ears clung to every sound, trying to imagine where he was and exactly what he was doing out there. The condo grew quiet for several minutes and she assumed he was finished cleaning up the mess. Then she heard the guest room door click shut and something inside of her broke. Turning her face into the pillow, she wailed silently. Her fists balled in the covers. She couldn't take any more.

EVELYN awoke in a daze. Her throat was sore and her lips were dry. As memories of the previous day came crashing back, a heavy ache settled over her chest. Moving quickly, she climbed out of bed and used the bathroom. She was still in her clothes from the night before.

Uncaring of her appearance, she went to find Lucian. As she left the bedroom she heard his voice speaking quietly.

"No, not an efficiency. I want a fully furnished studio or condo. There has to be a doorman. I want her to feel safe there . . ."

Evelyn's heart plummeted to her feet. Was he kicking her out?

"I also want to make sure there is an account set up in her name for emergencies and any incidentals. I won't be able to keep in contact with her and I need to know I haven't forgotten any-thing."

She was going to be sick. Unable to listen to any more, she turned back to the bedroom and quietly shut the door. Heading straight to the shower, she turned on all four showerheads. She didn't want him to hear her crying. This was her fault and she always knew what they had couldn't last forever. He had been quite specific when they first agreed to their arrangement. No lying. No going back to that section of the city.

After a long shower, her nose was clear, but her head seemed stuffed with cotton. She took her time brushing out her hair. Unsure of what the day would bring, she dressed in sneakers, jeans, a light shirt, and her warmest sweater. The sweater was a heavy black cable-knit Lucian had given her last Christmas when they went to a tree farm. That would keep her warm if she ended up back on the streets.

Taking a deep breath, she opened the door and went to face the music.

Lucian was off the phone and reading over papers at his desk. He was fully dressed in a suit and his hair was dry. He must have woken up very early.

"There's breakfast for you there."

Silently, Evelyn turned and saw a covered dish awaiting her at the small bistro table. She had never been so frightened to speak. Terrified that if she uttered one word her world would come tumbling down. Sitting at the table, she poured a cup of coffee from the insulated carafe and lifted the pewter cover from the dish. A box of cereal, a sliced grapefruit, and a muffin, all things that could have been ordered hours ago.

She picked at the muffin, not really having much of an appetite. Her back was stiff and she stared out the window as if she found the tops of buildings fascinating. Giving up on her breakfast, she sipped from her coffee cup.

"Did you have any plans today?"

She started and splashed hot coffee over her fingers. Hissing from the burn, she quickly put down her mug and grabbed the linen napkin.

Lucian was there in an instant. "Jesus, Evelyn, did you burn yourself?"

She was shaking terribly and couldn't meet his eyes. "It's fine," she said, brushing away his touch.

"Here, let me." He pushed her hands away and examined the red mark on the soft part of her hand between her index finger and thumb. He brought her hand to his mouth and placed a kiss there. Her eyes immediately welled up with tears.

"There, all better."

His stare drilled into her. She shut her eyes, afraid to meet his penetrating gaze.

"Evelyn, look at me."

"I don't want to."

"Please."

Her lashes fluttered open and she slowly lifted her face.

"Aw, baby, don't cry."

She couldn't help it. A tear slid past her lashes and down her cheek. "I'm sorry."

"I know," he whispered, wiping away the track.

"Are you throwing me out?"

"What?" His voice was a rasp, his surprise at her question apparent. "God, love, no, I'm not throwing you out. Why would you even think that?"

She didn't have the courage to tell him what she overheard when he was on the phone that morning. Shaking her head, she said, "Because I wasn't honest with you and I went back to Lower Folsom."

"But now everything's out in the open, right?"

She nodded.

"Then let's put it behind us. Our time's too precious to waste arguing. Promise me you won't do anything like that again."

"I promise."

He tipped her chin up and gently kissed her lips. More tears fell as she pressed her lips to his, needing him desperately in that moment. His arms wound around her and she was lifted out of the chair. Lucian dropped to his knees, taking them both to the floor.

"Why do you have so many clothes on?" he asked as he stripped the bulky sweater off of her. "Were you expecting a blizzard?"

"I didn't know what to expect," she admitted as he got her down to her jeans and bra.

He stilled. "Evelyn," he said slowly, "you know I would never just throw you out. Tell me you know that."

She didn't know that, but she nodded anyway. When the actual end of their relationship came there was no telling how it would go.

He reached for her face and ran his fingers over the arch of her cheekbone. "I'm an asshole. I shouldn't have reacted the way I did yesterday. It's just . . . I lost someone before. The thought of losing you, of anything happening to you, I . . . I can't bear it."

She knew very little about Monique, his ex. All she knew was that he shared her with Slade the scumbag, and now she was dead. He never talked about her. She didn't know if he loved her. She didn't know how often he dreamed of her or thought of her. She didn't even know what the woman looked like or how she died. She only knew that for some reason Lucian felt responsible.

He pulled her into his arms. "I'm sorry. Let's forget about yesterday."

They hugged for several long moments. His mouth slowly pressed kisses into her shoulder, her neck, and down the center of

her chest. Lifting her slightly, he undid the back clasp of her bra
and slid the straps down her arms. He kissed over the swells of
her breasts, down the valley in between. Undoing her pants and
pressing them low on her thighs, he kissed over the sharp curve of
her hips and to the top of her sex, but never once touched her
nipples or her clit.

Evelyn arched toward his mouth, begging him for more with
her body. "Lucian, please. I need you."

"Shh." He bit at her side, a soft reprimand for trying to take
control. Finally, his tongue slowly licked over her needy sex. She
moaned, her back bowing off the carpet. He slid his arm under
her thighs, banding them together, pressing them to his chest as
he licked again. Slow, long strokes of his tongue teased the sensitive bud.

Her fingers sifted through his soft hair, holding him to her, and
he bit her thigh. She squeaked.

"Hands above your head." She groaned, but did as he asked.

The gentle torture continued and her skin glistened with
sweat. The feel of her coarse jeans being yanked from her legs was
like coming up for air after diving to the bottom of a swimming
pool.

His mouth traveled slowly over her hip as he cradled her close.
"Come to the bedroom," he whispered.

She was putty in his hands. He scooped her up and carried her
back to their bed. She nestled into his shoulder as he carried her,
needing the reassurance that they were okay.

Taking his time, he covered her. His lips feasted on every
sensual point of her body, licked at every sensitive curve.

She arched into him, wanting him inside of her, but Lucian
remained in steady control as he slowly awakened every part of
her soul. His warm breath heated the sensitive curve of her neck
as he kissed her and fit himself between her legs.

She wrapped her limbs around him, holding tight as he gradually filled her. "Lucian," she breathed, her lips pressing into his strong chest.

He held her to him. "I love you so much, Evelyn. I can't imagine being without you."

They made love, taking their time and savoring every gentle thrust and quiver. The steady build of desire finally broke and washed away all her remaining tension.

Wave after wave of intense pleasure assaulted her, blacking out all rational thought, taking her body to a place her mind couldn't intrude. Time ceased to exist. All that mattered was Lucian. When he came, he did so on her torso, heat coating her rosy breasts, marking her with his scent. Her name fell from his lips and echoed off the walls. She never heard anything so beautiful in her life.

She loved him. God, she loved him. She hoped he truly meant what he said, because if he ever wanted her to leave she didn't think her mind, or her soul, would survive. Her body would never be the same after belonging so completely to Lucian Patras. Unfortunately, neither would her heart.

ten
·····

RESERVATIONS

B Y Thursday, Lucian still had not left the condo for more than an hour on his own. Evelyn was beginning to get offended. Every time he did run out, housekeeping conveniently came by. She was being babysat like a child.

She hadn't heard any more talk about an apartment, but that was probably because she'd barely been able to use the bathroom alone all week. Tuesday night she lay awake beside him, a sickening thought playing in her head.

He's renting an apartment for another woman.

He wanted it furnished. He wouldn't be able to be in contact with this female for certain amounts of time. Once the thought entered her mind, she tried to discredit it, but the seed had been planted. Was he having an affair?

She was too afraid to ask, afraid he might confirm her suspicions, or worse, lie to her. The only thing that distracted her from the suspicious hurt knifing through her gut was her instinctual need to survive. It became imperative that she find a new job. She needed to be able to support herself, and she was not going back to St. Christopher's if she could avoid it.

She started playing around with her new craft materials. She wasn't sure what she was aiming to make. She didn't use her favorite piece. Rather she played with the others, in case she messed something up somehow.

This was the only distraction from her fears that Lucian was somehow keeping something horrible from her. Using the wire, she formed loops and wound the metal around the sea glass in different, intricate designs. She used various widths of wire and tightly wrapped a thicker strand with thinner wire in order to re-inforce it. Before she knew it, she had a bracelet.

She clamped the ends with clasps and soldered the details into place where she could without detracting from the artsy appear-ance. When she showed Lucian what she'd created, he turned her wrist this way and that and seemed quite impressed. So she made another one and another and eventually tried making a pendant and a ring.

Lucian put a call in to his jeweler and had an interesting bar delivered that helped with sizing and allowed her to form the band in a perfect circle. After she made about eight pieces, each one unique, she decided to make something with her favorite piece of sea glass.

Lucian sat, working at his desk as she sorted through her jar of sea glass. She couldn't find her favorite, so she carefully poured the pieces out on a black velvet cloth. It wasn't there.

Stupidly, the missing piece breached some protective wall she'd been hiding behind. Symbolic of every anxiety she had of losing the grip on everything she loved, she completely overreacted to the missing piece of sea glass. Her search became frantic.

She'd never owned beautiful things until recently, and she found a peculiar attachment to this piece, now missing. Panicked, she climbed down from her chair and began searching the floor.

"Evelyn, what are you doing?" Lucian asked, not taking his eyes from his paperwork.

"I'm missing one." She dragged her fingers over the carpet, clearly seeing it wasn't there. Lifting back up to her worktable, she dumped canisters of typewriter keys, jars of silverware, and her pliers all onto the surface. "It's not here!"

He was suddenly behind her, his warm palms weighing on her shoulders, gentling her alarm. "Hey, *what* isn't there?"

"My favorite piece, the one I love."

He paused. Why did that word keep intruding in her neatly organized life? Lucian seemed to flinch every time it passed her lips, never in reference to her feelings for him.

He cleared his throat. "The purple one?"

"Yes!" It was irrational to care so much that a piece of glass was gone, but she did.

"I'm sure it'll turn up." Rather than help her, he walked away. At the sideboard he poured himself a cup of coffee and watched her with a curious look on his face. It irritated her that she was overreacting, but she couldn't help it. It also annoyed her that he didn't seem to care.

"I think you need to get out of the condo for a bit."

She scowled at him. "I don't want to get out of the condo. I want to find my fucking piece." Her crass words were overdone and frosted the air between them like shards of ice, cooling the otherwise pleasant morning.

His mug clanked down with a snap, and he walked into the bedroom. She continued to sort through her belongings, slowly righting her canisters and restoring the items she had spilled.

Lucian returned with a new tie dangling from his neck and a suit jacket on. "I'll be back in a little bit."

"Where are you going?" There was accusation in her voice. Something coiled for a fight deep inside of her.

"I need to take a ride downtown to meet with someone."

Someone.

Her body stilled, and she had the sudden urge to throw herself at his feet and beg him not to go. He was going to go see *her*. The girl he was renting an apartment for. Anger was overthrown by dread. "Okay," she said slowly, not sure why she wasn't stopping him. Perhaps she needed to see if he would actually go, so blatantly, right before her eyes.

As he adjusted his cufflinks, pain, jealousy, fear, and anger twisted inside of her until it took everything she possessed not to fall apart in hysterics.

"I should be back shortly. Housekeeping—"

"Lucian, do me a favor and give the babysitters the day off."

His lips thinned. Rather than argue, he turned and left. She was in a miserable mood. Maybe she did need to get out. But where could she go? Everything was messed up and she feared leaving, feared she might not be welcomed back.

A glimpse of a faceless woman in their home rushed through her mind, and she nearly heaved. Her face pressed into her palms and she groaned. It couldn't be someone else. There had to be a better explanation for why things felt so strained between her and Lucian. There just had to be.

After about twenty minutes of wandering around the suite as though she were lost, she found herself staring at the messy papers strewn across Lucian's desk. Illiteracy was something she hated. Although she was learning to read, the sight of so many written words, a language she was blind to, intimidated her and made her feel helpless.

She needed to know why he was renting an apartment. If he was seeing someone else, she needed to know. She needed to be prepared for the worst.

Flashbacks of the first day they met came hurtling to the fore-front of her mind, stilling her hand. Lucian's desk was off limits, but they were not the same people they were then. He trusted her now, right? Then why did the thought of rummaging through his papers feel like such an untrustworthy crime?

Her hand reached to a stack of notes he had scribbled. *Cursive*. She was lost. The sudden shrill bark of the desk phone in the quiet condo had her jumping back. With a shaky hand she reached for the receiver.

"Hello?"

"I'm sorry."

Relief flooded her. "I'm sorry too. I don't know why I acted—"

Lucian sighed. He sounded as though he was in his limo. "This has been a stressful week. Why don't we get out of the city for a while?"

"And go to your house?"

"Yes. I want . . . I want to escape for a while. I want us to have time together without thinking about anything but ourselves."

This was the cleansing they needed. He wanted to clean away the residue still tarnishing their trust. "Lucian, you know I won't lie to you." *Please just be honest with me.*

"I know. I just . . . sometimes I worry about what comes next."

His cryptic words made her frown. "What do you mean?"

"I have a gift for you, Evelyn, tonight, but . . . but you have to promise me—no matter what—you will go to the country with me immediately afterward."

Where else would she go? "I promise."

"Good. Pack a bag and get dressed for dinner. Nothing too sexy. I'll be back in about an hour."

She laughed. "Since when are you against sexy?"

"Just . . . for tonight. Please."

Something was off in his voice. If she didn't know better, she'd say he sounded scared, but that was impossible. Nothing frightened Lucian Patras. "Okay."

She packed a suitcase for the week and showered. She didn't own a lot of clothing that wasn't sexy and for that she blamed Lucian, so she hoped the outfit she chose was appropriate for wherever they were going.

Black tailored pants hugged her hips and hung loose at the calf. She selected a dainty pair of sling-back heels that matched a black bangle bracelet. She wore a sheer white blouse with large black polka dots and a collar that tied in a big ruffled bow. She resembled one of those stewardesses who direct people on a plane.

As she waited for Lucian to return, she boxed up some of her crafts. No matter how much he said he wanted to get away from it all, he wouldn't be able to put work aside for an extended period of time. He would bring work with him, so she figured she might as well bring something to keep herself busy.

The door opened and she turned to find Lucian. "Hi."

"Hi," he said, his gaze journeying from her shoulders to her feet. He sighed. "You're too beautiful."

She frowned and then laughed. "Blame the man who buys my clothes."

"This has nothing to do with your clothes. We could put you in a burlap sack and you'd still be the sexiest woman in any room."

Heat rushed to her cheeks and she lowered her gaze. His words were sweet, but there was no hiding the look of sadness in his eyes.

"What's going on, Lucian? You look like you're about to walk the gallows."

He drew in a slow breath. "Did you pack?"

She tilted her chin in the direction of her suitcase.

"Good. I just need to throw some things in a bag. I'll call Dugan and he'll come get our luggage. Then we can go."

"Where are we going?"

"To the estate, but we have a stop to make downstairs first. Dinner."

There was that look again. It scared her. "Lucian," she said, walking to him and wrapping her fingers over his. "Whatever you have planned, you don't seem to be looking forward to it. Let's just go to the estate and forget about things for a while."

He kissed her. "That's a very sweet offer, but no, I need to do this. I'm doing it for you. Just promise me, like I said, that as soon as our dinner's wrapped up we'll go to the estate and this tension between us will go away."

She didn't know if one could force tension like this out. It seemed an invisible, heaving beast was snarling over them with bated breath ever since the day they had fought. Sure, they weren't fighting anymore, but Evelyn felt as though she had welcomed something into their life that now wouldn't leave. "Okay, Lucian."

He called Dugan and went to the bedroom to pack some of his things. When he came out he was wearing his slate gray power suit, the one Evelyn had come to refer to as his "don't fuck with me" suit. He wore it whenever he had a big meeting or negotiations. The posh material outlined his shoulders to perfection and fit his waist magnificently. He looked like the offspring of *Forbes* and *GQ* all rolled into one. He never lost when he wore that suit. What was he negotiating?

"Ready?"

Dugan arrived at the condo, removed their bags, and Lucian held her back as the elevator closed behind the chauffeur. He turned her and his lips, warm and sure, pressed over hers.

There were various levels of kissing, Evelyn had come to discover. There were the kisses like cute little snippets that played over lips like plucked petals, whispering childlike flirtations. Then there were kisses that left no room for argument, the kind that demanded your soul and would settle for nothing less. Then there were kisses hinting of dirty deeds in dark nights, the kind of kisses that curled one's toes and had the potency to black out one's mind, leaving a girl never quite sure if she had been kissed or fucked.

Then there were kisses like the one she was receiving now, kisses that ran the gamut of all emotions too intense to speak. Lucian's hold was relentless, his touch proclaiming his potent need. His mouth whispered sweet desperations, and she tasted his fear like a drug flowing into her until desperation caught fire and the fear abated. Kisses like this were confusing. It was a kiss of heroic suicide. The kind soldiers gave their young brides before going to war, knowing they might never have a chance to kiss them so again.

Evelyn grabbed at his neck and pulled him into her. She didn't know what made him kiss her this way, but if he felt this was the kiss they should share, then she'd better give him her all.

Deep breaths drew from his nose as it pressed into her soft cheek. His fingers and palms cupped her face like a chalice. He made love to her, right there in the hall, with only his mouth, and as the meaningfulness evolved, the mystery of the cause became all the more frightening.

He was afraid of something and his distress breathed into her. She didn't want to let go. She wanted to save him.

Several minutes later they broke apart. He pressed his forehead to hers and stared into her eyes. "I love you, Evelyn. I want you to know, no matter the mistakes I've made in the past or the mistakes I'm sure to make in the future, I've never loved anyone the way I love you."

She nodded, too speechless and confused to comment back.

He cleared his throat and slowly released her. "We better go. We have reservations."

With all of this cryptic, ominous emotion floating around . . . she had reservations as well.

eleven

·····

"It takes two to make an accident."

~F. SCOTT FITZGERALD
THE GREAT GATSBY

LUCIAN led her through the lobby and toward Vogue.

"We're eating in the ho____" She had thought they would be going out.

He nodded. "C_____ neant for a home court advantage, Evely

Something _____ since they got off the elevator. Any _____ now thoroughly hidden away, replac_____ uredness. Lucian was back to the man ot_____ fear and obey.

His palm rested _____ possessively, at the base of her spine. He opened the do_____ Vogue, and the scent of exquisite fare wafted to greet her. Patrons sat in their fine attire, sampling the French cuisine and chatting softly beneath the dim amber lights.

He directed her toward their usual table in the back, where the seating was more private and intimate. Sounds of silverware and whispered discussions fell away as they entered the less occupied room. A man with brown hair sat with his back to the door, awaiting them at their table.

She didn't recognize him, which wasn't unusual. However, her mind naturally crossed off the colleagues of Lucian's she'd met, knowing this was someone new.

They approached the table, and Lucian slipped his hand into hers. He cleared his throat and the man stood. The moment he turned to greet them recognition dawned. Evelyn gasped.

"Parker?"

He smiled and held out his arms. She went to him, wrapping her arms around his waist and pressing her cheek into his chest. She failed to notice the moment Lucian's grip on her hand fell away, too caught up in her friend's presence. He was thicker, bulkier, his scent a little cleaner. The beard he had the last time she saw him was now gone. His hair was no longer in his eyes. She could barely believe it was him.

His arms wrapped around her back, cocooning her in a warm, familiar way. The weight of his cheek pressed into the top of her hair. "Hey, Scout," he whispered in a hoarse voice.

When had she started crying? She sniffled and wiped her eyes. A lopsided smile pulled on her lips and she batted away her tears. "What are you doing here?"

Her fingers petted over his clothing. He looked as though he robbed a thrift store dealing only in Ralph Lauren. A white dress shirt fit him well, the cuffs rolled to the crease of his elbow and top button undone to display the hollow of his throat. His belt showed over his fitted gray slacks where his tailored gray vest drew up as his arms held her shoulders. A trendy blue tie with horizontal white stripes hung loosely at his neck. He always had that youthful cover model look, a little grunge with the hand-me-downs of polished society. But seeing him in pressed clothing was altogether different than seeing him in a corduroy blazer with elbow patches and a worn, moth-eaten sweater.

His green eyes glittered, the corners creasing with mirth. Her hand rose to touch his hair. "You cut your hair."

He smiled. "I was due. Why are you crying?" His finger grazed her cheek.

She shook her head. "I thought you were dead."

"Oh, no, Scout, I would never die without first having the courtesy of telling you."

She laughed and wiped her eyes. "Where have you been?"

"It doesn't matter," he whispered.

"It does to me."

"*So we beat on, boats against the current, borne back ceaselessly into the past.*"

It took her a moment, but she got it. So like Parker to start quoting works of literature. "Are you claiming to be Gatsby?" she teased.

His expression sobered. "No," he said softly. "I'm still Parker, trying to float on and hoping to land in the right part of my past. I've decided to stop fighting the tide." He looked over her shoulder at Lucian, and Evelyn stepped back, immediately recalling his presence and perceiving her closeness to Parker as wrong in Lucian's eyes.

"Gatsby, for all his efforts and greatness, never could manage his own destiny," Parker whispered.

She had plenty to say to that, but remained quiet as Lucian retrieved her hand and said, "Let's sit down."

They sat and a waiter filled their glasses. As Lucian ordered the wine, Evelyn leaned close to Parker and whispered, "Are you off the streets? You look so different. Tell me everything! I can't believe you're sitting here."

Her fingers continued to trace the sleeve of his shirt, barely touching, but needing to prove he was really there all the same.

Lucian reached for her fidgeting hand and held it in his, suppressing her urge to keep touching Parker.

Parker cleared his throat. "Well, I got a job."

"That's great! Doing what?"

"It's an office job, actually. It's been a day-to-day thing for the past few months. I'm learning my way quickly and I've already gotten two promotions. I just put a deposit down on my own place."

The pride one might imagine for such an accomplishment was absent. While Evelyn put weight in financial stability, Parker always disqualified it as more of a means to an end. She laughed at the familiar stubbornness. All those pretty clothes did nothing to disguise how unimpressed he would always be by the rich.

"Careful, Parker," she teased. "In those fancy clothes someone could mistake you for one of those wealthy snobs you so detest."

He looked down at his chest and grimaced. Brushing an invisible piece of lint off his cuff he said, "Tragic, isn't it?"

"I think you look good."

"Let's order," Lucian interrupted, waving over the waiter.

He had been quiet since they arrived. Although he was in complete control of himself, it occurred to her that *he* had done this. He had arranged for her to see Parker. Lucian must have had to hire someone to find him, because Park was clearly not spending time at the tracks or the shelters anymore.

She squeezed Lucian's hand, trying to quietly express her gratitude for such an incredible gift. He smiled at her, but said nothing, just gave her hand an affectionate squeeze back.

The waiter returned and left to inform the chef of their order. Lucian was very reserved. He watched Parker in a manner that cloaked the table with an unsettling mood Evelyn found easier to ignore than acknowledge. Parker was her friend. Lucian had to come to terms with that.

Her mind was still reeling at the fact that he was there. "So where are you working?"

"I'm working for a company in the West End. You know how I feel about work. Let's talk about other things. Are you happy?"

The simple question dropped like a sinker into a pool, ripples tickling all of them with its implication. She smiled softly. "Yes, I'm happy," she said quietly, sending Lucian a gentle flick of her eyes.

Parker looked at Lucian and something in the air shifted. It wasn't a challenge, but rather a silent understanding of sorts. She squirmed in her seat. "Lucian hasn't even told me how he found you."

Parker turned back to her. "It seems Lucian does business with my boss."

"And who's your boss?"

"Evelyn's been making jewelry," Lucian chimed in. The sharp twist of topic made her frown. He lifted her wrist and displayed her bracelet. "She made this. She has quite a talent, wouldn't you say?"

Parker examined the bracelet, his finger dragging over the metal band and brushing softly across her pulse. "Lovely. You made this?"

She blushed. "It's just a hobby."

"Don't minimize your talent, Evelyn," Lucian said.

"Do you make other stuff?" Parker asked.

She shrugged. "I'm just sort of playing around with some junk I bought at a sidewalk sale. It's nothing, really. I'd much rather hear about what you've been up to."

"How's Pearl?"

She was getting whiplash from mentally volleying between topics. Why did it seem the two men in her life who openly disliked each other had formed some sort of alliance to shut her out? "Pearl's good. Great actually."

"Clean?"

"For now. It's a guessing game what tomorrow will bring. Lucian found her a great rehab. She hates it, of course."

Parker nodded, understandingly. "At least you don't have to visit the tracks anymore. I have no doubt you will do whatever it takes to keep her in the facility she's in now." His statement was directed at Lucian. She frowned. Of course Lucian would want to keep Pearl where she was receiving the most care. Why wouldn't he?

"Evelyn and I are leaving town for a while," Lucian suddenly announced.

"How long?"

Her eyes widened when Parker boldly asked of their personal plans. They nearly fell out of her head when Lucian entertained his question with an answer.

"A week or so." Lucian didn't explain himself to anyone.

Perhaps he was being accommodating so she and Parker could find time to reconnect as friends, but she very much doubted that. This was likely a one-time thing. Lucian wouldn't be comfortable with her and Park hanging out, yet she couldn't shake the odd sense they were talking in code.

"We're going to Lucian's country estate, getting out of the city for a while. You should come visit. I can show off my culinary skills."

Lucian chuckled and lifted their entwined hands to his mouth, kissing her fingers. "You don't have culinary skills, Evelyn."

Parker's gaze followed the affectionate gesture.

"Don't tell him that or he won't visit."

"I'm afraid I have to decline," Parker said. "I have some things I need to work out over the next week. There is a merger I need to prepare for and I'm afraid I'll need every free minute I have left." He turned and sent Lucian a pointed look. His eyes softened as he returned his gaze to her. "But I do intend to see you the moment you return, Scout."

She smiled. "I'd love that."

The waiter returned with their dinner and the conversation revolved around light subjects, the weather, Pearl, names of acquaintances from the past, Lucian's redevelopment of St. Christopher's.

"We should do this again sometime," she said as their plates were cleared.

"When do you see your schedule opening up, Hughes?"

Parker looked at Lucian, and there was something knowing and cynical in his gaze. "I believe it's safe to say you will be hearing from me again by the first of the month."

Lucian's jaw ticked. "Perhaps by then we'll have reason to celebrate once more."

Evelyn frowned and Parker's eyes narrowed. "That soon? I think you overestimate yourself, Patras."

That was it. She couldn't take any more. "What the hell are you two talking about?"

They both looked at her, but neither made a peep. Lucian signed the tab and stood, helping her to her feet. "It was an experience, Hughes."

Parker stood and reached for Evelyn's hand. "Scout . . . I'm sorry I made you worry. Here." He handed her a business card with only his name and number, no company name or even accenting designs. "Call me if you need anything."

She took the card and placed it in her purse. Why did everything seem so final all the sudden? All affability seemed to have slipped away the moment they stood.

Parker hugged her and she had a hard time letting go. When he stepped back, Lucian retrieved her hand.

"We'll be seeing you, Hughes."

"Count on it," Parker said, and then he was gone.

twelve

·····

A SINKING STONE

AS the limo pulled out of the city, the weight of a sinking stone settled into Evelyn's belly. Lucian was quiet until they were within a few minutes of the estate.

"Do you expect we'll spend some time with your sisters?"

His expression told her that his mind was occupied elsewhere. "I suppose. I hadn't really thought about that. I figured we'd use the week to focus on the two of us."

"Lucian, are you all right?"

His smile failed to reach his eyes. "Yes. Sorry. I just have a lot on my mind."

"You know you can talk to me about what's bothering you."

"I don't want to worry you."

That didn't reassure her. She scooted closer to him and played with the buttons of his shirt. "Thank you for finding Parker for me. It was a wonderful gift," she whispered, brushing her lips along his jaw.

He shifted and looked down at her. "Let's not talk about

Hughes right now." He patted her thigh and gazed out the window. She frowned and dropped her hand from his collar.

When they arrived at the estate, Dugan carried in their luggage. Lucy, the maid of Lucian's estate, awaited their arrival, and Evelyn followed Lucian into the great room. He went to the bar and poured himself a drink. "Do you want some wine?"

"Are you planning on getting me drunk?"

He took a long sip of the amber liquid in his glass. "I plan on getting myself drunk and figured it would be rude to do it alone."

There was no teasing tone to his voice. Her posture straightened. "Lucian, what's going on? Don't tell me it's nothing, because I know you're lying. Ever since we had that fight last week I feel like you've been keeping something from me."

He refilled his glass and drank it down. Ignoring her question, he went to sit on one of the club chairs. His tie was undone and he looked too disheveled for what their day had entailed.

"Do you know that I'm a prick, Evelyn?"

Her brow knit tightly. She'd never seen him act so peculiar. "You're not a prick."

He laughed. "Oh, yes, I am. Be smart. Know who you're dealing with. I'm a first-rate cocksucker who will do anything to get what he wants without thinking of the consequences."

She took slow, measured steps and lowered herself to the chair beside him. Something was wrong. "Did you lose a deal?" she whispered, trying to make sense of his mood.

"Oh yeah, I've lost."

She reached to comfort him, but he stood. At the bar he filled his tumbler again. This time when he sat, he brought the decanter with him. She waited for him to say more. He sipped his drink and she could actually see the brandy setting in. His cheeks became rosy and his eyes a bit glassy.

"What did Hughes mean when he said that thing about boats and waves?"

"*So we beat on, boats against the current, borne back ceaselessly into the past.* It's the last line of *The Great Gatsby*. He read it to me last summer. Haven't you read it?"

"No." He stared at the ice in his glass as he tilted it side to side. "What did he mean?"

"Parker? Who knows. He's always quoting something or other. How he applies literature to his own life is beyond my interpretation."

"Fitzgerald wrote that, no?"

She nodded.

"What do you think the author meant? Tell me the story."

She really didn't have the energy for this. They were supposed to be focusing on them, not having a literature lesson. But, for whatever reason, Lucian wanted to talk about this, and she decided to tell him.

"Well," she said, drawing her knees onto the cushioned seat. "Daisy's husband's having an affair and everyone knows it, except Daisy and the mistress's spouse." She paused, her throat tight, distracted as she recalled the mysterious apartment. She shook away the uncomfortable thought and continued with her synopsis.

"Nick, the main character, is trying to make something of his life. The whole story's an ongoing struggle revolving around challenges that stem from wealth or a lack of wealth. Nick lives in a poorer part of town next to a man named Gatsby, who's rich from bootlegging and in love with Daisy, but he doesn't find happiness. There's betrayal and drama and no one really finds a happy ending. I don't know why it's considered such a great classic."

"And do you suppose I am the laughable Great Gatsby trying to manage my destiny?"

"Lucian," she said slowly, waiting for him to look at her. "You're Lucian. Who cares what Parker meant?"

"What was it he said? Say it again."

She sighed. *"So we beat on, boats against the current, borne back ceaselessly into the past."*

He sipped his drink. "Do you know who Parker's father was, Evelyn?"

His question came out of left field. She blinked, unable to connect the dots. "He was a criminal."

Lucian chuckled, but there was no humor in the hollow laugh. "We always remember people for their worst, don't we? Parker's father was a legend among the gods of my field, a master of real estate. He had a gift for buying and selling at just the right moment. He could set the market on an upward trend as quickly as he could send a name into an abyss of failure. That's how much buyers treated his word as creed. He killed himself after he was busted for insider trading, but I don't believe that was how he made his fortune. He had a gift. I think he turned to insider dealings when he lost his gift and feared *losing* his fortune."

"Why does any of this matter? Parker hates money. He thinks seeing it as anything more than a means to an end is the fastest way to corruption. He hates his father and anything to do with him."

"But Parker will be rich all the same."

She laughed at the absurdity of such a prediction. "How do you figure?"

"Because no matter how hard he fights the current, he will be *'borne back ceaselessly into the past . . .'*"

"Do you know who Parker's working for, Lucian? Is he in trouble?"

He shut his eyes and sighed. "Ah, will your heart ever stop bleeding for him, Evelyn?"

She stiffened. "He's my friend, Lucian. If he's gotten into some sort of trouble I'd expect you to help him."

He opened his eyes. Those black orbs stared through narrowed slits at her. "He's a man, Evelyn. If he fucks up his life, it's on him. You see him as a vulnerable boy. I assure you, he's not. He's got teeth sharper than razor blades beneath that charming smile. Don't be a fool."

She stood. "You're drunk and now you *are* being a prick. I'm going to bed."

She turned to walk out of the room and he said, "You'll see. Your shining white knight is cloaked in secrets. One day you'll see him for who he is. Let him sell you his bullshit about money being corrupt. It's only as corrupt as the person who wields it. Every man is capable of manipulating others. Give them money and you've given them power. It's a sword to reach farther and cut down obstacles more swiftly."

She didn't know what he was talking about and was developing a headache. Rather than sit there and listen to the nonsense of a drunken man, she turned and went to their room.

EVELYN'S body was turned onto her back, but her eyes didn't open. Lucian's weight settled on top of her as the blankets lifted. His mouth, hot and searing, fastened to her taut nipple, and she arched. Soft suckling sounds filled the darkness as his arms lifted her upper body off the bedding. His cool hair tickled her collarbone, and the scent of stale brandy prickled her nose.

There was nothing aggressive in his touch. He seduced her from her sleep with gentle kisses and caresses. What was becoming of them?

The weight of his erection balanced on her belly. He embraced her, but did not trespass. Who was this man and what had happened to her domineering Lucian? Only at her own physical invitation did he enter her.

There were no words. He pressed into her, not to build pleasure, but to remain deep in the foundation of her being. Like the kiss in the condo the night before, there was something frightening and desperate about the way he touched her now.

She wanted to scream with bewilderment. She couldn't go on like this. Lucian either needed to confide in her about what was going on with him or she didn't know what would happen to them. This couldn't all be the result of her going to find Parker. He was keeping something from her and it was killing him.

They made love in the dark, and that stone she seemed to have swallowed sloshed about her belly, never letting her forget its presence. It was a tiny ball of tension, but there all the same, intruding on the serenity of her life, irritatingly present at every step like a pebble in her shoe.

SHE awoke to the scent of bacon and eggs. Her muscles pleaded as she rose from the mattress. What time had he come to bed last night? They had made love for a while. It was soft and gentle, but within the shadow of something dangerous.

Evelyn never had a relationship before Lucian, but she had the foreboding feeling that he might be readying her for a breakup.

Did this have to do with the apartment he was renting? She decided she would get some answers today.

After a quick shower, she donned a pair of cotton pants, a top, and sneakers. She headed downstairs and grinned at Lucy, who was dusting the furniture in the entryway. She found Lucian behind the six-burner stove, shuffling fluffy yellow eggs in a copper pan.

When he noticed her he smiled. "Good morning, beautiful. Breakfast's almost done."

She took a seat at the table and poured herself some coffee from the carafe. Lucian carried a plate of steaming eggs to the table and a pitcher of juice. "Lucy's upset with me. Apparently she had her own breakfast planned for us, but I told her I needed to do some groveling for my behavior last night and I would be the only one cooking for you this morning."

At least he wasn't planning on acting like nothing happened. He sat and they quietly ate. He was watching her but not saying anything. Finally, she plunked down her fork and stared at him. "Since the brandy is locked away now, I'm going to ask. What the hell is going on, Lucian? Don't lie to me either. I know something's bugging you. You've been acting weird since last week."

"I know and I'm sorry. I had a lot on my mind, but I decided last night I needed to get over myself."

"What does that mean, get over yourself?"

"It means I was being an ass and I'm over it. We have this whole week here and I want to leave everything else behind and make the best of it."

"You say that like things were terrible before. If you're not happy—"

"No, Evelyn. I'm happy. I love you and as long as you know that, even when I act like a jerk, we can get through anything."

"It just seems like something's changed. I . . . I heard you on the phone the other day, talking to someone."

He frowned. "And?"

"I . . ." She wasn't a weakling. She had never been the type to beat around the bush, but the pain of actually imagining he was seeing someone else cut deep. "I . . . I just want you to be honest with me."

He waited for her to go on.

Looking away, she bolstered her courage and the words rushed out. "Are you seeing someone else, Lucian?"

"*What?* Why would you ask me that?"

"I don't know. You've been so distant lately. I don't know what to make of all these mood swings you've been having. I just want things to be the way they usually are. If you want to see other people—"

"Evelyn, I *do not* want to see other people. God, how could you even think that?"

She looked at him. He appeared genuinely shocked she could assume such a thing. In a small voice she said, "What if I'm not enough?"

"What are you talking about?"

She shrugged. "Before . . . you and Slade and Monique."

He sighed and pinched the bridge of his nose. "That was nothing compared to what we have. It was totally different."

"I know. My point is, maybe that's the problem. You never talk about her. You've pretty much shunned Slade since we've been together."

"Slade is a regrettable part of my life on more levels than I can explain."

"He was your friend."

"Was."

She swallowed. "What about Monique?"

"What about her?"

They never talked about her. "Did you love her?"

Lucian leaned back in his chair, but looked away. "In a way. She was with me for so long she became a part of my life, but it isn't the same as what I feel for you. It never would've been either. With Monique it was . . . different."

"Because of Slade?"

"Because of a lot of things. Monique was work. She was materialistic and loved me for my name. Sometimes I think if I had been just an average Joe she would have left me and run off into the sunset with my partner."

"I don't understand how a relationship can work between three people."

"It doesn't. If Monique were still alive I don't think we would have been together at this point. I'm too possessive to share. I think I could only share her because I knew deep down she didn't love me and I didn't love her. I cared about her, but that was it."

"Do you have any pictures of her?" She needed to see what this woman looked like.

"Of course I do, but Evelyn, why do you care?"

"She was a part of your life for several years. I feel like I'm not entitled to ask about those years because they belonged to another woman."

"I never belonged to her."

Silence settled around them. She didn't think the topic of Monique would be one to come up again anytime soon, so she asked, "How did she die?"

No matter how much he claimed not to love Monique, he clearly felt responsible for her. His expression melted into etched lines of regret.

"She loved fast cars. Slade spoiled her. One day he brought home a beautiful Harley Davidson. None of us had ever ridden before, but Monique was impatient. I hated that bike the minute it was delivered. It was too big for her. I told her she was not to ride it and she threw a fit. I think Slade enjoyed that she often went to him for sympathy when I was too firm. Luckily, he also told her she needed to learn how to ride before she went off on her own. We arranged for a professional to come to the house and teach her the basics. He was supposed to come back the following day to give her a lesson.

"Monique didn't wait for him to return. I had a meeting and Slade was in the shower. He didn't hear her pull away. Dugan was driving me back from the city when we hit some traffic on a road that was never busy. I think I knew the moment I saw the flares lined up along the shoulder and the strobe of red lights flickering against the windshield.

"She died on impact. Slade bought the bike, but I think he blames me for not having the foresight that she would ride no matter what. What was I supposed to do, take the keys? I forbade her to ride that damn thing, but she didn't listen. Monique liked to play the submissive, but she had more control issues than any woman should. I'm still mad at her for being so damn stupid."

"I'm sorry."

He looked at her. "I think that's why I have no interest in games. I need to have control and know I have it without question. I don't want a puppet, but I need to be with someone who has the faith in me to give me final say. All this guilt I have from Monique and Slade, I know it's misplaced, but knowing that doesn't take it away."

They were quiet for a while, and Evelyn finally said, "All of my life I've had to make decisions. I've had to decide how we would eat, where we would sleep, and constantly worry if my mother was going to get stoned or die trying. I've been making those decisions since I was a baby, and I'm tired. You could be an average Joe for me, Lucian. I don't want you for your money. But I have to admit, the way you take control, the way you decide for me—maybe I should find it offensive, but I don't. I love it. I trust you to never intentionally hurt me. I believe you love me and will always do everything in your power to protect me. I can't surrender my free will completely, but I can almost guarantee if you told me not to do something I would listen, because I think you are one of the smartest people I've ever met. And, after this past week, I don't ever want to disappoint you again."

The side of his mouth curled up in a half smile. "And what if I told you *to* do something?"

She recognized that playful look in his eye, found relief in it, as the tension seemed to fade with its presence. "That's fun too."

"Come here."

He scooted his chair back from the table and parted his knees. Standing, Evelyn moved between his spread thighs. His hands gripped her hips and massaged. "You're looking very sporty today, Ms. Keats." His finger dipped in the elastic band of her pants.

Leaning forward, he pressed his face into the flat apex of her thighs. Through the fitted cotton, moist heat of his breath warmed her skin. "I want your pussy, Evelyn."

Her shoulders rolled with a reverberation from her center that tickled up her spine. Her voice was a mere rasp. "Have it."

Without needing more of an invitation, he shoved her tight pants over her hips with her panties, beneath the rounded curve of her ass. The cool air of the kitchen chilled her folds. That was all it took; one look, one command, one touch from Lucian and she was ready for him.

The thrill of their intimacy touched on so many levels. Physical transcended to emotional and back again. Her feelings for him ran so deep, a strong ache burst inside her chest at that look of need in his eyes, sending chills over her flesh and shivers up her spine.

His grip returned to her now nude hips as he yanked her close. Leaning into the apex of her thighs, he drew an audible breath at her arousal followed by a satisfied groan. The heat of his tongue had her cocking her hip to the side as heat trailed up the crease of her thigh just before his teeth nipped at her waist.

Her breath quickened as long fingers bunched the material of her shirt, pressing it up and over her belly. His tongue traced the concave slope where her ribs stretched beneath her flesh.

Nipples drew into two taut little buds. An urge to rip off her top and demand he suckle her breasts until they felt bruised and satisfied built within her, but he was in charge and taking his time. Sharp teeth bit at her side in a superficial nip, causing her to jerk. He brought her body to attention in the blink of an eye and could keep it poised along the sharp edge of something decadent for ages, drawing out every lick, kiss, and touch to such an acute sense of pleasure it blended with pain.

"Lucian . . ."

"Yes," he said slowly as his mouth worked its way back down to her other hip.

"You're torturing me on purpose."

"Yes." His agreement was tinged with assumed arrogance. Evelyn smiled over his dark hair. *Cocky bastard.*

"Let's go upstairs."

His tongue made slow work of teasing its way to the delta of her pussy. He was purposely avoiding her clit, which was now straining against her flesh, begging for attention. Her pants formed a tourniquet about her thighs, adding to the pressure building in her body and hampering her ability to squirm and add friction in hopes of some relief.

"No," he said, biting slowly at her ass cheek.

She could hear the presence of others in the house. "But Lucy . . ."

"Do you think Lucy doesn't know what we do at night? I've made it quite clear to my staff that I fuck you on a regular basis, Evelyn."

"But what if she walks in?"

"Mm, wouldn't that be interesting?"

She swatted at his arm. "No. It wouldn't."

He chuckled and sighed. "I suppose I can restrain my exhibitionism to a degree."

She smirked and arched her brow. No matter what, Lucian

would always push her sexual limits, but she loved that about him. Loved the way he pushed her to those freeing moments of surrender.

She squeaked in surprise as he suddenly stood and threw her over his shoulder. "Lucian!"

"Quiet." Playfully, he swatted her ass. "You'll attract the servants."

Her gaze followed the shiny floor as he carried her through the foyer and into another part of the house. She recognized the Oriental carpet as the library's. A door slammed and the room was suddenly bathed in light as the swish of the heavy blinds sounded. Lucian used his foot to maneuver the upholstered ottoman in front of the twelve-foot paned window.

He flipped her off his shoulder and before she could right her equilibrium, he was kissing her. Fingers roughly tugged at her clothes. She toed off her sneakers as he backed her to the ottoman.

"Sit."

As her naked bottom fell onto the cushion, her back arched over the soft bench. Her legs were yanked wide and his mouth fastened on her sex, his touch dark and intense. He fucked her with his tongue and fingers until she was a puddle of wanton cries, begging to come.

Finally, using his thumbs, he spread her folds, licked deep inside her sex, and used his fingers to stimulate her clit. She came in a rush, and his mouth lapped up every bit of her excitement.

Her eyes, which had been wedged shut, snapped open as he pulled her off the ottoman. Turning her toward him, he bent her over the cushion belly first. She simply pressed her cheek into the cool upholstery, catching her breath as she waited.

Lucian stripped, tossing his clothing to the floor. His bare foot pressed into the ottoman and his hand gathered her hair from her face, lifting her gaze to him. His other hand fisted his hard cock.

Knowing what he wanted, she opened. He thrust between her lips all the way to the back of her throat. Standing, as though lunging with one leg lifted, he fucked her mouth hard. She gripped the edge of the ottoman and took great pleasure in every moan and grunt that passed his lips.

He suddenly withdrew his cock. She wasn't finished with him, but he had other plans. Hands grabbed her limbs and maneuvered her body. She was turned, back again arched over the ottoman, hair spilling to the floor, legs sprawled over the edge. Lucian lifted her ankles to his shoulders and she formed a bridge, palms pressing into the carpet beside her head for support.

His cock filled her in one quick, hard thrust. Her body curved, her backside lifting off the bolster as he held her ankles wide. The angle had him slamming into her G-spot with each thrust. Half-spoken prayers and curses left her mouth with each panted breath. Gibberish slipped past her lips without thought, until she simply shouted, "Yes, yes, yes, yes, *yes*!" and came harder than she might have ever come in her life.

thirteen

CHECK

THE week passed entirely too quickly. By their second day, Lucian gave the servants some much-needed time off so that the two of them could be more at ease at the estate. Having always grown up with servants, their presence didn't affect him the way it affected Evelyn. Used to living with a man who never stopped moving and whose presence was always requested, she found a much-appreciated silence to their days, filled with tender glances, affectionate touches, and long afternoons of making love.

The mornings were chilly, but the days were growing warmer. They had taken to spending the afternoons out back looking over the vista.

Lucian tried to educate her on the various types of wine, but she wasn't impressed. All wine tasted like fruit and dried-up flowers to her. She wasn't very sophisticated when it came to her palate. Food quieted hunger and drink quenched thirst. Intoxication, she discovered, was just fun. She always tended to enjoy most the bottles he had her sample last, because by that time she was drunk.

Evelyn giggled as Lucian traced a cut strawberry over her

mouth. His lips curled gently as he leaned in to lick away the berry-flavored juice. "Mm, you are delicious, Ms. Keats."

Head resting on his broad shoulder, she lowered her lashes and let her mind fly away, drunk on berries, wine, and all things Lucian. "Why, thank you, Mr. Patras."

His fingers played at the hem of her linen dress, tickling her knee with each pass. He audibly breathed in the fresh spring air. "Can you smell that? The lilacs are blooming."

Her lashes fluttered as she looked around for the flowers he was referring to. "Where are lilacs?"

"Over the hill there. They were my mother's favorite. Every year she would have the servants cut bushels of them and fill the house. She hated winter, and once the house filled with the bursting fragrance of lilac, I always knew her mood would be a little bit lighter."

"What was she like?" she asked, shutting her eyes once more, allowing the sun to warm her face.

He sighed retrospectively. "My mother was like one of those paintings you see in a museum, beautiful but overlooked somehow because it was placed beside too many famous portraits."

"Was she sad?" She asked only because whenever Lucian mentioned his mother his voice took on a lamenting quality that pulled at her heart.

"She wanted nothing more than to be happy, but for some reason she needed my father to be present for that."

"Did they not have a good marriage?"

"My father saw everything in life as either a merger or acquisition. My mother was no exception."

"You never got along with your father, did you?"

"No."

There was no way she was touching that. "Tell me a happy memory from your childhood, Lucian."

He eased back, his hand gliding to her hair and pulling gently in a way that made her sleepy. "When I was nine we went to the circus. Isadora made a big stink about the animals being mistreated. She has something of a bleeding heart for creatures that can't defend themselves. I was unimpressed with the idea of watching a bunch of acrobats. Mostly because I was going through a bratty stage and I was irritated both my parents were absent.

"Louis, our old butler, had driven us. When the show began I was unprepared for the fanfare. There is something about the circus that's simply . . . majestic. Real people climbing to heights that hurt to look at and performing feats that no ordinary man could do. I was entranced the moment it started.

"It wasn't the lion tamer that impressed me. He had a whip and a chair. Had he gone at the beast on his own, perhaps then I would have found his performance more remarkable, but no. It was the young woman on the tightrope that fascinated me most."

Evelyn smiled, trying to imagine a young Lucian at the circus. It didn't compute. In her mind he was born middle-aged, a smaller version of his intimidating self, holding a swirled, pinwheel lollipop, and swimming in a too-large power suit.

"Why the tightrope?"

"Her feet were so small. She held a stick, but required nothing from anyone else. I remember glancing around. Clowns raced on tricycles, an elephant paraded over the sandy ground below, people shouted and clapped as an acrobat did cartwheels and flips. No one seemed to see her but me.

"To my left, Toni bounced on Louis's knee, cotton candy chapping her cheeks in sticky pink. I watched the woman on the tightrope tune out everything and focus on getting from one end to the other. It must have been a hundred feet wide, the tent. I feared she'd fall. There was a net, but I wanted her to succeed, stay above the others. I wanted her to walk on the narrow line because no ordinary person could. I think I held my breath the entire time.

"When she reached the center point, she fell. I jumped to my feet only to realize it was part of the act. She caught herself with her legs and hung as someone tossed up a paper fan, a parasol, and a unicycle. She used her teeth, hands, and feet, whatever she had in order to hold the items and right herself. I was blown away. When she reached the end of the rope I felt such overwhelming pride and happiness for her accomplishment. Then she climbed down and I actually saw her up close. She was no more than twelve, a child.

"That evening, I returned home dreaming about running away with the circus and feeling more inspired than I ever had before. It was the first time I actually grasped the concept of inspiration. I went in believing the show would be for babies and I saw performances that mimicked dreams. The scent of roasted nuts, hay, and sugar, colliding with the smells of animals and people all crammed into an enormous tent. I loved it all, from the East Indian music to the glitzy costumes."

She smiled at him, loving the way his voice took her there, to a place she had never seen. "It sounds magical."

"That's a word for it. Magic."

"I've never been to the circus. I used to think of Patras Hotel as the big top."

He glanced down at her, laugh lines creasing his eyes. He'd gotten some sun. "You did, did you?"

"Mm-hm. I loved watching the fancy performers put on a show for the ordinary people. I was in awe at the glamour of such a life."

"And how does it feel to be a part of all that glamour now?"

"I feel like I'm playing, a little girl allowed to try on fancy costumes and make-believe I belong."

His brow creased and his smile faltered. "You do belong, Evelyn."

Her lips curved softly, appreciating his effort to convince her otherwise. "No, Lucian. No matter how much I dress up and put on airs, I'll always be the girl born in an alley."

Lips pursed, he whispered, "Then I will always be the little boy afraid of my dad and sad for my mother."

They sighed. Lucian lowered himself to rest his head on his arms and stared at her. After a while he said, "People change, Evelyn. We all grow and adapt and learn. Eventually we all break out of the mold we were assigned to and find a better fit. You never fit at the tracks. I see them and I see you and there *is* a difference, whether you see it or not."

She said nothing. Was there a difference? She'd hated living on the streets and did everything she could to escape, but did she fit here, with Lucian? The problem with being homeless was never truly knowing what home felt like. The warm feeling she got when around Lucian was the closest she could guess to what having a home felt like. Belonging.

Once Parker had read her *Goldilocks and the Three Bears.* Perhaps she was Goldilocks. Everything she tried was either too big or too small, too hard or too tight. She wanted nothing more than to discover what it truly felt like to find just right.

They made love under the warming March sun, the cooling breeze rich with the scent of lilac. Later they napped and awoke for a low-key dinner followed by some television and a quiet game of chess that led to the two of them making love before they made it to their room. For as nice as Lucian's bed was, they never seemed to make it there.

It was a perfect week. Whatever had been stressing Lucian seemed to stay in the city. Evelyn was afraid of what would come when they returned home. She hoped whatever the cause of his tension, it was concluded and irrelevant now. Lucian always had so many deals going on. These past few days were how she always wanted things to be.

It was wonderful to be with someone who loved her without expecting anything in return. All of her life she'd survived on a formula of trade, tit for tat. No one ever gave without wanting in return. Sadly, that even applied to her mother. But Lucian seemed to simply want . . . her.

For the first time in her life she felt like she belonged to herself. It was a new and extraordinary feeling.

They visited Pearl one afternoon. That was the only downside to their week. As usual, Evelyn left in tears. Her mother showed no gratitude for the shelter she'd been given. She never acknowledged Lucian with anything more than scorn and often blamed Evelyn for her misery as well.

Evelyn didn't know how to make things any clearer. They were *helping* her. Pearl would've died last winter if not for Lucian and Dr. Sheffield. There was not a doubt in her mind that if her mother ever returned to the streets and her hard way of living, pulled between selling herself for drugs and being so stoned she'd sometimes sleep in her own waste, she would wither away to nothing and die. How a return to such a pitiful existence tempted her mother, she would never understand. But it remained one of Evelyn's greatest fears.

Before Lucian, the only thing she was given in this life that was solely hers was a mother. It didn't matter how sick or screwed up Pearl was. She was hers.

In a life of uncertainty, that one absolute made a world of difference. Even Lucian, no matter how much she depended on him and trusted him, could never be as bonded to her as her own mother. Emotions changed; genetics remained the same forever.

It took months for Evelyn to finally trust Lucian enough to believe he wouldn't someday suddenly turn her away and leave her desolate with nowhere but the shelters to return to. She wasn't sure when exactly she gave him that trust. She just knew one day it was there when before it wasn't. And even now, old insecurities sometimes reared their ugly heads.

Although Lucian would likely tire of her eventually and move on—a thought that caused her physical pain—she knew he would never let her return to the streets. He would never just up and abandon her. But, being a realist, it was one of the reasons she knew she needed to return to work.

She was approaching a time to make a decision about her life. She couldn't simply exist through him. She needed her own identity. That didn't mean they had to split up, it was just something she never had and knew she wanted. Evelyn wanted to be as independent as that acrobat from Lucian's childhood. She needed to know she could do it on her own.

She desired that sense of self without the stress of hunger, survival, and constantly seeking shelter. She watched women her age every day go about their lives with a sense of purpose. Evelyn wanted to find out what *her* purpose in this life was. It couldn't be to simply satisfy Lucian and protect her mother. She needed to do something for herself, and that need knocked more and more as she adjusted to the security of her new life.

She had some ideas requiring her to meet with a few dealers about her jewelry. Patrice and the girls at the salon had commented on her work and asked her to make them bracelets.

She mentioned her plans to Lucian about maybe selling her items and asked him if he thought it was a good idea, trusting him to tell her if he thought it was stupid. He didn't. He said he would think about it, but then went on a tangent about production and marketing and stuff that had nothing to do with the creating and design aspects. Suddenly feeling in over her head, she decided to just make trinkets for friends for a while.

Friends. She had never really had friends. The realization had her smiling several times throughout the week as she let it sink in. Lots of things were sinking in that week, things she never spent much time reflecting on in the city. Perhaps it was the peacefulness of the estate that helped her see things a little more clearly.

She'd come such a long way from where she was. Like Lucian said, she was breaking out of the mold. Even Parker had found himself a job. Everything just seemed so . . . perfect. And with that sense of perfection came a stark and frightening paranoia. Nothing lasts forever.

They were due to return to the city tomorrow. While she was sad to leave the estate, Lucian now seemed high-strung, almost hyper. Perhaps he was getting cabin fever and anxious to return to work. She wasn't used to seeing him that way. He was nervous, but also euphoric, as though something big was on the horizon.

She watched him throughout dinner, wondering if he had heard from a colleague, maybe gotten some good news about a deal or something. They finished dessert and he cleared away the plates with an asinine grin on his face.

She laughed. "What's with you? You've been grinning like that all day."

He stilled as if to consider her statement. Shrugging, he said, "I'm happy."

As he cleared the rest of the dishes, he paused to brush several kisses to her lips whenever he leaned over the table, but every time she tried for more he pulled away.

"I'm going to go change into sweats," she said, standing and carrying the last dish to the sink.

Lucian stilled.

She looked at him, trying to make sense of his mood. "Is that okay?"

"Of course. Do you want to have a match after you're done?"

"Sure."

He turned and kissed her slow and long, leaving her head a little fuzzy as she walked upstairs. After slipping into an over-sized white crew-neck sweater and a pair of navy blue yoga pants, she pulled up her hair and headed down to the library. Music was softly playing and the lights were dim.

She paused at the door when she saw the candles flickering from the sconces on the walls. "You're trying to throw off my game by distracting me with ambiance, aren't you? I've gotten too good for you. I knew I would." She buffed her nails on her shoulder. "Prepared to be defeated."

He chuckled and pulled out the heavy, ornate chessboard. Evelyn settled onto the floor across from him as he lifted the lid off the velvet-lined box and carefully removed each ivory piece. She was always white.

"Do you remember our first game?" he asked.

How could she forget? Heat crawled up her throat as she sipped the glass of wine Lucian had poured her.

"Yes." As the crystal rim pressed to her lips she hid a smile. "You may have captured my king, but if I remember correctly, I still walked away with my panties intact."

His hand froze over the ivory bishop he was placing beside her queen, and he chuckled. "You looked at me with those big doe eyes. What was I supposed to do?"

"Exactly what you did, be a gentleman and let me walk away with at least a shred of dignity."

"That shred was a thong. My thoughts were anything but gentlemanly," he mumbled as he lifted the lid off the box of onyx pieces. "Do you remember what I said to you that night?"

"That the king can do whatever he wants?" She smiled cheekily and he smirked.

They really were comfortable with each other. She never had

to worry about what she said or fear he would laugh at her for being so uninformed about normal everyday things.

Evelyn knew things most people never needed or wanted to know, like how to tell if meat was rancid, or which storm drains flood and which could be used to block the wind on below-freezing nights. Yet she was clueless about things that were common knowledge, like the fact that the news was on television every day at five, or that every single person in the world now basically had a computer, or whatever the hell a Tickle Me Elmo was. But no matter what, Lucian never held her ignorance against her or made her feel less than anyone else.

He placed the onyx queen on the board beside his king. "And what about this old girl?"

"Oh, well she's got all the power, of course."

"She must protect her king, and never stray too far, Evelyn. That's key."

"I do believe I've kicked your ass before when she abandoned the king and ransacked your front line, Lucian."

"You won that time because your foot was on my cock and I wanted your mouth there. You said I couldn't touch you until the game was over."

"Excuses. Excuses." She rolled her eyes.

"You've only beaten me three times. Each victory I was under extreme duress!"

She laughed. "Oh, is that it then? You really are a sore loser, Mr. Patras. I believe it was you who told me chess is a lyrical exchange of aggression and surrender. You must learn to surrender a bit more gracefully, sir."

His laughter bubbled up and faded into silence as their gazes met.

"What?" she asked, unsure what to make of the serious expression on his face.

"You remembered my words."

"I love your words. You have a great vocabulary and way of putting things."

"Why such an obsession with language, Evelyn?"

She shrugged. "If I could use big words and sound intelligent, people wouldn't think I was stupid or know I was illiterate."

"You were never stupid and you're learning to read and write better every day."

"I know," she said quietly and cleared her throat. Her gaze fastened to the board, now set and ready for a match.

"Who is the king's greatest asset?" he whispered.

Her eyes went to the queen. She loved this board. The pieces were so ornate and beautifully hand-carved with little faces. She even loved the opalescent gleam swirling over the checkered surface of the board. She'd come to think of the board as half hers.

"The queen," she whispered softly, admiring the priceless carvings.

A shadow passed over the board and Lucian placed something in the center. "Be my queen, Evelyn."

She sucked in a breath as a sickening dread rushed through her. Her eyes jerked to the tiny satin box, and then to his face. His expression was an unreadable mask, but his eyes showed a myriad of emotions, hope, fear, anxiousness, love.

"Wh-what?"

"I love you. I don't want you to stray too far. I want you to be the solace I come home to each night. Protect me. Let me be your shelter and protect you, always. Be my queen and let me take care of you. Marry me."

Her mouth was producing too much saliva yet her throat was too dry to swallow. Tension settled onto her shoulders like a heavy weight, and she found it suddenly difficult to breathe. He leaned forward and opened the box.

She gasped. It was her missing sea glass, the piece she loved, smoothed into two perfect pearls nestled around a humongous diamond. It was in the traditional kite shape she knew there was a name for, but at the moment words were beyond her grasp.

He lifted it out of the box and his fingers slightly trembled. Lucian Patras didn't tremble. He was an oak.

"If you don't like it, we can pick another. It's my mother's stone. Do you recognize the pearls?"

They were stunning, perfect spheres swirled with plum, jade, and cerulean blue. She tried to speak, but no words came out. Forcing her dry throat to open, she cleared it, and rasped, "My favorite piece."

"Because beauty can be found anywhere, Evelyn. It doesn't matter where it comes from. I think those glass pieces are more beautiful than the six-carat diamond. Let me put it on you."

Without thinking, her hands jerked out of reach.

"Evelyn?" He frowned at her.

"I . . . I need to go to the bathroom." She scrambled off the floor and fled the library before he could stop her. Passing the powder room near the den, she ran up the steps and directly to the rarely used hall bathroom. Her unsteady fingers quickly locked the door. Pressing her back against the heavy wood, she breathed and massaged her temples.

"Shit, shit, shit, shit, *shit*!" she hissed.

This was horrible. This was a nightmare. She couldn't marry him! Then when he decided to leave, which she knew he eventually would, things would be so much more horrendously messy. Why was he doing this to them?

And he would make her sign a pre-nup and people would find out where she was from and call her horrible names like gold-digging whore. She couldn't breathe. She needed air.

Rushing to the window, she pulled back the curtains and

broke a nail trying to open the window. *Stupid lock!* Once it was unlocked it went up a lot easier. She sucked in gulps of air, but that still wasn't helping.

She went to the sink and turned the cold knob. Cool water rushed over her wrists. She splashed her face and returned to the window. The night air chilled her damp skin and some semblance of calm set in.

She had no idea how long she was in there. Her face was chilled to the bone when she left and all of her nails were bitten down to the quick. The scent of extinguished candles swept through the hall as she approached the library, and the lamps were now turned on.

Lucian looked up as she stood in the doorway. His arm draped over the couch and an empty glass dangled from his hand. His gaze fell on her and he frowned.

Neither of them said a word. She opened her mouth, but what could she say? She looked around the room for the box holding the ring, but couldn't find it.

She'd never known such awkwardness. It seemed to take shape all around them, jostling their tense bodies, cementing their feet firmly in place. Paralysis took over and she was pretty sure that someone could set her clothes on fire in that moment and she would find it difficult to move.

Finally, he broke the silence. "You know, I played this moment through my mind, came up with a hundred different ways you could've reacted. I gotta say that wasn't one of them."

"You took me by surprise," she mumbled.

"Well, now that you know what's coming, do you think we can discuss it?"

"Lucian, I . . ."

"Evelyn, this isn't something I've ever done or ever considered doing before. At least do me the courtesy of telling me what's going through your mind. I mean, I have no idea what to make of this. Did you just need to find your bearings? Are you flat-out rejecting me? Is it the glass? The way I asked? Were you just caught off guard? I want nothing more than to slip this ring onto your finger and make love to you as my fiancée, but you feel a million miles away. Talk to me."

In truth, she was only a few feet from him. She fought the urge to turn and run away again. Jamming her stubby thumbnail into her palm, she forced herself to step into the room.

She awkwardly sat on the edge of the couch, her body poised for fight or flight. "God, you don't even want to sit with me. What the hell's going on?" he asked.

Run. "I . . ."

"Do *not* even say you need to use the bathroom again."

"Sorry, you just took me off guard."

"So you've said. That *is* the traditional way to propose, I'm told."

Propose. She never once imagined herself married. The scenario simply didn't work in her head. Where some girls played with dolls and dreamed of white dresses, she played with branches that looked like people and dreamed of warm clothing. She had never been more unprepared for a moment in her entire life.

"Lucian," her voice was barely a whisper. They were only supposed to play chess. "You don't want to marry me."

"Don't tell me what I want, Evelyn. I don't make hasty decisions."

"Okay, maybe you want to get married, but why would you want to marry me?"

He looked at her as if she admitted to something as heinous as boiling puppies for fun. "Why wouldn't I? You're smart, fun, beautiful, you make me happy. Evelyn, I love you. Don't you get it?"

She shook her head, dumbfounded. "No, I don't."

His frustrated expression crumbled to a look of insecurity that was so unfitting on Lucian's face. He frowned, his lips thin as he worked out his words. "Evelyn, do you . . . do you love me?"

She shut her eyes. Pain knifed through her as if something unbearable sat on her chest. She couldn't say it. Once someone had another person's love, they took advantage of it, took it for granted, killed it. It was giving someone ultimate power. "I care for you—"

"Don't give me that bullshit! It's a simple question. Do. You. Love. Me? Yes or no?"

"I . . . I don't say that."

"Well, do you feel it? I love you. Give me something here. We've been together for months. I tell you almost every day. I see the way you look at me. What we do, it isn't always fucking. I've felt you make love to me. Why can't you just admit it?"

"Because I've only ever said that to one person and she's done nothing but hurt me my entire life!" Startled by the anger in her voice, she covered her mouth. He was cornering her emotionally and she didn't like it. He seemed undeterred.

"I'm not your mother. I would never use you the way she does."

"You don't know that. You've known me for less than half a year, Lucian. Marriage is supposed to be forever. I'm too much of a cynic to believe in such things, and you're too much of a realist to consider a man like you marrying a girl like me feasible."

"Stop referring to yourself as some sort of anomaly. You're just as good as everyone else. Fuck the past," he hissed and took her hands in his. "I love you," he whispered. "I know you love me too, whether you admit it or not."

"I'm sorry."

His expression slowly darkened and his eyes narrowed. "Marry me, Evelyn."

Was she talking to a wall? "Lucian, I can't."

"Yes, you can. It's a simple yes. You agree to be my wife and we get married. It doesn't have to be tomorrow or even this year, just say yes and when it's time we'll say vows. I won't rush you. I promise. I just need to hear you say you'll be my wife."

She'd never seen this desperate side of him before. It threw her. He was being irrational. "That isn't how it's supposed to be, Lucian. Listen to yourself. You are asking me to promise my life to you."

"Fuck how it's supposed to be! And I know what I'm doing!"

She jerked back. "What's wrong with you?"

He ran his fingers through his hair, leaving it standing on end. "Nothing. Everything. Fuck!"

She flinched. "Maybe we should go to bed."

"No!" He grabbed hold of her wrist, startling her. Next thing she knew he was on his knees. "Evelyn Keats, I love you. I promise to always be faithful to you, take care of you, honor you with every bit of my being far past my last breath, so long as you agree to be my wife. Will you marry me?"

She didn't know if she should cry or be scared. Was he having some sort of episode? "Lucian, you're starting to freak me out."

He reached in his pocket and withdrew the box. His hands shook as he removed the ring, letting the box fall to the floor. He gripped her fingers and moved to slide it on her finger. "Just let me put it on your finger. It's only a ring—"

She jerked her hand away and stood. "No! What's gotten into you? Lucian, you're moving way too fast and you aren't listening to a word I say."

She stepped around him and stormed to the door.

"*Evelyn, wait!* Please, don't leave. I just . . . I . . . would you please just wear the ring? For one month, that's it. Then you can throw it away for all I care. We won't call it an engagement ring. It'll be just another piece of jewelry you wear. One month."

"What the hell is the matter with you?" Unable to listen to any more, she turned.

"Goddamn it, Evelyn, I can't let you say no! I know you don't understand, but I need you to wear this ring. I'm fucking begging you."

He was a stranger, sitting there on the floor, desperation making his eyes wild. She didn't understand what was happening, but she knew, no matter what, *that* ring was never going on her finger after this display. Something was going on here and she had no idea what, but she wondered if Lucian was having some sort of breakdown.

"Lucian." A tear rolled down her cheek. She was truly concerned for him. "I don't know why you're acting like this, but I am not going to marry you. I'm not ready. And frankly, neither are you. I honestly don't know if I'll ever get married."

"Evelyn," he said slowly, his gaze on the floor. "I know all you want to say is no right now, but let this be one of those moments when you trust me to decide what's right for us."

She didn't understand why he wouldn't accept her answer. There was something behind his insistence that wasn't adding up. "I'm sorry, Lucian, I can't."

His expression tightened. "You gave me your word you wouldn't tell me no."

"In bed! I never promised to sign over my free will! Now, stop this. My answer is no. I'm not discussing it anymore. I have a headache and I'm going to bed."

"Evelyn . . ."

She had every intention of walking out the door without turning back and letting him cool off, but something in his voice stopped her. She turned and didn't know what to make of the uncertainty showing in his eyes.

He swallowed. "If you won't take this ring, we . . ." His head shook. "When we return to Folsom . . ."

"Lucian, you're really scaring me. Should I call your sister?"

"No." It was barely a whisper. She never saw Lucian cry, didn't believe he was capable of such a thing, but when he looked up at her she swore she saw tears shimmering through the defeated look in his eyes. "We need to take a break."

Ice zipped through her veins, pulling her spine straight and sucking all her breath away. "What? Why?"

"If you won't say you'll marry me, we need to take a break."

What kind of fucked-up reasoning was that? She scowled indignantly. "*Why?*"

"Because . . . we just do. One month apart without communicating. After that month we can get back together and—"

"What the hell are you talking about?" Now she was mad. "Why are you making all these rules? None of this makes any sense. Lucian, I'm *sorry* I'm not ready for marriage. Five months ago I was a totally different person. You need to give me time to adjust to all this. I barely know how to be normal, let alone be someone's wife. You're being unreasonable."

"Will you wear the ring?"

A sharp ringing sang in her ears. She wanted to punch something and scream. "I told you. No."

"Then we need to take a break—"

"Because I won't marry you?"

"There's an apartment. It's paid for. I'll pay the rent as long as you want, but I hope this only takes a month—"

This was not happening. The apartment *was* for her! She saw red.

"Fuck you, Patras!" She practically spat the words. "I won't be manipulated and I don't do ultimatums. What's wrong with the way things were? Why this sudden need to get married? And now you're *kicking me out*! Don't bother. I'll fucking leave."

Her hands were trembling. She had to remain angry or she feared she would die. She couldn't acknowledge the hurt lancing her chest, the horrible, aching disappointment and heartache taking over her body. She needed to keep moving.

"Evelyn, I love you. It won't be forever. Thirty days, I swear it, and we can return to normal. I give you my word—"

"Who does that? This is ridiculous! I don't understand why you would want a break at all if you already know you'll want me back. Why do we need a break? You're messing with my head on purpose."

She wiped her eyes and realized her cheeks were wet. *Fuck.*

Lucian stood and slowly approached her. She didn't want him to touch her. She'd break if he laid one finger on her, but she would shatter if she tried to move. She was holding it together by a thread.

We were only supposed to play chess.

Her finger brushed away more tears as he stepped close. His hands took hers. A moan uttered past her lips, a bit of the pain seeping out.

"I'm sorry, love. Please don't cry."

Her shoulder shook. "Why are you doing this?"

His eyes shut for a long moment. When they opened they shimmered with unshed tears. "I have to."

"I don't understand."

"I know. It's just something I have to do. No matter what, Evelyn, I *will* be here in a month. I'll spend every day thinking about you, wondering if you're okay. It's going to kill me not to be able to call and hear your voice."

"Why? Why can't you call me? Lucian, please . . . you aren't making any sense."

He kissed her knuckles, whispering over her fingers as though praying to himself. "Promise you'll come back. No matter what, promise you won't . . ." He bowed his head, gripping her fingers tight and pressing them hard to his lips. There was something he wasn't telling her. "I need you, Evelyn. I'm nothing without you."

Why? *Why? Why? Why?*

After all of his lectures on honesty being necessary for trust, he expected her to trust him now when he was obviously keeping secrets from her? She yanked her hands from his, her anger back in spades. "Then don't do this to us. When you love someone you don't throw them away for no reason!"

"I'm not throwing you away. God—"

"Then what the fuck is this? You're sending me to live in some apartment for a month—" The apartment he had been on the phone talking about. Her fists beat into his chest. "You planned this! You knew you were going to send me away and gave me no warning! I trusted you to never abandon me without warning and that's exactly what you're doing!"

He caught her fists and restrained her. "No, Evelyn! I planned on coming here and leaving with your promise to be my wife."

"So you're punishing me?"

"This is more a punishment to me than anyone!" he roared.

With some superhuman strength, she yanked her hands away. She glared at him with scathing anger. "I respected you. I thought you were a man of your word. I *trusted* you." She stepped back. "I can barely look at you now. I don't believe you. I think you knew I'd say no. You did this on purpose because you're too much of a coward to break up with me."

"I am a man of my word! If I wasn't a man of my word we wouldn't be having this fucking conversation! And I don't want to break up. I want you to be my fucking *wife*!"

"You're talking in riddles. I'm done trying to figure you out.

This whole night was ruined the minute you took out that ring. You know what I think? I think you're a coward no matter how you deny it. The Lucian I know would never let someone he loved walk out on him. No. He'd make it impossible for them to leave. You've been acting different for a while now. I think you wanted to break up and were too much of a coward to say it. I think you were purposely *trying* to push me away. You knew proposing marriage would do the trick. Well, I'm not a coward, Lucian. I'm not some charity case you need to feel responsible for either. We don't need a break. We're over."

She turned and left the room. Lucian chased her into the hall. "Evelyn!"

She spun on her heel. "I hate that fucking name! My name is Scout! Do you hear me? Scout! Stay away from me. I can't even look at you right now."

"I won't be able to fix this for a month. Please, don't let it end like this."

She walked, not stopping until she was safely away from him and in their bedroom—correction, *his* bedroom. As the door slammed, shards of glass seemed to slice open her heart. She collapsed on the floor and let the pain inside of her swallow her whole.

fourteen
·····
ROARING SILENCE

THERE was a contrary existence to sadness. How could something so hollow weigh so much? Evelyn lay supine on the bed, face fused to the pillow with the salt of dried tears, unsure of the time and confused about the day of the week. Nothing had ever felt so horrible.

She stared at the backs of her eyelids so long she began to question if darkness was truly black or a blinding white. Misery cloaked her like a lead blanket, yet she was so empty she wondered how she didn't float away. Pain stabbed her heart, but oddly she was numb, like a person who crashes to the ground so fast they die on impact.

Nothing made sense.

He did this to her, but why? Because she wouldn't marry him? It couldn't be that simple, yet there seemed to be no other explanation.

He wanted this. He wanted them to end.

He hadn't come to her after she stormed off last night. Not once did he knock on the locked door or try to take back his ridiculous edict. Every torturous second was another crack in her broken trust.

His prolonged avoidance only made his stubbornness more annoying. *Screw him.*

She lay awake all night, waiting for this nightmare to end, but it never did. Just before she dozed off, as dawn crept over the horizon, she thought nothing could possibly be worse than the feeling inside her. She was wrong. She slept only a short time, but upon waking she learned of a new agony.

As her mind pulled out of the cobwebs of sleep, she realized the horrible dream was reality and that was worse than knowing it the night before. It was sharper, fresher, with a layer of disappointment added to the pain that sleep hadn't mitigated. Would it be like this every morning from here on? A repeat of last night's episode? She couldn't bear the thought.

Sleep became a waking matter she simply wandered through in some subconscious state. She never truly rested. The unsettled turmoil of her mind forbade it.

Moments of quiet were interrupted by sudden intrusions of thoughts so unwelcome she would roll to her side and moan. No cry was strong enough to expel her agony.

Sometime that morning she admitted to herself how utterly stupid she had been. Just twenty-four hours ago she was so sure of herself, imperiously proud of how far she'd come.

Some achievement. She didn't know what to do.

Her mother would be useless. And so help her God, if Lucian threw Pearl back on the streets, she would never forgive him. *Never.*

Perhaps Parker could help her. Perhaps Patrice, she thought, but how pathetic to go traipsing through Patras as the woman who was tossed away. Maybe it was just another stupid move on her part, thinking she still had some pride left to lose.

Fuck him and his apartment. She didn't need anything from him. She could make it work. She should have taken that damn ring and pawned it.

That quickly her mind switched gears, shutting off her anger and reminding her of how hurt she was. The whiplash of those unannounced emotions sneaking in and taking over was enough to make her vomit. She turned her face back to the pillow and began to sob.

What would she do? She had no one. Lucian was also her dearest friend and he was abandoning her. The actuality of her circumstances hurt more than the reality. Betrayal was a sharp object lodged in her heart.

Those words he was so desperate to hear her say were there, beating around in her tired mind, ready to come out now, but she forbade it. Now they were unwelcome for a whole new reason. She would never admit how much she loved him, because he had done exactly what she knew he would do. He pushed her away.

She must have faded into some sort of dazed sleep. Her eyes were open as though she had never shut them, yet she lost herself for some time. Things were calming down. Survival instincts were stepping in and quietly trapping all the irrational thoughts of desperation tearing through her insides like butterflies in a net.

Her unaccompanied existence now appeared unending, depressing, a huge, heaving giant breathing over her. She should just give up already. She was so tired of fighting. No one would miss her if she disappeared. But she was coming back to reality enough to know that wasn't the answer.

She would fight, because that's what she'd been doing since the day she was born, fighting to live, fighting to survive, fighting for the love no one ever gave her without conditions. She was a scrapper. She was not some polished woman named Evelyn. She was

Scout. She had survived much worse than this. All she needed to do was get up and move.

So why did that seem so terrifyingly daunting?

WHEN dusk arrived she showered and took time to really wash herself. She went through her clothing and belongings and selected only sensible items like jeans, sneakers, thermals, and sweats. She cleaned up by sweeping all her useless cosmetics into the trash can.

Rather than wasting time on frivolous things that only disguised her as someone else, she pulled her hair back in a long ponytail and removed all her jewelry except the bracelet she made. She wanted nothing from him, but knew she couldn't be stupid and cut off her nose to spite her face.

When she was ready, she fought back her sadness. Staring fiercely at her pathetic reflection, she hissed, "You will *not* cry. You're stronger than that. Get to Folsom and get the fuck out of here. You never have to see him again."

With a deep, shaky breath she lifted her bag and unlocked the bedroom door. The house was quiet. She slowly took the stairs and noticed a few items by the door, Lucian's briefcase, his coat, some files. He wouldn't have been able to pack while she was in the room with the door locked.

She placed her things near the door, but away from his pile. Turning, she jumped when she spotted him watching her from the other end of the foyer. They stared at each other for a minute. He looked terrible. There was no question in her mind he hadn't slept.

"Are you ready? I'll get the rest of your bags."

"This is all I'm taking," she said, proud that her voice didn't waver.

"I can have your other things sent to the apartment—"

"I'm not going to your apartment."

"Evelyn—"

"Don't call me that."

His lips pressed together. Exhaustion seemed to radiate from his pores. "This can all change if you just agree—"

"You're not the person I thought you were. I will never agree to be anything to you ever again. I'd like to go ho—return to the city. Now."

He nodded and began shutting off the lights. She waited by the door as he went upstairs to retrieve the last of his things, several times blinking back tears. There was no reason for this that she could think of. No point in taking a month apart—*on a break*—only to get back together. This month apart would tear them apart. There would be no mending things.

She hated him for doing this. She hated him for making her love him. She hated knowing this was the last time she would ever see the estate again, ever know this kind of peace again.

Her thoughts climbed over memories, committing them to some shadowed corner of her mind she could examine later, when she was stronger. She wanted to remember certain moments of their time together, never wanted to forget the scent of fresh lilacs or the feel of lazing in his arms on a rainy afternoon.

It was never about the money or the comfort. It was about sanctuary. It was about the peace that came with surrendering her trust to a man and letting him guard her heart for a change. She never imagined something could feel so wonderful. However, she never knew such extreme misery as having that love and trust trampled on by the one person she believed incapable of such cruelty. It was complete betrayal and she needed to stop romanticizing things and get real.

He returned and fished out his keys. "Here," he said, holding out a long envelope.

"What's this? Severance?" She scoffed. "Keep your money, Lucian. It was never about your wealth. It was never about getting something more from you. It was just you. I just wanted you, but apparently I wasn't enough in return."

"Ev—" She cut him off with a glare. He said the name she had gone by all her life as though it left a bitter taste on his tongue. "Scout, I know you hate me right now, but I swear on my life I will make it up to you. Go to the apartment just until you get on your feet. You can even pay me back for the rent if it makes you feel better."

He was so full of crap. Lucian would never let her pay him for something like that. However, she was grateful he pushed the offer. As much as she wanted to tell him to go fuck himself and prove she didn't need him, she was smart enough to know she did. At least for a little while.

"This is just the paperwork for the apartment, the key, and some other things."

She raised an eyebrow.

He sighed. "You need money, Ev—Scout. Take it. Please." She'd asked him to call her Scout, but hearing that name cross his lips only made their entire affair seem more tawdry and concluded.

"One last chance, Lucian. Tell me why you're doing this."

"I . . ." He looked away, and she knew there would be no explanation beyond the same bullshit he had fed her last night.

Her teeth ground together, and she snatched the envelope from his hand. Her pride stung too much to see his satisfied expression, so she grabbed her things and walked out the door. She was surprised to see Dugan waiting there.

"Dugan."

He nodded. "Ms. Keats." There was no *how was your vacation?* Or *are you excited to return home?* He knew, and she wanted to hug him in the hopes he might be the one true friend she had made through all this. Perhaps he could sympathize with her and tell her it would all be all right.

But he wasn't her friend. He was a chauffeur for crying out loud, a chauffeur loyal to the man fucking her over. Tears bit at her eyes, so she lowered her head and climbed in the car, where she could wipe away the evidence of her heartache in privacy.

Lucian followed a few minutes later. Evelyn never took her gaze off the window. There was not a single sound aside from the engine purring and tires rolling over the long highway back to Folsom.

When they arrived in the city, some sort of fear and unspeakable panic choked her. It became difficult to breathe, and she actually feared she might faint.

Lucian's hand covered hers and she jerked it away. "Here, drink this." He handed her a bottle of water, which she grudgingly took. She was incredibly thirsty and hadn't realized it.

They went off the beaten path to Patras and headed into one of the nicer residential sections. She knew where it was, sort of, but not really. He was going to drop her off here, like a dog sent off to the pound.

Her fingers itched and tightened into fists. She suddenly had the urge to claw his eyes out. It took everything she had to remain still.

They pulled up outside a pristine brick complex with decorated flower boxes on each window. It was an older building overflowing with historical charm. There seemed to be three floors and along the side, stacked like little cakes, were three garden balconies. Was this her new home?

"Would you like me to walk you up?"

"I would like nothing less."

She reached for the door and he engaged the locks. The cab of the limo filled with a resounding snick.

She seethed, despising the impotent position she was in. A hopeless pawn sent out to the slaughter, that's what she was. Never a queen, only ever a toy sent to amuse the king.

"Lucian—"

"Just let me say my piece and then you can go. In thirty days I will be back for you. If you have any trouble or need anything at all, I want you to call Dugan if you don't wish to call me. If you do want to speak to me, all you have to do is call and I'll come back for you, but you have to ask. I've left you Dr. Sheffield's number as well and a few others in case you need them." He took a deep breath. "I know I have no right to ask for any favors, Evelyn, but . . . please, don't do anything hasty. What we have is real. It isn't something time can break. Please, just . . . thirty days and I will fix everything."

"What we have is *nothing*. Time won't break it. You did that on your own." She unlocked the door and climbed out. As the door shut behind her, she broke and sucked in a breath that escaped on the wake of a swallowed sob.

"Ready, Ms. Keats?"

She looked at Dugan and tried for a smile. "I know he wants you to see me in, but I can't. I need to walk away now." She approached him and went up on her toes, pressing a kiss to his cheek. "Thanks for everything, Big D. Sorry I never got to make you pee your pants from laughing."

"You will."

Sweet of him to act like they would be seeing each other again. She didn't have the energy to refute it. Turning, she headed through the glass, maple-framed doors. Her fingers shook as she opened the envelope. She wouldn't look back.

She pulled out a note, several credit cards, and a key. Third floor.

A man at a desk cleared his throat. "May I help you?"

No. No one could. "I'm Evelyn Keats."

"Ah, Ms. Keats, welcome. Do you have any other bags?"

"No, just this."

He nodded. He was an older gentleman with wiry gray eyebrows and soft blue eyes. "Very well then, miss."

Her smile fell short. She nodded and continued on.

There was an antiquated elevator that carried her to the third floor. It was a small, private establishment. She realized there was only one apartment per floor. After taking a deep breath, she unlocked the door and stepped in.

She wasn't prepared for what she found on the other side. All of her belongings, her favorite blanket from the penthouse, her iPad, her clothing, everything had been moved there. That's when it truly hit her.

He was never coming back.

A thousand knives stabbed her from the inside out. She gripped the counter and fell slowly to her knees. It didn't matter that the place was beautiful. It didn't matter that he had arranged for her to have everything she needed. There was only one thing she needed, the one thing she couldn't have. Him.

lucian

fifteen

ABSOLUTE PIN

A pin against the king where no piece can move
without putting the king in check

L UCIAN watched her disappear into the apartment complex and
used every bit of his will not to rush out of the car and go after
her. His jaw ticked as he fought back his rage. She was gone and
there was no promise of getting her back. Never before had he
regretted being a man of his word.

His mind went back to that horrible day last December. Evelyn had been missing for two weeks and the temperature had
dropped to arctic levels, the city practically shut down by a blizzard. He'd never felt so helpless in his entire life. Then his fortune
changed and he had likely made a deal with the devil himself in
order to find her.

Parker had been sleeping outside of the shelter, which had
been condemned, doors closed and leaving the homeless without
shelter during the worst storm of the decade. Lucian was at his
mercy and the other man knew it, took pleasure in it.

Parker had looked like shit when Lucian found him. There
was no warm welcome as Lucian approached him on that horrid
morning.

A rattling cough preceded his sardonic greeting. "Well, well, if it isn't Prince Charming. She's not here. No one is."

Dropping all underlying disinclination, Lucian looked at him with all the humility he possessed. "Do you know where she is?"

The other man glared at him for a moment, clearly taking his measure. Lucian poured all his worry and concern into the space between them, and Parker sighed. "No. I don't. I haven't seen her in three days."

Three days. That was something. Eleven days less than the time that lapsed since Lucian had seen her.

"Where was she?"

Parker's lips pressed tight into a thin, silent line between the scruff of his beard.

"I want to help her, Parker. I swear it. I . . . I care for her."

"Maybe she doesn't want to be found."

Lucian hesitated a moment, then leveled with him. "Look, I know how you feel about her. I could let her go and give you my blessing, but you and I both know I can offer her more. If you really love her, let me help her. Help me find her. Please. I swear I only want to do right by her."

When several minutes passed and Parker said nothing, Lucian figured he wouldn't help. Then Parker surprised him by saying, "You hurt her."

"I did," Lucian admitted.

"I don't know what you did or said. Scout has a habit of fixing everyone else's problems and not letting anyone help her with her own. What I do know is that whatever you did, it hurt her bad. Scout doesn't cry and you changed that."

Guilt and shame cut through him. "I'll make it right," he vowed, more to himself than to anyone else. "Please just help me. I'm begging you here, Hughes."

Parker smirked. "Not something a guy like you does often, I imagine."

"You've got me. I'm putting it all on the table. My hands are tied here. I've been driving around for days searching for her. I'm out of ideas. You have an idea of where she might be. What do I have to do to get you to help me?"

The other man's lips pursed and his green eyes jerked away, then back again. He exhaled noisily. "Fine. You want to help her? Well, I don't trust you. Guys like you don't do anything without an ulterior motive. Scout needs . . . stability. She'll do anything to get it. Problem is, she associates stability with money."

"She's right."

"Says you. Judge me all you want, but I want to see you fail. However, if you fail so does she, and that's not what I want. I want her to have the life she's after. I want to see her keep a good job, have her own home, and never have to worry when she'll eat next."

"I can do all that for her. That's the plan."

"Ah, but I won't see it." Parker stood and Lucian noticed him limp slightly. No matter how strong he pretended to be, it was obvious his circumstances left him quite weak. "You're an audacious fellow. I have a proposition for you. I'll take you to her, but I want to be there when she gets everything she wants. I want to see all those dreams of hers come true. I want a job. You give me a job and I get back on my feet. At that point, you give me a fair shot at her. I'm not saying right away. I'll need some time. But when I'm ready, I say the word and you back off and give me a fair shot. One month where you don't interfere."

Not a chance.

Lucian learned a long time ago how to act unaffected during the negotiations stages of a deal. "She may have a problem with that, you realize. Evelyn doesn't like being maneuvered without her feelings being considered."

"Then I suppose we both lose."

Lucian's eyes narrowed. Patient Parker had a very shrewd side to him. Something told Lucian the other man had no problem letting him walk away and never telling Evelyn he was here. Every hour of cold made a difference. This wasn't a situation where one could wait out the other.

It would backfire on Parker, of course. Lucian never broke his word once given, but Parker would somehow break the deal on his own. There was something about the kid that didn't stem from growing up on the streets. Something . . . informed, innate. Once he'd secured Evelyn, he'd find out exactly who Parker Hughes was.

"Okay, Hughes. You've got yourself a deal, but let me give you some free advice. One, she'll eventually find out you only agreed to help her after securing your own chance at gaining something, and I give you my word I won't be the one to tell her this. Two, she won't like it when she does find out. Three, I haven't gotten where I am today by giving in easily. A challenge is just that to me. And four, I always get what I want."

"Keep your fucking advice, Patras. All I'm interested in is a job and your word."

"You have it." Lucian extended his leather-clad hand.

There was one other condition, however. All bets were off if Lucian got Evelyn to agree to be his wife. Never in a million years had he expected she'd shoot him down.

The anger boiling up inside of him surpassed regret. He couldn't regret agreeing to let her go. His promise likely saved her life.

Now he was indebted to the asshole. Perhaps he even owed Hughes credit for saving Evelyn's life. Knowing that made it impossible for Lucian to back out on their deal.

He'd given his word in exchange for finding her. She was worth him honoring his vow. The only silver lining was that in thirty days Parker's true colors would likely shine through, and Evelyn would see once and for all what a prick the man truly was. Unfortunately, that wasn't enough to quell the horrible thoughts running through his mind.

What if she chose him? What if she loved Hughes and never really loved Lucian? What if he'd lost her? It took every ounce of willpower Lucian possessed not to say fuck all and go get her, but he'd made such a disgrace of their relationship in the past twenty-four hours that there would be no reasoning with her now. Their path had been set, and he had thirty agonizing days to survive before he could put things back to right.

He reminded himself that if he hadn't promised to let her go for one month, he never would have found her. Swallowing hard and pushing down every instinct to go after her, he gripped the armrest of the limo door until it practically ripped off the car.

Dugan climbed behind the wheel and rolled down the privacy screen. His chauffeur didn't quite understand what was happening. A loyal employee from the start, Lucian didn't know how to feel about Dugan's now sour attitude. It wasn't his business, but the man clearly had come to care for Evelyn, because there was no mistaking the disapproval in his eyes.

"To the hotel, sir?" Dugan asked coldly.

"No."

The chauffeur tipped his head in surprise in the rearview mirror and waited.

"Drive to Leningrad."

Dugan's brow rose beneath his cap, surprise evident on his face. It had been months since Lucian had any doings with Leningrad Enterprises, but at the moment he had some pressing business to take care of.

The limo coasted through evening traffic and slid neatly into a spot outside of Leningrad. Lucian left the car before Dugan made it to his door. "I'll be back in five minutes. Wait here."

Passing the doorman without his usual cursory nod of hello, Lucian brushed past the front desk and security with a curt raise of his chin. His leather-soled shoes clicked over the lobby's marble floor as he made his way to the elevators. Claiming an empty one and shooting a glare at the man who thought to ride with him, Lucian hit the close button and seethed all the way to the fifteenth floor.

The stainless steel doors parted with a soft ping, and a secretary smiled up from her reception area. "Mr. Patras, what can I help you with today?"

Lucian walked past. "I'm here to see Mr. Bishop. I'll only be a moment."

When he didn't stop for an invitation, the receptionist jumped up from her seat. "Sir, Mr. Bishop is in a meeting." He continued at his clipped pace. "Sir!"

When he reached the corner office, he entered without the courtesy of a knock. His blood was on fire, and if one person got in his way they would regret it for only a split second, because then they'd be dead. The door slammed on the receptionist's objections, and the two men in the room looked up in surprise.

"Lucian, what are you doing here?"

He glared at his once good friend. "I'd apologize for interrupting, but at the moment I find it hard to give a fuck if I inconvenience you."

Slade's face darkened. "This isn't the time—"

"Oh, it's the time," Lucian growled.

Slade looked back at his company. "Mr. Chang, I apologize. If you'll excuse us, I'll have my messenger run over the paperwork before week's end, and we can revisit things on Monday."

The small Asian man sitting across from Slade nodded his

head in agreement and stood. Lucian stood like a grizzly in the corner, jaw locked, fists clenched at his sides, while he waited for the other man to leave.

When the door finally closed, Slade turned on him. "*What the fuck, Lucian? Are you insane?*"

"Fuck you. This is your fault, you disloyal, cocksucking—"

"*Ho!* You have some nerve coming in here and calling me names."

Lucian closed in on him. No matter how fearless Slade tried to appear, he backed up. It was the only smart thing the man had done in ages. "Why? Why help him? Do you hate me that much? I fucking loved you like a brother, and you singlehandedly helped that shit get to a position where he could stick it up my ass."

"He's a fucking kid, Luche. Don't be such a puss."

Two strides and the desk was the only thing separating them. His palms pressed into the oak surface as he leaned closer. "You know he's not just a kid," he said through clenched teeth. "Don't act ignorant. You knew exactly what you were doing. The minute you found out who he was, you jumped at the first opportunity to fuck me."

"The position was open—"

"Bullshit. You hired him, fed him, clothed him, promoted him, all for what? So he could come after the one thing I love?"

"Don't come in here waxing poetic about what you have with that girl."

"I love her. Do. You. Understand? I fucking love her and now she hates me."

Slade sneered, "I didn't agree to trade her off like some fuck toy. That was you—"

White noise squealed in his head as he rounded the desk. Once he had Slade's shirt in his fist he stared hard into his eyes, practically nose to nose. "Call her that again and see what happens."

"What? Are you going to punch me again? Go ahead. What's happened to you? You used to be a classy guy, Luche. This girl has you so fucked-up—I heard about the deal with Chrysler you lost. Everyone's talking about it. Lucian Patras, Folsom's renowned tycoon, screwing up for the first time in his life. They all see it. Maybe you weren't born on a dollar after all."

"I don't give a shit about Chrysler right now—"

Slade brushed his hand off with a look of complete disgust. "That's the problem. All you give a shit about is *her*. If she loves you so much, why are you so afraid some kid's going to take her away? If she goes to him, you know exactly what that makes her."

"He never would've had the chance if you stayed out of it! He needed money, security. He said once he had stability, *then* he would collect. Do you know how long it would have taken him to get to that point without your interference?"

Slade threw up his hands. "And then you would have been in the exact position you are now. Don't try and peg your own stupidity on me." They were both shouting, careless of anyone listening in or the fact that this was a professional office.

"He wouldn't have had the chance. He was fucking homeless, asshole. I gave him a job as a fucking bellboy. That was my agreement. You promoted him to an executive position without even knowing him. Don't act like you didn't know exactly what you were doing. If he stayed working as a doorman it would have taken ages for him to get to this point. I could have married her by then!"

"*Married her?*" Pure revulsion contorted Slade's face. "Jesus Christ, you've actually lost it."

"I *will* marry her, make no mistake. This little game you're playing, it won't work. I just have one question for you and then our business will be concluded once and for all." He shook his head and glared at the man who'd once been his friend. "Why?"

"Why what?"

"Why do this, Slade? Monique's dead. It isn't as though I'm keeping you from a life with her. She did that herself. Move on. For God's sake, move the fuck on. For you to betray me like this . . . you were my friend, but I'll never see you as anything more than an enemy from here on out. I just need to know why."

Slade pressed his lips together and scowled.

Lucian scoffed. Shaking his head, he looked away and quietly said, "You don't even have a reason, do you?"

"Oh, I have my reasons."

"Then tell me. What did I ever do to you to make you hate me so much?"

Slade looked as though he had something to say, but was torn about whether or not to put it out there.

Lucian gave a dry laugh. "Might as well say it. Whatever sort of fucked-up friendship we had is over. No fixing it now." He stared at Slade for a long moment, wondering when he'd become so deceitful, then scoffed. "You don't even have an excuse. Pathetic."

The other man remained silent.

Lucian turned away and when his hand touched the knob of the door he said, "Send my assistant a number. I'm buying out your share of Patras. I won't work with someone I can't trust."

Slade still said nothing. Lucian opened the door and stepped out, but paused. "And Slade . . ." Turning, the other man met his glare. "You ever betray me again and I will make it my life's ambition to personally take over and destroy everything you love. I did it to my father, don't think I won't do it to you."

He should already be making plans to dismantle Slade's life, but their history made him hesitate. Slade being a scumbag didn't make it any easier for Lucian to drop to that level. However, he knew he would make Slade's life an unending nightmare if he were incapable of fixing things with Evelyn.

Truth be told, there was nothing he loved more than her. She trumped all, and anyone who got in his way of having her risked their life.

Slade knew when to step back and recalculate. He was outmatched. It was like a mom-and-pop burger joint taking on the Golden Arches; one was all emotion and the other was sheer power. Slade was a professional. Patras was a brand, a name trusted by generations. He was the wealthiest man in the city, and Leningrad's yearly profits were a pittance to him.

He shut the door and strode back to the reception desk, where two uniformed security guards were waiting. "I'm leaving in a minute," he growled. "Before either of you boys put a hand on me, why don't you ring up Mr. Bishop and ask him if that's wise?"

He turned and headed down the hall, past several gawking eavesdroppers, and toward a long line of executive offices. When he found the one he was looking for, he pushed on the half-open door and waited.

Hughes sat facing the window, speaking on the phone. He turned at the sound of Lucian's arrival and stilled.

"I'll call you back." He hung up the phone. "Patras?"

"The clock starts now. You have thirty days, and then all bets are off. I gave you a job. I gave you time. Now I want this over. And Parker, make no mistake, I don't share. Once your time's up, you come near her again and I'll kill you."

The little shit's mouth kicked up to one side. "She wouldn't marry you, huh? Don't deny it. I know you tried."

"She'll marry me. Make no mistake."

Parker let out a dry laugh. "You really don't know her at all. She isn't the woman you've dressed her up to be. How does she feel, knowing you used her in a bargain, trading her like tender to a merchant? She's nothing more than an object to you, and I bet she's finally realizing that."

His jaw locked. "I didn't set the bargain. That was you. You had the upper hand and you're the one who set the stakes. I told you I'd leave it to you to tell her, because it's you who she'll see harboring an ulterior motive. Your arrogance only proves you're the one who hasn't got a clue as to who she really is. My only intention was to save her life, *under any* conditions. You're the one who would have let her freeze to death unless you had something to gain. *You* saw her as an object to barter. I saw her as a person worth saving *at any cost*. I'd sacrifice my own happiness for hers any day. I'll leave the pleasure of telling her to you. I think she'll be a little less impressed with you once she learns what a shrewd, manipulative creep you really are."

Lucian hit a nerve with that one, pricked a hole in the other man's ego so full of hollow, triumphant arrogance. It showed in his voice, the way it shook with emotion.

"You would have killed her eventually," Parker said vehemently. "I know what men like you are like. My father was like you. Otherwise you never would've let her go, just to be a prick. In my mind *I* was the one saving her. If you think I would've let her freeze to death you're nuts."

Lucian laughed. "And tell me, how does a man who can't even afford a coat get a girl off the street? You couldn't shelter yourself, let alone her. I found you in a fucking flowerbed, hiding from the wind while she was shivering and crying over her dying mother. Exactly when would the knight in shining armor mentality kick in, Hughes? Just admit it, you had nowhere to go and you were as helpless as you've always been when it came to her safety."

"*Were*, that's the key word, Patras. And I have lots of coats now. I don't need all your money to impress her. I'm not a shmuck. All I need is a roof and some time."

His jaw popped. "Well, you've got thirty days."

Parker's eyes narrowed. "You can't contact her. That was the agreement."

He almost sounded like he was questioning Lucian's word, which only irritated him more. He never broke his word. "Unless she comes to me," Lucian stipulated, per their original agreement.

"She won't."

"Don't be so sure, kid. And be warned, she returns to me—which she will—hurt in any way, and I'll be coming for you."

"You don't scare me, Patras."

"That's because you're still a naïve kid. But I know you want to play with the big boys and wear the big-boy pants, so I'll cut you no quarter. Thirty days, Hughes, not a second more."

sixteen

BIND

A stronghold, usually created by an advanced pawn,
which is difficult to break

LUCIAN'S knee-length trench whipped across his legs as he stood within the shadows, just outside of the golden halo set by the streetlamp. It was a good neighborhood with a Rittenhouse Square feel. There was hardly ever crime in this section of Folsom, and most residents were affluent to say the least. She would be safe here.

White light showed from behind her sheer drapes. He waited for even a silhouette to pass, something to let him know she was all right. There was nothing.

Of all the difficult decisions he ever had to make, this seemed to trump all. Would he lose her? She was confused, angry, but there was a reason. He just couldn't tell her. Once she found out the truth, she'd see his reasoning.

He was a coward. How did one explain to the one they loved they'd been bartered like a valuable trading card, loaned out like a car? He had never been so disappointed in his choices, but every time he recalled that freezing afternoon he'd gone searching for her, he could think of no other option around the fucked-up position they were in now.

During his most intense moments of arbitrage, he never experienced fear like what was living inside of him now. The clock had started. Parker would go to her—once he found her—and wasn't it sweet that Lucian had left her so vulnerable and in need of a friend? His stomach soured, bile swelling to a point of wooziness at the mental image of Parker laying his hands on her, hugging her, holding her, listening to her while she cried about what a prick Lucian was.

The chances of Parker getting his way left Lucian light-headed with worry. He wouldn't break his word, couldn't. It was written into his bones to always stand true to his vow. But nothing had ever tempted him more. All he had to do was go back on his word and he could fix this. But if he wasn't a man of his word, he was only another step closer to being his father.

Parker had played his part well. The way Evelyn described him, she saw him as an innocent man, carefree and understanding, nothing like himself. Lucian knew better. Parker was not one of life's players simply moving the game along. He was nobody's pawn.

He had come from a long line of impressive men. Crispin Hughes was a name Lucian had grown up hearing from the time he was a boy. It was said by many that Folsom was run by two men under the presumption they were Christ: the two Christs of Folsom, the gods of the city, Christos Patras and Crispin Hughes. The irony that he now was coming head to head with the son of his father's nemesis only left more of a bitter taste in his mouth. He was too afraid to actually appreciate the irony of it all.

Just as Lucian had been groomed to someday take over Patras Industries, so had Parker been groomed to take after his own father. The only difference was Patras was still a name people respected, trusted.

The Hughes scandal was huge. Crispin Hughes tried to

swindle conglomerates like Marquee, Velázquez, and Typhoon Industries. The minute he was caught in foul play with one, he was caught by all. Everyone stopped to analyze their doings with Crispin Hughes, and once one lawsuit came, the rest followed.

Lucian was a young man when the news broke of Hughes. Police had swarmed their family's mansion and taken him out in cuffs and a smoking jacket. Every channel reported on how the man never dressed, because he was certain they had no case. Within a day the courts commandeered his possessions and all of his computers were confiscated. Once the investigation started, Crispin Hughes lost a bit of his cocky attitude. The trial went on for years, and then one day, the news broke that Parker's father shot himself.

Loretta Hughes was a sweet woman, far too gentle for the likes of her husband. The bulk of the Hughes family had left Folsom during the trial, leaving only Crispin's wife and young son to handle the press. Parker was far younger than Lucian, but he remembered seeing his picture on the front of the *Tribune* and thinking, *He's just like me. That could have been me.*

Lucian had been going through his own grief at that point, still mourning the loss of his mother and trying to overthrow his father in a bout of misplaced anger and revenge. Men like his father and Crispin Hughes loved the industry. They were the visionaries of their time, gifted beyond measure when it came to business and cursed to the depths of their souls when it came to love. If something couldn't be measured in material worth it didn't exist in their eyes.

After years of watching the mockery of his parents' marriage, Lucian had no intention to follow in his father's footsteps in that realm. He would date, perhaps cohabitate, but for the most part he'd always intended on remaining untethered.

Evelyn changed all that. He didn't want anyone else and was

certain he never would. He sensed her antipathy to the finality of marriage. He knew she wasn't ready. He likely would have never proposed so soon had it not been for Parker's interference.

The man had placed him in a stranglehold, forced his hand in matters where she was concerned, and while Lucian assumed proposing marriage was a precise way to avoid separation, he had been wrong, an outcome he now believed Parker had predicted.

It was beyond frustrating to think Parker knew Evelyn. He knew Scout, some confused kid, a scrapper looking for something more.

Lucian knew Evelyn, the eloquently spoken beauty whom any man would be proud to stand by. True, Parker had him at a disadvantage and had somehow managed to manipulate him and take the upper hand, but Lucian had faith in Evelyn. She was better than him and she was better than Parker. She would be the only one capable of ending this, and he had to believe she would make the right choice. She wasn't Scout anymore, and surely she realized that.

The light behind the curtain switched out and with it, Lucian extinguished his hope that this was just a nightmare. Twenty-nine days to go.

LUCIAN looked over the portfolio Jeff Burnet placed in front of him. He had been staring at it for over five minutes now, seeing the man's expertise in advertising displayed beautifully in the contrasting colors highlighting the plans and drawing buyers' eyes to the pros of the project, yet all he wanted to do was tear it to pieces and demand he come up with something better.

It had been four excruciating days, and things had not improved. He'd gotten worse, far worse. He hated being in the penthouse by himself. His first hour home he'd thrown her craft desk and broken it. He asked Dugan to order a new one. Evelyn's presence was everywhere, on their sheets, in his closet, under his sink. There was no place she hadn't left her mark.

He decided only to use the penthouse for sleep, coming to the office before the doors opened to the public and working long past closing. He'd taken to having his meals delivered to his desk, dining out by himself for late suppers, and last night he had lost his nerve to go home to his empty condo altogether.

He spent the night at his place of work, sleeping on the stiff couch in his office. He showered and shaved that morning in his executive bathroom and found several suits hanging in his closet, a cautionary expense from his days as a bachelor. Freshly laundered dress shirts hung like empty skins all in a row. The lower drawer of his desk was filled with brand-new T-shirts, underwear, and socks still in their packaging and tissue. How much longer could he go on like this?

Jeff cleared his throat. "Would you like me to come back, Lucian?"

Lucian turned the page, not really paying much attention to what he was seeing. Jeff had worked for him for almost a decade. Lucian trusted his ideas, which had been validated by their profits over the past several years. "No."

He turned the page again. Everything was perfect. Lucian could find no room for improvement, which for some reason pissed him off. He shut the portfolio with a slap and met Jeff's eyes. "Do you feel this is the best you can give me?"

The man's expression hitched. He seemed to consider his answer before giving it. "I put three months into that, Lucian. It's everything you asked for."

"That doesn't answer the question. *Is this* the best you're capable of?"

Jeff frowned. "Do I feel it's the best I've ever done? No, but

I've done over one hundred pitches for you. Every one can't be the best or my favorite—"

"Why?" he snapped. "Why shouldn't everything you put on my desk be the best, Jeff? Do I come in here, day after day, and give only a percentage of what I'm capable of? No. I work my balls off so that things can get done around here and you and all the other people who depend on me can get paid." His voice had risen by the end of his reply.

"Look, Lucian, if you want me to give it another look—"

"I want the best you're capable of! Why should I have to wait longer because you slacked off? I gave you three fucking months to do your job. You should have done it right the first time!"

Jeff stiffened. "That's damn good work there. Go ahead and look around if you think you can find better."

"Perhaps I will," Lucian threatened back. "Maybe it's time to rearrange some things around here. People are getting a little too cozy, and I won't have Patras taking the brunt of everyone's indolence. I expect perfection and nothing less."

"Are . . . are you implying you want a new ad exec? You wanna look around, fine, but my contract isn't up for another six months."

Lucian didn't want a new advertising executive. He liked Jeff, liked his work, liked his wife, Debbie. He was invited to his children's birthdays.

"Contracts . . ." he mumbled, leaning back in his chair.

Jeff waited a few minutes. "Lucian, are you all right? You don't look too good. Your color's a bit off and you look tired. Maybe you should call it a day, go home, and get some rest."

"I don't need rest, and the last thing I need is to go home."

Several moments passed in awkward silence. The mood of the room seemed to settle and slowly right itself. "Look, if you want me to redo the ad I will. I can have something back to you by the end of the week. I have some other dormant ideas I was playing with that I could expand on and see how you like them—"

Lucian pushed the portfolio forward. "No, this is fine. It's good. Take it down to Silberstein and have him order the space. I want it up by April first."

Jeff's mouth opened and shut. He took the portfolio and stood. "You sure?"

"Yeah."

He hesitated a moment before leaving. "Look, Lucian, this weekend we're having a little get-together. Deb and the kids would love to see you. Why don't you try to make it?"

Lucian forced the muscles of his face into the closest impression of a smile he could manage. "I'll let you know. Thanks, Jeff."

A while later, after he finished up with Jeff, his intercom buzzed. "What?"

"Mr. Patras, Mr. Callahan's here to see you."

He sighed. "Send him in."

Lucian eased back in his chair. A moment later the door opened and Shamus stepped in, his perpetually flushed cheeks lifted. "Luche, how's it hanging?" As he took a seat at the club chair in the corner, he cocked his head, a crown of golden curls falling to the side. "Did you sleep here?"

Lucian stood to join him. "Yeah. I've been avoiding the condo. Evelyn and I are on a break."

Jamie's eyebrows lifted. "Since when?"

"Four days ago."

"That explains the rumors."

Lucian frowned. "What rumors?"

"That you've lost it."

He wasn't surprised. He'd been screaming at employees all week, setting unobtainable standards, making good workers feel incapable and less than they were. Somehow he thought that would make his own life seem less pathetic. It didn't.

"I've been on a bit of a rampage."

"Ya think? Georgette looks one loud noise away from bursting into tears, and Seth is running around with sweat stains under the arms. Lucian, if you're that miserable, go get her back and apologize for whatever stupid thing you've done."

"It isn't that simple." He settled into the couch and crossed his legs at the ankle. God he was tired.

"Is it really that complicated?"

"Yes."

Jamie waited for an explanation. He was Lucian's best friend. He might as well tell him before he heard it from Slade. "I made a deal. When Evelyn left last fall and I couldn't find her, I made a deal so that I could save her."

"What kind of deal?"

"The stupid kind. I'd spent days scouring every alley, dilapidated building, and shelter in Folsom. She was nowhere to be found. The temperature dropped to below freezing and I panicked. She has a friend, from the shelter, a guy."

"An ex-lover?"

Lucian's eyes narrowed. "No. She's never been with anyone but me. He's just a friend, but he'd like to be more."

"He's homeless?"

"Was. I ran into him on the street and asked him if he knew where she was. He had a better guess than anyone. He knew, but refused to tell me."

"Was she safe?"

"No. The little prick knew that too. He had no way of helping her and we were due another blizzard. He made me an offer. If I agreed, he'd tell me where she was."

Jamie's head slowly drew back. Hesitantly, he asked, "What was the offer, Luche?"

He sighed and shook his head. "I had to give him a job."

"That's not bad."

"Wait. I had to give him a job so he could make money and get himself off the streets. I gave him a job as a bellboy at Patras, but told him the minute he fucked up it was done. That was only one part of the deal."

"What's the other part?"

"When he was ready, once he felt he'd gotten back on his feet, I had to break up with Evelyn for a month. One month, no contact, during which time he could take a shot at her."

Jamie's brow crinkled as his upper lip seemed to snag on an invisible hook. "Are you out of your mind?"

"No. Yes. I was desperate. It was fucking freezing. It had been over a week and I'd used every resource I had to find her only to come up short. What choice did I have?"

"There had to be a better one than that."

"Tell me," he said in exasperation. "You tell me what the better choice was. He had me by the balls, Shamus. What was I supposed to do, let my dick and my pride get in the way of saving her life? I love her and there was no way she was coming out of that decline without my help. Her mom's sick. She was dying and Evelyn would have frozen to death right beside her rather than leave her."

"What's wrong with her mom?"

"A ton of shit; mainly, she's an addict. I found her lying on nothing but cardboard, coughing up blood, in an old abandoned mill by the tracks. I thought she was already dead when I got there. Evelyn wouldn't leave her, so I carried her out of there, had Sheffield take a look at her, and now she's checked into rehab. She hates me. She would've died had I not carried her out of there, but

she's too fucked-up to care. The woman is a selfish cunt and uses
Evelyn, but she's all Evelyn's ever had and she won't abandon her."

"So now what? Evelyn found out about all this and dumped
you?" Jamie asked.

"No, not completely. There were conditions to the agreement.
A bellboy makes practically nothing. Sure, Patras employees are
paid about twenty percent above the norm, but do you know how
long it would have taken to get an apartment in even the shittiest
part of Folsom on that salary? I didn't think there was much of a
rush. To protect myself further, I stipulated that the minute Evelyn agreed to marry me, all bets were off."

"*Marry you?* Lucian, since when are you the marrying type?"

"Since Evelyn. I love her. Why shouldn't I marry her?"

"Because you've never been with anyone longer than a year."

"I was with Monique for three years."

Jamie rolled his eyes. "Yeah, you, her, and Slade playing your
twisted game of house doesn't count. Marriage is between two
people. There's no gray area to escape to when things get tough.
You know this. I remember when we were kids, every time your
mother would cry because your dad ran off somewhere with
Tibet, you'd swear you'd never get married."

This was all true, but he didn't feel that way anymore. Evelyn
changed all that. "Well . . . it's a moot point now. She doesn't
want to marry me."

His friend's eyes bulged. "You asked her?"

"Last week. She shot me down—about twenty times."

"Why? Doesn't she know you're Folsom's most eligible
bachelor?"

"She doesn't give a shit about any of that. She said she wasn't
ready, doesn't know if she'll ever be ready. The funny thing is, the
more she said no, the more I realized how badly I wanted her to
say yes."

"That's because people don't tell you no enough. You just want it because you can't have it and you don't like being told something's out of your reach."

"No, I want her because I love her, because without her I'm incomplete. She makes me a better person. She grounds me. Being with her is nothing like being with Monique or anyone else for that matter. She's . . . perfect."

"Then what the fuck are you doing here? Fuck that little bellboy punk—"

"I can't. She almost got herself killed the other day looking for him. He'd been MIA, and she was convinced he was in trouble. She had no idea he was now working and doing better than he had been in years."

Jamie rolled his eyes. "Scout's too good for a bellboy."

"He quit working for me. Found a much better job, but she didn't know any of this. She was a mess. No matter how much I despise the little shit, he's her friend. She's stubborn, you know? She'd keep sneaking off to find him. I knew where he was and I couldn't take fearing she'd keep going back to the tracks looking for him where he no longer was, so I arranged a dinner."

"Cute. You set them up on a nice little date, did ya?"

"Fuck you. I was there. She was happy. In a way it was worth it."

"Give me a break, Lucian. You're smarter than that."

"You would think, but lately I've proven to be incredibly dumb. When I contacted him he told me he was going to be collecting, *soon*. I saw it in his eyes. He wanted his shot and I couldn't let that happen—"

"Wait, wait, wait . . . You gave him a job, when? November? How the hell does someone go from absolutely nothing to bolstering their confidence into taking on the likes of Lucian Patras?"

"Slade."

Jamie stilled. "Slade? How's he have anything to do with this?"

"He fucked me. Somehow he ran across the kid and found out about our arrangement. I don't know what Slade's issue is with Evelyn. I don't really care anymore. I'd rather take a pike up the ass than ever see him again. He found out and gave the kid a job."

Jamie scowled. "What kind of job?"

"A good one, making about ten times what he was making at Patras."

Jamie shook his head. "Why? Why would he—"

"The kid's Crispin Hughes's son."

His friend let out a long whistle and sat back in his seat. "Fuck."

"Yeah." Lucian tipped his head back until his neck was resting on the back of the couch. His hand scrubbed his brow. "So I proposed, she said no, I freaked, thereby freaking her out in the process. Giving Hughes any more time would have only put the odds more in his favor. I didn't want him to be any more comfortable. The kid's a prodigy. I've looked into it. It's in him, same as it was in his father, same as my father instilled it in me. So I told Evelyn we needed to take a break."

"I imagine that didn't go over too well."

He laughed without humor. "No. She hates me. I've fucked things up so bad I don't think any more damage can be done. She wanted to know why. What the hell was I supposed to tell her? That I'd loaned her out to her friend?"

"Fuck that, Luche. Screw this kid. I don't care who his dad was—"

"I gave him my word."

Jamie groaned. "You and your fucking word. He's a Hughes! Do you think he'd keep his word?"

"He isn't like his father. Smart like him, yes, but I have a feeling he's not dishonest."

"Aw, that's nice. I'm sure Evelyn will appreciate his honesty when he tells her he wants to sleep with her."

"What the fuck could I do?" Lucian yelled.

"You should have told her the truth!"

His insides tightened. "I can't. I couldn't. It's no use now, because part of the deal is that I don't contact her, but before . . . I refuse to be the one to tell her what's really going on."

"Why? If honesty is such an important trait to her, don't you think whoever explains things will ultimately be on her good side?"

He met his friend's gaze. "Imagine how it will go when she finds out. First she'll be irate. If I told her, she wouldn't listen beyond the first confession. She'd be out the door and I'd be right where I am now. I know what he has planned. He's her *friend*, sweet Parker who'd never harm a fly and thinks of everyone before himself." He scowled. "She has him pegged as some sensitive, selfless, poetic sort of guy. I assure you he's anything but. He's as shrewd and selfish as his father. Only my intuition that he hated Crispin leads me to believe he'd loathe coming off as anything less than noble to Evelyn. I think it would kill him to be seen as anything remotely similar to the man who raised him, and right now I wouldn't mind him dead.

"All I was worried about that day was finding Evelyn and making sure she was safe—by *any* means. *Parker* had conditions. He could've helped her. He knew that's what I was there to do, but he found a way to press his advantage. I was at the mercy of anyone who knew where she might be, and he used my disadvantage for his own purposes. Evelyn's the furthest thing from a pushover. Her life's been too hard for her to be naïve. Once she has all the facts, and believe me, she will, she'll realize what he did."

Jamie was quiet for several minutes. His hands were folded as his elbows rested on his knees. This was his pose for deep contemplation. Finally, he said, "So, she finds out he put the deal on the table. That's one black mark. She then finds out that, had you not agreed to his conditions, she would've frozen and her mother would've likely died."

"Correct."

"Okay, but Luche, that doesn't guarantee she'll come back to you. It doesn't guarantee that before she finds all that out he may have already gotten what he's after."

Lucian's throat went dry and he swallowed. "I know," he rasped, baring every bit of worry in his expression for his friend to see.

Jamie sat back with a jerk. "Fuck, this is a goddamn mess."

"You're telling me?"

"No. I can see you don't need anyone telling you what a cluster fuck this all is." He scrubbed his face with his palms then stilled. "What did you do to Slade?"

"I'm buying him out. Fuck if I'll do business with that prick ever again. I reminded him the only reason I'm in this predicament is because I'm a man of my word. I then gave him my *word* that if this ends badly for me, I would make it my life's ambition to destroy everything he loves."

Jamie shook his head. "He's an idiot. Why the fuck would he get involved?"

"Because he wants to fuck me," Lucian said snidely, still not understanding Slade's reasoning. He wasn't even sure he had a good reason. All he knew was that Slade used to be a good guy until he turned so cynical and bitter.

Jamie threw up his hands in exasperation. "We're supposed to be friends. Do you think this is because of Monique? Good God, he needs to let it go!"

"I know."

"You had no more to do with her death than he did. It was a fucking accident. Jesus. Do you want me to talk to him?"

"Don't bother. The selfish prick's gonna do what he wants. Besides, it's too late to change things. I've got twenty-six days to sit here with my thumb up my ass and hope I don't kill anyone in the process. He better pray that doesn't happen, because the minute murder is on my radar, I'm coming for him."

"Why don't you get out of town for a while?"

"And do what, write poetry about the one who got away? No. I need to work."

"Well, your staff's terrified of you at the moment. If you're going to work, work. Don't make them pay for your mistakes."

Lucian got quiet. "I really fucked up," he confessed in a whisper. "What if I can't get her back, Shamus? What if this kid really is better for her and she sees that?"

"Knock it off. You're Lucian Bloody Patras. You've gotten everything you've ever set your sights on. What makes her different?"

He thought for a moment, then met his friend's gaze. "She may be poor, but she's the only person I've ever met with as much determination as me. She's my match, and for the first time in my life, I finally understand what others fear when they face me in a board meeting. If she's determined never to be with me again, take my word, she won't."

"I find it hard to believe there's anyone in this world with as much determination and tenacity as you, Luche. I like Scout. You're right, she's a feisty thing, but she loves you. That fact is clear to anyone who sees you together. You're tired. Get some rest. Once you have a clear head you'll see things better. I don't give a shit who this kid's daddy was. He's not you. Christos was always a little classier, with a little more stealth, and a little more honesty than Crispin Hughes. That sort of thing sticks with its lineage. Evelyn may be your match, but Hughes isn't. She's not the one you have to take out. He is. The thirty days will be over before you know it and you'll have this fixed in no time."

"God, I hope you're right."

"I am."

seventeen
. . . . .

DECOY
A chess tactic used to lure a piece to an unfavorable square

A S the week progressed, things only grew worse. After dressing down an employee in front of the entire lobby, which unfortunately also included the man's fiancée, who worked on another floor, Lucian decided to head home. It was Friday and for the first time in God knows how long, he was home. Pathetic. So he decided to drink.

He drank whatever was sitting in the decanters on the bar, and then he called room service and had them bring him more. He drank until he couldn't walk without knocking into things, and he couldn't stand without the room tipping on end. He drank until his vision played tricks on him, and then he decided it was best to simply sit. So he sat and had a long discussion with himself about what an asshole he was.

His eyes were shut and his head rested on something. He thought he had last sat down on the couch, but couldn't quite remember. He wanted to check, but his eyelids were simply too heavy to move. When there was a knock at the door he groaned.

"Who's it?" he slurred.

Nothing.

He decided to fall asleep, then the knock sounded again. "Who's there?"

When he began to doze off and the knock sounded a third time, he tipped his ass off the couch and forced his eyes open. The world swirled and he moaned until it eventually righted itself. Pressing himself up on his knees, he groped the coffee table, hoisting himself on his feet. Like a marble making its way down a wobbling maze, he staggered, bouncing off the walls, down the hall to the door.

He stretched his eye muscles by blinking hard, then tried to find the peephole. Something sharp shifted in his gut as his hand went to the knob. Cursed fingers yanked on the door only to realize the latch was engaged. He undid the latch and threw the door open.

Unbelievable.

Through his off-kilter, blurred vision he saw three Evelyns standing before him, trying to combine into one as his eyes fought for focus. "Jesus."

She gave a slight finger wave, but said nothing. He reached and caught air, then reached again and felt the warmth of her skin. Sweet heaven, she came back.

He yanked her inside and slammed the door, pressing her into the wall. Her dark hair was down and she had a lot of makeup on. She seemed so different even though it had only been a week. His fingers ran over her shoulders, feeling her, testing that she wasn't some sort of conjured dream.

"I can't believe you're here," he whispered as he kissed her jaw, her throat.

Peeling away her coat, he threw it to the floor. Her touch was aggressive, needy. His mouth found hers as she yanked the knot of his tie the rest of the way loose. It slid from under his collar with a whoosh, and then her cool, nimble fingers worked the buttons of his shirt open.

His tongue pierced between her lips and went deep, reclaiming her. She tasted different.

"Never again," he whispered between kisses, parting his mouth from hers to draw her shirt quickly over her head. Something caught his eye, but he was too drunk and lost in the exquisite moment to wonder what it had been. "I'll never let you go again."

His cock was rock hard. Her fingers curved over the bulge in his slacks, and he moaned as she fondled him through his clothing. His palm cupped her breast and he stilled. His dick, now fully engaged, seemed to control his fingers as they pinched her nipple, but his brain objected. Something wasn't right.

She took over the kiss, aggressively gripping his neck and backing him into the wall. Lucian was never one to be directed in sex, yet he went docilely as his simple, brandy-sodden mind worked to understand why this was suddenly so, so wrong.

The wall halted her progress as his back hit it with an ungraceful thump. He watched her dark head as she kissed her way down his chest and dropped to her knees. His cock was already free and in her hands.

"Mmm, you're so big," she purred in an unfamiliar voice as she prepared to take him into her mouth.

Something snapped. She yipped as he roughly grabbed a fistful of hair, holding on by a thread so as not to fall into a violent rage. He yanked until her face tipped into view. Through clenched teeth he growled, "Who the fuck are you?"

She whimpered and released him. "My name's Sherry."

Appalled, he flung his fingers out of her hair, which was not nearly as soft as Evelyn's, and stepped away. After quickly righting his pants, he paced. The hall was dark. As he flicked on the switch, he turned to face her.

"Jesus," he uttered. She had the same length of hair, the same delicate bone structure as Evelyn, but her eyes were not crystal blue like hers. No, this woman's eyes were brown. She also had freckles showing under a great deal of makeup. Her breasts were larger by at least two sizes, and there was a tattoo of a raven on her shoulder. That must have been what caught his eye at first, telling him something wasn't right.

He wished like hell he were sober. He couldn't think. The woman sat on the floor, watching him, looking like she wanted to bolt, but he still held her shirt in his fist and blocked her exit.

"How did you get up here?" he demanded.

"I . . . I had a key."

Impossible. Only hotel staff, Evelyn, Dugan, and himself had keys to the penthouse. His alcohol-sodden brain cleared as if by magic. "Who sent you?"

Her lips pressed together. She lowered her head. "I was paid to do whatever you wanted. I'm sorry you're disappointed. If you give me my shirt I'll go."

"Fuck that. I want to know who sent you here and I want to know now. Someone gave you a key."

When she said nothing, he barked, "Prostitutes are paid. You either tell me who bought you or I call the cops and have them haul your ass downtown."

She burst into tears. "Please don't do that. This was a mistake. I'm sorry."

"Who hired you?" he growled.

She sniffled and covered her breasts. "I don't know his name. He's a client. I've only serviced him a few times, but he's nice and I never thought he'd put me into a dangerous position. Please don't hurt me or call the cops."

"What does he look like?"

Her voice hitched as she drew in a stuttering breath. She

looked at him with teary eyes. "Young. Brown hair. Green eyes—"

"Motherfucker." He turned and forked his fingers through his hair. "How did you meet him?"

She sniffled. She was clearly terrified. Either that or she was an actress before she became a hooker. "He called my agency and asked for someone who looked like me."

That cocksucker. Lucian shot out a humorless chuckle at the man's audacity. "What, they didn't have a girl with her blue eyes?"

"He requested blue eyes. He asked if I could get contacts," she admitted in a whisper.

Disgusted, Lucian walked passed her and threw his ass into a chair. After a few minutes, she followed him. "Sir, if you give me my clothes I'll leave."

Lucian looked at her standing with her coat covering her naked breasts. It was uncanny how much she actually resembled Evelyn. "He fucked you?"

She blushed and lowered her gaze to the floor.

"I take it that's a yes," Lucian said slowly.

"I've only been with him a few times. After tonight I don't think I'll ever take his call again."

He shook his head. What could he say? "I don't imagine he'll be calling you in the next twenty-three days anyway. How much did he pay you to come here?"

She gazed suspiciously at him. "One—two hundred."

Doubtful. Luckily he could play her little game too. Lucian reached into his pocket and pulled out a wad of cash. He counted out five hundred and tossed it on the table. "That's yours if you tell me everything you know about him. I promise not to hurt you and you won't have to work for the money he gave you. Sorry, but you're not my type."

She gave him a measured look, then gradually approached the table. Small fingers scooped up the money, and she carefully sat on the chair across from him. He tossed her the shirt.

After she put it back on, she asked, "What do you want to know?"

"Start at the beginning. How did you meet?"

She adjusted her clothes and tucked her hair behind her shoulders. "Like I said, he called the agency asking if we had anyone who fit a description. He wanted thin, long chestnut hair with hues of auburn, blue eyes, early twenties. They sent me and two other girls. He sent the other two home and invited me in."

"What happened during that first meeting?"

Her cheeks flushed. "Um, what usually happens . . ."

"He fucked you?"

"Well . . . yes."

Lucian tilted his head. "What's the 'well' about? He either fucked you or he didn't. It's a yes-or-no question."

"Um, first we talked for a while. His time eventually ran out, but he put more money on the table and asked me to stay until morning."

"And did you?"

"Yes."

"What did you talk about?"

"He was, um . . . inexperienced I guess you could say." Lucian chuckled and she paled. "Are you going to turn me in?"

"No. My issue is with him, not you. Tell me more."

She licked her lips and sat back. "Well, he said he didn't have a lot of experience and he wanted to know how to . . . please a woman."

"He was a virgin?"

"Not exactly. He wanted to learn how to . . . make love. He said his experience was only with, well, quickies, I guess."

Lucian growled. "Go on."

"We started with kissing and he asked a lot of questions, what I liked, what I didn't like. Then we moved on to other things. He was very insistent that I not, um, you know . . . fake it."

"I bet he was," Lucian mumbled, shaking his head. "Continue."

"Well, we slept together that night, and then he asked me to come back every two weeks. He said he would hire me more if I kept our arrangement between us and left the agency out of it. I'm not supposed to do that, but I sort of, um, liked him." She shrugged, a gesture Lucian imagined some men found cute.

"So he could pay you less, no doubt."

"Well, yeah, but that wasn't what it was about. At the agency's rate he would only be able to afford to see me every few weeks. If I cut them out, I took home everything I got. So, since he was nice, I . . ." She suddenly looked upset. A tear fell from her eye and she batted it away. "I came to see him every week, sometimes twice a week."

Lucian watched her critically through narrow eyes. Then it dawned. "You liked him."

"I'm a call girl. Emotion doesn't play into it."

"But it did for you, didn't it, Sherry?"

She sniffled and wiped her eyes again. Her frustration with her emotions was evident in the way she kept readjusting her posture, searching for ways to hide her upset. Giving up, she confessed, "He was just so nice. He made me feel special. It wasn't just about the fuck for him. It was about the touch, the kisses, the looks. Clients don't usually look at me the way he did. I swore he was falling for me, but then . . . then he sent me here and I don't understand why. I assumed you were friends."

"Certainly not friends." He sat back and crossed his ankles. "He was learning how to seduce a woman and practicing on you."

The statement stung her, he saw. She shrugged, pretending indifference and failing at it. "I guess."

"Will you go back to him?"

She didn't answer for a long time. Quietly she whispered, "I think I'm in love with him."

This woman was sent to fuck him, physically and metaphorically, yet he pitied her. She was caught up in a game she didn't understand. Parker used her to up his game when it came time to seduce Evelyn. All other thoughts got interrupted by the king of all thoughts. "Was he a good lover?"

She met his gaze. "He wasn't when I met him. I was the first person he ever . . . took his time with. Once he learned how to savor it, it became incredible, for both of us. He was the first person I ever made love with, so yes, I think he's a good lover."

He drew in a slow breath that shook inside his ribs. "Did he bring you to orgasm often?"

She blushed. "Every time."

His back teeth clenched. "What did he expect to gain from you coming here?"

"I don't know. He told me not to call him. Said he would call me. He said he wanted me to remember everything we did, every way you touched me, how you looked at me, then he said he would invite me over one day and I was supposed to report on what we did when he asked, no matter who was present, but I wasn't to admit that I'd been paid."

"Son of a bitch," he hissed. That shit wanted it to get back to Evelyn that he'd been unfaithful during their time apart. Fuck that. He needed to think. Here was a woman under the misconception that she loved Parker, yet she knew nothing about him. He'd used her to get closer to another woman.

"I want to tell you something, Sherry. You've been honest with me and I want to be honest with you. Parker Hughes is not in love with you."

Her face tightened and she blinked back more tears.

Lucian continued. "He's in love with a woman who looks remarkably like you. He's trying to seduce her and he used you to enhance his skills in the bedroom. If he succeeds, you'll never hear from him again."

Her shoulders shook as she cried silently. "How do I know you aren't lying to me?"

"Because I'm in love with the woman he's after. He sent you here thinking you were a close substitute in her absence. I'm sorry, but you're not. You see, when you love someone, only their touch will do. It's only in their scent you find intoxication, *their* kiss that tastes so perfect. It has nothing to do with you, but everything to do with her."

"Believe it or not, I know what you mean. I felt the same way with him. I loved going home and still being able to smell him on my clothes."

"Will you tell him about our discussion?"

She frowned. "I don't know. I don't know what to believe. I thought he cared for me, but if what you say is true, well, I don't want to help him. It's just, I may seem stupid to you, but I don't really believe he would do that. You're a stranger. He's not."

"A stranger he sent you to fuck. Does that sound like the actions of a man in love with you?"

She was silent. Poor girl really did have her heart wrapped up in that little fucker. Lucian wasn't stupid enough to say anything that shouldn't go back to him. There was a huge chance love would outmaneuver reason, and she would help Parker again no matter how Lucian warned her.

He sighed. "Look, I can't tell you what to do. I can't even convince you of what I know. What I can do is make you a promise.

I promise you, Sherry, that if you do what he asked, if you confess things that happened tonight in mixed company, it will only work to screw us both. When you speak to him next, I predict he'll try to persuade you to lie about what we did. He'll want to hear that I easily fell into bed with another woman and he'll try to convince you to say so in front of the woman I love in order to push us further apart. The problem is, the further she is from me, the closer he can get to her, and where does that leave you, Sherry?"

He didn't want to say much more. Who knew how sane Sherry really was? The last thing he needed was some jealous, confused hooker going after Evelyn.

"What do you expect me to do?" she asked.

"I expect you to go to him the next time he calls, which you will. I'd advise you not to, but I can see it in your eyes that you'll need to see for yourself what a prick he is. I don't really expect anything from you, Sherry. Except for your honesty when it comes to reporting back to him about what we did this evening. The only reason I touched you is because I've been drinking and I mistook you for someone else. The moment I realized you weren't her, I stopped. Nothing happened because I will not do that to her."

"Who is she?"

"Someone I hope you'll never meet. And, Sherry, I'm a nice guy, but I'm also a powerful guy. Whatever you and Hughes have going on is between the two of you. I'll be able to find you if I want to. Don't get her involved and make me find you. You'll regret it. Do you understand?"

The girl's expression fell from intent focus to terror. She scooted toward the edge of the chair.

Cutting her some slack, he said, "Put my key on the desk and you may go."

She stood, slowly walked to his desk, and dropped the key.

With her back to him, she slipped on her coat and took her time doing up the buttons. As she turned, she said, "Thank you. I have everything I came for. I hope we never meet again."

"As do I."

A moment later the door closed and the elevator pinged softly. Parker must have acquired a key during the brief time he worked at the hotel as a bellhop. Lucian knew he could no longer waste away his evenings drinking. He needed his mind sharp.

Parker Hughes was not a man to underestimate. His ploy tonight had only showed Lucian that having the odds tipped in his favor was not enough. No, Parker would do everything he could to fuck him over, and Lucian would never underestimate him again. If he couldn't go to Evelyn, he needed to get the hell out of Folsom.

eighteen

FLIGHT SQUARE

A square in which a piece can move in order to escape an attack

THE jet squealed through the air as it careened toward the earth, altitudes decompressing the cabin with every inch of descent. When the wheels finally skidded along the tarmac, Lucian undid his seatbelt.

"Look, Isadora, I'm landing. I'll call you once I check in at the hotel."

"Lucian, don't you dare hang up on me," his older sister snapped, using her most stern voice. "What's going on with you? You haven't been to Paris in years and all of a sudden you announce you're taking a holiday to go visit Daddy of all people."

He stuffed his papers into the briefcase sitting beside him at the table. "I'm not visiting Christos and Tibet. I simply needed to get away and decided Europe was the place to go."

"Away from what?"

"All of it."

Isadora was silent for a beat. "Luche, are you okay? Jamie told us you and Evelyn had a disagreement and the two of you were taking some time apart."

He paused. Fucking Shamus. "When did you talk to Jamie?"

"He, uh, he came by last night. He's been visiting a lot lately."

Lucian scowled. "What the hell for?"

His sister drew in an audible breath. "Okay, listen, don't freak out. She's twenty-three years old—"

"Are you fucking kidding me? Toni? What the hell happened to that ass wipe she was dating?"

"Oh, come on, Lucian. You knew that was never going to go anywhere. You should be relieved. Could you imagine if she would have married him and we had to put up with him all the time? At least we know Jamie—"

"Whoa, whoa, whoa, *no one* is getting married."

"Calm down." She growled. "I knew I shouldn't have said anything. We all knew this would eventually happen. The two of them have been dancing around each other for years now. She's not a kid anymore, Luche."

"Why didn't Shamus tell me? He should have fucking asked."

She snorted. "Because you ask? Come on, get real. Besides, he wanted to tell you this week, that's why he popped into your office, but he said you already had enough on your plate with Evelyn. What's going on with you two, by the way?"

The captain opened the door to the cockpit and nodded, informing Lucian it was safe to exit. He adjusted his phone between his ear and his shoulder and stood, looking around for anything he might have left behind.

"Don't change the subject, Isadora. How long's this been going on with the two of them?"

"Only a few weeks." She lowered her voice. "Lucian, I don't even think they've slept together yet."

"Good God, I don't want to hear about that!"

"What? It isn't like I'm telling you they're going at it like rabbits. I thought that might be a relief."

"Fuck." The idea of Shamus and his sister was one he had tried to avoid for years. Isadora was right. It was only a matter of time.

Toni and Jamie had been doing that bullshit playground flirting ritual since they were young. The only difference was he and Jamie were a lot older than Toni. However, Toni—the little brat—took great pleasure in pointing out that she and Evelyn were the same age. "Fuck."

"Stop saying that," Isadora scolded.

"Well, what the hell am I supposed to say? My best friend wants to screw my baby sister."

"Damn it, Lucian! She isn't a baby."

"I should have known this was coming. Now that I think about it, Shamus has been breaking my balls about her being an adult now, more so than usual. He could've just come out and told me what his intentions were like a man, so I could've punched him in the face and moved on, but no. He had to be a tissue about it and let my older sister tell me."

"I don't think he wanted anyone else to tell you. They're probably going to be mad I blabbed."

"Well, they can get over it. And while they're at it they can get over any ideas they have of this continuing. Toni's too young for him."

"Okay, Grandpa. Listen, you go check into your hotel and call me when you get settled. I'll be sure to inform the two lovebirds of your disapproval while you're away. I'm sure it will put a halt to all their intentions. You are the center of the universe after all."

"I'm the patriarch while Dad's—"

"Well, I'm the matriarch and older than you by quite a few years, so I'm overruling you. Besides, I think it's sweet."

"Oh, spare me."

"Oops, here they come now. I gotta run, Luche, we're going shopping. *Au revoir!*"

"Isa—" The phone went dead. He stood at the bottom of the steps and went into his contacts. He pulled up Jamie's number and texted:

Prepare for an ass whooping when I get home. MY SISTER? Really??

A second later his phone vibrated. He looked at the screen.

Sorry. I tried to warn you.

I'll start hitting the gym again to prepare, because I'm not walking away.

Lucian growled and slid his phone in his jacket pocket. It wasn't that Jamie was a bad guy. He just had similar appetites to his own, and Toni wasn't the type of girl to be bossed. She was the furthest thing from submissive and Shamus, that voyeur pervert, only slept with girls who gave him control of the ropes. Literally.

Maybe it won't work out.

And maybe Hughes changed his mind.

His sister was right. He had to get real.

"Bienvenue, Monsieur Patras. Votre limousine est de cette façon," an attendant said as he waited for Lucian, his bags already loaded on a cart.

He followed him to the limo. *"Merci."*

Jacques, a long-term employee of Hôtel Patras and the last chauffeur he had had when in Paris, stood awaiting him at the door to the limo. *"C'est bon de vous revoir, jeune Monsieur Patras."*

He took the chauffeur's extended hand. "Good to see you again, too, Jacques. How have things been in my absence?"

"Très bien, monsieur. Et où allez-vous aller aujourd'hui?"

Where would he be going? Good question. He supposed it was only proper to visit his father first since it had been about five years. He sighed. *"Je voudrais voir mon père et le Tibet, s'il vous plaît."*

"Ton père va être content."

"I wouldn't be too sure," Lucian mumbled as he climbed into the limo. While most fathers were happy to see their sons, Lucian had never been the typical son. Christos Patras also was not the typical father. As the limo pulled away, he shut his eyes and prepared for the worst.

nineteen
· · · · ·

RESIGN
To concede the loss of a game

JACQUES pulled into the rounded cobblestone drive of his father's primary residence, and Lucian climbed out of the car. The brick façade of the mansion stretched high and wide. Nothing in America was this old and therefore could never be as beautiful. The chauffeur lifted his bags from the trunk.

"Oh, don't bother. I won't be spending the night. You can take my things to the hotel and I'll call when I need a lift home."

Jacques frowned at his English.

"Shit." Lucian thought for a moment. Changing gears, he recalled the French lessons he'd been forced to endure since the womb. *"Je vais dormir à l'hôtel."*

Jacques raised an eyebrow. *"Mais votre famille est ici."*

Exactly. If his family was here, he wouldn't be. At least not with this side of his family. The driver nodded his understanding, not masking his disapproval well, and placed the luggage back in the trunk of the car.

"Je vais telephone l'hôtel quand je suis prêt," he said, waving the chauffeur off. Jacques slowly pulled out of the stone drive, leav-

ing Lucian alone on the steps of the mansion. "No time like the present," he grumbled as he climbed the stairs and rang the bell.

"*Juste une minute,*" a female voice called from the other side of the door. When the door opened, Claudette, his father's maid, stood on the other side, her hair a bit more gray, her build a bit softer. She looked at him and he saw the moment he'd been recognized. "*Oh mon dieu, Lucian! Que faites-vous ici?*"

"*Bonjour,* Claudette," he greeted, and she reached up, grabbed his ears, and pulled him down so that she could kiss both his cheeks.

"Your *père* shall be so pleased to have you here! 'Is son 'as finally returned. It is *magnifique!*"

She tugged him over the threshold and stripped him of his jacket. "'Ave you been in Paree long, *mon garçon?*"

"No, I've just landed."

She covered her smile with her fingers. "And you decided to visit your *père* first? You 'ave grown up, no? And 'ow 'andsome you 'ave grown."

Lucian refused to let this butterball of a woman make him blush. He was Lucian Patras for Christ's sake. He did not blush.

Claudette hung up his coat and turned to face him again. She tilted her head to the side and studied him for a moment. "Ah, but what is this, Lucian? You are *déprimé.*"

He frowned at her. She was the only woman who refused to speak to him as an adult. She met him when he was twelve and treated him as such ever since.

"I am not depressed, Claudette," he assured her.

"Do not lie to me, *garçon.* I see it in your eyes. What has you so?" She suddenly jumped and smiled. "And you 'ave come to see your *père*! Per'aps whatever it is that weighs on you can act as a bridge to mend this silly rivalry the two of you share."

They walked toward the back of the house, their steps echoing to the tops of the fifteen-foot ceilings. Christos called Lucian's taste gauche. Lucian called his father's taste pompous Parisian chic.

Claudette leaned close and whispered, "Is it a woman? You have the sad look of a man *amoureux*. Has she captured your poor tortured heart and scorned you, my sweet *garçon*?"

He pursed his lips. "You've been watching too much daytime television, Claudette. Perhaps my father needs to give you more to do."

The swat of her hand landed on his arm where she gripped him affectionately. *"Ne vous l'osez!"* she hissed. "Bite your tongue."

He chuckled.

They stopped outside of the tall French doors that marked his father and Tibet's private living quarters. She turned to him and drew his face down to her height. "Now you listen to me, *garçon*," she whispered. "Your father is not a young man anymore. I do not want any fighting, *comprenez*? You bicker with 'im and you answer to me." Her pudgy fingers slapped his check twice. "Now, you go 'ave a nice visit and then come see me, and I will see about getting you some fresh croissants. Lord knows what you 'ave been eating in zee States."

She smiled and turned away. As the echo of her soft footsteps dissipated into the depths of the house, he could make out the slight rumble of voices coming from a television. He was here. There was no turning back now. He turned the brass knob and knocked as he pressed the door open.

"Oui?" his father called from the next room, his voice as gruff as always.

Rather than answer, Lucian walked toward his father's voice and stood in the doorway. His dad's graying hair had begun to thin. It wasn't a bad way to go, Lucian thought, figuring in a few decades his hair would likely look the same, being that he was about as carbon copy as a son could be.

When he cleared his throat, his father continued penning the line of whatever he was writing and, without being rushed, glanced at the door. When he saw who was there he stilled.

"What the hell are you doing here?"

"It's good to see you too, Christos."

Lucian stepped into the room. It was furnished in a nouveau riche style that had Tibet's mark all over it. The only thing in the room of any real value was the desk his father was writing at and now scowling from.

"Are the girls all right? Did something happen?"

"Isadora and Toni are fine. It wouldn't hurt you to call them once in a while."

"Has Antoinette finished her degree yet?"

Lucian settled into a dainty blue chair that was predictably uncomfortable. "No, she's changed her major again."

His father crossed his arms. "You and Isadora give her too much freedom. She needs direction, that one, too headstrong. Isadora was always more like your mother."

"Yes, it's quite unfortunate Toni takes after her father more than her mother."

Christos's eyes narrowed. "Well, come on then, why are you here? I know you didn't just come to visit."

"I had business here," he lied.

"What business? I keep in touch with your manager at the hotel here. There are no matters pressing enough to require your presence."

Lucian pursed his lips. "Do you think my employees would keep you informed if there were matters requiring my attention? You're no longer the owner. You're the man I bought out and they're quite aware which Patras signs their checks."

His father waved away his words. "Family squabbles do not interest the French the way they do the Americans. You're my son.

They see you as my subordinate. As your father I'm deserving of their respect and, in their eyes, I hold more authority than you, regardless of who signs their bloody checks." He practically sneered the last part of his statement.

"Fucking Europeans," Lucian mumbled under his breath.

"So why are you here? Is it money? Are you in trouble?"

"Wouldn't that make you happy."

His father surprised him by snapping, "No, it would not make me happy. Unlike you, I do not wish my family to fall upon harder times. You may have taken over my livelihood, but it takes a lot more to leave a Patras penniless. I asked, because if you needed money I would give it to you."

Lucian rolled his eyes, not falling for the fatherly act. "I'm sure you would. At what? Fifty percent interest? Sixty-five?"

"Goddamn it, Lucian, must every word between us be in anger? Surely you didn't come all this way just to frustrate me."

Something in his father's voice gave him pause. He studied him. This was the same man who walked away from every single one of his children directly after the death of their mother, leaving them with governesses and tutors to guide them into adulthood. He didn't give a whit about their problems.

Toughen up! his father would yell, whenever they even mentioned something they found unjust. He wasn't old enough to have a change of heart forced by mortality. Besides, one had to have a heart in order for it to change.

"I needed to get out of the city and I haven't been here in five years. It doesn't hurt to surprise employees every once in a while, check on how things are really going."

As his father nodded a look of sadness flashed in his eyes. "True. Well, it was nice of you to stop by while you were passing through. Tibet will be sorry she missed you."

"Is she not here?"

"No. She's been dealing with some medical issues of late and today was the first day she actually felt more like herself in some time. I sent her out shopping, thinking the fresh air ought to do her good."

"Yes, well . . . tell her I'm sorry I've missed her." Truth be told, he was relieved by her absence.

His father scowled. "She's your stepmother, you insensitive brat. Aren't you even going to ask what's wrong with her?"

And so it began. "That woman will never hear a title from me with the word *mother* in it. I had a mother and she killed her—"

"Do not go pinning that on Tibet. Your mother had cancer. *Cancer*, Lucian. You act as though Tibet was pricking pins in a voodoo doll for Christ's sake!"

"She might as well have been!" he roared back. "She was letting you stick your prick in her when you should have been taking Mother to medical appointments!"

His father shook his head, and just like that all the steam seemed to leave him. "This is the way it will always be between us then?" He rubbed his brow and in a softer voice said, "I loved your mother, Lucian. I loved her and took care of her the best I knew how, but I loved Tibet too. I loved her in a different way. A way I didn't know existed until I met her. By then it was too late. Your mother was already my fiancée."

Lucian turned away, discarding all the same old bullshit. If not for Tibet his mother would have never suffered as she had in the end. Rather than facing her disease with the courage of her spouse and his strength available to her when she was at her weakest, she suffered through treatments while battling a broken heart.

He'd never forget the night his mother was up vomiting after a treatment. Lucian had sat with her, terrified as only a young boy could be seeing his mother so weak. She was on so much medication she was babbling about things he didn't quite understand.

"She's the cancer, Luche," she had told him. "She is a cancer to this family, to my marriage, and to you children."

"Try to rest, Mom."

"I'll rest when I'm dead."

Her words angered him. He was only a boy. A world without his mother in it was unimaginable. The idea of being raised by his heartless father who showed up only to criticize them was unthinkable.

Then there was the infamous Tibet. His mother spoke of her often. She had been a name spoken in their house from the time he was a child, yet he had never set eyes on her.

Lucian had tried to settle his mother that night, asking her to please not get herself worked up. "You need to rest, Mom. Sleep and the pain will be gone in the morning."

She laughed dryly. "You kids think it's this disease that's killing me, but it's her, her and your father. I loved him, Lucian. Do you know how much I loved him?"

She began to cry. "Why wasn't I enough? That's what I want to know, Lucian! Why wasn't I enough? I stood by for years while he carried on with his affair and pushed all of us aside to make his fortunes. When he fell on hard times, I was there. And where is he now? Huh, where is he?"

She had swung out her hand in anger and knocked the tray from the night table, the sound attracting the maid and Isadora. His sister climbed onto the bed and held their mother as she wept like a little girl. He backed out of the room as she cried, "Why wasn't I enough? We will never be enough. He always has to have more, more, more."

WHEN he was a child, Isadora ripped the arm of his favorite bear. He beat her with a toy car and his father then beat him, instilling

in him that a man never raised a hand to a girl. It didn't matter
that Isa was bigger than him. Lucian had been four. It was the first
time he ever felt enraged. However, that time was purely child's
play to what he felt that night his mother fell to pieces in his sister's
arms.

It was then he vowed to always be a man of his word—unlike
his father—and he also vowed in that moment that if his mother
did not live through this, he would personally go after everything
his father loved. That was a promise, and he kept it.

He looked at his father now, that old rage bubbling up inside
him again. "It was a mistake coming here." He stood.

"You're leaving?"

"What do I have to stay for? I must have been nuts when I
thought being here would do me good, having some crisis of conscience, or perhaps looking for some sort of parental guidance
that has never existed between us. I'll call a cab and be out of
your hair—"

"Why would you need guidance, Lucian?"

He faced his dad and noticed genuine curiosity in his expression, but he couldn't trust it. Christos only moved in methods of
advancement and malice. There were no softer sides.

Lucian sighed. "Forget it. If I don't see you . . ." He left the
comment open, knowing it would likely be another five years before he saw his father again. He turned for the door.

"Wait."

He stilled but didn't face him. His father waited as well, and
then finally said, "I lied. Tibet's not sick—"

Lucian spun on his heels. "Who lies about something like
that?"

"I am. I've been sick for quite some time. Had a heart attack
back in November that put me on my back for a while. They did
some invasive bullshit, opened me up." He drew a line over his

shirt, showing where his incision had been. "A few weeks ago I caught a bug. I tell you, once you have a heart attack, little shit like the common cold can feel like the plague. Today's the first day I've been out of bed in a month."

His father appeared thinner, now that he was standing. Lucian believed him. There was no reason not to, even if he did just lie about Tibet being the one that was sick. Still, for all the sympathy he felt for his mother when she had come close to death, he felt drawn in the opposite direction for his father. Yet an innate part of him wanted to go to his dad and comfort him, let him know he was there and everything would be fine.

"I don't want the girls to know," his father said. "No sense in worrying them." He was quiet for a few beats, then in a small voice he said, "Or worse, telling them and realizing I mean so little to them now that they don't seem worried at all."

Weight crushed down on his chest, only angering him more. *Fuck.* "Guilt? Really, Dad? Bad form." He drew a quick comparison in his mind between Pearl and Christos.

His father let out a breath of laughter as his mouth quirked in a half smile that didn't reach his eyes. "Sorry. Pathetic, I know." He sat back in his chair, and this time Lucian took notice of how winded and lethargic he seemed. He returned to his chair as well.

Christos cleared his throat. "So many times I wanted to call you kids and just say . . . hell, I don't know, just say *something*. Isadora's a woman now. You're busy with business. I remember what that was like. And Antoinette . . . my sweet little Annie . . ."

"She hates being called that," Lucian informed him.

"Well, she's my baby. I can call her whatever the hell I please." The words should have come out with a hint of laughter, but they didn't. Instead they were laced with what sounded like anger. "I'm too weak to even fly. I can't even get on a plane to see my

own damn children!" His hand thumped on the desk. "I know if
I asked you kids to come to me you wouldn't. I have three children and not one of them likes me."

Lucian pressed his lips together. All of his instincts were
rallying up his sympathies, but for whom? This man was the same
person who made him feel worthless on so many levels, made him
feel like he would never be good enough. For all Lucian knew he
was destined to be something totally different, but his father's
lack of faith challenged him directly where he'd landed. He had to
be a success just to stick it up his dad's ass.

Yet here he was all boo-hoo woe is me. Well, where the hell
was he when Isadora found out she had a lump in her breast? Or
when Toni got in a car accident when she was seventeen? How
about when he . . . Lucian came up short when he searched for
some life-threatening moment in his own existence.

The only thing Lucian had ever truly suffered was losing Evelyn. The pain of burying Monique couldn't equate to what he felt
when he thought about losing Evelyn.

He looked at his dad and found his expression anxious. What
could he say? You were a shitty father and husband?

"Tell me why you're here, Lucian," Christos whispered. "You
came all this way. Don't expect me to believe it was for nothing. I
know you didn't come to see me, but you came here hoping to
find answers. Let me help you. Let me at least be there for one of
my children."

A knot twisted inside of Lucian's stomach. He couldn't deal
with any more guilt or stress or he was going to have an ulcer before the month was over.

The trustworthiness of his father was up for debate. He didn't
know if even a come-to-Jesus moment was enough to change a
man like Christos Patras. His father feared no god. On the

contrary, he thought *he* was God. So the entire idea of him suddenly caring about what was going on in his children's lives was too foreign for Lucian to digest.

Lucian was trained by the best to overtake the best. He had to be the better man in order to outmaneuver his dad the way he had. He knew what being a man of business entailed. One had to know how to read people, pick up on any weaknesses, and put pressure there at just the right time in order to proceed in the desired direction.

His mind drew back to another time in his childhood, before his mother had gotten sick. He was seven, sitting out back on the veranda, hiding because he was crying. When he heard his father's heavy footfalls he quickly dashed away his tears.

"LUCIAN! What are you doing out here? Your mother's looking for you."

He drew up the tail of his shirt and wiped his nose. Scrambling to his feet, he bowed his head instinctively, knowing his father would not be empathetic, and scurried by. He came up short when his father caught him by the collar.

"Are those tears? Patras men don't cry, Lucian. You'll never get anywhere in this world if you don't toughen up."

Lucian clenched his teeth, wishing he could strike the giant that held him immobile. "Yes, sir."

His father released his collar and narrowed his eyes, critically watching Lucian's flushed face. "Is this about that dog?"

That dog! His name was Rex and he was their family pet. Rather than get into an argument, he pressed his lips together, but frustration boiled beneath his skin.

His father shook his head. "Damn dog, I told your mother

*that was a terrible idea. Now look at you kids, every one of you
an absolute mess because some animal's dead."*

Lucian's heart sank. His father was nothing like the rest of them.
He was cold and unfeeling. Everything he spoke of had to do with
business and money. He never simply stopped to just be a father.

"I should have saved everyone the worry and shot that thing
long ago, put it out of its misery," his father said as he turned
away and headed back toward the house.

A white haze of anger took hold of Lucian. His crooked, chewed
fingernails bit into his small hands as they fisted at his side. His
tongue pressed to the roof of his mouth as he sucked in a deep
breath through his nose like a dragon draws in smoke after
breathing fire. Hate was a living, seething thing coiled inside of
him, and he had to get it out.

Like a locomotive running off its track, Lucian bellowed as
deep as his young lungs would allow and charged at the man. His
fists crashed into his back, and for a moment he felt his father's
shock before it transitioned into anger.

"I hate you!" Lucian shouted as his fists pummeled the giant.
"You're mean and heartless! No one here loves you! You don't
care about anyone or anything but your stupid money!"

His arms were restrained as he thrashed and spit. His father's
anger quickly shifted into something disturbing. As if deranged,
his dad was suddenly smiling at him. "Good, boy. That's it. Be
angry. Let it all out. Tears are for pansies, and no Patras man is a
pansy. You see, love weakens a person, makes them vulnerable.
Never put yourself in that position, Lucian. You open yourself up
for those lesser emotions and you open yourself up to be dominated. Power is control, and having control leads to more power.
Love corrupts power."

As he drew in one enraged breath after another, he wondered

how a man survived all those years without a heart. He jerked his arms away, forcing his shoulders out of his father's grip.

"That's you. I don't ever want to be like you! You have no heart."

His father stood and smiled. It was odd, that was perhaps the one moment of his life he recalled seeing pride in his father's eyes, but it was for all the wrong reasons.

He nodded. "Go ahead and hate me, son. I'll survive. I've made it through worse. If I have to be the one you hate in order to teach you that it's okay, then so be it. I will not have a son who cries. Love weakens us, but hate focuses our drive. Embrace it, trust it, let it move you to top of the heap."

"LUCIAN? Lucian, are you even listening to me?"

Lucian turned to his father, so much frailer than the giant he once was. Now Lucian was the giant, yet that brought him no comfort in moments like this.

He did the math. His father was about his age when he'd given him that load of crap about love and called it advice, using his age as a reference point on wisdom. Lucian had no answers, likely because everything he knew of emotion and the human heart was stilted, being that this man beside him was the only male role model he had growing up.

He shook his head. "I'm sorry, what were you saying?"

His father frowned. "I said you can talk to me. I'm your father. I want to be here for you."

Not good enough. His mind played over all of the bullshit his father had spouted over the last couple of decades. This man truly believed that lulling a person into a sense of comfort, getting them to bare their soul, was only a means to an end. He was the python of manipulation, seemingly still but large, waiting until the precise moment to sink its teeth into its prey, strangle it slowly, and swallow it whole.

Lucian shook his head. He had to get out of there. He was being sucked in, and he was smarter than that. "That's not going to work for me, Christos."

He didn't let his father's surprised expression interfere with his exit this time. He stood. "My days of being a sucker ended a long time ago. Find someone else to buy into your bullshit."

He hated that the man looking back at him was not the arrogant, heartless giant from his memories, but an older, withered version, sharing the same eyes and nose.

"You don't mean that," his father rasped, eyes unblinking, face crestfallen.

Lucian wasn't sure what he meant, but he couldn't make a decision like that while his head was a mess and he was working on six hours of jet lag. His dad never had empty sleeves. That was what he spent his life observing, learning. There was always an ulterior motive with him, a way to climb on the weak and slither to the top. He would not be another stepping-stone for this man.

"I gotta go."

"Lucian," he pleaded.

He twisted again, this time angry and needing someone to unleash on. Why not let his father have it? Lucian had taken his abuse for years. Let the old man see how it felt when someone bigger pushed him down. Better he take the brunt of Lucian's wrath than his blameless employees. At least with Christos, he could peg some of the blame. Perhaps he was why Lucian could never have a healthy relationship.

"What?" he shouted, and his father sunk back in his chair. "What could you possibly have to say to me? That you love me? *No, never that!* You don't love. You find hate a better-suited emotion for advancement. Well, how's this? I hate you. I've hated you since I was a boy and you're so heartless and single-minded you nurtured that hate, taught me to harness it. I don't know how to feel anything else for you. I can barely make sense of my emotions because you taught me to hide them. I don't want to hide them anymore. But you know what, *Dad*? When I see you I feel more than hate. I feel sadness. I pity you. You have three children and don't know a thing about a single one of us.

"You think you're the only one with problems? I could give you a list of problems we've worked through over the years—without you! We don't need you, and if you suddenly feel the need for family, well, I can't help you. You pushed us all away years ago. So I really don't know how to comfort you through these moments. I've never known how to comfort you."

He was breathing heavy, waiting for his father to yell back, but he only stared at him like he was some sort of a monster. He uttered an oath. When he couldn't take that look in his father's eyes another moment, he snapped, "Say something!"

Christos cleared his throat, but his voice remained a hoarse rasp. "What do you want me to say, Lucian? That you're right? Okay, you're right. I was a shitty father and I know even less about raising children today than I did then. Truth be told, you all scared the piss out of me. You were so damn small and delicate. I was afraid I'd break you all. I thought when you got older . . . But by then the bonds were already there. Your mother was the nurturer. I was the provider. I wish I had an explanation for you, but I don't."

Lucian shoved his hands in his pockets and shifted his weight, unsure of what to do or say.

His father laughed. "Aren't we a pair? Two emotionally stunted men discussing our feelings."

He pursed his lips. "Speak for yourself. I'm only emotionally stunted when it comes to you."

That slight bit of sarcasm left his father's eyes, extinguished by yet another cutting truth. Perhaps he was getting too old for this verbal sparring that had always been their sole means of communication, but Lucian didn't know how else to talk to him.

Christos lifted the papers on his desk, aligned the edges, and made a show of stacking them. Without meeting Lucian's gaze, he mumbled, "Perhaps you could stay here, at the house, rather than at the hotel. Tibet would love—"

"Christos—"

"Right. You have business to attend to." His disappointment seemed so real. "Will I see you again before you leave?"

He was suddenly exhausted. "I . . . I don't know."

"I'd like to, see you again that is."

There was something frightening about the way his father said that. He was being melodramatic. "I'll . . . I'll let you know." He quickly turned and exited the room, cutting off any further comments from his father.

When he reached the hall, he saw Claudette. She left whatever she was doing to come to him. "Did you 'ave a nice visit, *garçon*?"

"Is he sick, Claudette? Really sick?"

She turned away, then back to him. Lowering her gaze to the ground, she wrung her fingers and whispered, "Your father is not well. Madame Tibet cries often. We thought we might have lost 'im during these last few weeks."

"Why didn't someone call us?"

She met his gaze. "Would you 'ave come if I did? I do not know what would be worse, me going over 'is head and contacting you when 'e asked me not to, or seeing the hurt in 'is eyes when I confessed calling 'is children, but not a single one of them came to 'im."

He didn't answer. He wouldn't lie to her and he couldn't honestly say if he would have come. "May I use a telephone?"

She looked disappointed, but showed him to the closest phone. His cell service was shit this far out in the country. Claudette shut him into the library, and he found the phone on the table by the window.

As he dialed the hotel, he looked through the curtains. He stilled when he saw Tibet sitting on a cement bench in the garden. She must have returned from shopping.

He frowned. She was crying.

Tibet was a tiny woman with dark black hair and tiny features. Her nose was long and her lips thin and tight like a bow. Her brows were narrow and arched naturally high. She was a beauty of the European sort, a native of France.

He stared as she dashed away a tear with a handkerchief. She was alone. He'd never seen much emotion from her, or perhaps he never really looked. This was the woman who destroyed his parents' marriage.

"*Bonjour, Hôtel Patras. Puis-je vous aider? . . . Bonjour?*"

Lucian stared at the phone. He was rendered mute a moment as he waited for his brain to kick in. It didn't. His mouth was the first part of his body to work, and he was shocked when he heard himself say, "This is Lucian Patras. I need to reach Jacques Dubois. He's a chauffeur there."

"*Oui*, Monsieur Patras, I can reach Jacques for you. He is still on zee road. Shall I telephone him for you?"

"Yes, please tell him to return to my father's estate with my belongings. I'll be staying here."

twenty
. . . . .

JEU SUR

Translation: Game On

THE Parisian culture was something that had always appealed to Lucian. He adored watching the people from the benches bordering the River Seine, loved the scent of fresh baguettes flowing from café windows. The fluid language was familiar and eased his mind like lyrical poems even when he was overhearing a mother chattering on about her list for the market. He loved Paris, but had never been more miserable in his life.

Meandering up the cobblestone thoroughfare, he sneered at couples as they embraced and strolled along beside him. Bistros opened their doors to patrons, beckoning guests to dine on their cuisine, but he wanted nothing to do with such vulgar displays of culture. Everything he'd eaten in the past week tasted like ash on his tongue. Even the most delicate and buttery pastries filled his mouth like flavorless mush.

The skies weighed like dull blue cotton, and the manicured grounds sat like graves beneath his feet. Nothing was as it should be in the most romantic city in the world when he had no one to

share it with. The idea of being there alone never bothered him
before, but it bothered him now.

A group of young women dressed in their slim heels and swank
Blemar Pierre dresses tittered by. One dark-haired beauty offered
him a shy wave behind the backs of her friends. Lucian couldn't
even muster a smile. He was miserable, and he knew the cure to
what ailed him was nowhere on that continent.

What was he doing there? Wasting time dancing around his
family issues, knowing there were so many more pressing decisions to be made, like deciding what held more value, his word or
the woman he loved.

Stupid question. Evelyn of course was more valuable. How
could he have let things come to this? What was she doing at that
very moment?

He thought coming here would put some distance between
him and his issues, but all it did was make him feel less in control
of himself, a feeling he loathed above all things.

She was his, and he had pushed her aside in some twisted
attempt to do the honorable thing. He paid her no honor with
such actions. She would eventually find out, and he was a fool to
assume Parker Hughes would be the only one responsible for her
hurt.

Lucian was as much to blame as the boy. They'd both acted
like self-serving pricks. So why was he still over three thousand
miles away from her? Why was he still letting fate decide what
was best for him? She was his, damn it. It was his job to protect
her. What if this was killing her?

He shivered as a chilling thought ran through his mind, not
for the first time. What if she was fine? What if she was over him?
Perhaps she truly hated him and now moved on to other endeavors? For all he knew, she and Hughes were laughing at his expense right at that very moment.

Lucian ground his teeth together and shouldered his way through a crowd. He needed to get back. He was as useless as tits on a bull sitting here with his thumb up his ass in old fucking *Paree*. He hadn't even done business since he arrived.

He couldn't think straight. Nothing made sense. His head was so twisted up. He was adrift and desperately needed to get back on track.

He took a cab back to the mansion, and Claudette greeted him at the door. "Your father is sleeping," she informed him.

He needed to get a call out to arrange his flight home. "I'll be in the library."

She nodded and stepped aside, taking his coat.

As he shut the door to the library he turned and stilled.

"Lucian." Tibet stood by the dainty table by the fireplace. "I'll be finished here in a moment. I was just trying to figure out some of these insurance papers." She was flustered and appeared to be crying again.

He awkwardly stood with his hands in his pockets. For seven days he had successfully avoided being alone with the woman who ruined his mother's life.

"I'm sorry," she apologized again. Her trembling hands gathered several papers and hurriedly pushed in her chair.

He sighed. It was her damn house. He could be nice. "You don't have to leave on my account."

She eyed him curiously and nodded, lowering her small frame back into her chair. She mumbled something in French. Tibet was many things, but timid was never a label that fit her.

Taking a deep breath, he stepped into the room. "Is there something I might be able to help you with?"

She shook her head hopelessly, her mouth tight, but pushed the papers in his direction.

He approached the table and took the top page. They were life insurance papers. His stomach sunk like a lead balloon. He swallowed. "These are for Dad."

She sniffled. "*Oui*. I can't seem to make sense of things. Christos told me to take care of things, but . . ." Her shoulders quaked. "I do not want to make plans for my husband's death," she sobbed.

Discomfort had him holding his breath. He searched for comforting words and came up short. Was he really that sick?

The papers were all written in French. His mind switched to metric as he reviewed the policy. He needed to take himself out of the equation in order to comprehend what he was reading. "Everything looks to be in order here, Tibet."

She sniffled and took the paper from him. The next paper she handed him reviewed burial arrangements. Fuck. He found himself lowering into a chair.

His fingers sorted through the stacks of papers. Medical bills, scripts, statements for physical therapy; it was all so overwhelming. He rubbed his head and frowned.

"It was very nice of you to stay here, Lucian," she suddenly whispered. "Your father enjoys having you here."

His mouth tightened. They'd barely spent time together and he was leaving as soon as the arrangements were made. "I appreciate the welcome."

Tentatively, her hand settled over his. He stared at her small, dainty fingers, still beautiful for a woman of her age. It was the first time, to his recollection, that she'd ever touched him. "He loves you."

His throat worked to swallow. "Well, he's never said so, but I'll take your word for it."

She withdrew her hand. "Christos is not a man who says such words easily. I don't believe he understands what it truly is to love, but his heart knows it, and the funny thing about love is that your mind doesn't need to think in order to love someone. You just do it. Sometimes we even love someone when we know we shouldn't."

He knew she was referring to loving his father. "I think this calculation is wrong. The copay was thirty euro, yet the doctor has you down for fifty. You may want to call them about that."

"Thank you," she whispered, tucking the paper into a folder after making a note at the top.

They sat in silence for the next several minutes as Lucian reviewed his dad's forms. As he reached the last one, Tibet seemed tired, but a bit more in control of her emotions. As he handed her the last of the papers, she asked, "Does she love you?"

He frowned. "Who?"

"The woman you are running from?"

He stilled. He was not running. "I'm not running."

She waved her hand. "Of course you are. That's what you Patras men do; you run when your heart distracts you from business."

"You're wrong—"

"Then why is she not here with you? Or why are you not there with her?"

"How do you even know there is a her?"

"A woman knows such things, Lucian. You are a man in the torturous claws of love."

He sighed and leaned back in his chair. His eyes scrutinized her sincerity, and he found no reason to believe she was being anything but sincere. Still, he wasn't sure he could have this conversation with Tibet.

When he didn't reply, she said, "I still remember the first time I saw you as a boy. You were devilishly handsome, running through the lobby of the hotel. I watched from afar as your family checked in. Antoinette was not yet born. I remember thinking, *He's going to be even more handsome than his father.*"

He didn't want to think about moments like that. She shouldn't have been there.

"Your mother had come to Paris for that visit. After the three of you left, your father told me he could no longer continue our affair."

"As always, he proves to be a man of his word," Lucian said dryly.

"He kept his word . . . for a while. But eventually our paths crossed again and we were right back where we left off, in love. You see, Lucian, when you love someone, you do so without choice. It is a force of its own and no amount of time or distance can dissolve such feelings.

"Your father wanted to be a good husband, and I never wanted to be a mistress. I tried not to love him and he tried not to love me." She laughed. "I do believe he was quite irritated with his inconvenient emotions. Over time, we realized there was no use fighting what we felt. Our lives became incredibly easier once we simply embraced it."

"How altruistic of you both."

"Yes, we were selfish, but our lives were far from perfect. He would never leave your mother. He loved her too, and that was something I was never able to compete with."

"Lucky for you she died," he said coldly. Did she think she was earning his compassion?

"I was very sad when your mother passed. So was your father."

"I should hope. She was his wife and the mother of his children."

She sighed. "She was a good woman and I regret very much what I did to her."

"I'm sure you do." His insincerity was clear.

"I just want you to know that I'm sorry. I know you all hate me, but I want you to know I love your father very much, enough to go behind his back and tell you he's sorry for the way he abandoned you children. Do you know what it's like, to hold your husband's hand, a hand you held for over thirty years, when you fear he will not make it through the night, and hear him confess his one regret is you? It is a horrible feeling.

"I love him more than I love myself. I gave up any hopes of a family to be with him. Unfortunately, he did the same. I do not think he realizes what he said when he was ill, but I will never forget. His one regret in this lifetime is choosing a woman over his children."

Lucian's breathing was labored. What difference did any of this make? His father had made his choice years ago, and now he had to live with it. Was she telling him this in hopes that he would offer her some form of comfort?

"My mother also had regrets when she died. Suffice it to say, our family's fucked-up, Tibet, and you knowingly married into it."

She nodded. "I did. I just thought you should know that he loves you."

She stood, and he frowned as she gathered her papers and made to leave. "Why did you tell me all that?"

She turned, a sad look on her face. "Because your father is a difficult man to love. I imagine you are too. Our hearts choose for us, and mine chose Christos. Whoever you love, Lucian, love her well. Do not cause her pain because you are too afraid to face your emotions."

She couldn't be more off. "I'm not afraid of love. I'm not my father."

"No, you're not. Did you know my father was very much like yours? We never got along and he was a very cold man. We tend to do that, fall in love with people who are as emotionally broken as the ones who raised us. When it occurred to me that you were in love, I found myself wondering, is she like your mother or your father?"

His blood chilled. *Holy shit.* Evelyn like Christos? No. "She's not like either of them."

She shrugged indifferently. "Perhaps. But perhaps she is a bit of both of them. Your mother loved your father to a fault while your father has always been terrified of love. If she's like either of them, you shouldn't be here. You should be with her, because I imagine your absence is killing her."

"I'm leaving tonight," he announced.

She nodded. "Good. As much as your father wants you here, I believe there is someone else who needs you more. Go to her, Lucian, and love her with all of your heart. Don't let life complicate it for you. Love is simple. It drives itself. But I'm afraid you have to be present for it to flourish."

She left then. Lucian stared after her. Tibet was a mistress. Her moral compass was crap, yet she was obviously a romantic. He couldn't fathom his father's relationship. It had been complicated and tainted from the start. His regret was a result of his own actions, and Lucian couldn't be bothered to fix the many bridges Christos had burned in his long journey to the top.

What he did gain from Tibet's confusing story was that love was complicated enough between two people. He'd seen what happens when three were involved. He'd experienced it with Slade and Monique. Even when three hearts were accepting of the situation, it was awkward. His mother had not consented to Tibet being an addition to their marriage, yet she tolerated it and left this world miserable and alone.

There was no way he was going to repeat his parents' past. He didn't share. He loved Evelyn and she loved him, whether she'd admit it or not. If she fell in love with Parker as well, he was doomed.

His heart raced as he dialed his pilot, Ken. He couldn't get out of there fast enough. He told Ken there was an urgent situation and he needed to return home as soon as possible.

"Sir, we have the engine being looked at now. There was a short somewhere and we're doing our best to locate the problem."

"How long?" Lucian asked.

"Should be worked out in a day or two."

He ground his teeth. "Fine. I want someone working on it round the clock. Call me as soon as we're ready to go. I'll be waiting."

He hung up and fixed his stare on the door. His father would have another day of his time. Lucian would try to be civil and perhaps they could make some headway. It wasn't going to be long, and as soon as he got the call, he would be gone.

parker

twenty-one

·····

GLITCH

THE cool glass flashed his reflection as he stared at the dark window of his apartment, waiting. He'd become a master of waiting, yet his patience had grown reed thin. Waiting for winter to end, waiting for Scout to come around, waiting for her to become a woman, and now he was waiting for the key to it all. Parker was sick and tired of waiting, especially because everything he'd been waiting his whole life for always seemed to be interrupted by Lucian fucking Patras.

Unbelievable. A week had passed since Patras announced the clock had started, and Parker was sitting around with his thumb up his ass. He should've known better than to assume Patras would simply hand Scout over. No, that would be too easy. He had to hide her away like the quintessential needle in a haystack.

Parker was taken completely off guard by Lucian's appearance at Leningrad. It was killing him, not knowing what brought on the happy couple's parting so suddenly. Something had to have transpired. The Lucian who burst into his office was nothing like his usual cool, arrogant self.

Parker smirked, his eyes narrowing in the marbleized reflection on the glass. He liked knowing Scout was likely mad at Patras. However, his satisfaction faded fast, as it always did when he considered her predicament. On the tails of his smug amusement always came the awareness that she was likely hurting as well. Hurting because of Patras, but nevertheless hurting. He needed to find her.

When Patras showed up at his office like a man possessed, Parker knew she'd left him. No man looked that haggard after voluntarily cutting a woman loose. It should have pleased him, but for the first time Parker's confidence wavered.

There was such bleak desperation in those dark, haunted eyes. It could have been his superciliousness. A man like Lucian Patras wouldn't take well to being turned down by any woman. Yet, there was something personal hidden in the frantic set of his eyes, something sad. Perhaps the man really did love her.

If he truly loved her, Parker's plight would only be more difficult than it already was. He turned and faced his small living room. This was no penthouse. He'd found a modest place, and it was the first roof he'd had over his head in years. Great pride should be riding him, but all he felt was trepidation. What if this wasn't enough for her?

He shook the thought away, trusting his instinct that he knew Scout better than anyone, and while money held importance to her, material things did not. So long as she had shelter, warmth, and food in her belly, she'd be content. All the other extra shit was just distraction.

Men like Patras were masters of distraction, magicians over the meek, drawing the eye with glitz and ostentation. But Scout was anything but meek.

He still recalled the first day he'd met her. She was small and thin. She'd been crouched low, tying a tattered lace of a boot too many sizes too big for her small foot. Parker had been still adjusting to a life without walls. His mother was dealing poorly with their new lifestyle and mourning the loss of her husband.

HE glanced down at his shoes. They were warm and cushioned with support. "Wanna trade?" he asked the small girl. When she glanced up at him, he stepped back. Her eyes were crystal blue and lined with far too much cynicism for a girl of her age.

"Get out of here," she snapped, and he frowned.

"Those shoes are too big for you."

"Who asked you?" she said smugly and went back to lacing the boots.

"Mine are a little tight."

She glanced at his shoes and then to his face. "Who are you?"

"Name's Parker Hughes. My mom and I are staying over there for a while until we find a new place."

She laughed. "Once you come to the tracks, you don't leave. Better keep the shoes you got. Mine gots holes and you won't likely find a better pair than the ones on your feet. Winter's coming. Your feet freeze, and you'll be limping all the way to spring."

She had a crass way of speaking he found intriguing. She looked about five years younger than him. Her face was dirty and her long, dark hair disheveled, yet her hands were clean.

"What's your name?" he asked.

She knotted her lace and stood. She was a little thing. Her jeans were serviceable, tucked into the boots and drawn with a rope around her waist, a thermal shirt tucked sloppily beneath, and a flannel tied low around her hips. She slung a canvas bag over her shoulder.

"I'm Scout."

"Scout. Like in To Kill a Mockingbird*?"*

She frowned. "I ain't killed nothing."

"It's a book."

Her expression remained tight, but something in her eyes shifted. "You read books?"

Parker's brow pinched as he nodded. "Yeah. I love to read."

"About birds?"

"About anything. Do you like to read?"

Her tiny shoulders pulled back. A curious look took over her small face as she hardened her expression. "Sure. I read all the time. That's why I'm smart. Smart enough to not go trading good shoes right before winter."

"Scout!" a scratchy voice called, and they both turned.

"I gotta go," she said, shifting her bag again.

"Do you live here?" She was the first kid he'd seen in weeks. Granted, she was years younger than him, but he missed talking with people close to his age.

She jerked her head toward a dim corridor. "We stay at the end there, but don't you think of coming by and snooping through our stuff. I got ways of keeping back creepers."

She was being quite serious, staring up at him with those witchy blue eyes. He fought back the pull of a smirk. She mesmerized him from the hard set of her mouth to the way she carried herself in those rugged boots. She was rough and nothing like the girls he'd grown up around. No bows and lace for this little scrapper. She was all sharp edges and intimidation. He doubted she'd ever held a book in her life.

"Well, Scout, it was nice meeting you."

Her brow crinkled. As her gaze moved over him, he waited. Her eyes settled on his watch. She lifted her chin. "You steal that?"

He looked at his wrist. "No. It was a gift for my fourteenth birthday."

"Probably shouldn't wear that 'round here. People go thieving *on new folks with expensive things. Could probably get some good money for that. I'd hide it away and pawn it when you need food or clothes."*

"Pawn?"

"Yeah. Sell it."

His life sure was not what it used to be. "Maybe I'll do that."

THAT winter he did pawn his watch, but only to buy Scout a coat. They'd become friends, but she always kept him at arm's length until the day he found her with Slim.

Parker had noticed the man leering at Scout in a way that made him uneasy. He tried to always know where Scout was, but soon became equally as interested in where Slim was. His instincts had done him good. It wasn't long before Slim proved to be as creepy as he appeared and Parker had to step in.

She was too young for the tracks and too beautiful for a girl of her age. Parker always kept an eye on her, watchful of the older men who looked a little too closely at young Scout.

Over time, she'd changed in subtle ways that only made the job of protecting her more difficult. When his mother died, she'd come to him and sat silently beside him through the night. She never said much, but she missed nothing. After losing his mother, he and Scout sort of stuck together, like a team. The only time she went missing was when Pearl needed something.

He had mixed emotions about Pearl. Parker knew what it was to lose a mother. He'd lost both his parents, but losing his mom hurt the worst, mostly because she was a victim.

Pearl was nothing like his mother. Over the years she became harder, colder, but no matter what, Scout loved her and he loved that about her, her loyalty. Scout didn't turn her back on those she cared about. He liked that he fell into that category.

Parker liked to believe he was a man of the mind. He learned at an early age to value less earthly things, a beautiful sunset, the sight of a father holding his child's hand, words of love written from heroes to their far-off lovers just before a battle.

He had a romantic soul and Scout had one too. She loved stories. His favorite days were those spent taking her on an adventure in the public library. They'd visited Atlantis, traveled back in time, flew the Jolly Roger, without ever having to spend a penny or leave that braided carpet.

She was enraptured by fiction. "You're magic, Parker," she'd told him one rainy afternoon. "I think this carpet is magic too. All we have to do is sit on it and your voice flies us away from Folsom, to places where we are rich and warm and feasting like kings."

Her vocabulary and grammar had improved greatly once he started reading to her. It wasn't easy for her to confess she couldn't read. He'd always suspected she couldn't, but it took years for her to admit it. When he promised to teach her, she hugged him fiercely. It was the first time she'd ever touched him and it had been years since he'd been hugged.

It wasn't long after those physical boundaries had been crossed that he started seeing Scout differently. He became a bit more protective, territorial. She was still young, not yet an adult, but he'd decided once she came of age he'd press his luck and introduce her to other things.

He'd dreamt many times of kissing her. She was so innocent. When that time came, he didn't want to frighten her. Knowing Scout, if she was kissed and didn't want to be, she'd break his nose. He started reading her more adult stories with romantic plotlines by the time she was seventeen. During the intimate moments, she'd blush and fidget.

Then one day she'd caught him in the alley with another woman. He was an adult and technically doing nothing wrong, but the repulsed look on Scout's face when she'd caught him haunted him for a long time. She truly was innocent.

He grit his teeth and paced his apartment. A man like Patras likely had a twisted definition of love. Scout deserved a love that was pure, without condition. He couldn't imagine Patras using a slow hand to teach Scout about things she'd not yet learned. It was almost an intolerable thought, the two of them together. He was furious when he'd found out she'd given herself to a man like Lucian. She was his first.

Scout gave herself to a man who knew nothing about her. He hated that she was so enchanted by money. She could be quite the fool and he'd told her so last fall. He wanted to tell her only whores sold their bodies for riches, but he didn't have to. She connected the dots on her own and he could see in her eyes that sleeping with a man like Patras did not come without the price of her pride.

Scout had dignity in spades, and Parker saw the mistakes she was making. However, until he was in a position to put another solution on the table, his hands were tied. He never expected her to fall so willingly into the arms of Lucian Patras. She was stronger than that, and the fact that he'd miscalculated her emotions for the other man irritated him to no end.

I'm the one who waited. She should be with me.

Patras was a spoiled, rich prick much like those Parker had once called "friend." Their lives only felt the tremors of the stock market. Real human emotions never broke the surface. How could Scout fall for such shallowness?

She needed a man who could relate to her plight. Respect the journey she'd made thus far in her life and see her for the accomplished person she was. Lucian would never be able to grasp what her life had been, but Parker had been there beside her for almost a decade. Waiting.

It wasn't fair to have someone step in before he had the chance. Parker had waited because Scout was innocent. He didn't feel the need to rush her. He hated acknowledging he'd missed an opportunity. But he would have another, and there was no way he was letting a man like Lucian Patras walk away with Scout's heart.

However, when he caught a glimpse of the uncontrolled, savage rage in the other man's eyes, Parker wondered if he had made a deal with the devil himself.

He knew how Patras saw her. She was a beautiful bauble, a possession. Something must have severed whatever fucked-up arrangement they had. She wasn't meant to be a rich man's mistress. She was meant to be cherished and respected. She was meant to be loved.

Lucian admitted to loving her last winter when he was so desperate to find her. Well, Parker had strong emotions regarding Scout too. Patras didn't deserve her. She was too trusting, too good, and too naïve to know better. Patras was a disease to humanity. Such men believed only in advancement and would climb over anyone to reach the top, including innocents like Scout.

Parker had a plan. He needed money, because Scout saw money as freedom. Parker saw money as a noose around the neck, tightening and choking his peripheral, cutting away all humanistic qualities until nothing but greedy breaths for more sneaked by. It was a challenge not to fall under its spell the way his father had. However, if money was what she needed in order to see him as a man, then so be it.

He'd intended on working his ass off. Not as a bellhop like Patras would've enjoyed. That was only a small stepping-stone. He had plans of finding a better job as soon as he found the means. Running into Slade had been nothing short of a miracle.

Slade Bishop was a shrewd man. It was no wonder he and Patras hung in the same circles. And, for whatever reason, Slade was out to get his partner. Parker didn't care. He was smart enough to let the other man's vindictive nature work in his favor. They'd quickly formed an understanding—fuck Patras and get him away from Scout.

Parker didn't know what the other man's issue with the couple was. He didn't care, so long as no one hurt Scout. All he cared about was getting her safely away from all of them.

He could support her. He could give her a life off of the streets and under a roof. He'd do whatever he had to in order to put food on their table and shelter over their heads. He'd keep her clothed and warm throughout the colder months and he knew—he just knew—he could win her heart.

Once he secured a good-paying job, he quickly fell into step with the rest of the rats in the race and forged a fast route to the top. It wasn't easy. In everything, Parker liked to keep a strong hold on his dignity. He had to be smart and cunning in order to find success in a swift and honorable manner. But all was fair in love and war.

He found an apartment he could afford in one of the safer sections of Folsom and rapidly came up with a deposit. His furniture was functional and simple. His bed was the warmest thing he'd slept in in ages and it was a blessing to once again have a stove to heat his food.

It was easy to get wrapped up in the game of it all. He *was* his father's son and as such, he saw numerous opportunities to make money.

Slade claimed Parker was a prodigy when it came to the market. Parker didn't see this at first, but soon realized others who'd been watching capitals and trends for years simply couldn't read the stocks the way he could. It was something he'd learned to do as a young boy when his father would hand him the business section at the breakfast table and quiz him over their morning meal.

He felt the fiscal heartbeat of the world as though it pounded from his very own chest. It was a pulse, once identified, impossible to turn off. The rhythms were easy to track. Simple tremors led to ripples and he had a gift for forecasting exactly how the chips would fall.

The day he told Slade to pull out of Winslow Cherokee Pharmaceuticals was the day he earned his promotion and corner office. The company had dealt out a contract with an overseas drug company that had taken some criticism for medications intended to curb the effects of dialysis. Lab rats were dying, and Parker saw this as a risk factor.

Winslow Cherokee ignored the warnings, bought in with the questionable company, and just like that, statistics came back, people were hospitalized, and the drug was recalled.

Stocks fell like stones from the Empire State Building, and Leningrad was saved from the collapse of Winslow Cherokee because of Parker's quick intervention.

The partners were beyond impressed with his ability to not just know the brand names they promoted, but to see past the numbers and actually know the pulse of the companies themselves. He memorized the names of each CEO of every company they represented, studied their fiscal histories, and seemed to be unstoppable when it came to spotting the invisible red flags.

His clientele list had grown to a hefty figure, a number that men who'd been with the firm for years could envy. Parker didn't give a shit about any of his clients. He needed to make money and if making them money made him money, then so be it. In the past four months he'd piled away what most middle-class men made in two years.

Now it was time to collect, but what he wanted most was hidden away where he couldn't find her. Where could she be? She wasn't at Patras. She wasn't at the shelter. He knew Lucian could be a selfish prick when life required it of him, but something told him—something about that look in his eyes that day he stormed into his office—that he would not leave Scout stranded with nowhere to go.

He'd hidden her somewhere. Parker just didn't have a fucking clue where.

He paced his apartment waiting for Sherry to return. She was his only hope. He didn't know what else he could do. He'd never counted on not being able to find Scout. Not that he expected her to be handed to him on a silver platter, but the other week when they sat down to dinner he assumed they would reestablish contact and she'd keep him in the know.

Unfortunately that hadn't happened. Lucian warned him he was taking her out of town. Did he leave her there? Was she even in Folsom?

The elevator dinged and Parker tensed, his eyes staring hard at the door. Three knocks and he let out a harsh breath.

"Thank fucking God."

He opened the door and there stood Sherry. The resemblance was uncanny. "Hey, handsome," she purred as she stepped inside.

"Hey, how'd it go?"

"Umm, well, it didn't go like we had planned."

"What does that mean? Did you fuck him?"

She plopped down on the couch. "Nice, Parker. No. It only took about a minute for him to realize I wasn't her. He probably would have realized it sooner if he wasn't stone drunk."

He cursed under his breath and sat next to her. "Did you get it?"

She pursed her lips and arched a brow. "No *hello*? No *how have you been? I've missed you?* No kiss."

"I don't have time for this, Sherry," he snapped and dragged a frustrated hand through his hair.

She looked crestfallen, but a woman like Sherry was made of tougher stuff. She quickly straightened her spine and reached into the breast pocket of her coat. Her fingers withdrew a slip of paper folded in thirds. "Is this what you're looking for? Lucky for you it was on top of his desk. I nabbed it while buttoning up my coat. You owe me, because if he would have caught me . . ."

He snatched the paper from her and quickly unfolded it. His eyes greedily scanned the words. It was a lease signed by Lucian Patras himself for a Ms. Evelyn Keats. He kissed her. "You're a genius!"

She looked uncertain. "Listen, I know you're all goo-goo gaga for this girl, but I gotta tell you, that man isn't someone you should underestimate. He's sort of scary."

"What makes you say that? Did he do something to you?"

Her mouth opened and shut. He leveled her with a hard look.

"Sherry, tell me what happened."

For the first time ever, he noticed Sherry looked unsure, scared. "I . . . I just worry you don't know what you're getting yourself into. That man's intimidating as hell. He knew you sent me."

"Did you tell him?"

"Well, I didn't have to. He asked. There was no point in lying."

"What else did you tell him? I need to know."

"Okay, calm down." She took a deep breath. "He said you would never get what you were after. He told me to warn you off."

"That's because *he's* scared." The words came out to reassure her, but he knew they were partially meant to reassure him.

"Parker, I don't think he was kidding. I think if you try to mess with a man like that you're going to wind up getting yourself hurt or worse."

"He's a goddamn hotel owner, not the mob."

"He's fucking powerful, that's what he is, Parker. He has more money than Midas. You should have seen his place."

"So what?"

"So, I just think you should watch out. What's so special about this girl anyway?"

What *wasn't* special about Scout? "Don't worry about it. Did he say anything else? I need to know everything that transpired from the moment you walked through the door."

She considered her answer, and that pissed him off. He paid her to do a job. She was working for *him*.

She swallowed. "I don't think I want anything to do with this anymore, Parker."

He wasn't expecting that, but that was fine. He'd hired Sherry to serve a purpose. He'd hoped he could get Patras to fuck her. She looked so much like Scout, just a little harder and less pretty, but she had the same dark hair and the same bone structure. She also had more sexual knowledge than a tantric how-to book.

He'd found her while using one of the computers at work. Her agency was simple enough to reach. Once he'd slept with her the first time, he arranged a private deal with her. She helped him figure out how to properly touch a lady. It was a lesson he needed to learn.

Parker was no white dove, but he surely couldn't treat a woman like Scout the way he treated the women of his past. Growing up on the streets, sex was about one thing: release. It was a free pastime he'd indulged in often, but he never made love.

He'd never slept with a woman completely unclothed. Sex was always about getting off and getting done without catching frostbite or something worse.

Sherry showed him how to use a gentle hand. She'd taught him how to hold a woman. Some nights he paid her to simply lie with him. He'd stroke her arms and curves and she'd tell him what she found especially appealing and comforting. When it came time to be intimate with Scout, he wanted to offer her all the tenderness a girl like her could possibly need.

Scout was an extremely independent woman. She'd need to maintain a certain level of control. He wanted to be the perfect lover for her. When they finally made love it would be tender, and giving, and everything it should be.

"Parker, are you listening to me?"

He turned to Sherry, her brown eyes rife with concern. "Sorry, no. What did you say?"

She grasped his hands tightly. He should probably start pulling back from her, limiting the ways he let her touch him. Now that he had Scout's whereabouts he wouldn't need her anymore.

"I said why can't you just forget about this girl? She's got this whole other mess going with that guy. You're handsome and well-off. Why don't you find someone a little less complicated?"

He gently pried his hands from hers and touched her cheek. "You don't understand, Sherry. She's in a bad way with this guy. I have to help her."

"What if she doesn't want to be helped?"

"She can't go back to him. A man like that would destroy her. I need to save her."

She scowled at him. "Why do all men think that women need saving when the most dangerous thing to us is men in general? You're all capable of ruining us. Who's to say you're any better for her than this guy?"

He frowned. "I am. I'm to say. Lucian Patras is a greedy, manipulative, self-serving prick. He collects pretty things he covets so no one else can have them, and then when he loses interest in them he throws them away or puts them on a shelf until they lose their value."

"And this girl . . . this Evelyn, you want her for more than just satisfying some need to possess her so other men can't."

He grit his teeth. "Her name is Scout, and yes. I want to love her."

Sherry paled. "The lease said Evelyn. What if she doesn't love you?"

"I can make her love me."

Her gaze dropped to her knees. Softly she said, "Really, Parker, I thought you were a smart man."

"What's that supposed to mean?"

When she met his gaze there were tears in her brown eyes. "It means that you can't make someone love you any more than you can choose who you love, especially when their heart is elsewhere. I should know."

When a tear tumbled down her freckled cheek, regret washed over him. "Honey, you know how I feel. I've never kept it a secret from you."

"I know. I just . . . it's been three months."

"And for three months I've never changed my course or my plans," he reminded her gently.

She nodded tightly. "I know. And here I am, just another fool in the room, wishing I had the love of someone in love with someone else. Stupid, right?"

"She doesn't love him." He was only concerned with Scout's feelings.

"How do you know?"

"I don't, but I know if she falls in love with him it's a mistake."

She sat quietly for several long moments. It was too late to go to Scout tonight, so he let Sherry have this time. No sense in rushing her off.

"Will I ever see you again?"

"I . . . I don't know. If my plans go accordingly . . . no."

She gave a sad laugh and wiped her eyes. "I never should have agreed to help you. I never should have let things go this far."

Wanting to comfort her, he tucked a stray hair behind her ear.

"You knew what this was, Sherry. Was it so bad, letting a guy be nice to you for a few months?"

Her head shook. "No, but going back to men who see me as only a vessel will make every other encounter from here on out so much harder. Every time I let a stranger touch me I'll think, Parker didn't just touch me, he made me feel. Parker didn't just look at my body, he saw *me*. Parker didn't just fuck me. He made love to me. I've never had that before and I'll never have that again."

That wasn't necessarily true. When he looked at her he searched for someone else, and when he made love to her, it wasn't her he was holding. "I'm sorry."

She sniffled. "I should go."

"Will you be okay?"

"I'll be fine."

He didn't know if she was being honest or brave, but he had his own problems to worry about. He had to save Scout. Saving Sherry wasn't on the agenda. "You know you can call me at the office if you ever need anything."

"What I need you aren't willing to offer, Mr. Hughes."

"I never led you to believe this was anything more."

She nodded. "And I suppose that should make it all right. Pardon me if I find it cold comfort in the face of reality."

Guilt pinched at his nerves. He shoved those emotions away. He'd spent ten years on the street, held his mother while she died crying about the injustice of it all. There were plenty of sad cases on every corner. Sherry's sad life wasn't his fault. "You offered a service and I paid you for it."

Her face fell and all her color drained. Perhaps his words were a little too honest for her to cope with at the moment.

She stood. "Wow. I don't know what's more frightening, the idea of that man getting his claws into you or the idea that you may actually deserve whatever he does. Whoever you are, you're not the man I thought you were. Good-bye."

He stood as well. "Wait." She paused by the door, but didn't turn around. "I owe you money."

Her back stiffened. "Parker Hughes, if you dare hand me a dollar right now I'm afraid of what will happen. Enjoy your life. Send my best to the poor girl you're after." She opened the door and shut it without a second glance.

PART EIGHT

scout

twenty-two
. . . . .

WALLS

SHE was definitely under some form of paralysis. If she knew how to move, she would get up and find a phone, then perhaps try to call Dr. Sheffield, but she couldn't. So she lay there and continued to cry.

Under a ceiling of untouchable stars, she lay with no walls holding her in. Something was holding her physical body together. Her mind had unhinged many days ago. She was floating, lost somewhere between two names, and neither one told her who to be.

It was evening and the sun had set. Her fuzzy mind worked to count the days. The first night she'd slept on the floor by the door. The second night she moved to the couch. The third she stared at the pristine bed awaiting her tired body but was too afraid to touch it.

Days were lost to sleep and nights were filled with anxious need to do *something*. So tired. Waking hurt, and she dreaded the moments before her conscience roused her physical body. All she wanted to do was sleep.

Seeing the thought he had put into her apartment was agony. The walls she had envied all of her life were suddenly suffocating her. She needed to get out.

She'd taken to sleeping on the balcony. It was cold, but she wasn't as claustrophobic under the blanket of sky. Walls. She hated those fucking walls.

It was day eight, she believed. Eight long, lonely days and she wasn't quite dead yet. She'd formed an addiction to sadness. When her mind slipped away and took a reprieve from the desolate introspection of her life, she felt its absence. Interestingly enough, Scout realized, even when she'd been one of several, sleeping on a mat on the floor of an overcrowded shelter, she was never really a part of anything.

She was and would always be a loner. She didn't fit in at the tracks. She didn't fit in at St. Christopher's. And she didn't fit in at Patras. So where was she supposed to go? She wanted Pearl, but didn't know if her heart could tolerate her mother's cool welcome. Getting to Pearl was a daunting task as well, so she shoved off any plans of visiting her mother.

As she stared up at the clouded night sky, she tucked her quivering shoulders under her blanket. The apartment was filled with parts of her that only existed through him. She hated it. Spring was coming, and she found solace in the terrace garden where she spent most of her time gazing at the empty, cold sky, wondering what the point of it all was.

She'd sleep with no recollection of letting go, only waking up. Her body temperature adapted to the gentled elements, and she simply adjusted her blankets and snuggled deeper into the soft cushion of the lounge chair she was slowly becoming fused to.

She had everything she needed. A wool cap, her thick cable-knit sweater, heavy socks, a blanket, and her picture of Pearl. The tattered sketch was no longer stiff. The lines were smudged from too many foldings and fingers brushing the paper. It was her most cherished possession, and in times of sadness it always comforted her.

She didn't need to look at the image to see that long-ago day in her mind. It had been cold and rainy, and Pearl had again stuck that ridiculous rubber hat on Scout's head. The artist had captured the desolate look in her mother's eyes, but that was not what Scout saw when she looked at the drawing. No, she saw her mother holding her hand, a silent promise that they would make it through anything. And they did.

Rain never lasted forever. After every harsh winter she'd experienced from the outside looking in, there came a rebirth of life. It seemed that was all Scout had ever done, get reborn time and time again.

She was tired of starting over. She was tired of fighting and clawing her way to the top. For the first time ever, she lacked the reserve of determination she'd been known for all her life.

She hurt. She hurt, not the way an empty belly aches or even the way a scrape burns. She hurt from someplace hidden deep inside of her, and she had no idea how to make the terrible ache go away.

He'd deserted her when he promised to love her. She didn't want to think about *him*. The problem was she couldn't recall how she used to think before *he* interfered in her life.

Her eyes shut out the stars moving behind the clouds and, mercifully, she slept. Her thoughts subsided for broken moments in her timeless mind.

There was a sound. Something woke her. Her lashes slowly fluttered open. Her nose was chilled, her lips tucked under the wide satin trim of the blanket. She scanned the area without really moving. When she saw nothing out of the ordinary, she shut her eyes and tried to return to her dreamless sleep. That's when she heard it.

"Scout."

Her breath sucked in and her eyes pulled open. A dream, she must have been falling into a dream, her consciousness pulling her back just before she stepped over the threshold of sleep. Curling farther under the blanket, she searched for a warm place to tuck her hands.

"Scout! You up there?"

That was real. She frowned. *Parker?* Her lips moved, but no sound came out. Her voice was so neglected she had to concentrate to talk. With shaky limbs, she sat up and cleared her throat.

There was a whistle, a familiar whistle, the kind of whistle that rang out "Shave and a Haircut."

"Two bits," she rasped, her whispered reply floating away on the fingers of a far-reaching breeze. Her sleepy mind snapped to life.

Scout clumsily staggered to her feet, catching the blankets before they fell to the cold cobblestone floor.

"Parker?"

"Scout?"

Her mouth parted, as though too skeptical to smile. "Parker!"

"Scout! I'm down here."

His voice was like the sweetest music to her ears. Her legs propelled her to the edge of the garden balcony, and there was an extraordinary release of tension from her shoulders. There he was, as real as ever, in jeans, Converse, and a cozy crewneck sweater. So very Parker.

Her face split with the greatest grin. Muscles she hadn't used in days protested, but gave way as the first sense of happiness washed over her in what felt like an eternity.

"Oh my God, Parker! Is it really you?" How did he find her?

"Of course it's me, ass. Let me in! I've been waiting down here forever."

Was he really there? Did Lucian tell him what happened? Maybe he came with a message from Lucian? No, that didn't make sense. Who cared? He was here!

"I'll be right down!"

She turned and bolted on her bunchy socks to the glass door. Not realizing how weak she'd become, she struggled to slide it open. Once it gave way, she shouted for her own reassurance, "I'm coming!" Part of her feared he'd disappear like a mirage in the desert.

Ignoring the familiar pieces of her life appointing the apartment, she ran to the door and pressed the intercom. It buzzed. "Park?"

She released her finger and waited, bouncing in place. It buzzed back and a scratchy version of her friend's voice said, "I'm in! I'm coming up." It was late and the doorman must have gone home.

Scout turned and caught her reflection in the mirror by the door. Her cheeks were gaunt and her eyes appeared overly large for her face. Her hair hung in ratty waves over the shoulders of her sweater, her brows hidden beneath a tight wool skullcap.

She looked like a ruffian. She looked like a kid. Her lips, unadorned with any gloss or any artificial color, curled upward in a slow half smile. She looked like Scout.

The sound of the elevator in the hall drew her back to the present. Her fingers quickly twisted open the locks on her door and flung it wide.

He stilled and smiled at her. He seemed as shocked to be seeing her as she was at the sight of him.

"How did you know I was here?" she whispered, her breath coming fast.

"I always know where you are. How else can I watch over you? I lost you for a few days there, but I'm here now. Are you okay?"

No, she was definitely not okay, but she was a world better now that he was there. Parker. Her friend.

Her trembling lips formed a thin line as too many words tried to force their way out and each one seemed to fail. She shook her head sadly and fought back a sob clawing its way up her throat.

His smile faltered and his brow pinched. "Oh, Scout . . ." He held out his arms and she ran to him.

It was magical to be held. For days she'd known a side of loneliness that was fathomless, unending, and so terrifyingly hollow. To feel the warmth of another body holding her now . . . it was remarkable.

All of her defenses came tumbling down the moment her mind recognized his familiar scent, the way he protectively sheltered her with his body. It was all so nostalgic and so incredibly needed. She simply gave in to the vortex of emotions eddying inside of her and didn't think.

His lips pressed into her temple as she cried. When her knees gave out he scooped her up, carrying her like a baby into the apartment. "Hey, hey, it's okay. I'm here. Scout, please don't cry . . ."

Her nose pressed into the warm skin beneath his collar, her tears leaving salty tracks from her eyes to her lips. Pain cut through her as she admitted what a fool she'd been.

"You were right. He used me. He wanted me to be something else, and when I couldn't he sent me away."

Parker tensed and stilled. She wiped the back of her hand under her eyes and sniffled. She was a mess, but beyond caring. Her pride was trampled the minute she stepped foot into this horrid place. She was a fool. Her fall from grace was an excruciating tattoo on her heart, a branding still raw that would permanently stick with her, reminding her love was cruel and she was a fool.

He sat down on a piece of furniture and tightened his arms

around her back, rubbing in soft, wide circles over her thick sweater. "Scout, have you been crying like this the whole time? You've been here for days. Have you eaten?"

She stilled and drew back. "How do you know how long I've been here? Did Lucian send you? Have you talked to him?"

Parker scowled at her. "No."

The atmosphere cooled at his clipped reply. She looked down and noticed how inappropriate their position was. She was straddling him and he had his arms around her. Pressing her lips tight she pulled to the side, intending on easing off of him. His grip tightened. She made an uncomfortable sound in her throat and he let her go.

Embarrassed, she slid beside him and tucked her hair behind her shoulders. "Sorry. I . . . I've been really emotional lately. I shouldn't have jumped on you like that."

Fingers traced softly over her denim-clad knee. He grinned sadly at her. "Hey, that's what friends are for. I came because I was worried about you. Whatever you need, I'm here for you."

She felt her brow furrow as she slowly attempted a smile. Everything was blurry. Confusion and too many questions of how he'd found her spun in her mind like clouds turning a day to night. "Did you see him?" she whispered and Parker's face shuttered.

"What if I did, Scout? The guy's a jerk. Seriously, who does that?"

She frowned. Had he seen him? "You know what he did?"

Parker scoffed. "I can imagine. I mean, you're here and he's in Europe—"

"*Europe?* With who?" Something vicious and cold came alive inside of her. He was in fucking Europe? They just broke up! "How do you know all this?"

His mouth opened and closed. "I . . . I work with people who do business with him. I mean, the guy's everywhere. People talk."

"And you heard he was in Europe?"

"Paris, actually, for an extended visit."

She could almost see the black webbing tightening over her heart like a suffocating cocoon, squeezing so tight she thought she might die. "Did he go alone?" she choked.

Parker's expression looked uncomfortable. His fingers gently pinched at her chin as he eyed her sympathetically. "I don't know many people who visit the most romantic city in the world alone."

The cocoon tightened and something inside of her suddenly shattered under the vise of misery. And that was when she threw up.

Her head flipped forward, and right there, on the polished wood, whatever little bit of food she had in her belly came spattering out. Parker leapt to his feet. "Holy shit, Scout! Where do you keep the paper towels?"

She spit and whipped the back of her hand across her lips. Moaning, without answering, she rolled to her side and collapsed on the sofa. Parker moved around, mumbling and cleaning up her mess, then thrust a glass of cool water in front of her face.

"Here, drink this."

She sat up weakly, took a sip, then pushed it away. Why bother? He was with someone else. She stared numbly at the wall. A flat screen was mounted against the exposed brick. What a waste. She didn't watch television. All of this stuff was a waste, severance to ease his guilt for pretending to love her. He *never* fucking loved her.

She vaguely registered a much more flustered Parker sitting down beside her. He seemed unable to meet her gaze. He fidgeted as though uncomfortable in his own skin.

Folding her hands and wedging them between her knees, she awkwardly sat through the silence, aware of her friend intensely observing her. "Sorry," she mumbled.

"Scout, this isn't like you. I . . . I figured you'd be upset, but . . ."

"I fell in love with him, Parker. I swore I wouldn't, but turns out I don't always have control of everything."

He blanched. "You don't love him. I think you loved the *idea* of him."

She turned and shot him a withering look, but she was too raw to act tough. She felt her face puckering into something that surely looked pathetic. Her words should have come out with a touch of hostility, but there was no bite left in her.

"What's that supposed to mean, the idea of him? Meaning because he's rich? Thanks a lot, Parker. I can see you're still thinking as highly of me as ever—"

"No, not his money," he said, holding up his hands. "I just think . . . Patras is a complicated man. From what I understand, his last relationship was a train wreck at best. I just don't think he's the right guy for you, Scout. It has nothing to do with you. It's him. Men like that don't ever truly commit to anyone but themselves." He sighed. "You can't love him."

I know.

She frowned and stared at her knees. "But he was committed. I was the one . . ."

Without touching her, Parker eased forward, his gaze searching hers. "If he was so committed, he wouldn't have told you to go, Scout."

The truth of his words hit her like a hammer to the chest. She was so tired. So emotionally exhausted, simply mangled, yet a part of her rejected his accusing words. Defensively, she snapped, "If he wasn't looking for commitment, why did he ask me to marry him?"

Parker jerked back, his face losing a bit of color. "He actually proposed?"

She couldn't stop the laugh that slipped out. It was a protective blanket to her wounded ego. "Don't look so shocked, Parker."

"But I am . . . I mean, I'm not shocked someone would want

to marry you. You're incredible. I just . . . can't believe he actually tried."

"Why? Why wouldn't he try?"

"I guess I never honestly believed his feelings were sincere . . ." he admitted quietly.

She shrugged. "Well, maybe they weren't. When I said no, that was it."

They sat in silence for some time until she softly whispered, "Maybe I should've said yes."

Parker sat up and grasped her hands with a desperation she wasn't prepared for. "No, Scout. No. You're young and beautiful and deserve the time to make up your mind. Fuck him. Look at you. You look miserable. That's his fault! He did this to you. That's the real him."

She shook her head. No, Lucian was not some evil person. He was intense, but also gentle. She couldn't believe that after so much time she didn't know the real him. She knew a side of him the rest of the world didn't see. That was why none of this made any sense. "You don't know him."

He looked appalled. "Are you defending him?"

Her vision glazed with tears again. "No, I suppose that's stupid. It's just . . . none of this makes any sense. We were happy, I thought."

He scowled at the floor, and then faced her, all hostility gone. "Well, enough of that. You have a roof over your head, food in the pantry, fuel in the furnace, and more than we could have ever dreamed of. You don't need some arrogant billionaire to make you happy. Screw him. Prove that you don't need him, that you can move on just as well."

That's right. He was in Paris . . . moving on.

She looked around the apartment. It was cozy, but nonetheless luxurious. She wasn't naïve enough to believe the artistically rustic furnishings and distressed, exposed walls diminished the value of a place like this. That was Lucian, trying to find a place that didn't appear too lavish, knowing the more posh it appeared the less comfortable she would be. But he wasn't fooling her.

Those chipped sconces by the door likely sold for a thousand dollars a piece. This place wasn't run-down and then fixed up. It was purposefully aged to give wealthy people an earthy impression of themselves without sacrificing any of their security. How ridiculous, making a classy building appear seedy for the whims of the rich.

She sighed. "This isn't my place. All of these things"—she swept her hand in front of her—"he bought them. None of them are mine."

"Don't cut off your nose to spite your face, Scout. What you have here is food and shelter. You have clothing. He owes you this and more for what he took from you. You'll be able to sleep safely at night and work a job during the day. This is an advantage you didn't have before. See it as such."

Work. She told herself every day that she needed to find a job. "I'm just . . . so sad, Parker. I can't find the energy for anything."

His green eyes narrowed and his lips pressed tight, as though holding in a foul word that soured his mouth. He shifted until his knees were on the floor and his gaze locked with hers. "You listen to me, Scout. You're tougher than any girl I know. I know he hurt you and I wish I could've somehow saved you from that, but what's done is done and now it's time to move on. Fuck him. He's all the way across the world. Do you think he's worried about you?"

Sharp pain knifed through her, and she sucked in a jagged breath.

Parker went on, ignoring her visceral reaction to his cold words. "Our people survive, Scout, and that's what you need to do now. You need to stop moping, assess the damage, and survive. If you don't want this place, then leave. Come stay with me. I'll take care of you."

The last thing she wanted was another man taking care of her. While these things didn't technically belong to her, they were given out of affection, not obligation—*maybe*. Somehow that brought about a sense of entitlement, more so than taking charity from Parker would.

"I can't live with you, Park. I need to be on my own."

Disappointment briefly flashed across his green eyes, but he shook it away. "Fine, but I'll help you, Scout. I'll help you find a job. I'll help you remember how to smile. I'll help you laugh. And so help me God, I'll help you forget about him."

A world without Lucian Patras seemed bleak and pointless. However, a part of her wished she could somehow, magically, shut off all her memories of him and act as though he never really existed.

Her heart was growing addicted to sadness and becoming more and more reluctant to let his memory go. But her mind was shoving all thoughts of him away, making her insides a tumultuous and uncomfortable place. It was too painful.

She was losing her mind, suffering some sort of mental break, she was sure. With Pearl as her mother, those types of occurrences wouldn't be too far off the mark. For the first time ever, she was scared for her own well-being.

She *needed* Parker to help her get through this, but she couldn't explain why. It was too much to put into words. He'd think she'd completely lost it if he knew that she, his driven little friend always scrapping to get ahead, found it meaningless to even live in a world that did not include Lucian Patras. No, Parker would never get that.

She swallowed, shut her eyes, and nodded. "Okay, Parker. I'll take your help. God knows I need it. But I can't stay with you. If you want to stay here, you're more than welcome. I'd like the company."

His eyes searched her face and slowly he grinned. "Okay, Scout. You got a deal."

twenty-three
.....

A NIGHT WITHOUT STARS

THAT was what her life had become, a night without stars. Scout could still smile, but it was an empty expression, pained by so many tiny fractures along her heart. Her laughter, for the most part, was hollow. She tried in vain to recall what happiness felt like, but the mere thought triggered a string of memories that seized her breath and put unbearable pressure on her heart.

She didn't want to break. Her mind filled with unholy images of her heart splitting like sheets of ice choking a river, ripping apart until gaping blackness showed through. Not being able to process recollections of the past few months without pain meant her recollections of happiness were, for the most part, gone, blurred, buried beneath the ice that had so thoroughly smothered her heart.

But happiness had once existed in her. She just couldn't imagine it.

Parker decided to spend the night. He was prepared to sleep on the couch, but when she said good night and headed to the balcony, he froze. "Scout?"

It wasn't like she never slept outside before. She was more comfortable there than under the roof of some apartment that didn't belong to her, surrounded by walls and memories she couldn't bear to face. She shrugged, unable to meet his gaze without feeling embarrassed. "It's suffocating."

Quickly turning away from his confused face, she padded over the threshold to her lounge chair. She was very tired. All she seemed to do anymore was sleep, which was fine with her. She welcomed the numbness.

Settling under the blanket, she breathed. Her eyes counted the stars in the sky. There weren't many, yet they were innumerable, infinite. If a sky was without stars, would it still be called night? Could there be laughter without glee, smiles without joy? Like a starless night, she was falling into something dark and unremarkable, a smudge that blocked the warmth of the day.

So unmoved by all things lately, she couldn't find the nerve to really care. Sometimes darkness was peaceful. She was the starless night, cold, still, without a single flicker. It was so tempting to drown in the oppressive darkness swathing her mind. The thought was enticing enough to make her sigh and shut her eyes, darkness pulling her under.

A shadow passed over her face, and she cracked open her lashes. Parker was standing over her, frowning.

"Are you really sleeping out here?"

Her shoulder lifted beneath the blanket. "It's safe up here. It's not too cold. Why not?"

He scoffed. "Because you have a home to sleep in."

She didn't have the energy to defend her crazy behavior at the moment, so she just stared back at him. He sighed and lifted the covers. "Move over then."

Surprised, but slightly glad for the company, she shifted to the left of the wide lounge chair and Parker scooted in beside her.

As she shifted her hips, searching for a soft spot to settle in to, his soft sweater and familiar scent warmed her senses. Heat collected between them. They'd never rested so close. It was different, yet for some reason welcomed by her body.

Parker's lean form fit against hers. "Thanks for finding me, Park."

"I could never lose you completely." His breath was warm over her cheek.

Scout shut her eyes. Images of Lucian played with visions of her past, visions of Parker, of the tracks, of her life as it was before billionaires and broken hearts.

Her mind stumbled as fingers gently tugged the hair peeking from the brim of her wool cap. She blinked into the dark.

This was new. Parker never really touched her before. It was foreign, but at the same time familiar. She should probably scoot away, but something about his touch, the presence of another body close to hers, was selfishly coveted and she couldn't ask him to stop.

She relaxed, letting his gentle touch soothe her in a way no one else had offered her comfort in days.

"It's okay to talk to me about it, Scout," he whispered.

She didn't open her eyes or acknowledge his statement, but heard it all the same.

"I'll be there for you, through anything. I care about you and don't want you to be sad."

I know.

She did know, but offering words of validation, proof of a rational train of thought, only made her feel like a traitor. Part of her believed she needed to feel this pain right now, as though it were a rite of passage to teach her that this was why she should not have fallen in love.

Thoughts blended into nothingness, and slowly her consciousness faded and fell away. She became aware of time passing only as the distant sound of vehicles occasionally moved over the streets below. She slept. For the first time in days she truly slept.

Her nose tingled, winter's kiss pressed upon her chilled face. Her back was burning up and a heavy weight rested across her legs like lead.

Lucian? No. Parker.

She opened her eyes and caught the pink haze of dawn tingeing the blue night into shades of crimson over the city. The temperatures had dropped overnight, and vapor formed as each breath passed her lips.

Something was different inside of her, lighter, almost hopeful. Was it because Parker was there?

"You up?"

Scout slowly rotated her head until Parker's green eyes came into view. They were very close, closer than they'd ever been. Small flecks of brown, olive, and gold swam in his emerald irises. She nodded.

Neither of them moved. She wondered if he was cataloguing all the awkward traits of waking up so close to her. His gaze moved over her face. "Your nose is red."

She sniffled. They should probably go inside where it was warm, but she feared climbing out from the protective blanket.

Suddenly his body stretched, hard planes curving along her softer parts. His head tipped back and he groaned, shaking slightly as his muscles extended. Then he was standing.

The absence of his body's heat was jarring. A chill immediately took his place. She snuggled under the blanket and watched him continue a round of motions meant to awaken his limbs.

"This sleeping outside shit is for the birds, Scout. I think I've done enough involuntary camping in my life to know better. I'll take a roof whenever it's offered."

"You could have slept on the couch."

He shrugged. "I came to be with you. You were out here." His back cracked. The cold definitely had a way of making a person stiff. "I've got to use the bathroom. Do you have anything to eat here?"

She stared up at him. Didn't he know her world was in shambles? Who could think about food at a time like this? Yet, her life didn't seem as much a mess as it had yesterday.

"There's stuff in the pantry and the fridge. Help yourself."

A few minutes after Parker disappeared into the house, she shifted into a sitting position and slowly stood. Wrapping the blanket over her like a shawl, she headed inside.

He sat at the counter, hunched over a bowl of cereal. He'd put on weight since last fall.

"This milk's about to expire. You better use it up."

She frowned.

"So," he said with a mouth full of mushed flakes. "Should we go job hunting for you today?"

"Don't you have to work?"

"I took off until Monday. I figured you probably needed a hand. Sorry it took me this long to find you."

She still didn't know how he'd managed that. "How did you find me?"

His shoulder lifted with nonchalant grace. "Word gets around."

He was being cryptic, but before she could ask more, he said, "Do you get a paper? We should look over the want ads."

"I don't get the paper." She shot him a telling look. What would an illiterate person want with the paper?

"Don't give me that look. You can read."

"Parker—"

"Scout," he said knowingly, mimicking her tone. "I've heard

you read. Don't act like you're illiterate when you haven't been for quite some time."

She scoffed. "Compared to you I am."

"So? Just because you aren't the best reader doesn't mean you can't. Eat breakfast and we'll go get a paper."

"I'm not hungry."

His head tilted and his spoon stilled, a pile of bran-colored flakes dribbling close to the edge. "Scout, don't be a waif. When food is offered to you, you take it. You know better than that. Don't be dramatic."

He shoveled the spoonful of cereal in his mouth, and she scowled at him, half tempted to tell him to get out, but at the same time terrified he might leave. Her face tight, she marched into the kitchen and retrieved a bowl. She ate beside him in silence, calling him all sorts of insensitive names in her head.

Her stomach rejoiced at the sustenance being offered. She was starving. Her brain just forgot to relay the message.

THERE were several job openings in the area, but only a few Scout felt capable enough to apply for. She and Parker sat on the carpet in the living room, various pages of classifieds strewn around them.

"You should think about getting a license. There are lots of openings for drivers."

"I don't have a car," she said.

"They give you a car or a truck."

"I don't know. That all takes time. I need to make money now. I don't want to stay here longer than I have to."

Parker's eyes met hers. "Did he give you a time frame of when you had to . . ."

She frowned. He said he'd be back in a month. She didn't want to still be there by then, especially if he didn't come back for her. Her heart would never survive more broken promises. "No. I'd just rather cut all ties."

His gaze lowered. Turning away from her so she could no longer read his expression, he said, "Yeah, that's probably a good idea. You know, you could be my roommate. I have a place. It isn't much, but . . ."

"Thanks Parker, but I think I want to do this on my own. I know what it feels like to have the rug pulled out from under me. I don't want to be in that position ever again. You know what I mean?"

"I would never abandon you like he did."

She didn't believe that, but didn't see the point in telling him. "I just need to do this for myself."

He nodded tightly. "How about waiting tables?"

"I'd have to write."

He sighed. "You're going to have to write with almost any job, Scout. We can work on it."

"I can deal with a job that requires minimal reading, but writing's different. I'm slow and incredibly self-conscious. I can't spell."

"Who cares? Not everyone's a good speller."

"I'd just rather not have a job that requires it."

He looked back at the want ads. "Here's an opening for models. You could be a model."

She hit him in the arm. "Shut up."

"I'm serious. You could!"

"I don't think so."

He shrugged and grumbled something. "How about a clerk at a grocery store? Clemons is hiring."

She thought for a minute. She'd have to scan things, but as far as reading, there wouldn't be much required of her that she could think of. "How much is the pay?"

His lips pursed. "About an eighth of what you'd make modeling."

"Forget the modeling!" She snatched the paper from him and searched. "Where is it?"

"Here." He pointed, scooting closer.

"Eight dollars an hour, that's not too bad. I made more at Patras though. Maybe I should see about getting my old job back."

A sour taste filled her mouth the minute the words left her. No, she couldn't work in Lucian's hotel ever again. What if she saw him? What if she saw him with someone else? Nausea swirled uncomfortably in her stomach.

"I don't think you should work at the hotel again."

"Yeah, I know. It was just a thought. This looks good."

Parker took the paper and tore out the advertisement. He jotted down a list of things she'd have to write on a résumé, like a fake social security number, her address, a sentence or two about why she would be a good candidate for the job. It would be much easier to fill out an application if she had the answers spelled out for her.

"Do you have a phone?"

"Yes." She went to the counter and found the phone Lucian gave her. "I don't know how much longer it will work." It was sad seeing her empty mailbox. "Here, the number's on the back."

Once they had everything organized, Scout cleaned herself up. She didn't know if she would be interviewing on the spot, so she chose soft brown pants, a cream sweater, and camel-colored boots. They were clothes of courage Lucian had bought her. She needed courage.

She didn't feel like putting on makeup, but she had to do something about the bags under her eyes, so she dabbed on some concealer she found in her purse and smeared a bit of gloss over her lips. That would have to do.

. . .

THE stockroom of Clemons Market was cluttered and smelled slightly of cardboard and some sort of citrus oil. Mr. Travis Gerhard, a man who looked to be in his early twenties, was the assistant manager. After she filled out her application, he directed her to the stockroom he referred to as his office.

There was a chunky brown desk in the center and schedules surrounded by other notes tacked all over the yolk-colored walls. The drop ceiling had watermarks, and the gray metal filing cabinet wedged in the corner was dented and scraped along the side.

He leaned back in a wrinkled leather chair, his loafer-clad foot crossed over his knee. He wore a pale pink, short-sleeved button-down dress shirt with a gray tie that might have been a clip-on. He didn't look old, but he carried himself as though he were in his forties.

His top lip was covered with a brown mustache, and his eyes were magnified behind thick, wire-framed glasses. His hair was parted severely on the left of his crown.

As he read over her application, the quiet stockroom filled with the incessant flick, flick, flick of his pen as he twitched it between his fingers, tapping the edge of the paper.

Her memory retreated to a familiar place where a similar pen flicked. She was suddenly in Lucian's office, beneath his desk. Her mind jerked out of that vivid memory and back into the present.

"It says here you're twenty-three?"

"Yes, sir."

He nodded, but didn't look at her. "What did you do when you worked at Patras? That's quite a different atmosphere than what you can expect at Clemons."

You aren't kidding. "I was in housekeeping."

"And why did you leave your last job?"

Fuck. "I, um, I could still go back there. I left on okay terms. I just . . . it wasn't for me."

He looked at her then, his plain eyes swimming behind the augmented lenses of his glasses. "Being a floor clerk is no easy job, Evelyn. I wouldn't want you to assume this job will be any easier."

She held back an eye roll. "I'm sure it isn't. I'm a hard worker, Mr. Gerhard. I just didn't fit in so well with the people at Patras. I wanted a change of setting. That's all."

He smiled softly as if he had a secret. His smile didn't show teeth. It was really just a curve of his hairy lip. She smiled back nervously.

"Call me Travis." Leaning forward, he placed the application on the desk. When he spoke, the scent of spearmint-laced coffee wafted at her, but she remained still, plastering a serene expression on her face.

"Evelyn, I think you might be a good addition to our team here."

Relief rose within her like a swarm of butterflies, but she held her breath as she noticed the manager's reluctant expression. She waited, foot tapping incessantly, as he went on.

"You'll be under a trial period for the first ninety days, in which you'll report to me and I'll be keeping a close eye on your performance. Clemons is a family name, and our customers depend on the community feel they get here that they don't necessarily find at the more corporate grocers. It's important that you always smile and make the customer feel as though they're important. That's the Clemons way."

"Yes, sir."

"Dress code is gray slacks and Clemons pink-issue dress shirt with a Clemons apron. Your appearance matters. If you're ever working around the deli or fish department, you're expected to wear a hairnet and gloves. You'll likely be at the register for now, although you will have to stock from time to time."

He stood and went to the dented filing cabinet. The drawer made an obnoxious scrape as it slid open and rattled closed. When he returned to the desk, he was holding another form.

"You'll need to fill out the proper tax forms and return with them before you start. Payday is the second and fourth Thursday of each month. Lateness is docked, and days off must be cleared ten days in advance."

He slid the tax paperwork across the desk. She'd have Parker help with that. When he leaned back, he examined her. There was something very artificial about him, like his skin was made of wax. His eyes creased the way eyes did with a smirk, but he wasn't smiling under that mustache, from what she could tell.

"I want you to know that I'm the type of manager who cares very much for my employees, Evelyn. If you have any problems I want you to come to me with them."

"Uh, okay, Mr. Gerhard."

His mustache curved. "Travis."

She nodded. "Travis."

"Good. How does Monday sound?"

After a sharp and fleeting thought of Tamara Jones, her GM at Patras who was so normal and sweet, Scout plastered on a smile. "Monday sounds great."

"Great! Welcome to Clemons."

She took his extended hand. It was dry and chafed her palm. She breathed in the unwelcome scent of spearmint and coffee.

Parker waited on a bench around the corner from the store entrance. He was reading a tattered paperback. As she approached he looked up. "Hey, how'd it go?"

"I got it!"

He smiled and stood, pulling her into a brief hug. "That's great! When do you start?"

They began walking in the direction of her apartment. "Monday."

"Good. How was the interview?"

She burrowed her hands into the pockets of her corduroy jacket as they strode briskly along the walk. "Fine. My boss is sort of weird."

"Well, you like weird bosses, no?"

Her face tightened at his joke. "Lucian wasn't weird. He was . . . unconventional."

"Pretentious."

She frowned and nudged him with her shoulder. "No, I mean he was unexpected. He isn't the way people see him."

They crossed the street in silence. "I think you glorify him for reasons he doesn't deserve."

Keeping her gaze down, she shrugged. "Maybe, but I can't see him as the untouchable man the rest of the world sees him as. He isn't like that. He's caring and loving and—"

"I don't need to hear any more. Tell me why your new boss is weird."

They turned onto her block. "I don't know. I think he's around our age, but he acts older. He's serious in a way I just don't get. How intense could the world of groceries be?"

"Maybe it's been a rough berry season?"

She laughed as they entered her building. "I have paperwork I need to fill out."

"I'll help you with it." They took the elevator in silence.

Parker casually removed her coat after unlocking the door. She stilled, not expecting him to do such a thing.

The apartment was quiet as it always was. She couldn't wait to be gone from there. Be gone from all things Lucian. She faced Parker and came up short. He was right behind her.

She waited for him to say something. The sun was fading and they should probably turn on a lamp. Thinking that was the perfect reason to turn away from his confusing stare, she did just that.

The spell broke, and he moved to the pantry and began rummaging in the kitchen. "We should have gotten some milk while we were there."

She took a seat at the counter and watched him as he pulled out various containers and stacked them on the counter.

"Do you plan on cooking something?" she asked.

"Aren't you hungry? I'm starved."

She said nothing. She considered her hunger, but her appetite was being a finicky bitch. She knew better than to turn down food though. "Do you know how to cook?"

"Sure. What's not to know?"

"I don't know. I mean, I can heat up canned stuff, but I don't know how to use kitchen things. The oven scares me, and once I put something in the microwave and a huge blue spark snapped."

He laughed. "How about grilled cheese and tomato soup?"

Scout smiled as her stomach clenched in agreement. "Sounds delicious."

Parker threw down a mean grilled cheese. The soup was from a can, but perfectly thick and warm, heating her insides up just right. They ate and talked about safe topics like the weather, St. Christopher's, and Pearl.

"Have you been to visit her lately?"

"Not since I left. The place she's staying at is far."

"I could take you," he offered.

She met his gaze. "How?"

"I could rent a car."

"Parker, that would be a fortune. It's not in the city."

"So. I have money."

"Don't waste your money on me—"

He caught her hand before she could reach for the other half of her sandwich. "Hey, it wouldn't be a waste. It would make you happy and that would make me happy. Money's meant to be spent, Scout. Let's go see Pearl. I miss her."

The fact that he could actually say that and mean it did things to her insides she didn't quite understand. Pearl was such a troubling part of who she was, yet Parker got it. He'd always gotten it. Pearl was her mother and that was that.

She smiled shyly and nodded. "Okay, I'd like that."

After dinner she helped Parker do the dishes in comfortable silence, then took a shower. As she stood in the door to her bedroom, she stared at the large, undisturbed bed dominating the space.

He left her and was never coming back. The dull familiar pain came as usual with the thought. She missed him.

Scout changed into soft cotton pants and a loose fitting T-shirt. She sat on the edge of the bed, brushing her hair, her gaze routinely being pulled to her bag. Her eyes skittered to the door and back to her bag.

Slowly she placed the brush on the nightstand and picked up her bag. She dug in the deep pockets until the weight of her phone filled her hand.

Examining the object for several long minutes, she thought. What was he doing at the moment? Was he alone? Was he happy? Did he still think about her?

Her thumb slid over the screen, bringing the device to life. Under Contacts she found four numbers: Lucian Cell, Lucian Office, Penthouse, and Dugan. Other than that there was nothing.

Three bars showed in the top left of the screen. Her thumb trailed longingly over his name. What if she called?

Before she considered what she was doing, she pressed the

number that said Lucian Cell and brought the phone to her ear. It went immediately to voice mail.

"Hello, you've reached Lucian Patras. Leave a message after the tone."

The sound of his voice was like a blade slicing through her. Warmth pulled like blood, and pain ran cold, turning her veins to ice. She ended the call and tossed the phone aside.

She couldn't keep doing this. She needed to move on. He was in France and apparently not alone.

Standing, she went to the living room and found Parker sitting on the couch. Lamplight pooled around him. He was reading. As he heard her approach, he looked up from the pages of the same tattered paperback and smiled gently.

"Hey."

"What are you reading?"

He flipped to the faded cover. "*To Kill a Mockingbird*." He gestured to the space beside him and Scout settled in.

This was good. This was familiar. This, reading with Parker, was one of her favorite pastimes.

"Should I start back at the beginning?"

His finger was wedged against the spine, showing her he'd already read half the book. "Just catch me up."

He sighed happily and placed his arm over the back of the sofa, drawing her close to his side. Again, she noticed the odd way he'd taken to touching her, but her skin was so starved for contact, she didn't object.

The cover of the novel was faded green and orange with a crude brown tree taking up space. He'd mentioned this book to her the day they first met. Her lips curved as she recalled the arrogant way she'd talked to him, thinking he was just some punk trying to steal her shoes.

"Well, the story takes place around the thirties. There are two kids and their father's a lawyer. He's trying to teach the kids that you always fight for what's right even when you know you can't win. The main character's name is Scout."

Scout turned and looked at him. "Like me."

"Yes." He smiled and pressed her back into the curve of his shoulder. "Atticus, the father, gave Scout a small gun, but he told her she couldn't shoot the mockingbirds because they're harmless. That's where the title comes from. As the story goes on, Atticus takes on a trial defending a black man accused of raping a white woman. The kids go to the trial and are convinced of the man's innocence, but Atticus loses because the world is unfair."

"It's a book about crime?" Scout asked, confused. By the title she'd thought it would be about birds.

"It's a book about people and understanding others. Boo, the neighbor, is a recluse. He's terrified of the real world because he was never allowed to be a part of it, but he isn't a bad man. Scout's father tries to teach her about life, but there are so many miscarriages of justice along the way."

Parker shrugged and slid his thumb from between the pages. "That's it basically. Scout learns life is unfair and good people protect those more vulnerable than the rest."

She scowled at the plain cover and eerie tree. "Do you like this book?"

"Not particularly."

"Then why are you reading it?"

"I like Scout and Atticus."

She smiled. "Why do you like Scout?"

His thumb rolled over the beveled leaves of the cover. "She's tough. She doesn't care about social niceties, but is fascinated by human nature. She defends those who can't defend themselves. And she's fun."

Heat crested her cheeks. He was describing her. "And what about Atticus?"

"Atticus is great. His moral compass leads the story. He holds respect for anyone that deserves it, even the poor. He's . . . consistent."

"Was your dad like Atticus?" They rarely spoke of his family, but she was trying to understand why he would like such a story.

He laughed without humor. "No, my father was nothing like Atticus. My father was greatly influenced by others' wealth, and he had about as much moral fiber as a rock. Atticus believed that a person's nearness to evil destroyed innocence."

"Do you see me as that Scout?"

His lips curved slightly. "In some ways. Sometimes I guess I think of you as Scout and myself as Atticus. I want to protect you from evil and keep you innocent."

Her brow knit at his words. She wasn't expecting an answer like that. Leaning back, she scowled at him. "I'm not a child, Parker."

"I know." His agreement was quick and somehow sad.

Just once, she'd like to point out to him all the not-so-childlike things she'd done in her life. Maybe then he would stop acting like her keeper. Her anger quickly dissipated. She didn't want to fight. "Are you going to finish it?"

He looked down at the book, its frayed, yellowed pages smoothed into a thick block. "Eventually. I've read it so many times I can just enjoy parts here and there. I don't need to read it through. Did you want me to read it to you?"

"No."

His expression appeared crestfallen, but his mouth curved into a smile that didn't reach his eyes. "Do you want me to read something else?"

Her mind played over everything he'd just said, his words

about poor little Scout trying to make sense of the unfair world, how majestic and wise Atticus was. She thought back to an argument she and Lucian had not too long ago. Her eyes narrowed. "Why don't we read *The Great Gatsby*?"

She wasn't sure why she was suddenly in such a prickly mood. Perhaps she was just *poor* Scout trying to make sense of it all.

His brow lifted. "We've read that before and you didn't like it."

"I know, but like boats and all . . ." she loosely quoted.

"Are you making fun of me, Scout?" His expression was playful, but she saw a flash of insecurity in his eyes.

"Were you making fun of me when you said that?"

"When I quoted Fitzgerald?"

"Yes. '*So we beat on, boats against the current, borne back ceaselessly into the past.*'"

He frowned. "No, I was merely pointing out that we all are meant to be a certain way."

Lucian's words fell from her lips. "Maybe we're all meant to choose who we are, but we have to break out of the mold we were born into to get there."

"I think life's easier if we just accept who we are."

"And who am I, Parker? Do you see me as some naïve little girl who stupidly throws herself against the currents of this fucked-up world only to get trampled in the end?"

He stiffened and sat up. "God, no, Scout. Why would you even say that?"

She threw up her hands. "How should I know what you think?" There was no need to snap, but it felt good. "You go around spouting all sorts of literature instead of speaking clearly. You compare me to the children in the grown-up stories you read. Do I really come off so hopeless and naïve?"

His head shook. "Why are you suddenly angry?"

She didn't know. All she knew was that she wanted to scream because maybe he was right. Maybe she was just a dumb kid, too innocent to play in the real world. She blinked and, to her mortification, a blurry line of tears clouded her vision. She didn't want to be the kid. She wanted to be the recluse, if she had a choice at all.

"Scout, I adore you. You're not a kid to me. You're my friend. When I quoted *Gatsby*, I was trying to be an asshole to Patras. He had you convinced he was this nice guy, and it was killing me to see you falling for his bullshit act—"

"Don't criticize him when he isn't here to defend himself. You don't know him."

He looked as though she'd slapped him. "Are you serious? Scout, he isn't here because *he left you*. How can you defend him? Whatever, we don't need to talk about him. I don't care about him. I care about you. Please, don't think that I would ever make fun of you. You're my friend and I . . ." Whatever he had been about to say faded away. "Just . . . don't. Okay?"

She sniffled and they sat in uncomfortable silence for a moment. Parker looked as though he wanted to hug her, but seemed unsure. Finally, she admitted, "I hate that he can make me cry like this. I'm not used to being this emotional."

"I know you're sad," he whispered.

The heel of her palm rubbed at her eye. "He isn't coming back for me. I don't know why I defend him when he clearly doesn't give a shit about me. I just want to forget I ever knew him. I want to start over and get away from everything that reminds me of him, but my life is so empty without him. It'll take years to rewrite those memories with new ones. He's everywhere I look."

Parker gazed around the apartment, his eyes cataloguing all the things that weren't really hers. "I told you. You could live with me."

"I don't want that either. I want to be my own person."

"Well, you can be. Get rid of all this stuff that reminds you of him and get new stuff."

"I don't have any money," she said as though she were talking to a two-year-old.

"Well, you now have a job. You'll get money. Things take time. It took me months to save up for my own place, but I did it. I don't have much furniture, but it's a home and it's mine so long as I continue to pay the rent."

He pressed his lips tight and drew in a breath. "Scout, if you lived with me, you could pay half the rent, and then the place would be half yours, as much as it is mine. You don't need any of this shit he left you."

"Parker . . ." She shook her head, but wasn't really sure why she was so against the idea. She was miserable there, because she knew the place was really Lucian's. What would he do if he came back from his little honeymoon in Paris and she wasn't there? Would he know if she left? How long would it take for him to find out she was gone?

What if he never came back and she withered away there, waiting for him?

She glanced up at Parker, who was anxiously awaiting her reply. "Is there enough room for both of us—"

"Yes."

He seemed to really think it was best she leave her place. He was probably right. She'd been there for almost two weeks, and the place never stopped being oppressive. Every corner revealed a hidden memory of Lucian, the door a looping nightmare of the moment Dugan deposited her there like a broken dove.

Anger and shame suddenly burned through her. She gritted her teeth with a renewed sense of pride. She would *not* be one of Lucian Patras's thrown-away, soiled and broken doves.

Yes, she loved him, but he left her. She gave him all that she could give of herself, and it wasn't enough for him. Yet, she never looked for more than what he could emotionally offer her.

She needed to get back to being strong. She needed to forget about this little detour into the lap of luxury and get back on track, back to reality, get back to being Scout.

She leveled her gaze on Parker, full of fresh resolve. "Okay. I'll move in with you, but I'm going to pull my weight. I have an account with two hundred thousand dollars in it. It's not mine, but I can—"

His eyes momentarily bulged, then he shook his head. "Scout, I know what it would take for you to touch that money. Leave it. We'll keep track, and once you start getting checks from Clemons we'll square up. I've saved a ton of money since I started working. You can pay me back."

She smiled. Parker understood her pride wouldn't allow her to take, even from him. She was glad he didn't fight with her about such things.

Energy suddenly coursed through her limbs. "Should we pack?"

He looked surprised. "You want to leave tonight?"

She met his gaze, knowing her smile was full of sadness, and admitted, "I hate it here. Everything reminds me of him. I want to forget him, Parker. You're helping."

His expression was gentle, but unreadable. Slowly, his fingers coasted over her cheek. "Okay, Scout."

twenty-four
.....

"With him, life was routine; without him, life was unbearable."

~HARPER LEE
TO KILL A MOCKINGBIRD

PACKING was an anticlimactic affair. Parker followed Scout around the apartment for the more pathetic part of an hour as she shifted through belongings like a thief and took what she felt was either earned or necessary. Unfortunately, it was only by mentally classifying herself as a whore that she could justify her right to take certain things she couldn't leave behind. In the end it was a trade, one mental insult as her penance in exchange for whatever item she wanted in her bag.

Certain things were expressly given as gifts, for Christmas or her birthday. Those items were not as difficult to take, but were, for the most part, cumbersome and useless and therefore left behind.

She filled a small duffel with sensible clothes. It was getting warmer, so she was able to pack more, bringing only a few sweaters. Her toiletries were thinned down to the basics: shampoo, deodorant, a razor—she would never be able to go back to not shaving—and some very basic cosmetics.

Parker had filled four paper sacks with food. "Don't you have food?"

His shoulder lifted and fell. "Sure, but this stuff will just go bad. Why waste it?"

He had a point. She grabbed another sack and began to fill it.

"How far is your place from here?" She probably should have asked that before.

"We'll have to get a cab. It's not far. You'll still be able to walk to work, but it's late and we won't be able to lug all this crap."

BY the time they arrived at Parker's apartment, it was almost eleven. Scout's adrenaline had not stopped pumping since she made up her mind about moving, but she knew a crash was coming. When Parker left with most of the bags to hail a cab, she quietly shut out the lights and locked up the apartment, locking away that part of her life once and for all. She left the key inside, not wanting the temptation of returning hanging over her head.

As she waited for the elevator, a sense of dread filled her as though she were consciously drowning herself. It took every shred of false dignity she could muster to get on that elevator and walk away. As the doors to the elevator shut and her body descended to the first floor, she felt as though a part of her life had been ripped away and entombed forever.

Gone. Lucian and everything connected to him was no longer a part of her life.

It was possibly one of the most painful moments of her life, and she would have buckled, rushed back up to her apartment, had Parker not been there to tug her along.

He loaded her things in the back of a yellow cab and she silently sat, allowing him to direct the driver. So long as she kept moving she wouldn't be carried away with the tide.

They pulled up beside a nondescript brick high-rise. Parker

handed a few dollars to the driver and unloaded the bags. She filled her arms and followed him through the glass double doors.

The halls smelled like a mixture of ethnic cooking and paint. Gray carpeting stifled the sound of their footfalls as they made their way to the elevators. The place definitely wasn't a dump, but it was nothing like Patras or even her vintage-inspired severance apartment. Parker's place was . . . functional.

He seemed nervous as they took the elevator up. "How long have you lived here?" she asked.

"A couple months. It's not fully decorated. I was more concerned with getting off the streets. I've saved a lot, not really sure what the point of decorating would be."

The doors opened and they stepped onto the landing. Parker shifted the bags in his arms and dug out a metal key. He unlocked a deadbolt then the knob and toed the door open. "After you."

Scout slowly stepped over the threshold and waited for him to turn on the light. There was some mail on the floor, which he immediately scooped up. The lights switched on, and she turned.

The space was small, but open, with very little clutter. Two tall windows dominated the main area, and Parker had stuck a table for two in the space between. A radiator hummed from beneath one curtain. A wall of appliances with only a small gap of counter space made the kitchen. A plain couch sat along the other wall. There was a simple wooden table with a lamp and books stacked around the floor. No television.

"This is the living room slash kitchen," he said, stowing the sacks of food on the kitchen table.

It was nothing special, but it was nice. She was slightly envious of what he'd achieved on his own. She could see Parker being completely content there. She dropped her bags on the table as well.

He led her down a short hall. On the opposite side of the wall that held the couch sat a bed. This was his room. It was a good size, about the size of the main room, which was really two rooms, the living room and kitchen. Next to the bedroom was the bathroom. It was white, simple, and to the point.

Parker dropped her duffel bag on the bed. "That's it."

She looked at him. "That's . . . that's it? Parker, this is a one-bedroom."

"I know."

She suddenly wanted to cry. "You said it was big enough for both of us."

His chin lifted defensively. "Well, it's not a luxury hotel, but it's certainly big enough for two people. We used to share one room with two hundred homeless people, Scout. I'm sorry if this isn't good enough—"

"No, that's not what I meant!" She ran a hand through her hair and breathed. *Enough with the tears!* "I just thought when you said it was big enough that you meant we'd each have our own room."

"You can have this room. I'll take the couch."

"No," she said adamantly. "This is your place and—"

"This is *our* place and I don't care."

"Well, I do. I'm not putting you on the couch."

There was a long, stubborn silence.

"We can share the bed," he suggested, looking at his shoes.

"Or we could take turns, follow a sleeping schedule."

He looked ready to argue, but didn't. "Fine. You take the bed tonight. I'll take it tomorrow night."

"Deal."

They stood facing each other, neither looking the other in the eye. Was this a mistake? She supposed she could go back to her apartment, but the thought of facing all those memories again was repugnant. Besides, she'd fully cut the ties, gave herself no recourse by leaving the key behind. *Shit.*

Parker moved to the dresser against the wall. The apartment

was small, but underfurnished. Only the most functional items filled the space. He opened a drawer and removed a pair of sweats.

"I'm gonna shower."

He left her there, and soon the squeal of water rushing through the pipes filled the walls. Scout quietly explored, first putting away the food in the kitchen, then peeking in the coat closet. There wasn't much.

She smiled at the various piles of books here and there. When she found a closet full of freshly pressed suits in the bedroom, she was caught off guard. First, the suits reminded her of Lucian. His clothes often returned to the suite in clear plastic bags similar to ones hanging in Parker's closet. Secondly, she didn't understand why Parker had a closet full of suits.

The water shut off and steam billowed out of the bathroom into the hall. She turned and faced another unexpected sight.

Parker stood, chest wet and hair damp, in a pair of low-slung sweats. She'd never seen him unclothed before. Although she had no point of reference, she knew he had put on weight. He was lean, but not rail thin like she'd assumed in the past. His body was cut and smooth.

His arms were muscular in a very natural way. His shoulders were broader than what they appeared under his clothing. She swallowed and quickly looked away, her skin feeling abnormally warm.

"I, uh, have some extra blankets in the closet there," he said as he slid the suits across the rung. His voice sounded hoarse.

When he turned, his arms were filled with blankets and an extra pillow. She was very disoriented.

"Why do you have suits, Parker?"

He frowned. "For work."

She felt incredibly selfish and stupid for not knowing what he did. "Where do you work?"

"In an office downtown." He shook off the statement. "It's a job. I make good money and I've done really well for myself after only being there a short time."

"What do you do in this office downtown?"

"I watch the market and handle hedge funds."

Her brow lifted. "You know how to do that?"

"Yeah. I used to watch my dad follow the market when I was younger. He taught me when I was a boy."

Parker had a *real* job. She was so impressed and speechless, she hugged him.

His shoulders tensed, then relaxed. His arms slowly wrapped around her. His skin smelled of clean soap. "Hey, what's this for?"

"You. I'm so proud of you."

He laughed uncomfortably. "Thanks. I'm proud of you too."

He seemed reluctant to talk about his job. She stepped back and shoved him. "Don't act like it's nothing. You have a *real* job. I bet you even have benefits and a retirement plan working in a fancy office like that." When he blushed she smacked his shoulder again. "I knew it! Parker, that's incredible. You must be making a ton of money."

His expression grew hard. "I make enough to survive. It isn't about the money, Scout. It's a means to an end. That's it."

She shook her head. This was the same argument they always had when it came to money. "Call it what you will, you have it, and because you have it, you have security."

He stared at her, unblinking, an odd expression on his face. Self-consciously she touched her hair and looked away.

"I have security," he agreed. "I could afford to take care of you."

She frowned. Where had that come from? For the first time ever, she wondered if Lucian's theory about Parker was true. She suddenly felt like she might have made a huge mistake. *He's just your friend and he knows that.* "Park, I . . ."

"I know. You can take care of yourself. I've never doubted it, Scout." That wasn't what she was going to say, but before she could correct him, he surprised her by adding, "I just want you to know that you don't have to worry about me being another bum. I'm not. I know you hated being homeless. I should've gotten us off the streets a long time ago. I could have. I just didn't see the point. I hate the business world, but I'd do it for you."

She frowned. "You mean for you."

"Right." He lifted his armful of blankets. "I'm exhausted. I stupidly allowed myself to get manipulated into sleeping outside last night. I'm gonna hit the hay."

She smiled and let him pass. As he made up the couch, she quietly watched him. When he stood, makeshift bed in place, she said, "Parker?"

He turned and she could tell he hadn't realized she was watching. "Yeah?"

"Thank you. For everything."

He matched her smile and nodded. "Anytime, Scout. Anything you need."

twenty-five
.....

SUSPICIONS

THEY arrived at the New Day Rehabilitation Center a little before noon. "This place is nice," Parker said as he held the
lobby door.

Scout carefully signed them in at the front desk and handed
Parker a visitor's pass. "Yes. It's a shame Pearl doesn't see it for
what it's worth."

He pinned the visitor's badge on the lapel of his tweed jacket
and offered a sad smile. His hand gently coasted over the sleeve of
her sweatshirt. "She will . . . eventually. It takes time."

Scout led them down the long corridor. Doors were decorated
with bunnies and cutouts of colorful flowers. She envied the childlike decorations because they reminded her of what a grade school
might look like, although she had never attended school.

Pearl's door was open, and they found her sitting in a chair by
the window in her room. "Momma?"

She turned. Her complexion was so much more alive than it
had been in the years past. "Scout." Pearl smiled but it didn't

reach her eyes. Her face was a bit fuller. She no longer looked the eighty pounds she had been when they admitted her.

Parker stepped in behind Scout. "Hi, Pearl."

At this, her mother's eyes lit. "Parker! My, my, you looking good. What brings you here?"

"I came with Scout."

Pearl looked back to her. "Where's that other man?"

"Lucian isn't here."

"Good. I don't much like him. He bosses me and I don't like to be bossed."

Scout shot Parker a quelling look when he snickered. "How are you feeling, Momma?"

"Old. I wanna go home."

Scout sat on the clinical-looking bed dressed in bleached linens. She should probably see about getting her mother some colorful blankets. "I'm working on it. I've moved into a new place."

"I don't see what there is to work on. I gots a home. Never needed no invitation to go home before."

"Momma, you can't go back to the mill. We're going to get a new home, as soon as I save enough money. You'll have your own room and we'll make it our own like we never had before."

Pearl crossed her arms over her narrow chest and made a rude noise. It was nice seeing her dressed in put-together clothing that fit her body and matched. "I don't need no fancy home. I got my own stuff. Or I used to until that bossy man stole it all."

"Lucian didn't steal your stuff, Momma. Whatever was salvageable is here."

She shook her head and mumbled, "There ain't shit here that belongs to me."

Parker sat beside her. Scout picked up a brochure resting on the bed tray. There was a picture of flowers and writing on it. "What's this?"

Pearl shrugged unknowingly. Parker took the pamphlet.

"It's an activity schedule. Pearl, do you do these things? They have art classes and pottery. That sounds like fun."

"What am I gonna do with art classes, Parker? I don't want to hang out with those people. The nurses all talk to me like I'm four."

He put the pamphlet down. He might as well throw it away. Pearl would rather stew in her room than socialize with people she thought were better than her. She would never ask someone to read it to her, and Pearl could only read street signs with pictures.

"How are you feeling, Momma?"

Her mother's gaze drilled into hers. "Achy. Hungry."

"Did you eat?"

"They'll be bringing me lunch soon. Made me go see a dentist. I got teeth pulled and thems is sending me out to get some new teeth."

Scout knew immediately this was not a perk offered by the center, but something Lucian had arranged. Dental work cost a fortune. She had gone to the dentist for the first time that winter and had a cavity filled. Pearl's teeth—the few she had left—were in bad shape from doing so many drugs.

"You'll look beautiful with a new smile, Momma."

"What's I got to smile for, Scout? Use your head."

Parker looked uncomfortable. He cleared his throat. "Scout got a new job, Pearl. She's working at Clemons Market now."

"That man finally stop paying you?"

Scout's cheeks flushed. Anger surfaced hot and tense under her skin. "He wasn't paying me. I just worked for his company for a time."

She laughed coldly. "You giving him some and he buying you stuff . . . it's all the same."

She couldn't bear to look at Parker. Her eyes prickled. How

was she supposed to convince herself that she'd been more than Lucian's glorified whore if her own mother didn't believe her?

"Lucian and I broke up."

"He find someone else?"

Scout's jaw trembled. "Maybe," she rasped.

The weight of Parker's hand on her arm was a comforting presence. He squeezed and she met his gaze. She found sympathy swirling in his green eyes. "He'll never find anyone as good as you," he softly whispered, surprising her. She smiled back, sadly.

"Now that you ain't with that rich man no more I suppose I'll be leaving here."

Scout turned back to her mother. "No, Momma. You can stay as long as you'd like."

"I'd like to have left yesterday."

Again, she bit her tongue, not wanting Pearl to know the choice to stay or go was hers. She quickly changed the subject. "I'm living with Parker for a while."

Pearl smiled at that. "You two finally saw some sense."

He lowered his head and Scout saw color chase up his neck. "No, Momma, it's not like that. Parker and I are just friends."

"So says you. Parker looks like he might disagree."

"Momma!"

"It's okay, Scout," Parker quickly said.

Her gaze jerked to his. Her expression tightened as she gave him a pointed look, waiting for him to correct Pearl's assumption. When he didn't, she frowned.

Scout stared at him, a world of questions swirling through her mind, Lucian's accusations about Parker's feelings front and center. No. They were friends.

"Parker . . ." She shook her head.

He smiled softly and squeezed her hand. The motion carried more affection than she was comfortable with. All of his casual touches over the past few days seemed to have accumulated into a heap of confusion she kept sweeping to the back of her mind.

She withdrew her hand and stood, moving to the window so she could look anywhere but at him. Pearl said something and she vaguely heard Parker's voice as he replied. Scout frowned as she stared through the glass. They were friends. Only friends.

They stayed with Pearl for about an hour. Scout's head was a mess with questions. He couldn't like her like that. Their history was too long, too comfortable, and intimacy only spoiled simple affection. And she loved Lucian.

Although Lucian left her. She needed to stop thinking about him in terms of still being a part of her life. She was better off going back to her old way of thinking, when she didn't love anybody. But no matter how she tried to turn off her emotions for Lucian, she couldn't.

As they took a cab back to the apartment, she thought about last night. Had she really called him? She dug through her bag in search for her phone. It was so painfully telling that he hadn't called her back.

"What are you looking for?" Parker asked from beside her.

"My phone."

His expression blanked and he turned away as she pulled it out. Her finger ran over the screen, but nothing happened. "That's weird." She tried to turn it on again. When it didn't work, she grew frustrated. It had been on the charger all night.

She hit the main power button and held it, but nothing happened. "What the fuck?"

Parker faced her. "Not working?"

"No. I can't even get it to turn on."

"Those phones are temperamental. Maybe you need to get a new one."

She continued to hit the button, but nothing happened. She

opened the back of the phone and slid out the battery and popped it back in. Nothing. "Damn it!"

She tossed it angrily back in her bag. Great. A horrible thought crossed her mind. What if Lucian tried to reach her and couldn't? Not that he would call her, but if he wanted to for some reason . . . The phone was under his name. She couldn't get another one on the same account. It was stupid, but not having that phone felt like her last lifeline to him was severed. She wasn't ready for that yet.

"Can we stop at a phone store?"

Parker glanced at her. His lips parted and he hesitated. "Why don't you just wait a few days and see if it fixes itself? Maybe the charger wasn't working."

Maybe, but she'd feel better if someone who knew what they were doing checked it. "I'd rather just take it to a professional. It shouldn't cost anything for someone to just look."

His expression was placid as he nodded. Parker directed the driver to a phone store near their place. When they arrived, there was a young guy named Brett at the counter, who looked at the phone. He removed the back and frowned. "This phone's gotten wet."

"What? That's impossible. I never keep it anywhere near water."

He flipped open the back panel. "See this patch—how it's red? That tells us if it's been near water. That's really red. It looks like this phone's been submerged in water."

"I didn't get my phone wet," she gritted. It had to be something else.

The clerk shrugged. "There's nothing I can do. Once a phone's been soaked like this, it's junk."

"But how can that be?"

"Sorry. If you give me your account number I can see what kind of plan you had. If it was insured I can get you a replacement so there isn't an interruption in service."

She didn't know the account number. Frustration choked her. She felt completely cut off from Lucian.

With a shaky hand, she took the phone. "That's okay. I'll just take it anyway. Maybe it will start working again if it dries out."

"Oh, it won't work again. It's dry. The damage is done."

She knew that, she just couldn't seem to accept it. Taking the phone, she dropped it into her bag. Her eyes prickled with tears.

"Do you want to get a new phone? Set up a new number?" Parker asked. He wouldn't understand. Having a phone wasn't the point. She wanted *this* phone, in case Lucian needed her.

Fuck! She didn't even know his cell phone number. Everything was gone.

She shook her head. Her eyes frantically blinked. "That's okay. Let's just go home."

Parker kept glancing at her as they walked home. "I'm sorry about your phone."

She shrugged. "Don't be sorry. It's not your fault."

They walked in silence back to the apartment, neither of them feeling much like talking.

twenty-six
. . . . .

DARK KNIGHT

SCOUT sat at the table, fingers curled around her useless phone, and stared at the surface. She was adrift, lost in a world she hated, floating along some destined path with no idea of where her fate intended to send her.

"Hey."

At Parker's soft word, she turned. He looked upset. Some odd emotion swirled in the depths of his green eyes. Was it regret? About inviting her here perhaps.

She gave a weak smile. Parker. He was an entirely different issue she needed to deal with. Everything had become so fragile. She wasn't sure how to read him, how to interpret the casual gestures he'd been making, but she knew they needed to get back to normal or this delicate hold she had on herself might crumble and turn the little peace she had left into dust.

She was drained from overthinking everything. Sighing, she tried again for a smile and failed. "Hey."

His gaze searched hers, and he hesitantly pulled out the other chair at the small table and sat across from her. "I think we should talk," he quietly said.

Yeah, they probably should, but she was just so damn weary of *everything*. Life had never been this hard. The constant struggle to survive was nothing compared to this ongoing emotional battle to keep breathing, to keep seeing purpose and moving ahead. She could barely muster the attention she needed to form the proper facial expressions. How was she supposed to have a conversation about hypotheticals she might be imagining? The wrong words could make an awkward situation unbearable.

Her gaze connected with his and she waited. His hand slid across the surface of the table and curled around hers. She tried not to wince. More mixed signals. Maybe he was just trying to be supportive. The hand still holding her phone dropped to her lap, protecting the worthless device from others as though it were some sort of security blanket that could somehow protect her in return.

"Scout, I hate seeing you like this. It's killing me."

Did he think it wasn't killing her? She felt like her body had started rotting from the inside out, all bits of life slowly breaking away, starting with her heart. What was the point of all this pain?

When she said nothing, anger briefly flashed in his eyes, followed by some regretful expression. His face lifted, and he focused on her with what she could only identify as resolve.

"I'm going to make you forget about him, Scout. I won't pretend to understand what you two had, but I promise I can be better, better for you."

A better friend? Again, his words confused her. "Parker, I—"

"I know. I know you're hurting, but . . . try . . . try to move past that."

She scoffed. "I am."

"I can help you."

"You're my friend, Parker. I don't want anything to ruin our friendship." She lowered her head. "You're all I have left."

He drew in a deep breath and looked away. "I would never let anything destroy our friendship. We've been friends for almost a decade, been through freezing winters, sweltering summers, hungry springs, and dry autumns. We've seen children come into this world and watched acquaintances go out. You and I, we have an understanding for life that men like Lucian Patras will never grasp. You and I are the same, Scout. Nothing will ever change that."

Yet she couldn't shake the sense he was somehow trying to change everything.

She needed to clarify, needed to state the obvious and make sure he was on the same page. "You're my friend, Parker."

He squeezed her hand. "And you're mine."

She carefully extricated her fingers and he frowned. "I'd never jeopardize that."

"Me neither."

Why was this so difficult to talk about? Maybe because if she misinterpreted something and said the wrong thing she'd be putting it out there, and once something was out there it was impossible to pull back. She didn't want to inadvertently put ideas in his head.

She met his gaze. "Good. I'm glad we're clear on that."

When he looked back at her, something tightened in the air. Their eyes locked, both pleading for something, but something altogether contrary. Her heart began to race at the unwanted feelings his intense look brought about inside of her. It was different yet familiar. She looked away.

"You're too pretty for all the ugliness of this world, Scout. Too special. I want to help you find the beauty in life again. Help you find your smile again."

Heat rushed up her neck and she blushed. She didn't know what to say.

Her heart began to race as she briefly let her mind entertain the chance that he might be saying more than just words. She missed being touched, missed the feeling of being kissed, the rush of blood and surge of nervous energy that came with being intimate. What would that be like with a man like Parker?

The vision she tried to conjure was immediately rejected by some part of her. She simply couldn't see him as more than a friend, and maybe she was imagining all of these mixed signals. She frowned inwardly. This was also Lucian's fault. He'd suggested Parker had more than platonic feelings for her, and now she was paranoid.

Her voice was a choked sound. "I'm trying to get back to the girl I was. That's what I want. I want everything back to the way it used to be. I just feel so . . . I'm . . . broken."

His jaw clenched and she recognized the glimpse of anger flashing in his gaze. His hand again gripped hers. "You are *not* broken, Scout. Don't say shit like that."

Too much introspection, too many emotions, the abyss of fear broke and the pain suddenly seeped out. She'd kept it locked in for most of the day, but she was getting tired again. Something close to a dried-up sob slipped past her lips. "But I am. I'm not even sure if I left him or he left me, but I do know if he welcomed me back I'd go running to him."

"He's an asshole!"

"He's also incredibly sweet. He loved me the way no one else ever has."

He suddenly released her hand and forked his fingers through his hair. "You can't say that if you've never given anyone else the chance to love you."

Oh, God, please no. Don't take us there. "Why would I want to? This is the first time I've ever experienced love, and I've never known such pain or misery." She wiped her eyes. "I love my mother and she . . ." The ache in her chest bloomed. "Love is so powerful. It lifts you up and cuts you down. I hate it and want nothing to do with it."

He stood abruptly and began to pace. "It isn't natural to scorn love. That's what I'm trying to get you to see. *He's* the one that's broken. You can't go by what he showed you. You need to stop defining things in his terms. Love is the underlying motivator in this world, beyond wealth, beyond anything else; only love could drive a person to such a ceaseless place of want and need. It's the most powerful driving force of life."

"No, Parker, it's the most powerful distraction to our existence."

He came over to her chair and dropped to his knees. "Why exist at all if it's not beside someone you care about, someone to share it all with, the ups, the downs, the great moments and the hardships that cut us in two? We're meant to have partners in the world, Scout, someone to make us feel complete and right. Don't close yourself off because of one asshole. Time will fix things. You just have to be patient."

It shouldn't bother her, but every time Parker referred to Lucian by a nasty label, her mind conjured a memory that disproved his words. She thought of the moment Lucian burst into the mill last winter, how he scooped Pearl into his arms and carried her out of that hellish place. She remembered the day they celebrated her first birthday. Her heart tightened. He wasn't an asshole.

Or was he? She recalled the day he had embarrassed her in front of Shamus and the look in his eyes when he realized he'd upset her. His apology was so raw and clearly unfamiliar to his lips, yet he looked at her with humbled confidence and vowed to never do anything so thoughtless to her again. He'd kept that promise . . . for a while.

Her head was all over the place, no room for more. There simply was no space left to consider more of the unfamiliar.

Why did people try so hard to find love? It was awful and cruel when taken advantage of. And like all things of power, the temptation to abuse it was too easy. When someone loved a person, they surrendered everything so completely it was against human nature not to take advantage. And when they walked away, one was left exposed and vulnerable to all the ugliness.

Lucian had always been a danger to her. He did something nameless to her. He could tease her in a way that delivered her from life's challenges. How she wished she could find that deliverance now.

Being with him gave her a sense of falling that was more addicting than anything she had ever known. He'd conditioned her to crave that loss of control he created. He taught her to wholly surrender and simply be. It was without thought, and for the first time in her life, during those moments of intimacy, she saw herself in her rawest form.

And he crushed her.

"What are you thinking?" Parker whispered, still holding her hands.

The phone pressed between her palms was a weight she couldn't seem to let go. "I don't know. My head's a mess. I feel like I'm dying."

"I've watched you with quiet fascination for years, Scout. You're strong, driven. You have a fire inside of you that no one can bank. With time the hurt will fade."

She wanted to believe he was right, but her pain was so consuming it seemed impossible. She'd been someone else over the past few months. It was her, but not. And the woman Parker was describing . . . that didn't fit either. "You're glorifying someone I don't know, but I'm certain she isn't me."

"How can you say that? She is you."

She was turning into some pathetic, tortured soul. Why couldn't she see herself the way he saw her? Anger washed through her. Life was never this complicated.

Her face crumbled and she cried. The weight of all her confusion finally fell like an avalanche inside of her.

"Talk to me, Scout. I can't help you if you don't talk to me."

"Why?" She had so many questions as to why. Why had she not been enough for Lucian? Why did he need her to marry him? Why had he simply let her walk away? How was she still living with so much agony?

"Why what?"

"Why did this happen to me?"

He touched her jaw, dragging his fingers lightly to her ear and down her throat. "Because you're different and people see that. Patras saw it and he won't be the last. You're special."

"No, I'm not. I'm incredibly selfish. I only know how to think about myself."

"That's not true and you know it. Every choice you've ever made has considered others. You never make a single move without thinking about what consequences it might hold for the people you care for. You move with purpose and always try to predict how others will follow."

She was tired. "Like chess."

He frowned. "What?"

"You describe me like chess."

"I suppose that's a good way to put it."

"I can move whatever direction I want, yet I won't leave the king."

He released her and sat back, his expression suddenly hard. "And he's the king?"

Of course. She nodded.

"What does that make the rest of us, the sacrificial pawns?"

She smiled sadly. "If you asked Lucian, he'd call you a dark knight."

"Why's that?"

"Because you come off unthreatening, but really, you're quite stealthy." She was still amazed she was sitting in Parker's apartment, on *his* furniture.

He chuckled and arched his brow. "Stealthy?"

She smiled. "Yes. The knights appear to be focused on one direction, but are known for making swift, unpredictable shifts and hijacking the entire game. He said I should watch out for you."

"Maybe he's right." The momentary ease of their conversation evaporated. He'd done it again, slipped in some confusing sentence that had her questioning the ever-dependable presence that was Parker.

She met his stare head-on, a glint of assuredness making his gaze sharp in a way she'd never seen him look before. This was what Lucian had been referring to when he called Parker shrewd. It was a worrying side of him to see. Instinctively, she withdrew her hands from his grip.

"Parker." She swallowed. This time there was no misinterpreting the look in his eyes. When he eased forward, she drew back. "I can't."

"Scout, *can't* is a word outside of your vocabulary. And it's a very extensive vocabulary." He quickly brushed his lips over her cheek and stood, leaving her frowning. It was the kiss a brother would give a sister. She was mangling everything. She needed to just stop, stop thinking, stop worrying, stop her brain from overthinking.

She took a moment to scrutinize him. She didn't know why, but she continuously compared him to Lucian. Parker was so different from Lucian, younger, leaner. Parker was a handsome man. He had a sophisticated air and an earthy edge, while Lucian was all chiseled edges and sleek control. Lucian was contained authority, and Parker was reserved vigilance.

As she analyzed the soft curve of his lip, the dappled golden shade of his haphazard hair, she saw a man who was quite attractive. Her fingers went to her cheek, where his lips had briefly touched. Maybe she was the one mixing things up.

Parker saw her as a girl she no longer was. His opinion of her remained unchanged. She was the one who suddenly saw him differently. The boy she'd grown up beside was gone, and in his place stood a man she sometimes couldn't recognize. Perhaps if she could somehow make herself feel something for Parker, her heart would stop pining for a man who no longer wanted her.

No! Her mind immediately rejected that suggestion. But the thought remained. She trapped it away, labeling it as destructive and wrong.

As she struggled to predict how long she would hurt, she couldn't help but scrabble for anything that would numb the pain. Was this what Pearl felt like, helpless to have what she'd become so addicted to?

She was painfully aware of the fact she was holding on to something she no longer had. Her heart constricted. For the first time ever, she saw shades of Pearl in herself.

Like Pearl, Scout craved something she couldn't have, something that changed her, brought her to life in a way only she experienced, while onlookers pitied how lost she'd become. Did Parker pity her?

Lucian was an addiction, and the withdrawal was surely killing her. Seeing her situation in that light made her recovery absolutely necessary. She'd become as disoriented as her mother.

She drew in a slow breath. Parker continued to pace as her insides fell to pieces.

She sat on the straight-back chair and watched as he turned to face her. "Scout," he whispered.

What could she say? She was completely lost. She remained silent. She wasn't sure what sort of expression she wore, but it drew him close. He slowly held out a hand. Confused, she placed her fingers in his. *Make it stop. Make the pain and questions go away.*

"Let's get out of here," Parker suddenly said.

"W—where do you want to go?"

He grinned. "Let's go have some fun like we used to. I want to see you smile, and I decided my goal for the day is to get as many smiles from you as I can."

Grinning at the offered distraction, she nodded. Escaping sounded nice. It also sounded daunting. Scout didn't know if she could commit to a day of feigned happiness when on the inside, shattered bits of sadness were fighting to get out of her. But she agreed anyway. He was the only lifeline she had left.

"Okay."

THE temperature was in the low sixties. People ambled along the city walks without coats, and the soggy April ground showed little peeks of spring. Snippets of green flecked the wintered earth, and pale blooms of color were budding from the thawing soil. Trees were greening and the world took on a renewed appearance, as it once again was reborn beneath the sun.

They first went to Ninth Street Park, where a group of children were having a baseball scrimmage. Scout smiled at the ragtag appearance of their clothing. This was not an organized competition, but a joining of friends sharing in the nice afternoon.

Some kids had softened leather gloves and some merely used their hands. There were no bases, only a general understanding that certain lines in the sand stood for more than just tracks.

She and Parker sat in the run-down dugout of the field. Ninth Street was one of Folsom's many community parks, ranking among the less nurtured. The game didn't play for nine innings. Rather, it continued until the girls on the field lost interest and formed a small cluster by third base, where they giggled and watched the boys.

The boys continued to perform and compete. They strutted like young peacocks for their female counterparts, and for every bit of fanfare their efforts were well rewarded with chortles and flirtatious finger waves.

Scout smiled at the display, envying it for the natural promenade it was. No matter how old she grew, she would always envy the secure freedom of regular children at play, something she never experienced on her own but always watched longingly from a distance.

When the game seemed to conclude, even the boys putting aside their gloves and bats to join the clusters of girls hanging in the outfield, Parker stood and held out his hand. "Come on."

They walked along the path that bordered a pond. The breeze was stronger there, and Parker quietly slipped off his tweed jacket and slid it over her shoulders. They crossed a small bridge and stopped at the center to watch a gaggle of mallards swim by.

"The ducks will be having their babies soon," Parker commented.

Scout adored seeing the new ducklings each spring. She always found it impressive that in the rush of the city, when a mother duck led her ducklings across a road, everyone stopped until the last little webfooted balls of fluff safely marched to the other side.

They followed the trail until it led them back to the ballpark. The sun was setting behind the trees, and the children were all gone.

"Are you hungry?" Parker asked.

"Sure."

"Come on."

He took her hand and led her out of the park. She wasn't sure why she allowed him to hold her hand, but his lead excused her from thinking, and she welcomed his direction, found comfort in handing over control.

They walked to a middle-class section of Folsom, where several schools were located. The streets were cast in a late afternoon glow as the sun took up space somewhere behind the buildings that stunted the horizon.

"This looks good," Parker said as they arrived at a church.

Scout smiled. It had been a while since they'd done anything like this, but she knew the drill. They entered the small church, and in the basement voices echoed as parishioners gathered and enjoyed a weekend potluck. A man with receding gray hair greeted them.

"Hello, welcome to Our Lady of Grace. I'm Pastor Dan."

Parker placed his arm over her shoulders and extended his hand. "Hello, Pastor. I'm Parker and this is Scout."

"Nice to meet you." After shaking Parker's hand he reached for hers. She shook. "You're welcome to help yourself. Plates are over there, and feel free to walk around and meet the flock. In about an hour we'll be holding a casual service upstairs. All are welcome."

They nodded their thanks and made up plates. There were various home-cooked dishes sitting out in mismatched containers. Once their plates were filled, they found seats between two older women who asked various questions, some a bit intrusive about their relationship and some as simple as what they thought the weather would be tomorrow.

After everyone seemed to fill their bellies, Pastor Dan made an announcement, and the parishioners cleared their plates and moved to the upstairs of the church.

"Did you want to stay for the service?" Parker whispered as they tossed their plates.

Scout shrugged. It was expected, but no one would stop them from leaving if they chose to go, seeing it as being "Christianly" to share food with the hungry.

They quietly slipped out the side door just as a choir began to sing. It was amusing to her that they'd just found a good meal the way they used to, without spending a dollar. Especially since she now had a bank account holding hundreds of thousands of dollars, and Parker had a closetful of suits and had money as well.

Her jaw tightened at the reminder of the money Lucian put aside for her. Was that the price of his guilt? The price of her? No matter how far she'd fallen, her pride was worth more than the temptation of the money. She'd never touch a cent of it. It was ugly and offensive, and she hated him a little more for leaving it to her.

The sun set, and the sidewalks were no longer as congested. Scout pulled Parker's jacket tight over her chest. "We should probably get back. It's getting cold."

He nodded and, without comment, they strolled in the direction of the apartment. At about a block away, his hand casually slipped into hers again and squeezed.

Scout still didn't know what to make of this new, affectionate side of Parker. Perhaps he was only reacting to her outward breakdown. They had always been so respectful of each other's personal space, but Parker seemed to be purposefully putting an end to the way things used to be. Again, she chased the thought away, needing this momentary reprieve from her mind.

When they arrived at the apartment, he unlocked the door and let her step in first. His feet shuffled over the bare floor and when he found the lamp, the room glowed in soft amber. She stood by the entrance to the living room and stared at him. They each seemed to be having a moment of *now what*.

"I had fun today. Thanks," she said, breaking the heavy silence.

He smiled and took a slow step toward her. Her breathing was slow, but her heart raced.

Do something. She wanted to escape the moment, but his gaze held her in place.

"I had fun too," he whispered as he came to stand in front of her. His fingers lifted to her hair, picking up a strand. She followed his gaze as he examined it. He seemed mesmerized by the feel. She shifted uncomfortably.

Everything over the past few weeks was such a blur to her that she wondered exactly when she granted this unspoken permission and how permitted he assumed he was to touch her. Curiosity was a dangerous thing.

She *was* curious, but her distrust for her heart and common sense gave her temperance. She'd never again surrender to that driven, potent lust she experienced when she and Lucian first touched. Of course, that wouldn't be a problem with Lucian being gone.

When Parker touched her, like he was now, it was slightly different for some reason, and she had yet to determine if it was different in a good way or a bad way.

His gaze met hers and she recognized the intent there. Feet shuffled a step closer. She sucked in a breath. She should move. Green eyes stared deeply into hers, and there was that quiet moment of warning just before his lips touched her cheek, this time lingering a second longer than they had before.

Forcing herself to relax, Parker's scent filled her nose as his fingers released her hair, and he stepped away before she could determine what the kiss meant.

She lowered her gaze to the floor.

The echo of Parker's easy laugh filled the silence. Gentle fingers caught under her chin and tipped her face up. "I had fun today too," he repeated, and turned to get something in the kitchen.

He returned a moment later with a glass of water. After taking a sip, he tilted his head and frowned. "You okay?"

She nodded. "Just tired."

"You can have the bed again if you want. I don't mind."

She frowned. "No. It's my turn on the couch. Fair is fair."

"Sleeping on the couch sucks, Scout."

"If you can do it, so can I."

"We could share the bed."

Tightness slowly wove through her chest. Sharing a bed with Parker would not be a great idea. "I'll manage."

He looked like he wanted to push his argument, but thankfully he didn't. Tomorrow was Sunday and she had a lot to do to get ready for her new job. She'd been sleeping more than usual, but was still exhausted. Sleep would do her good before starting work.

They awkwardly moved around the apartment in silence, preparing for bed. There was a new element to her and Parker that apparently involved a lot of blushing and downcast eyes on her part and a lot of confusing stares and stolen touches on his. She feared they might be ruining something wonderful, and the thought was so sad, filling her with such a feeling of desolate helplessness, that she pushed it away. She could not lose Parker too.

twenty-seven
· · · · ·

SOCIAL INTERCOURSE

SHE wore a sequined mermaid-cut silver dress with a ruffled slit traveling up her inner thigh, toeing the line of indecency. Champagne bubbles tickled her nose, the smooth blown-glass of the flute a welcome weight in her hand. Music flooded the room, mingling with the gentle chatter of guests.

Heat pressed into her back. "Are you enjoying yourself, Ms. Keats?"

Her eyes closed as she leaned into him, a thousand worries and insecurities scattering into the wind like thistle on a balmy afternoon.

Hands coasted over her bare shoulders and turned her body. She walked as the heavy press of his palm settled on the small of her back and directed her through the crowd.

They were in an aquarium. The normal lights were replaced with dripping crystal chandeliers. Rafters were swathed in thick, satin reams of white linens, bunched with balls of wild lilies perfuming the air.

He led her to an isolated corner. Three walls were made of

glass. Clown fish and colorful beds of coral brightened the dark blues, pierced with silver beams of light. It was as though she were in some secret part of Atlantis, a magical underwater kingdom away from the rush and racket of the world.

She could see her reflection in the glass, silver shadows playing over her skin, giving her a celestial blue glow and turning her gown shades of cerulean and deep indigo. His hand traveled over the tight curve of her hip. The dress hung on her like a weighted skin bedazzled in gems. She was the pirate's treasure hidden beneath the deep blue of the ocean.

Heavy satin tickled her knee as it was lifted away from her leg. The cool air met her heated flesh as her inner thigh was subtly exposed, and fingers traced upward over her sensitized flesh. Angelfish passed by, undaunted by the display of delicious need and lust on the other side of the glass.

She needed him, needed his touch like a breath beneath all this water. Bubbles danced slowly from reefs, circling waving fronds and palms of green as they made a slow, tantric climb to the unseen surface.

Guests passed, their shadows meandering at the entrance of the quiet room. She wondered who the voyeurs were, them or the fish. Blurred silhouettes could barely be seen on the other side of the aquarium as guests took in the view. If they looked hard enough they would see them, see him touching her.

"Spread your legs."

Her sandal-covered feet, so sharply arched, stepped apart, giving him access. Her folds were bare. Only silk stockings covered her legs, tied with delicate ribbons to the garter that fit around her nipped waist.

Warm fingers slid upward and tickled her bare folds. "Are you wet for me?"

Her heart raced and her voice tripped past her tongue in a raspy whisper. "Always."

"Good girl."

The touch of his fingertips was a carefully rationed tease she wanted to steal and gorge her body on. She moaned, expressing her deep hunger to feel him inside of her. "Please."

"Please what, Evelyn?"

"Please touch me."

Gentle fingers continued to pet over her folds as he tsked. "We're at a very formal and public affair, Ms. Keats. Someone might see."

The side of her lips curved into a secret smile. That was her exhibitionist, always playing on the edge of propriety.

His movements were contrary to his words. "Part your gown for me."

Her shaky fingers found the heavy ruffled hem of her gown and slowly lifted, pulling the folds apart like a curtain to some hedonistic show.

"I should punish you for being so brazen," he threatened with little conviction.

His palm cupped the apex of her thighs, and his middle finger slid deep into her heated channel. Her body quivered and buckled. That first, long-awaited touch was always the most potent.

He slid his finger out and plunged it back into her, gently fucking her with his hand. "I love taking you like this, having you at my disposal to entertain me and satisfy my every whim. You love being that for me, don't you, Evelyn?" His words heated her temple as he whispered them against her flesh, each gentle puff of his breath teasing her hair.

"Yes."

"Do you see there, through the glass? If you look up you can see where the majority of guests are. I'm going to fuck you right before their eyes and they won't even know what they're missing."

Her teeth bit into the soft pout of her lower lip as she stifled her moans. She was so ready for him. Her body coiled with need as he wound her tighter and tighter. The scrape of his feet shifting over the polished floor preceded the slow glide of the zipper on his tuxedo pants as it lowered.

"Give me your glass." The champagne flute disappeared. There was a soft click. Her dress lifted, discreetly exposing the backs of her thighs. "Place your palms on the glass and don't move."

Cool glass pressed beneath her fingers as they stretched wide. Her skin was so hot, condensation gathered in the creases of her palms. A sharp crack followed by a quick sting bloomed over her ass. She gasped.

"That's for being so wicked at a high-class function, Ms. Keats. Shame on you, tempting me to take such measures," he whispered playfully. She loved the sound of his smile over his hoarse voice.

The blunt end of his cock teased down the crease of her ass as he slowly seated the tip of his erection in the opening of her sex. His finger slipped under the band of her garter and pulled it back, releasing it like the tight thread of a bow. As it snapped against the rounded curve of her ass cheek, she gasped as he filled her in one quick motion.

So full. Her eyes shut as his knees bent behind her. His hips pulled back and snapped forward, filling her in long, sure strokes. "Let me hear you."

Her teeth released the hold they had on her lip as she surrendered to him, allowing her moans to escape. With each plunge of his cock she gave a soft cry. Her breath beat against the glass, causing a cloud of vapor to form on the surface. Her hands slicked and whined, as the force of his thrusts caused her palms to drag ʔ the aquarium wall.

"Louder."

She cried out as he forcefully took her. His hand curled over the inside of her thigh and lifted her left foot off the ground. He had her suspended, one leg trapped on the outside of his strong knee and thigh, the other lifted, forcing her body open for his taking. Her hands offered little support, but his body was so snug behind hers, covering her like a second skin, she knew she wouldn't fall.

Her skin heated as her needy cries echoed through the quiet room, countered by a hard grunt that escaped his chest with each steady thrust. If she concentrated she could make out the voices of guests nearby, knowing it would only take one lull in a conversation to expose them. She had no doubt her cries could be heard if only someone cared to listen.

Fingers dug into her thigh and his pace increased. He drilled into her. Words whispered over her bare shoulders as he spoke of what she did to him. The flesh of her thigh was released. She had no doubt the press of his fingers left little purple kisses on the ivory expanse of her skin.

His hand slid upward and strong fingers found her clit. He grazed her tender flesh, and she nearly came out of her skin.

His sultry snicker was music to her ears. "Dirty girl," he whispered playfully and pressed a kiss just below her ear. "Feel what you do to me." He thrust. His hips pivoted and his cock caressed the walls of her sex.

She moaned and ground her body into his.

His teeth scraped her shoulder, and the fingers of his right hand found their way up the back of her neck, latching into the hair at her throat. Her head was jerked back at the same time his fingers advanced on her, bringing an onslaught of pleasure to her clitoris as he drove into her.

She cried out as she came, visions of glass shattering around them filling her fanciful mind, water washing them away on a tide of pleasure. His teeth bit into her shoulder, pulling her skin tight between his lips, marking her.

His release flooded her like a warm caress. Her body pulsed with his, milking every bit of his pleasure, swirling their beating bodies into a riptide of need that followed a continuum of throbbing ripples as their climaxes doubled and folded into one.

His chest pressed into her back as his breath huffed against her neck, ruffling tiny wisps of her now ruined hair. Her forehead rested on the misty glass, searching for coolness.

"I love you," he whispered with more affection than she could measure. "Don't ever leave me, Evelyn. Ever."

She woke up on a choking gasp and sat bolt upright. The living room was black as pitch. She was panting and covered in a cold sweat. Scrambling for the lamp, she fumbled with the switch. Her eyes fluttered and adjusted to the sudden brightness.

She caught her breath and waited to find her equilibrium. Her cheeks heated as she quickly stared at the doorway to the hall. Checking that the bedroom was dark, she slid a hand between her legs. She'd come in her sleep.

A wash of humiliation and guilt flooded her. That was a rule. She was not allowed to make herself come.

Those rules don't apply anymore, stupid. He left you.

She frowned and hid her hand behind her back. Actually, it was him who had made her climax, just not in real life. She shook her head. She needed to stop this. She needed to get past all of this, past him.

Sighing, she fell back onto the couch. *God, this sofa is uncomfortable.* Shifting irritably beneath the covers, she tried to find sleep again, but it was elusive. Her mind was now stuck on Lucian, on the conversations they'd had in the past, the moments that made her laugh, the things he had taught her.

He defined so much of who she was. She'd never known someone who played such a fundamental part in her identity.

She knew it was best to get over him, but her conscience was stubbornly holding on to him. It was a self-imposed torture. But in truth, the real torture would be letting him go. Moving on without Lucian meant saying good-bye. Pain had her curling into her pillow. Why did she have to love him so much?

She shut off the light and cried silently in the dark. It was time to let the past go and move on. She'd never get anywhere in life if she allowed a ghost of her past to have such a hold on her.

Life was like the game of chess, he'd taught her. "Social intercourse," he called it. Regular men were the pawns of the visionaries. Rooks were the voyeurs, the onlookers watching from their towers and announcing events to come. The knights were clever and alert, seemingly sleeping beasts with one eye open.

And then there was the all-powerful king, tucked safely within his court. Everyone vied to be near him, but only the truly deserving made it to his side. He needed his queen to stoically stand by his side and protect him. According to Lucian, that was her greatest charge in life. However, the queen was never tethered. She had the freedom to go if she pleased and very little could truly trap her.

She thought she was a queen, but perhaps she had only ever been a pawn.

As Scout fell back asleep, her last thought rang like an epiphany clamoring through the belfry of her mind. In life, everyone who encroached on the king got fucked—social intercourse indeed.

twenty-eight
· · · · ·

A NEW LEAF

SUNDAY was a mix of diversions. Scout woke up feeling, for the first time in weeks, refreshed. No longer would she be the wallowing sad case she'd allowed herself to become. No. She was starting a new chapter in her life. It was a new day and she had a new job and she decided it was time to break out of this funk and mold the new her.

She spent the morning filling out paperwork with Parker. Once everything was completed, she packed her bag and left to deliver her papers to Clemons.

Mr. Gerhard was in his cluttered office when she arrived and, again, he gave her the creeps. He seemed nice enough, but something was off. She was grateful she'd be working the registers on the other side of the store, far away from his office.

After Clemons, she visited a thrift store several blocks away and found a pair of gray slacks that fit. Locating the grapefruit pink Clemons dress shirt was another challenge, but she found ne at a local uniform shop downtown.

e was down to thirty-two dollars in cash. That was the last

of her honestly earned money. It was going to be a tight few weeks. She refused to use the card Lucian placed in the envelope.

He broke up with her because she wouldn't marry him. She didn't play games and thought he didn't either. So why had he left her all that money and put some invisible timeline on their "break"?

Deep down, if what Parker suggested was correct, she knew Lucian would never come back for her, not if he was in Paris vacationing with someone else. The thought of being replaced so quickly was unfathomable, but gutted her all the same. Still, it gave her a little more control to imagine him coming for her and her being gone, his guilt money sitting in an account, untouched.

No, she would not take a single cent from that man. The thirty-two dollars would just have to last until her first paycheck, which would come at the end of the month. It would be tight, but she'd starve before she tapped into that account.

Parker offered to spot her. She didn't want to borrow from him either, but she would. He'd keep track and let her pay him back. Still, she planned on doing everything in her power to *not* have to resort to borrowing.

It shouldn't be difficult. She'd lived on much less in the past. They had a pantry full of food. Their rent was paid. She had her uniform for work. And she could walk everywhere she needed to go.

By the time she returned to the apartment on Sunday night, it was dinnertime. Parker was making grilled cheese and tomato soup again.

"Hey, how did it go?"

She plopped her bag on the counter. "Good. I got my uniform and dropped off the paperwork."

"What time do you have to be in tomorrow?" He slid a crispy sandwich off the pan and onto a plate. She carried it to the table and returned as he served up the next one.

"I'm scheduled for seven to three."

He paused in ladling out soup. "So early?"

She swapped out the bowls. "Only on Mondays, Tuesdays, and Wednesdays. Thursdays I'm off and Fridays and Saturdays I work from nine to five."

He looked disappointed. "You'll be working every Saturday?"

She poured two glasses of milk and began following him to the table. "Yeah. Is that a problem?"

They walked to the table and settled into their seats. "No, I just figured you'd have off on the weekends. I was looking forward to doing stuff."

"Oh, well . . . I don't think I really get a say in my schedule until I'm there for a while."

She took a nibble of her sandwich and watched as he frowned over his soup. She understood working the weekend was not a favorable shift, but his disappointment surprised her. Why did it matter so much to him?

Lucian used to resent her time working, but they had an entirely different arrangement than she and Parker. Maybe she should say something to Parker about what was happening to them, but she still wasn't sure if bringing up the sense that they were changing was smart.

She intended to address the awkward turn their relationship had taken, but when she spoke, something totally different came out of her mouth. "What time do you leave for work?"

"I'm usually out of here by seven thirty, back by six."

That would be almost three hours to herself each day and all of Thursday. She kept her gaze on her food so as not to give away her relief. As much as she appreciated Parker letting her move in with him, she still valued time to herself.

As she swirled her crust in her soup, Parker said, "I was thinking tomorrow night we could watch a movie together. They have those Redbox rentals now."

She smirked at him. "Parker, you don't have a television."

He shrugged. "I could get one."

Her mouth fell open. "Park, you don't even watch TV. Why would you get one? So you could watch *a* movie and then use it as a bookcase?" She laughed and he smiled.

"Yeah, I guess that's dumb. Well, what would you like to do? I know how you are about money so I'm trying to be accommodating, but I think it would do you good to get out, Scout."

She stilled. "Oh." Did he mean hang out or go out?

He looked at her. "Scout, if it's a problem . . . I mean . . . I just want a chance to show you a fun time."

"I'm not so sure I have a fun side, Parker."

They smiled through an awkward silence. Finally, he said, "Let me take you out, Scout. For once, let me treat you when you aren't going to keep a mental tally of what I spend."

"Parker—"

"Please."

"I don't want you to throw away your money on me."

"I don't care about money. It's there to be spent. Truth be told, the only reason I have it is to prove to you that I can get it when I need it. It means nothing to me."

She put down her spoon. "What?"

"Come on, Scout. You know I don't care about wealth. I could be content with any roof over my head and a good book in my hands."

Yeah, she knew that. That was why Parker was dangerous. He just didn't have the natural hunger necessary to make it in this world. She couldn't figure out what had motivated him this far, but she didn't believe *she* was enough to provoke that sort of ambition. The fact that he somehow managed to get a job in the corporate world was still a shock to her.

For some reason his statement bothered her. It implied something she didn't want to face. Perhaps it was because she knew how much Parker disapproved of the world he was suddenly living in. It was like he was making a barb at her without really saying so. Parker could be passive-aggressive when he wanted to.

"Don't blame me for you having to work. I never told you to get a job," she said, taking another bite. Her food was getting cold.

"I know. I wanted a job."

"Well, then say you wanted a job. Be accountable for your own actions."

He frowned. "I am accountable."

Tension zapped up her spine. "Then what the hell did you mean by proving to *me* you could get it?"

"Nothing. It's stupid. I just meant that I have money, and you shouldn't concern yourself with how I spend it. You earn money for what you think you need, and I earn it for what I need. Who cares if they're different reasons?"

"I only care because you said it like I made you get a job or something."

He tipped his chin down and gave her an exasperated look. "What?"

He shook his head. "You. You're exhausting."

She drew back. "*You're* annoying."

His lip twitched like he wanted to laugh. His fingers idly dragged his spoon over the remaining soup in his bowl. "You need to learn how to laugh again, Scout. I feel like you're always so serious now."

"I know how to laugh. I do it quite freely around funny people. I can't help it if you aren't funny."

His mouth gaped. "Me, not funny? I am highly amusing, I'll have you know."

She tightened her mouth, refusing to smile. "Sure, Parker, you're hilarious—" Her words choked off as cold tomato soup suddenly spattered across her face.

"You have a little something on your cheek," he said, deadpan.

She dragged the heel of her palm along her jaw, mopping up the mess. "I can't believe you just did that," she whispered, reaching for her spoon.

He eased back in his chair, his eyes following her every move as she scraped up a spoonful of soup. Carefully, she raised her spoon and held the tip in a makeshift catapult. "You're dead," she warned, and flung it at him.

The moment it spattered across his face, chairs scraped along the floor. She squealed and giggled as he lunged at her. They fell to the floor in a clatter. Parker grabbed hold of her bowl and set it on her head like a drippy hat.

"Parker!"

He tickled her relentlessly. "Say it! Say I'm funny!"

She reached onto her plate and grabbed the other half of her sandwich and smashed it into his cheek, taking special care to shove the greasy parts up his nose. "Never! You're a dull, dull boy!"

He poked her side and they rolled over the floor. The bowl wobbled off her head and spun across the hardwood. He laughed as she giggled and threw an elbow in his side. Her right eye squeezed shut as tomato soup made its way past her lashes.

Parker tickled her until she was begging for him to stop. "Uncle! Uncle!"

"Say it!" He laughed. Breadcrumbs stuck to his eyebrow.

"Fine!" she cried, out of breath and developing a cramp from laughing so hard. He rose above her, breathing heavy, and looked into her eyes expectantly. She relented.

"You're funny," she admitted derisively.

He pursed his lips and pinched her hip and pinned her hands above her head with his other hand. Something came alive inside of her, something that reminded her of Lucian and scared the hell out of her.

"Fine! Fine!" In a more believable tone, she said, "You're funny. You're one of the funniest people I've ever met." *Now let go.*

His grin widened and then he slowly lowered his mouth to hers. *Oh no!*

She quickly turned her face and he stilled, his lips landing on her cheek. *Don't do this.* She made a sound in the back of her throat.

He sighed and pressed his head into her shoulder. "Scout . . ." Her name was a barely audible plea. What did he want from her?

Her breath came fast. His grip slackened, but her arms remained suspended above her head, his body still covering hers.

Was he asking permission? She was suddenly embarrassed, for her or for him she didn't know. She turned into the floor and scooted out from under him, into a seated position.

His hair was a mess and there were bits of sandwich all over his shoulder. Then he was there, good old Parker. He laughed and the moment was over. She snorted and brushed some of the crumbs away.

"You look like someone hit you in the face with a frying pan," he said, dragging his finger over her temple. He flashed a tomato-covered finger at her before popping it in his mouth.

Good. Keep it light. Normal. "That's exactly what a girl wants to hear," she teased, mopping her sticky hair off her face. "You're cleaning this up."

He smiled shyly. "If that's my penance for getting you to laugh, I'll take it. I have no regrets."

That's not all you tried to get. There was no mistaking what had almost happened there.

She rolled her eyes at him and shook her head, pretending a great deal of lightness she didn't feel. "I'm going to take a shower and wash this crap out of my hair."

He caught her hand, looking momentarily unsure. "Are you mad?"

She stilled. He shouldn't ask questions she didn't know how to answer. She was confused, but not mad. For a while there she was having fun. She hadn't even thought about Lucian until he restrained her, which was sort of her goal. She just didn't understand what she'd done to make him try to kiss her. She looked away, unable to meet his gaze. "Of course I'm not mad."

He leaned forward and pecked a kiss on her cheek—a completely platonic peck. "Good, because I didn't want to have to do it again." His expression said that was a lie.

What was happening? She stood. If she acted unaffected she could pretend it didn't happen. "Please try to abstain."

"Will you let me take you out tomorrow night?" he asked, the sudden change of subject surprising her.

Laughing had felt good. It was tempting to see if he could make her forget again. She needed the distraction.

He was right. It was his money to do with what he wanted. Besides, from what she understood, he was making a hell of a lot more money than she was going to be making at Clemons. She just needed to keep herself at a safe distance. "Okay."

"Great," he said with a wide smile. "We can celebrate your first day of work."

twenty-nine
· · · · ·

ENOUGH

WORKING at the grocery story was a cakewalk compared to keeping house at Patras. All Scout had to do was smile and scan items then place them into bags. There were even lulls when she was simply required to stand by her register until the next customer arrived.

The register was a little tricky at first, but she got the hang of it. When she didn't know how to do something, Nick, the guy working the next register, was more than eager to explain. Nick was nineteen and funny.

Mr. Gerhard made several appearances throughout the day. At one point he stood behind her, uncomfortably close, breathing his spearmint coffee breath over her shoulder as he explained how to refill her receipt roll. She only survived because Nick drew a mustache on his finger and mimicked their manager when he wasn't looking. It was almost impossible not to laugh.

All in all, she liked her new job. When she finished for the day, she felt a sense of promise. She could do this.

She returned to the apartment hours before Parker would get

home. They were going out that night to celebrate and, shockingly, she actually felt like she had something to commemorate. She was moving on.

Scout showered and dressed in jeans and a loose gray sweater that hung to her lower thighs. The elevator chimed softly just as she finished with her hair. Frowning, she glanced at the clock. It was only five.

Her heart suddenly raced as her ears focused on the sound in the hall. Shadows of feet showed under the door and the knob slowly turned. Parker stepped in and she exhaled. She had no idea who she was expecting, but she was relieved it was only Parker. Something in the past hour had set her on edge. She was oddly anxious.

"Hey," she greeted. He looked so different in his suit.

"Hey. You ready for tonight?"

She actually was. "Yup. Where are we going?"

He smiled and removed his jacket, draping it over the back of a kitchen chair. "I got tickets for a show."

Her lungs filled with excitement. "What kind of show?" She'd never been to a show. Well, that wasn't true. Once Lucian took her to a burlesque show. She flushed and shook off the memory. No thinking about him tonight. She was determined to have fun.

"It's a surprise. It starts in an hour so I figured I'd make something quick to eat before we go."

They ate sandwiches and guzzled down some juice. Parker locked the apartment, and then they were whisked off in a cab to the show!

The cab deposited them outside of Folsom's stadium. She'd never been this close to the enormous structure before. Vendors sold shirts as ticket holders bustled by. A man scalping tickets distracted her, but Parker kept his hand on her back and guided her to the doors.

It was loud once they made it inside. The floor was a wide,

cement ramp. People shuffled slowly to the top and everything smelled of popcorn. Her excitement had become almost impossible to contain.

A man in a striped staff shirt searched her bag and took Parker's tickets. They were sitting in row fourteen, section D, seats nine and ten. The seating made absolutely no sense to her and even less sense once they entered the main area.

Thousands of chairs formed an enormous bowl. It was a modern day coliseum. In the center stood a dark stage. Long cords hung from poles and there was no ceiling to speak of. A blanket of stars glittered back at them as Parker found their seats.

The chairs were theater style, the kind that flipped forward and snapped back the moment one stood. She took her seat and smiled. "This is so cool."

Parker laughed. "It hasn't even started yet."

"I know, but look at this place. It's incredible."

He patted her knee and grinned. They sat, listening to the roar of voices surrounding them, and Scout watched the various faces of people going by.

"Do you want something to drink?" Parker half shouted.

"Sure." She reached in her bag for a few dollars and he stilled her.

Shaking his head, he said, "Let me treat you."

She reluctantly withdrew her hand and nodded. Parker left to find them drinks and she continued to stare in awe at the stadium. People slid into the seats in front of her and she saw they held a pamphlet. The words she saw made no sense no matter how she tried to sound them out. She was too excited to think.

"The lines are insane here," Parker said as he returned to his seat. He held two cups of something golden and topped with foam. "I got you a beer. Is that okay?"

She'd never had beer. Lucian had always given her wine. "Sure. Thanks."

The beer had a very heady scent. The taste was much stronger than wine, more robust and grainy. She wasn't sure if she liked it, but she continued to sip it anyway. The lights flickered and dimmed. Her heart pumped as she settled into her seat.

The dark stage reflected silver shades of blue and soft chirping came from every direction. Scout turned her head, trying to find the birds, but saw none. Then music filtered over the gentle twittering. It was coming from speakers.

Her gaze returned to the vacant stage just as a dark shadow of a man came into view. The audience seemed to hold their breath as the man took center stage. Would he sing? Dance?

Scout jumped when he suddenly shouted something, too excited to make out the words. Then the stage careened to life. Men and women in bodysuits flipped onto the stage from every direction. Flames flashed and a ring of fire formed. She couldn't peel her gaze away, so she leaned into Parker. "Is this the circus?"

"Cirque du Soleil," he whispered. "The circus of the sun."

The circus! He'd brought her to a circus. Would there be acrobats? Clowns? Animals? Her gaze darted to the sky, and suddenly all the dark ropes and cords made sense. *The tightrope.*

She was breathless. Her body scooted to the edge of her seat as she stared unblinking at the performance in the distance. Drums rattled and the volume of the music below climbed to an intensity that vibrated in her bones. With a loud thump, the dancers fell to the stage, and everything went dark and silent.

The audience exploded with applause. Scout couldn't clap any more enthusiastically. Parker smiled at her as she applauded vigorously. She hadn't stopped smiling since they arrived.

A feminine voice echoed and the audience quelled. A woman

dressed in a medieval red gown took the stage. She sang in a different language, and her voice was incredible.

A sultry sound kicked in and the woman sang to the music. The beat picked up, and Scout gasped when the wall behind the stage was illuminated and hundreds of young ballerinas joined her. They paraded from one end of the stage to the other, performing beautifully.

When the tiny dancers left the stage, a glass tub was left in their wake. Scout knew it was much larger than it appeared, but from their seats it showed a tiny fishbowl with two fish swimming inside. When a woman, not a fish, swam to the edge of the tank, Scout's mouth dropped open. People. They looked like fish.

Another woman climbed out of the glass tank. They didn't dance, yet they performed in long stretches. They were contortionists. Their bodies folded in ways that shouldn't be possible. It was amazing to watch, so much so that Scout was afraid to blink.

There was something almost sexual about the way they performed. The rhythmic music was as hypnotic as their motions. The entire audience had been cast under a spell.

She glanced at Parker. He was as entranced as the rest of them. Every act was followed by a more impressive one. There wasn't a dull moment.

When the acrobats began to climb, the stage broke apart and rose higher and higher as dancers twirled like fireflies from impossible heights under the starry night. Scarves became wings, and bodies transcended like kites with long flowing tails. But that was not what impressed her most.

What made the show for Scout was the second-to-last act. A trapeze artist, a woman, broke away from the group of dancers and raced up a rope ladder that disappeared somewhere just before heaven. She reached a platform and performed pirouettes, reminding Scout of a jewelry box she once saw in a storefront window as a child, with a tiny spinning dancer on a spring.

Every face in the audience angled upward as if waiting for the rain to fall. The woman pointed her toe and suddenly stepped off the platform onto a rope.

Scout's breath came fast. She licked her lips, her own anxiety nearly unbearable as the performer took her first step. A net sat somewhere, a hundred miles below. It didn't matter. She was crossing the rope without harnesses or ties. It was sheer balance and determination that kept her poised there on the thin rope strung from heaven.

Her heart raced and suddenly Scout's eyes closed. She wasn't at the Circus of the Sun, but beneath the sun, her head resting on Lucian's lap as he told her of the impressive show he'd seen as a boy. She blinked and again watched the tightrope walker. He was right. It was the most impressive thing she'd ever seen.

He should be there with her, but he wasn't. She glanced to her right and studied Parker's profile. This was where her path had taken her. This was where she was. There were no safety nets in life or love, only spectators and the incredibly brave performers. She'd always longed to be a part of the show, never content with looking from the outside in.

Parker had found a way to break out of the mold and join the rest of them. It was time she did the same. He was her last ally.

Her hand slid to his thigh and he turned, first staring at her upturned palm and then setting his questioning gaze on her. She smiled and his expression slowly matched hers. This was where she was, and she wasn't going back. His hand slid into hers and he squeezed.

They held on to each other until the performers concluded the show, only letting go to applaud. The noise returned as the lights came on and he reclaimed her hand as they found their way back down the ramp and into the crowded parking lot.

The pavement was congested and noisy. Parker hailed a cab and told the driver the address to the apartment. A sort of calm settled over her as they drove. It occurred to her that she was okay with her decision to move on and let the past stay in the past. It was the healthiest choice she could make, being that she wasn't given many choices regarding her circumstances.

There had been enough tears, enough dreamless nights and sleep-ridden days. It was time to break away from the woman she'd become and figure out who she was meant to be.

"Did you enjoy it?" Parker asked softly as they neared the apartment.

Her face split with a genuine smile. "Very much. Thank you so much for taking me."

He seemed content with her answer and nodded, turning back to face the front.

When they pulled up at the apartment, Parker paid the driver and held the door for her. His hand slipped into hers as they took the elevator in silence. Scout didn't know what was going to happen once they made it inside, but she was done fearing the future so she could hold on to a meaningless past.

The amount of days no longer mattered. Fourteen, twenty, thirty days, he was never coming back. The pain would likely always be there, but tonight, for those brief, magical moments, she'd forgotten her hurt. Parker had given her that gift.

Parker unlocked the door and switched on the light. She placed her bag on the couch. Would he sleep there tonight?

Hands gently turned her shoulders. Parker's expression was unreadable. He stepped close and lifted her hair, carefully placing it behind her shoulder. Her breath stilled in her lungs as his eyes met hers.

He blinked. There were no words, but the question was there. Lowering his head, he slowly pressed his lips to hers. She stopped drawing comparisons and took it for what it was. Nice.

Her mouth slowly opened and his arms pulled her closer. Her body rejoiced at the feel of another's touch, no matter how much her mind objected. It was only because it was different, she told herself.

They kissed for several long minutes. Scout's body engaged and disengaged on and off. She was never able to fully lose herself in the moment, and that frustrated her.

Taking his hand, she backed into the bedroom. He eyed her curiously. She didn't want to *sleep* with him—couldn't—but it was silly to make him stay on the couch. "We can share the bed," she told him quietly. "But . . ."

He shook his head. "I'm not asking for more than you want to give, Scout."

Thank God, because she was still trying to process the fact that she and Parker were kissing. She couldn't handle anything more. She only wanted the relief he'd given her from her recent misery to continue. She'd figure it out later.

They took turns using the bathroom. Parker changed into a pair of sweats while she carried a large T-shirt to the bathroom and changed there. It hung past her knees and covered all her important parts. It was the least inviting thing she owned that she could sleep in.

She crawled into bed and he did the same. He leaned up to shut the light, and the mattress dipped. Her breathing echoed in her ears as she waited. Would they sleep? Would he try to kiss her again? She wasn't sure what she wanted.

The mattress whined as he turned on his side. "Come here," he said as he pulled her close. Her heart raced. The dark complicated things. This was Parker. Needing to remind herself of that, she went to him, her hand mapping out his shoulders, feeling the difference.

His mouth pressed into hers and there was suddenly a loud bang. She stilled. Frowning, she drew back. The pounding sounded again.

Parker's frown showed in a slice of moonlight pouring through the drapes. "What the—"

"*Evelyn!*"

Scout jerked back. Everything stopped: her lungs, her heart, the rotation of the earth. She held her breath, and then she heard it again. More pounding.

"Evelyn, open the door!"

Breath burst out of her as a million shards of her broken soul reacted to that voice. Parker cursed as she scrambled out of the bed. She ran to the hall and suddenly came up short. She glared at the hand holding her back. The pounding continued. He was going to break down the door. Parker turned her and pulled her back into the dark bedroom.

"Scout, listen to me." His eyes were frantic. "Stay here. I'll get the door, but just, please, stay here."

"Parker, let me go. It's Lucian. What if something's wrong?"

His grip on her arms tightened. "Please." He shook his head rapidly. "Let me make sure everything's all right before you do anything."

Her lips pursed beneath her tight brow. She couldn't catch her breath. What was he talking about? Lucian was here for her. Parker wouldn't let go of her until she gave him her word. She huffed. "Fine, but hurry, before he leaves."

He placed a brief kiss on her cheek and left, shutting the bedroom door behind him. She brushed away his kiss and pressed her face to the cool wood of the door. Her heart was erratic. She dug her fingers into the wood of the door, forcing herself to stay put.

"Evelyn!"

The locks clicked and as soon as they turned she heard the front door pull wide. "What the hell are you doing here?" Parker asked coldly.

Lucian's voice grew closer. "Get out of my way. Where is she? Evelyn!"

She cracked the door. Should she go to him? What did this mean? What about Paris?

"You have to leave," Parker snapped. "You aren't allowed to contact her for another two weeks. We had a deal."

She frowned. What was he talking about? He was going to ruin everything.

"Fuck the deal!" Lucian snapped. "Evelyn—"

"I'm here," she said, stepping into the hall. His eyes met hers and he breathed heavily. He looked like absolute shit. Her world spun. "What are you doing here, Lucian?"

His gaze lowered, traveling over her loose T-shirt, down her legs all the way to her bare feet. His jaw ticked as his face darkened. "Motherfucker," he hissed, then he turned. Everything happened so fast.

Lucian's arm cocked back. There was a crack, and the lamp crashed to the floor as Parker's body fell into the table. She screamed and jumped into motion.

"You son of a bitch!" Lucian growled, cocking his arm back to hit Parker again.

She tackled him. "Lucian, no!"

Parker scrambled to his feet. "Get the fuck out of my home!"

She held Lucian back, knowing it was her presence more than her strength that kept him from lunging for Parker again. He was seething. "You fucking touched her?"

"She doesn't belong to you!" Parker snapped, wiping his lip where it had split wide.

"The fuck she doesn't," Lucian growled.

Wait, what?

Scout looked around for help that wasn't there. She wasn't strong enough to hold Lucian back if he lost it on Parker again. She panicked. In a shrill, unrecognizable voice, she suddenly screamed, *"Someone tell me what the fuck is going on!"*

They both glared at each other. Breath stuttered from their chests as they faced off. Finally, Parker growled at Lucian, "I still have thirteen days left."

She shook her head. Turning to Lucian, she asked, "What's he talking about, Lucian?"

His dark eyes darted to hers as his nostrils flared. Slowly, he turned to Parker and arched a brow. "You didn't tell her."

"Tell me what?"

"Scout . . ."

She turned to Parker, very much disliking the contrite expression twisting his face. She waited.

"Go ahead, Hughes, tell her. Tell her what a stand-up guy you are, always looking out for her best interests."

She glared at both of them, waiting for someone to explain. "Parker?"

He shook his head. "I'm sorry." He swallowed. "I was only trying to protect you."

Lucian's dry laugh drew her attention. He straightened, but said nothing. She turned back to Parker. "Protect me from what?"

"From him," Parker growled.

She blinked, waiting for more, but it didn't come. She turned to Lucian. "Why?"

Lucian's face softened. His dark eyes blinked down at her, and she recognized the affection in his gaze, wanted so badly to drown in it. "Because he thinks he's better for you," he whispered in an almost sympathetic voice.

Her head shook. She scoffed. "What about what I think?" This was absurd. "Does anyone give a shit about what *I* think is best for me? Someone better start explaining what's going on, fast." When no one said anything, she stomped her foot and snapped, "Say something!"

"We had a deal," Parker quietly admitted. She pivoted, not liking the sound of that, and waited expectantly for him to continue. He wouldn't look at her, and something utterly terrifying clamped down on her battered heart. "Last winter, we made a deal. Lucian agreed to break up with you for a month so that I could try to get you to . . . care for me, the way you do about him."

Words stopped computing in her head. She shook, not accepting his explanation. "What?"

"I only wanted a chance to prove to you that I was the better man."

"So you're saying he gave me to you? No. He wouldn't do that." She turned to Lucian, waiting for him to call Parker a liar, but came up short when she saw the regret clear on his face. "What is this? Is this how you do it, like what you did with Slade and Monique?"

She couldn't wrap her brain around what she was hearing.

Lucian swallowed tightly. "I never wanted to agree to—"

"You're saying it's true then?" Her spine stiffened and her shoulders drew back. "You broke up with me so another man could try to fuck me?"

"Scout—"

"Oh, shut up, Parker. I'll deal with you in a minute." She turned her scowl on Lucian. "Lucian, tell me that's not true. *Please.*"

"It was freezing. I couldn't find you. Hughes knew where you were and I was desperate. He wouldn't help me unless I promised him something in return."

Her mind tripped over visions and scenarios that were far too bizarre to believe. This had to be some sort of a misunderstanding. "Whose idea was it?"

Lucian's lips formed a thin line. She turned to Parker and had her answer. "You said you were my friend."

Lucian grunted.

She turned on him. "And you said you loved me. What kind of man does something like that to the woman he loves?"

She found herself backing away from the two of them. They were despicable, the both of them. "Is that all I ever was to you? A bargaining chip to pass around when money didn't work?"

"God, no, Evelyn—"

"Then explain it to me in words I can understand!"

"I just wanted to find you," Lucian said pleadingly. "It was just before I found you at the tracks in the blizzard. You would have frozen out there. Pearl would have died. I swear to God my only intention was getting you home."

"So you could eventually give me away?"

"I never would have agreed to his conditions if I wasn't desperate."

"What exactly were your conditions, Parker? I'd like to know what price my *friend* puts on my survival."

Parker's face twisted with a multitude of emotion. "You weren't supposed to find out this way. We should still have two weeks together."

"You tricked me." Her fingers went to her lips. "All of this was to get me to go to bed with you."

Lucian stiffened and Parker's head jerked up. His green eyes pleaded as his head shook in denial. "No, I just wanted to show you what it was like to be loved."

"I was loved! At least I thought I was. Now I don't know anything!"

"Evelyn, get dressed. I'm taking you home."

Lucian reached for her, and she snatched her arm back. *"Don't touch me."* Tears rushed to her eyes. "How could you do this to me? To us? To everything we had?" Her chest tightened and she fought to get the words out. "I loved you."

All the blood rushed from Lucian's face. He stepped forward, but she stepped out of his reach. "Evelyn, please, come home with me and I'll fix everything."

She wiped her eyes and stared at their surroundings. "I don't have a home."

"Yes, you do, with me. Please, baby. I've been miserable since you left. I love you. We can fix this—"

"I'm not going anywhere with you. There is no *fixing* this. The two of you are perverted."

She glanced at Parker, but he wouldn't look at her. "And you, pretending you live by some code of honor. Your moral compass must have been broken that day." Turning back to Lucian, she analyzed her path of escape. She needed pants.

She spun on her heel and went to the room where her clothes were already put away in drawers. Yanking down her bag from the closet, she tossed it on the bed and began filling it with whatever she could find. When she found jeans, she slid them onto her legs. Her limbs convulsed with uncontainable emotion.

Both men crammed in the bedroom doorway, staring at her as she laced up her sneakers.

"Stay here, Scout, I'll go," Parker said quietly.

She stilled. "No."

"Where will you go?" he asked.

She didn't know. She wouldn't go back to her apartment. She'd go where no one could find her.

"Evelyn, come to the hotel. I'll give you a separate room. You can't just walk away like this."

She knotted her laces and stood. Her bag zipped with an obnoxious final zing. She turned and they backed up.

Parker stood aside, but Lucian blocked her exit like an immovable oak. "Get out of my way."

"No," he rasped. "I can't let you go. I can't lose you again."

Shaking her head, she looked up at him, tears running down her face. "You already lost me."

When he didn't budge, she said, "Please, move."

He was an anchor. She tried to shove past him and his strong hands caught her arms.

"Don't touch her!" Parker snapped, closing in on him.

Lucian turned and snarled, "You stay out of this." Turning back to her, he pleaded. "I can't let you leave."

Wasn't this a pretty picture? Lucian, the king, backed into the corner as the black knight stood poised and ready to attack from the left. She was prepared to do anything to knock them down.

The queen has more power than any other piece. She is the most coveted player of the game and can move any way she pleases.

Swallowing hard, she looked up at the man she had stupidly trusted with her heart and said the only word she hoped would get through to him.

"Checkmate."

His eyes closed and his face crumbled. Social intercourse. It was all a game. He'd taught her how to play, by rules she never chose, and he lost. He stepped aside.

She crossed the threshold and swung the front door wide.

"Scout!"

Lucian held Parker back. She never expected to lose him twice. She was free now. She finally understood she'd been manipulated, and while she was still standing, she was barely breathing. All her questions suddenly had answers, and she realized her unwanted ignorance had actually been a blessing in light of her reality. She'd lost the only two people she could ever count on.

As she stepped into the elevator, she turned and faced them. What a haggard pair they made. Good. As bad as they looked on the outside, she was a hundred times worse on the inside.

Lucian's dark, onyx eyes met hers. Those were the eyes that could make grown men crumble, with enough determination to dominate a city the size of Folsom. He set those eyes on her, his mouth a hard line, drawn with challenge. "You get a five-minute head start, Evelyn, while I settle some things with your friend here. And then I'm coming for you. I'm done playing games."

Not her friend. She had no friends.

The doors to the elevator closed, and her legs quaked with understanding. He thought she wouldn't get far. He thought he would come for her and nothing would stop him. But he was wrong. Lucian owned the heavens of Folsom, but he underestimated the depth of its hell. Scout was a master of hiding. She'd disappear before he made it to the street. She had to move fast, because once he found her, there was no telling what would happen.

The elevator opened again and like a queen conscious of the treachery that poisoned her court, in high dudgeon she walked on.

acknowledgements
.....

This book would not be possible without the wonderful readers in this world. I thank you all for allowing me to bring my characters to life and introduce them to your world.

I would like to send a special thank-you to Team Surrender for all of their extraordinary support: Becca, Carla, Nikki, Lori, Ivone, Regina, Michelle, and Mary—you are awesome! You make my job so much fun and I love you all!

And I would like to thank the incredible Tigerlilians. You know who you are. Your friendship means more than I can say and I love that the clubhouse has become the backdrop to every story I pen. Thanks for the love, the care, the friendship, the laughs, the round-table escapes, and the cupcakes. Your "unrestrained" presence in my life has made me smile many times while writing this trilogy.

· ·

Keep reading for an excerpt from
the third book in the Surrender Trilogy

COMING HOME

*Available now from InterMix and in print
from Berkley December 2015*

· ·

. . . . .

SHAM SACRIFICE
An offer of material, which is made at no risk

THE burst of pollen hit Scout's nose like a feather laced with pepper. No, she couldn't sneeze. If she sneezed, she'd get glassy-eyed and look as if she were crying when she certainly had *not* been crying. As a matter of fact, she hadn't cried for days. After what was likely the most trying five days of her life, Scout made a vow to never cry again. Tears were useless and, frankly, a big pain in her girlie ass.

As she shifted to the shade out of the warm May sun, her pale pink dress shirt was a light cover to her skin. Her heavy gray wool slacks, however, were not. Coming directly from work and living out of a small bag for the past week hadn't left her much choice in the wardrobe department. Pavement smacked beneath her Nikes along the busy Folsom sidewalks with each determined stride.

For five long days, Scout contemplated her predicament. She'd always aimed to be something more than homeless, but tolerated her circumstances all the same. Now, however, things had changed. There was no way she was going back to where she'd started.

Her memory was an endless revolving door of strife, covered in a bleary haze, smothering the prettier things in this world. Scout never had pretty things. Well, that wasn't true. Lucian gave her many pretty things. He also *gave her away.*

The pain hadn't subsided. It was very real and seething angrily inside of her. Scout simply made a decision to channel that anger into something worthwhile. And that was what today was all about, something worthwhile.

She was worthwhile. So worthwhile, it was possible to put aside the hurt and the sting of his betrayal to do something for herself.

For twenty-three years she had struggled to survive. At age four she was diving in dumpsters for the smallest scrap of salvageable food. At age seven she'd been scavenging while other girls her age played house and learned their ABCs. Scout never played house, because she didn't know the first thing about living in a home. And she never learned her ABCs, because her mother, the only person Scout ever had to look up to, didn't know how to teach her.

Pearl wasn't a typical mother either. She never baked cookies, sang lullabies, or kissed scraped knees. Rather, she cooked crack, mumbled ramblings of a stoned soul, and gave her body to men who funded her next high. Scout was likely seven by the time she realized if you gave certain things to men, they'd give you almost anything in return; yet she never wanted to go down that same degrading road.

Scout wanted to *be* somebody. Her needs were more basic. She wanted four walls and a roof to call home. She wanted a key for her own front door. She wanted a job, and she wanted money for food and heat, and clothing thick enough to keep her warm even in the coldest blizzard.

Now she was halfway there. She had a job working at Clemons Market. It wasn't a spectacular place to work, but she liked it. The people treated her nice. And her boss, even though he sometimes gave her the creeps, was tolerable.

Her last boss expected much, much more. *He* expected her heart. The son of a bitch got it too. Scout was still dealing with that emotional fallout.

Lucian Patras was likely a name she'd always know. He was a person quite difficult to forget. She tried. Lord knew she tried, but he was inside her, like a tattoo inked deep into her flesh. She couldn't wash him away no matter how much she wanted to.

Scout finally admitted that he'd used her, and with that shameful admission came some much-needed clarity. She could use him too.

She required a plan. Lucian had taught her many things. He taught her how to make love. He taught her how to socialize with aristocrats. He taught her how to play chess. And he taught her that she was more than a lost cause. However, he also taught her what it feels like to be truly fucked over.

She learned the agony of a broken heart, the torment of betrayal, and the misery of knowing the one person she wanted was the one she could never have. Her intimate relationship with Lucian was over.

One didn't have to be literate to read between the lines. She was given a chance to see behind the scenes as to how men of wealth play the game. She might not know how to count very well or be able to read heavy books, but Scout was not a stupid person. And she was a survivor.

Business was business, and so long as she kept the intimacy at bay, she could do what she needed to do. Scout's abbreviated taste of high society left nothing but a bitter taste in her mouth, and it was time to change the game.

Rounding the corner, Scout brushed her moist palms down the

coarse wool covering her thighs. She could do this. She'd thought long and hard about what she wanted and nothing, not even the infamous Lucian Patras, would get in her way.

The revolving door of Patras Industries reflected the bright rays of sun peeking through the high-rise buildings across the street. Scout's sneakers moved silently over the polished marble of the lobby floors, and her thumb pressed with purpose into the smooth button of the elevator.

After keying in the floor, she waited, her empty belly doing a row of summersaults having nothing to do with the rise of the lift, and everything to do with coming face-to-face with her past and finally having the balls to go after her future.

Cheeks puffed as she forced out a shaky breath, her clammy palms brushed over her blouse. "Your terms, Scout. Don't take any shit," she whispered as the elevator eased to a stop.

The door chimed softly as it opened, and she stepped onto smooth burgundy carpet. She looked nothing like she had the last time she was there. Her polished Mary Janes were humbled down to rubber-soled, serviceable shoes. Absent was the lace that once adorned her legs. This was not a mission of seduction, but an exercise in influence.

Same as before, she arrived at the reception desk with a deep hunger burning in her belly, but this hunger was something much more potent than any form of lust. This was a hunger for well-deserved recompense. No need to pretty herself up to get what she came for, what she deserved.

It might've taken her five days to figure out, but she finally understood. She held all the power. She was no longer an outsider. She'd been on the other side of the looking glass and realized she very well could stand on her own two feet. It was only a matter of declaring her intentions and not backing down. It was time to do for *her*.

"May I help you?" Seth, Lucian's personal assistant, greeted.

He clearly didn't recognize her, and why would he? She'd only met Seth once, several months ago. She'd been dressed to the nines and ready to seduce his boss. Without makeup she looked like a child. Her hair was pulled into a no-nonsense ponytail, and her Clemons uniform was anything but flattering. She'd also dropped well over ten pounds, which on a small frame like hers was not a welcome loss.

"I'd like to speak to Mr. Patras."

His eyes narrowed with rejection before he voiced his reply. "You need an appointment to meet with Mr. Patras."

"I'm sure I do not." Insecurities rattled her confidence, but she kept her chin up and remained polite. She had every right to be there. Convincing herself of such was step one. "Please tell him Evelyn Keats is here to speak with him."

Seth's eyes bulged. "Ms. Keats, I'm sorry. I didn't recognize you. Let me tell Mr. Patras you're here."

That's right!

He pressed a button on the intercom, and a tight shiver pinched her heart at the sound of Lucian's voice. "Yes?"

"Mr. Patras, Ms. Keats is here—"

It shouldn't have been possible to get from his desk to the door in such a short span of time, but the door to Lucian's office whipped open and his muscular frame filled the doorway, stress marring his expression and exhaustion weighing in his eyes.

Lips parted in obvious surprise, he stilled. "Evelyn." His voice was a mere rasp of the self-assured baritone he usually spoke with.

She nodded. "I came to talk—"

"Come into my office."

Her lips twitched as he cut off her request. She wouldn't let him obtain the upper hand. This was *her* show. She was there for a reason, and she couldn't let her heart distract her. That foolish organ had caused enough problems.

Aiming for poise, she nodded and carefully stepped past him. The office door shut with a sharp snick. Her mind replayed the first time they'd met. Lucian had stood like a giant, a thin veneer of control, masked in immeasurable power, seething behind her then, and he reminded her of the same giant now. Her sneakered feet quickly stepped away.

When he faced her, she saw he was still speechless, his eyes scanning her from head to toe. "I need to talk to you," she said quickly.

"Where have you been?" he asked, his gaze filled with bewilderment as it traveled back and forth from her feet to her face.

"That's not your concern."

"Evelyn." He leveled her with a look that said he wasn't in the mood for games. Neither was she.

There was no way she'd tell him she'd actually returned to sleeping on the streets, using her bag as a pillow, a playground for shelter, and a McDonald's for facilities. He'd see it as a weakness, and she couldn't stomach his pity. Her pitiful circumstances were only temporary and tonight she'd be in a bed once more, so long as she stuck to her plan and didn't let him intimidate or bully her.

Steeling herself, she met his gaze. "Lucian, I came to talk about other issues, not where I'm living."

"You haven't been at the shelter."

She pursed her lips. "No doubt you had your minions checking every crevice of the city for me. I'm a lot more resourceful than you give me credit for."

His brow softened as though her words wounded him. "Did you expect me *not* to look for you? I told you I'd find you."

"I expected nothing less. Luckily, your search can stop now that I've come to you."

He stepped forward and she moved back. "Don't." Her hand

shot out in warning. Regrettably, her request didn't come out as confident as she would've liked.

The hand reaching for her stilled and detoured to fork through his hair, tension clear on his face. He looked ragged, but still devastatingly handsome. The shadow on his tanned jaw should have looked sloppy, but only added another layer of sexy to his distinguished presence. His blue dress shirt had a white collar. Paired with the paisley red tie and black suit vest, he looked quite the tycoon.

"How long are you planning on keeping your distance, Evelyn? You're killing me. I've been going crazy since you ran off. I can't continue like this."

"And whose fault is that, Lucian?" she snapped, instantly regretting the show of emotion. *Keep it together, Keats.*

"I can't fix it if you refuse to let me—"

"There is no fixing it, Lucian! You used me and betrayed me."

"Bullshit!" he snapped. "I love you." His feet swiftly carried him across the office, incidentally boxing her into a corner. "I fucking love you, Evelyn. He had me at his mercy. *He* set the conditions."

He, being Parker, her once-dear friend turned Judas. Scout's understanding of their agreement was still foggy. Lucian had apparently been looking for her during a blizzard last winter and ran into Parker. After begging Parker to tell him where she was hiding, Lucian agreed to give her away for a month, with Parker driving some kind of bargain. Nope, still didn't compute. They were both guilty.

"And *you* agreed to his terms," she hissed. Fury at the injustice she'd been the victim of bloomed inside her, fresh and scorching. "I'm not here to talk about that. I don't care about your pitiful excuses. What's done is done. Either we discuss what I came here to discuss or I leave."

His gaze searched her face, likely hunting for some validation that she wasn't bluffing. Eyes that read opponents and colleagues with ease homed in on every visible strength and weakness she allowed him to see. Her jaw locked in determination.

"Go ahead and try to push me, Lucian. I'll be out that door so fast your head will spin."

He stepped back. *Good.* "What did you want to talk about?"

She glanced at the leather chair across from his desk. "May we sit?"

His dark eyes followed her gaze and he waved his hand in theatrical invitation. Irritation was evident in the set of his mouth and narrowed stare. Probably because Lucian was a man who didn't easily relinquish control. "By all means."

She sidestepped him, careful not to get too close, and he slowly returned to the seat behind his desk, his assessing gaze never leaving her. Her slight form sunk into the smooth leather chair. Her shoulders ached with the effort to remain stiff as she settled deeper into the soft seat. Exhaustion beat at her, threatening her resolve not to appear weak in front of him, but indignation and bruised pride stiffened her spine.

"What did you want to discuss?" he asked again.

This was it. Her entire life had been about survival, and now she wanted to survive in a more desirable way. She didn't need a billionaire to do that. She did, however, need a foundation to find her footing. Lucian could provide that foundation. While he may look at a woman like her and see someone vulnerable and in need of coddling, he was wrong. She didn't need someone to hold her hand. She simply needed a push, and then she'd manage on her own.

Taking a breath of courage, she said, "I want a loan."

His brow arched, telling her he hadn't expected such a request. "You're aware there's an account with over two hundred thousand dollars in your name? What could you possibly need that your bank account won't cover?"

That money had never been hers. Her dignity forbade her to touch it. Above all, Scout was practical. Lucian had more money than Midas and could afford to loan her what she was after. However, she was wise enough to know loans came with penalties and interest. Those were necessary stipulations to protect her pride. Unfortunately, Lucian's pride would likely face off with hers, and they were both incredibly stubborn.

"I don't want that money. I won't touch money earned on my back. I'm talking about an actual loan with interest and penalties and—"

He winced, then rolled his eyes. "Watch it, Evelyn. Tell me what you need. I'll give it to you. There's no need for this formal bullshit."

"I need my dignity back," she said succinctly, causing him to come up short. The "bullshit" that made this an official business deal was the only way she'd be able to stomach his help. It was just business. Taking those penalties away made it a favor, and she was done depending on favors from him.

"I see. And how much does one's dignity cost?"

"I'd like thirty-five thousand dollars."

His jaw ticked. "For?"

She met his challenging stare and tightened her lips. That was her business.

He sighed. "Evelyn, when an establishment finances another's endeavors, they're foolish not to question the investment."

"A second ago you were prepared to offer me anything I wanted. I don't see why my intentions should suddenly be an issue. This is just you being nosy. I'm not falling for it. Thirty-five thousand dollars is nothing to you. It's a new beginning for someone like me. Give me the satisfaction of at least believing you know I am capable of taking care of myself. I'm practical and I'm not stupid. Trust me to have a plan and I'll trust you to treat me fairly, like you would any other person asking you to invest in their future."

Those intimidating onyx eyes narrowed. "You're not any other person. Look at it as legal extortion. I have what you want. I'll trade you thirty-five thousand dollars for a bit of information."

Anger bloomed inside of her. Extortion indeed. She would *not* let him run her life. "I'll just go to a bank then," she bluffed.

"With what? You have no social security number, no identification, no birth certificate."

The molars in the back of her mouth clicked together. "I know you have those things. You're trying to manipulate me and, by doing so, only losing more of my respect."

He'd looked into getting her legal documents months ago. For him to be able to place a bank account in her name, he'd have needed to obtain some form of identification for her. Likely, he'd been holding it, too cowardly to hand over the documents before the big trade with Parker. If she had an ID, she could've fled a lot faster. That was Lucian, always the thinker and planner.

"I do," he agreed shamelessly.

"It wouldn't take long for me to go to a federal building and report them stolen. The numbers are on record, Lucian. Hard part's over. All you're doing is wasting my time. To be honest, your pettiness reeks of desperation."

His desk drawer slid open and snapped shut. Papers fluttered to the surface of his desk. He glared at her. "There."

Scout gazed at the documents. A neatly printed card with blue scroll trim filled her vision. Evelyn Scottlynn Keats. Nine digits formed her social security number below the neatly typed name. She was real!

Emotion had her chin trembling. So long she'd waited for such validation of her existence. So many obstacles could be overcome with those simple pieces of paper.

With unsteady fingers, she reached for the documents and stilled when Lucian's firm hand caught her wrist. Her gaze jerked to his.

The respect she held for him was in shreds, but giving her these documents that were rightfully hers mended a bit of the damage. She was gambling with his affections, asking for these things. If he didn't give them to her, he would annihilate any remaining faith she had in his goodness. She hated him for what he'd done, but deep down believed there was good behind the man. If he was so desperate to help her, it would have to be on *her* terms.

Don't deny me, Lucian. Please. She waited him out.

"I'll help you. But our other issues are far from concluded. Eventually we need to talk about what happened."

She glared at him and shook off his hold. "I'll ask that you keep your hands to yourself."

"And I'll ask that you drop the haughty performance you've been affecting since you got here."

Fingers snatching up the papers, Scout quickly removed her body from within his reach. Her brow tightened and her voice was dangerously close to cracking with emotion. "It's not an act. These are *my* papers and I deserve them. You have no right to keep them from me."

"And what of my money? Do you deserve that as well?"

"All I asked for was a loan. You can afford it. Either you help me or I go somewhere else."

"With what credit, Ms. Keats? No bank will sign over that amount of money without a cosigner."

He was likely right. He was also being mean and spiteful on purpose. Two could play that game. "I could always find another wealthy man willing to help me. After all, it was you who taught me *everything* is for sale."

He growled. "Watch yourself, Ms. Keats. I'm in no frame of mind to be pushed."

"Lucian." She took a deep breath. "I'm not forfeiting my morals for money. Even *you* can't afford them. You either agree to my terms and help me with a loan, or I'll figure out another way."

"Another way for what?" he snapped.

She wouldn't give him more information than necessary. She needed to do this for herself and if he knew her plan, he'd try to take over. Lucian was a leader—a very successful one—but she was sick and tired of following the tide. She needed to prove she could do this on her own. "For my future. I have nothing! I want to invest in *me*, since no one else gives a shit, and I need thirty-five thousand dollars to do that."

He stilled, his eyes narrowing, and she saw him weighing her words. Again he reached into his drawer, only this time he removed a heavy blue ledger. Long fingers flipped it open and reached for a pen. His hand swiftly moved over the check, the ballpoint scratching across the dense paper. The tear along each tiny perforation mesmerized her with its slow intent, but at last the slip fell free. He dropped the check in front of her with flourish. "There you go."

Scout stared at the check. The numbers read $35,000.00, but she couldn't read the script. She had trouble with anything that wasn't printed in capital letters.

Eyeing him suspiciously, she blinked as he arched a brow. "Take it. It's yours."

Her fingers hesitantly reached for the check. Once closed over the thick paper, she pulled her hands back to her lap. "I'll . . . I'll pay you back."

"I don't care about the money, Evelyn."

"Well, I do. I'll pay you back. Every cent. I'll make payments whenever possible. Once I've paid off the principal, we'll figure out what I owe in interest."

He rolled his eyes. "All right, but here are my conditions."

Her mouth opened. She shook her head, trying to scramble up the right words. "But you already gave it to me."

"I gave you a voucher. A check of that amount has to be cleared through me. What you have is trash unless I approve it when the bank calls."

"Fine," she gritted. "What are your terms?"

"Your payments will be made *in person*. I also require an address of where you're staying. These are simple requests, and any bank would demand a hell of a lot more from you. Be grateful that's all I'm stipulating at the moment."

Her jaw locked against what she wanted to say. He was trying to intimidate her. It wasn't happening. "Fine." He'd have to wait on the address.

"Good."

Several beats passed where neither of them said a word. She glared challengingly back at him, refusing to be bulldozed or bullied. She read Lucian's intentions in his eyes just as he likely read hers. She stood.

"I should be going."

All the intensity left Lucian's face. He shot to his feet. "Can I offer you a ride?"

She laughed. "Do I look stupid?" His expression was wounded. She sighed. "Lucian, I have no doubt the second I walk through that door you'll be on the phone with Dugan or some other underling, insisting they follow me. Can we skip the stalking for a change? I've been through hell and back over the past month. I think I'm entitled to my privacy."

"You know I can't do that."

"Why not?"

"Because I worry."

She shook her head. "How would you feel if someone followed you everywhere?"

"People follow me every day. I'm in the tabloids. I'm on the news. There aren't many places I can hide, Evelyn. You know that."

"And I know you hate it, so how could you intrude on my privacy in the same manner?"

"Because it's *not* the same. You're on your own and I'm only trying to keep an eye out." He suddenly frowned. "Why are you dressed like that?"

She glanced down at her Clemons uniform. Her hand quickly snapped off her name tag, and his eyes narrowed.

"You got a job," he guessed.

"I told you I plan to pay you back. I need money to do that."

"Where are you working? I would've given you your old job back."

"I don't want any ties, beyond this loan, to you or your companies."

His head slowly drew back, and she saw how her words wounded him. "Did what we have mean so little to you?" he asked in a quiet voice.

"Perhaps you should ask yourself that question." She picked up her bag and folded the check, slipping it safely inside the zippered pocket. "I have to go. Please don't have anyone follow me."

She turned and he called her name. "Evelyn."

Her resolve was waning and she had to get out of there. It was so hard seeing him and not touching him. Her heart wanted to run to him, feel his arms around her as she cried about the injustice done to her, but he was the culprit behind all of her heartache.

All she needed to do was think of how he'd betrayed her, and the pain was enough to drop her to her knees, cutting off all urge to step closer.

"Will you continue to pay for Pearl to stay at the rehab?"

His eyes narrowed. "The fact that you can even ask that shows how little you think of me."

What did he expect? He'd completely shocked her when he'd let her go and broken his promise to always protect her. She shrugged.

"Yes, I will continue to pay for your mother."

"Thank you."

He shook his head. "I'm glad to do it."

She remained facing the door, not wanting to look at him anymore. He stepped close but didn't touch her. "For what it's worth, I'm sorry."

"So am I." Quickly opening the door, she fled. Her finger pounded into the elevator button as if she were tapping out Morse code.

SOS. SOS. SOS!

Not until the doors of the elevator closed behind her did she turn and exhale. She did it.